I0762899

BY MEG SHAFFER

The Book Witch

The Lost Story

The Wishing Game

The
BOOK WITCH

The BOOK WITCH

A NOVEL

MEG SHAFFER

BALLANTINE BOOKS
NEW YORK

Ballantine Books
An imprint of Random House
A division of Penguin Random House LLC
1745 Broadway, New York, NY 10019
randomhousebooks.com
penguinrandomhouse.com

Hardcover ISBN 978-0-593-98358-4
Ebook ISBN 978-0-593-98359-1

Printed in the United States of America

3rd Printing

First Edition

Book Team: Production editor: Cindy Berman • Managing editor: Pam Alders • Production manager: Jane Sankner • Copy editor: Susan M. S. Brown • Proofreaders: Karen Ninnis, Barbara Greenberg, Muriel Jorgensen

Book design by Alexis Flynn

Illustrations by Andrew Shaffer

Chapter opener plaque art: Oleksandra/Adobe Stock

The authorized representative in the EU for product safety and compliance is Penguin Random House Ireland, Morrison Chambers, 32 Nassau Street, Dublin D02 YH68, Ireland. https://eu-contact.penguin.ie.

Dedicated to . . .

The librarians, booksellers, and teachers fighting the good fight to save our stories.

And to all the world's bedtime-story readers.

Me, poor man, my library
Was dukedom large enough.

—WILLIAM SHAKESPEARE, *The Tempest*

In the end, we'll all become stories.

—MARGARET ATWOOD

CONTENTS

READ ME

NOW HIRING

BOOK WITCHES TO PROTECT AND DEFEND WORKS OF FICTION

Ideal candidate should be willing to jump into and out of books, short stories, and the occasional epic poem.

Starting pay commensurate with magical proficiency, but spell-casting experience not required.

INQUIRE WITHIN

Book One

ROMANCE

CHAPTER ONE

Two Years Ago

All stories are love stories if you love stories.

And I do love stories. As a Book Witch, you kind of have to love them. It's on our recruitment posters, after all.

My name is Rainy March, and yes, it's a bad pun and also a weather forecast, and no, sorry, I can't change it now. It's already embroidered into my underwear and printed on my bookplates.

This love story starts with a phone call, one of those pivotal moments you don't realize will change your life until much, much later. It was two years ago on September 1st, back when I was a young and mostly innocent Book Witch of twenty-five. I don't even have to look at my case notes to remember the exact date. After all, you never forget the day you fall in love with a fictional character.

Of course, having a crush on a fictional character is nothing new. Sherlock Holmes used to get more fan mail than his creator, Sir Arthur Conan Doyle. Women would write 221B Baker Street proposing marriage to the fictional consulting detective, or simply offering their services as housekeepers to get close to him.

What I really mean is . . . you never forget the day a fictional character falls in love with you back.

Admittedly, I also remember the day in question was the first of the month because Koshka, my feline familiar, gets his flea and tick preventative applied on the first. Right before the phone rang, I had the boy wrapped in a towel and wedged between my knees on the bathroom floor. I can't say who was enjoying it less, me or my cat.

"Big baby," I said as he wiggled under me, slippery as a hot-buttered eel. "It'll take two seconds. Do you want to get a tapeworm? No. No, you don't."

From inside his bath-towel burrito, he let out a piteous whine.

"All this fussing from a familiar." The familiars of Book Witches are like normal pets except they can read. They certainly don't handle taking medication any better than normal pets. "It'll be over in a second, buddy." With one hand, I parted the thick silvery gray fur on the back of his neck while I popped the medicine cap with the other. "Be strong, comrade! You are Russian. Act like it!"

He isn't actually Russian, but don't tell him that. He's a Russian Blue and therefore thinks he's Russian. Another Book Witch might have saddled him with a cutesy cat pun name like Alexander Puss-kin or Furdor Dostoevsky, but as I suffer from a cutesy pun name myself, I refuse to inflict one on another living creature. Since the only Russian I knew at the time was the word for *cat,* that's what I called him. (Yes, I know *koshka* usually refers to female cats, but my Koshka is very comfortable in his masculinity. Oh, and if you want to pronounce it correctly, it rhymes with . . . well, nothing, but you say "kosh" as in the Hebrew word *kosher.* Capisce?)

The moment I had the medicine tube in position, the red hotline phone across the hallway rang. During that split-second distraction, Koshka wriggled out of the towel and bolted.

Defeated, I dragged myself off the floor. I was a fur-coated shell of my former self as I reached the doorway to the library, only to see that Pops had beaten me to the phone.

"Sullivan March here," he said, answering the call.

From behind his desk, my white-bearded grandfather gave me a wink. With his brown tweed suit and elbow patches, he looked like Santa Claus undercover as a retired English professor. But Santa Claus is a jolly old elf. Pops is a jolly old Book Witch, the first in our family to enter the storycraft trade.

He listened to whoever was on the other end of the line. By the dour look on his face, it was most likely our coven leader, Dr. Regina Fanshawe, who was older and white-haired but looked nothing like Mrs. Claus. More like a taller, angrier Dame Judi Dench. *Much* angrier.

Pops pulled his old brown leather case notebook out of the top desk drawer and flipped it open, jotting down notes. I leaned across the desk, hoping to see what he was writing, but when he caught me looking, he covered the page with his arm.

"Understood," Pops finally said. "I'm on it."

My heart sank as he hung up. That "I" in "I'm on it" didn't sound promising. I would've preferred a "we" or a "she."

Pops looked at me. "Well, that's interesting."

"What's the job? And can I do it?"

"Absolutely not," he said. "Not a chance. Not this job."

"Not a chance? Pops, need I remind you that I have been working the horror beat for months? Whatever this assignment is, I can handle it."

Not only had I recently survived the machinations of a monstrous mansion in Shirley Jackson's *The Haunting of Hill House,* but I'd also sparred with both Dr. Jekyll and Mr. Hyde and come out on top. And who was the only Book Witch in the world who knew the first name of the second Mrs. de Winter in Daphne du Maurier's Gothic classic *Rebecca*?

This witch.

"I don't think this is a good idea," he said, shaking his head.

"If I can handle vampires, ghosts, and Mrs. Danvers, I can handle anything."

"They will not send a young female Book Witch to Gangland Chicago. It's far too dangerous, Raindrop."

"Gangland . . . Wait, Pops . . . Is it the Duke of Chicago? Is he in danger?"

The Duke of Chicago, for those who haven't read the books, is the star of a popular noir mystery series. According to his backstory, the Duke had been the youngest of four aristocratic sons. He'd inherited the dukedom, however, after the tragic deaths of his three older brothers. Feeling as if he were doomed if he stayed in England, the Duke ran off to America and set up shop as a private detective in Chicago. Although christened at birth Bartholomew Maximillian Augustus

Fitzgerald Nicholas Ardingly, in Chicago he went by the moniker Nick Duke, Private Eye.

Everyone just called him the Duke.

And he was my favorite fictional detective of all time.

Instead of letting Mrs. Turner, our housekeeper, answer the door, Pops practically leapt to his feet with the energy of a man half his age. I, of course, gave chase. He wasn't going to get out of this conversation that easily.

"He *is* in danger, isn't he? Let me take the case. I've read all the books a hundred times. I know where the Duke lives. I know his favorite drink. I know his valet's name and birthday—Nigel, born August twenty-third, 1860. A father figure to the Duke and a constant source of irritation. Check the books. I know everything."

Pops opened the front double-doors to find Professor Dodsworth on our porch. The Professor had been a Book Witch longer than Pops, since the days when paperbacks cost fifty cents, hardcovers a dollar, and if you wanted an audiobook, you asked someone with a decent voice to read aloud to you.

The Professor held out a bag. I don't know how spies usually receive their mission dossiers—manila folders probably—but Book Witches in the Ink and Paper Coven get our mission documents in canvas tote bags from the local bookstore.

Before Pops could grab it, I snatched it away. "Thank you, Professor."

The poor man opened his mouth to say something, but I'd already closed the doors.

"Rainy—" Pops said in a warning tone.

"I knew it." Inside was a paperback copy of *Empty Graves*, Duke of Chicago book two. "I'm going."

"You can't. You're too close to the story. We both know you've been in love with the Duke since you were a teenager."

"Pops, that was years ago. I'm over him."

"Over him? Really?" He crossed his arms and eyed me sternly. "Did you or did you not attend a book conference last year playing a Duke of Chicago love interest?"

"I may have *allegedly* attended Murder Me Con, where I cosplayed as the femme fatale Hennie Fox from book six, *Chicago River Red*. I wouldn't call her a love interest really. She's a paid assassin hired to kill him, but in the end, she repents and turns herself over to the police, because she's in love with him in a sort of sociopathic way."

"Once a Ducky, always a Ducky," he said, taunting me with the nickname devoted readers of the Duke of Chicago series go by.

"You have a crush on Miss Marple. I know it. Grandma knew it. Even Miss Marple knew it."

At this point, the conversation turned into a staring contest.

Finally, I broke the stalemate.

"Come on, please? This is my dream assignment."

If anyone was going to save the Duke of Chicago, it needed to be me. If only to return the favor. A bit of my backstory, in case you haven't read my previous case files: My mother—a second-generation Book Witch—died when I was a baby. Growing up, I hadn't dwelt on my loss much until high school, when I began to feel her absence like a missing limb. Turning sixteen without a mother to teach me to drive or attend my apprenticeship graduation had been quietly awful. The only things that gave me real comfort were the Duke of Chicago books and that other, better, wilder life I led with him inside my imagination. Not that I could have told Pops that. He and Grandma had done everything in their power to give me the best possible childhood. Knowing I'd suffered even five minutes would've broken his dear old heart.

"Can you be professional here?" Pops asked.

"If I weren't your granddaughter, if I were any other Book Witch with my skills and background, you'd send me there in a heartbeat, and you know it. No one is more qualified for this mission than I am."

"You could get hurt," he said.

"And so could you. We've all been hurt."

I pulled back my right sleeve and held up my forearm to display the burn scar from my mission into Ray Bradbury's *Fahrenheit 451,* when I pulled a copy of John Steinbeck's *The Grapes of Wrath* from a book fire. Inside the world of the story, it was the last copy of the book left on earth. The act had left my right forearm scarred, but I never regretted it for a second.

"Watching you dive for that book," Pops said, "was the most scared I've ever been. And the proudest."

"Let me make you proud again." I pulled my sleeve back down.

He sighed heavily, and I knew I'd already won even if he didn't quite realize it yet. "They have tommy guns in there." He nodded at the book. "I lost my Mary. I can't lose you too."

Mary, his wife and my grandmother, had been a retired high school English teacher. Grandma had been very ill and suffering for several years, and her death, though heartbreaking, was a peaceful release for her. Unspoken was the fact that Pops had already lost his *daughter*—my mother—and therefore losing me too would be one tragedy too many for his heart.

I could've reminded him he was the only family I had left as well. I would have bet my entire book collection that I would miss him more than he would miss me, should something happen to him on a mission.

But I didn't.

"If I can handle Cthulhu, I can handle Chicago."

"I know, I know, but—"

"What's this about, Pops? I'm twenty-five years old, remember? Twenty-five," I repeated. "Not five. Not fifteen. I've been doing this job for a decade."

Most Book Witches begin apprenticing at age sixteen, but I had shown magical promise from childhood. Plus, I'd been so determined to follow in my mother's footsteps that I'd begun my formal training a year early. For ten years now, I'd worked as a fully licensed practitioner of storycraft. In other words, I knew what I was doing.

"Hard to believe," Pops said wistfully.

Time toyed with us like a funhouse mirror. When I looked at Pops, I saw the robust sixty-year-old man who'd walked me to school the first day of kindergarten, not an eighty-year-old with a broken heart and a bad hip. When he looked at me, he saw a girl with pigtails and a My Little Pony lunchbox. Time passes like the pages of a favorite story, drawing ever nearer the end whether we like it or not.

"You know you still love him," Pops finally said. "Nobody really outgrows their first fictional love."

"I can still do my job."

"What if he disappoints you? You should never meet your heroes, they say, and they say it for a reason."

"Either the Duke is as wonderful as he is in the books or he's not. If he is, I'll be a very happy witch. If he's not? I'll find a new book boyfriend. Poirot's single, right?"

I put my hands on Pops's shoulders—he was still strong for a man of eighty—and grinned. "Follow me," he said.

We returned to the library, and Pops made the call, putting it on speakerphone. "I'm sending Rainy," he told Dr. Fanshawe. "She knows this series inside and out. Any objections?"

There was a long heavy pause before Dr. Fanshawe replied.

"Rainy?"

"Yes, ma'am?"

"Your late mother was the best Book Witch I've ever had the honor of serving with," Dr. Fanshawe said. "I hold out hope that in time I'll start to see the resemblance."

"So do I," I said, my voice smaller than usual. No matter how many cases I cracked, I would never measure up to my mother in Dr. Fanshawe's eyes. I was good, very good, but even very good was nothing compared to perfection.

"Recite the Eight Black and Whites, please," Dr. Fanshawe ordered. It was the Book Witch equivalent of saying the Pledge of Allegiance, something only apprentices were asked to do.

"Are you—" I was about to say "serious" when Pops shot me a warning look. "—listening?"

"Go on," she said, her tone stern.

"Of course," I said, running through them quickly in my head to make sure I had the order right. Our rules are called the Black and Whites for two reasons. One, books are printed in black and white, so the name fits our aesthetic. But the main reason, so I'd been told many thousands of times, is that when you are a Book Witch, there are absolutely no shades of gray. The Black and Whites are to be obeyed to the letter.

"Black and White Number One," I began, "is to protect all stories without judgment, be they true classic or cult classic, bore or bestseller, fan favorite or forgotten flop.

"Number Two: When a fictional character escapes the story world, they must be returned as soon as feasibly possible, and their memory of our world erased.

"Number Three: The author's intention for the story must be preserved at all costs, no matter how much a fictional character may object."

Pops succinctly paraphrased Black and Whites Two and Three as *Never let the inmates run the asylum.*

"Number Four: Take no weapons into the stories, for the pen is mightier than the sword.

"Number Five: Never use the powers of a fictional character for personal gain."

In other words, don't go dragging the Owens sisters out of *Practical Magic* to fix your love life. For many reasons, come to think of it.

"Number Six: Never eat, drink, sleep, or take up residence in any way in a story, lest you become part of it."

Sleeping is especially dangerous. Many a Book Witch has fallen asleep in a story only to wake up certain the story world is *their* world. They are like the dreamers who can't be convinced they're only dreaming. Waking them is cosmic agony. Imagine someone telling you the world you live in is only a story in someone else's imagination . . . would you ever believe them?

I continued. "Number Seven: Real people belong in the real world. Fictional characters belong in works of fiction. Rare the twain shall meet."

Rules six and seven translate to "Get in fast, get out fast, and leave no trace." Just as fictional characters are not allowed to take up residence in the real world, real people are not allowed to live in story worlds. We can only hop into a book when work requires it, leaving the second the job is done. Imagine the discipline and self-control it takes a Book Witch to not jump into their favorite stories willy-nilly. I'd never once snuck into the Duke of Chicago's books before, and quite frankly, I think I deserved a medal.

"And Number Eight?" Dr. Fanshawe prompted.

"Never fall in love with a fictional character," I said, as if it was the most obvious thing in the world. "That's all eight. Can I go now?"

Even over the phone I could tell Dr. Fanshawe was wincing, already regretting what she was about to say.

"Very well, if only because we're running out of time. But take no chances. Don't do *anything* that will blow your cover," she said firmly.

"Thank you, I won't let you down."

Without missing a beat, she launched right into the mission. "Page eighty-seven has gone blank. We have reason to believe the Duke is being held captive in a speakeasy on Damen Avenue."

I turned to page eighty-seven. Sure enough, the page had turned white. I flipped to the next page, only to see that eighty-eight was starting to fade as well.

"The Bathtub?" I said. "Yes, I know it. The Duke meets his contacts there."

"Get him out and back on the plot at once."

"On it, boss."

"And be quick about it."

After Dr. Fanshawe hung up, I looked Pops in the eyes.

"I won't let you down either," I told him.

He smiled. "I know you won't. Be safe, Raindrop."

"Koshka!" I called as I ran from the library and up the stairs. "Come on. We're going to Chicago!"

My usual uniform of black leggings and a black-and-white striped sweater was not proper attire for Depression-era Chicago. No worries. Up in the attic, Pops and I kept a large wardrobe to blend into any story, any genre, any setting: A space suit for sci-fi. An elf costume for fantasy. Black cloaks and ball gowns galore for Gothics.

For this mission, I was thinking my Hennie Fox silver cocktail dress? No, too impractical. Then I spotted the tailored wool men's suit I'd worn for Agatha Christie's *The Mysterious Affair at Styles*. The suit was a decade out of date in the Duke's world, but better than trying to fight off gangsters in an evening gown.

I dressed quickly and tucked my hair up under a newsboy cap. If Pops didn't think Gangland Chicago was safe for women, I'd simply go as a man.

In the cheval mirror, I gave myself a onceover. My long dark hair remained firmly hidden under the hat. I'm about average height and a little too skinny (by Mrs. Turner's standards anyway), so in my suit I fully resembled a pale and slightly freckled teenage boy who just happened to have unusually long eyelashes.

"Ready?" I asked Koshka, who'd been impatiently pacing while I'd gotten dressed.

He meowed loudly in reply.

We returned to the library, where Pops had already taken my magic umbrella out of the wall safe and laid the damaged copy of *Empty Graves* open on the reading table, an onyx paperweight on each corner. It's much easier to escape an open book than a closed one. While you can get out of a closed book, it feels like taking off a scuba suit in a tight sleeping bag. And it's not much fun for the book either.

In this particular novel, the Duke of Chicago is tasked with rescuing a socialite who's supposedly been kidnapped by gangsters, only to discover a far more complicated and tragic truth. The book, originally published in 1948, had a deliciously campy cover with a beautiful redheaded femme fatale in a painted-on scarlet red dress holding a shovel.

"I'm going to try to land us in the alley next to the speakeasy," I told Pops. "Wish us luck."

"Good luck," he said. "And be home in time for dinner or Mrs. Turner will have a fit."

"Promise." I rose up on my toes and kissed him on the cheek.

"Koshka?" Pops said, addressing my cat. "If the Duke gets fresh with her, bite him."

"He won't even look twice at me," I said, scooping up Koshka.

"Don't listen to old Fanshawe," Pops said. "If your mother were here right now, she'd be as proud of you as I am."

But she's not here, I thought but didn't say.

"Thanks, Pops," I said. "Now excuse me, we have a story to save."

Pops passed me my umbrella and stepped back.

When performing an immersion, you always want to enter a story at the last possible moment before the damaged section. Never begin on page one, otherwise you could be wandering the story world for weeks or months—years even if you're in a multigenerational family saga. Dangerous business. The longer a real person lives inside a story, the more likely they are to forget who they are and where they come from. A Book Witch from a neighboring coven got himself stuck for two weeks in *Treasure Island.* Apparently, he talked like a pirate for a month after that. Not kidding, the poor man had to see a speech therapist.

With my cat in one arm and my umbrella in hand, I read aloud from page eighty-six, willing us to become one with the story. It was the scene where the Duke of Chicago spots the socialite dancing with an infamous gangster.

She was a beautiful girl, I read, *but so was Helen of Troy, and look what happened to the Trojans.*

With a flick of my thumb, I opened my umbrella. All Book Witches use black umbrellas instead of wands. Seen from above, an open black umbrella looks like the dot atop a lowercase letter "i." With my umbrella, I could make a portal through that tiny dot on the page and hide our presence at the same time.

And with the magic of storycraft, that's precisely what happened. Koshka and I vanished from the real world into the story world, slipping through the miniature black hole made by the dot on the lowercase "i" in the word "girl."

As we disappeared, I closed my eyes on a soft, warm September evening in Fort Meriwether, Oregon. When I opened them again, I was breathing the bitter cold and sinister air of Gangland Chicago.

CHAPTER TWO

Koshka and I touched down safely into the alley outside the Bathtub, the infamous speakeasy the Duke of Chicago frequented in his books. Bad gin, he said, but good information.

"You all right?" I asked Koshka. We'd arrived behind a pile of garbage about ten feet high. The stench could melt glass, but at least it gave us good cover.

Koshka leapt out of my arms, ready to work. He scouted around the garbage while I straightened my suit. Some Book Witches suffer severe vertigo when entering stories, but I've never had that problem. I assumed it was because the Marches had been Book Witches for generations now. Pops liked to joke we had ink in our blood.

Koshka trotted back, indicating the coast was clear. Above me, at the end of my outstretched fingertips, my umbrella hovered, keeping the portal between the two worlds open. When we left, we would have to find our way back to this alley. Should be easy enough. Get into the speakeasy, free the Duke of Chicago, then we would be on our way.

And maybe if I played my cards right . . . he'd give me his autograph.

"All right," I said to Koshka, "let's go. Stay close."

Together, we strolled out from the alley and mounted the sidewalk as if we belonged there. The few people out that night paid us little to no attention. Cats were a common sight in big cities, where rats and mice were legion. Coins clinked in my pocket and my face wore a tough customer scowl. I was merely another lost soul looking to drink my cares away.

Because Prohibition was still the law of the land, bars and other gin joints were hidden behind fronts. The Bathtub was in the basement of a haberdashery. I knocked on the nondescript front door of the shop, and a pretty but hard-faced young woman opened it.

"Yeah?" she said.

"I'm looking for a straw boater," I said, lowering my voice an octave.

"We got boaters. In the back."

She let me inside and locked the door behind me.

"I can find my way," I said.

"What about the ratcatcher?" she asked, glancing down at Koshka.

"He needs a boater too."

She put her hand on her hip and tossed her bobbed black hair. "Whatever floats your boater, honey."

Koshka and I headed straight back through the hat shop, passing fedoras and trilbies and derby hats galore. The Duke of Chicago favored a top hat for evening excursions. It was all part of his mystique. Anyone who's ever read an old detective series knows each detective has a special superpower, so to speak. Hercule Poirot was a former Belgian police officer who relied on his legendary "little grey cells" to solve his cases. Miss Marple lived all her life in the small village of Saint Mary Mead, a microcosm of the world where she became an astute student of human nature. The Duke of Chicago's superpower? A uniquely potent combination of money, looks, and charm.

The Duke always dressed to the nines, if only because he'd seen how people crumble in the face of someone they perceive as being of higher status. Fortunately, the Duke was unusually self-aware and humble considering his rank and background and only used his powers for good. Kind of like Batman, but with a better wardrobe, fewer gadgets, and no daddy issues.

We reached the stockroom door. The party raged on the other side. As soon as I opened it, the acrid scent of cigar smoke slapped me in the face. I breathed through my mouth as best I could as I made my way down a short flight of stairs toward the source of all the shouting and laughing. Nothing would have given me away as an outsider faster than a coughing fit. You needed asbestos lungs to survive the smoke-filled rooms of the early twentieth century.

We reached the basement. The place, no bigger than your average coffee shop, was packed to the gills just like it always was in the books. Women in flashy floor-length gowns danced cheek to cheek with men in suits to the raucous sound of a ragtime piano.

"Don't get your tail stepped on, boy," I warned Koshka, who slinked along the floor at my side. "Try to sniff out the Duke. Follow the scent of old money and class privilege."

Koshka weaved through dozens of pairs of dancing feet while I cozied up to the bar and ordered a Sidecar from the bartender. Did I know what was in a Sidecar? Not a clue. But a drink in hand would help me to blend in with the other toughs.

The bartender slid my drink across the bar. I nodded and paid the man with an old Liberty half-dollar that I hoped had been minted before 1930. I'd forgotten to double-check my vintage cash stash before I'd left, but he took it without looking too closely.

Leaning back against the bar, I tried to look inconspicuous as I pretended to sip my drink. The cocktail smelled like orange juice and ethanol, so I wasn't tempted to drink it. People dropped like drunken flies from poisoned bathtub gin during the Depression. Besides, drinking and eating were uniquely dangerous for Book Witches, as I mentioned. Although . . . if I were forced to choose a book to be trapped in for all eternity, I wouldn't mind if it were one of the Duke's mysteries.

Something brushed against my ankle. Koshka had returned and nipped my pants leg, signaling for me to follow him.

We passed a table where a woman in blue sat alone and forlorn. I placed my drink in front of her and said in my best bad Chicago accent, "You need this more than me, sweetheart."

"Thanks, handsome," she said, perking up. "Save me a shimmy later."

I winked at her. "You know it, sugar."

But there was no time for dancing. Koshka made a beeline for the enormous American flag hanging on the back wall. If I stopped to count I would have counted forty-eight stars, not fifty, because Alaska and Hawaii wouldn't be states for about thirty years.

When no one was looking, I slipped behind the flag and felt around the wall for a catch. A panel quietly popped open, and Koshka and I snuck into a dimly lit room. An oil lamp cast pale gold light across the stained concrete floor. I picked it up and turned up the wick.

There in the corner, I spotted a chair. A man sat slumped down, facing the wall, hands tied behind his back. And on the floor by the chair, a hat.

A top hat.

I'd found the Duke.

I lifted the lamp and spun a slow circle lighting the room's dark corners. He'd been left unguarded. Good. Slowly I approached him.

"Mister," I rasped. "You awake? Hey, mister?" This was my impression of an ordinary bar patron who'd innocently stumbled into this bare and menacing back room.

No answer.

"Mister?" I said again.

His head was down, his chin on his chest. Was he sleeping or unconscious? I want to pretend I stared at him for as long as I did because of concern for his health, but I was stunned speechless at the sight of him in the flesh. Even passed out and trussed up, the Duke of Chicago was ten times more handsome than I'd ever dared to let myself imagine. He had a face that belonged on the silver screen, with thick wavy dark hair that demanded a girl run her fingers through it and the most kissable lips in the long and storied history of kissing.

While his author, Tom Hightower, said in an interview he based him on a young Cary Grant, the Duke was a bit more of a young Gary Cooper live and in person. And I write from personal experience when I say nothing bad happens when one does an online image search for "young Gary Cooper."

"No wonder he can get anyone to do anything at any time," I whispered to Koshka.

"You aren't so bad yourself," the Duke of Chicago said as he lifted his head and stared directly at me.

"Oh," I said, which wasn't one of my better comebacks, but even the dictionary would be at a loss for words if the Duke of Chicago looked at it the way he was looking at me. "You're awake."

I should've known he'd been only faking unconsciousness.

He furrowed his regal brow at me.

"Either you are a young woman under that suit pretending to be a young man . . . or I am learning something surprising about myself. Or both." He tilted his head to the side. "Both. Most certainly both. And quite frankly, it's not that surprising."

I slapped myself across the face.

"What on earth was that for?" he demanded.

"Someone had to do it," I said. "All right, I need to get you out of here."

"The fiend tied me up too well," he said. "You'll have to cut the knots."

"Do you still have that knife strapped to your ankle?" I asked.

Traumatized by the carnage of the First World War, the Duke of Chicago famously didn't carry a gun. However, he always kept a knife on his ankle in the event of a kidnapping. For a fictional detective, being kidnapped and/or held hostage was a daily concern.

"I do, yes," he said, his tone suspicious. "But how did you know—"

"Um . . . I mean, who doesn't keep a kidnapping knife in their socks these days? I left mine in my other socks so I'll use yours if you don't mind—"

I bent down to get his knife, but at the last moment, he danced his leg away.

"I never let anyone touch my socks until I know their name. Strict rule of mine. Never steered me wrong."

"I can't tell you," I said. "Sorry."

"That's unfortunate. As I need to get out of here, I'll simply have to give you a name. I'll call you . . . darling."

"That works," I said. "And you're the Duke. Now if we could get back to the knife—"

"Just call me Duke, darling," he said, relaxing his leg for me. "And your friend?"

"Koshka," I said. "He thinks he's Russian."

"Koshka? Your four-legged Bolshevik is sitting in my hat."

I lifted Duke's pant leg. Sure enough, he had a slim knife hidden inside his right sock. "Sorry about the cat in the hat," I said.

"Don't apologize. It looks better on him than on me. Greetings, comrade," he said. "Добрый вечер."

"You know Russian?" I asked as I went to work, sawing through the thick ropes. The blade was sharp but small.

"Only enough to get me thrown in the gulag."

"The guy who grabbed you . . . what did he look like?"

"Pure essence of knob, if you ask me," Duke said.

"Can you be more specific?"

"Caucasian male, approximately forty years old, five feet, eight inches, average build, brown eyes, sallow complexion, Roman nose, short brown hair, widow's peak, birthmark on his right hand—"

"Did he smell like smoke?" I said before I got his weight and the name of his third grade teacher too.

"Yes, and he looked like his mother never once kissed him good night. Know him?"

"Unfortunately." It sounded like X, an old archenemy of mine. A Burner. We'd tussled more than once in the past.

"Why did he leave you here?" I asked. "Did he say?"

"He said nothing to me at all," Duke said. "My turn to ask the questions now."

"Shoot," I said, as I continued to saw at the rope.

"How did you know I was here? Who are you? Where are you from? Why are you helping me? Why can't you tell me your name? Who was that man who jumped me this afternoon? And any idea what he planned on doing with me? Oh, and are you married?"

"You need to know if I'm married?"

"I do, actually," he said.

"Not married."

"Wonderful. Now I feel free to say you have the finest gray eyes I've ever seen in my life," he said. "Storm clouds and silver. Try to blink less. It's like closing a curtain across the *Mona Lisa*."

"Thank you," I said, unblinking.

"Better," he said. "My other questions?"

My eyes started to dry out, so I blinked.

"I knew you were here because I'd been told where to find you. The guy who grabbed you was trying to stop you from solving this case," I said, which was vague but true enough. X was trying to stop Duke from solving this case and, knowing X, every other case forever and ever. "I can't tell you who I am, but I'm from Fort Meriwether, Oregon, and don't worry if you've never heard of it. Almost nobody's heard of it. I want you to solve this case, so I'm helping you. Wait, what was the other question?"

"What was Old Smokey planning on doing with me?" he repeated.

"He wants to stop your work," I said as I got Duke's right hand free.

"So he means to kill me?"

"I wouldn't be surprised." And I wouldn't. X could be coming back any minute to finish the job.

"If I had a dime . . ." Duke sighed.

As I kept working on the rope, Duke reached his free hand down for his hat. I assumed he meant to shoo Koshka out of it and dust it off, but he didn't. He petted Koshka between the ears. I'm not sure if that's the moment I started to fall in love with him, but I think it's safe to say that's the moment my cat did.

Finally, I freed Duke's other hand. "There."

He got to his feet and, instead of rubbing his abraded wrists, he simply straightened his jacket, vest, and tie, then ran a hand through his hair. "How do I look? Shipshape and Bristol fashion?"

"You make James Bond look like a hippie."

"I have no idea who or what any of that means," he said, "but from the adoring look in those storm cloud eyes of yours, I'll take it as a compliment."

"It was."

I held out his knife to him, but instead of taking it, he took my hand, brought it to his lips, and kissed the back of it. His own beautiful eyes—chocolate brown and delicious—peered deeply into mine.

When his lips touched my skin, I felt lightning surging through my entire body.

"Thank you, darling," he said. "I owe you my life and anything else you'd like to request."

"Rainy," I said suddenly.

"Is it?" he asked, still holding my hand. "Well, that's spring in Chicago for you. If you don't like the weather, wait five minutes—"

"No, my name. My name is Rainy March. I'm not supposed to tell you that, but I wanted you to know it."

"Rainy," he said, musing, "my favorite kind of long morning in bed."

The man could charm the pants off a statue.

CHAPTER THREE

Focus on the mission, I told myself. Step one—stop staring at Duke's face. Easier said than done.

Step two—get Duke out of the speakeasy and back on track.

I shooed Koshka out of the top hat. "Go scout around, boy. Make sure there's no . . . you know, kidnappers about," I told him.

Koshka raced from the back room through the wall panel.

"Your hat," I said. "Sorry about the cat hair."

Duke dusted it off. "No trouble at all. Shall we have a drink somewhere? My place?"

"No time. You're tracking Edith King, the socialite, right?"

He'd been adjusting his cuffs but froze when I said the woman's name.

"Aren't you a clever clock? This is a secret mission. How did you know that?"

"Long story," I said, although Duke's books were on the shorter side, about 250 pages each. "But it's imperative you get back on the plot. I mean, the job. Yes? Say yes. You need to finish this job."

It had been a few years since I'd read *Empty Graves,* but I remembered it well. Edith King hadn't been kidnapped at all but had arranged her own abduction to escape her wealthy, powerful, and very abusive husband. The Duke of Chicago, instead of "solving" the case for her husband, ends up aiding in her escape.

"You saved me, darling. Your wish is my command. And if you don't know what to wish for, I have a few suggestions." He grinned devilishly as he lifted his trouser leg and slipped his knife back into his sock.

"That . . . that is not what . . . No." Suddenly, I realized what was happening. I pointed at his chest and backed up two steps. "Wait a minute. Are you trying to seduce me?"

"Of course I am. Why wouldn't I? You're beautiful, brave, and, frankly, a little bizarre. All aces in my book. Everyone I meet seems so . . . so two-dimensional in comparison. You're the realest girl I've ever met."

The fictional character I'd had a crush on in high school, my book boyfriend, was trying to get me into bed? And not in spite of me being weird but because of it? Had I died and gone to Heaven? Was it Christmas morning? Did I save a genie's life and get three wishes granted in return?

"Rainy?"

"Sorry, this is weirder than when Ebenezer Scrooge sent me a fruitcake for Christmas. I'm having an existential crisis."

Duke waved it off. "Happens to the best of us. About that drink I mentioned, should we get it before or after?"

"Before or after what?"

"You tell me." His intense eye contact was making me uncomfortable, but in a fun way, like when you bike across a wooden bridge.

"You don't want to get involved with me. I'm a witch."

"You seem perfectly charming."

"I meant that literally."

"I don't believe it," he said as he buttoned his jacket. "I've seen witches in books. Your hat is flat and you don't have a single wart on your nose."

"I'll prove it," I said.

"How? Turn me into a frog?"

"Look into my eyes."

"With pleasure."

He and I locked gazes. Duke's dark eyes made it a little harder to read him, but as I tilted my head this way and that, trying to catch the light, I glimpsed the words still dancing across his irises.

"*They slipped briskly into an intimacy from which they never recovered.* This Side of Paradise. F. Scott Fitzgerald. That's the book you're currently reading."

"Good Lord, I am. Last night before bed. How did you—"

"The book leaves an impression in your eyes. I can read it."

"I'm dazzled. Absolutely dazzled. Let me buy you dinner so you can dazzle me more."

"You have a mission."

"Then we'll meet for a drink after I find Miss King." Thank goodness Koshka returned at that moment to remind me I wasn't there on a blind date.

"It's all clear," I said. "We have to go. Now."

"I respect your decision," he said, "but if I cry about it later, don't think less of me."

"You're incorrigible."

"You started it by being so beautiful."

Before I could say another word, he took me by the hand and headed for the door.

"They're going to notice you holding hands with another man," I whispered to him.

"Trust me, darling," he said, "down here, they've seen everything."

He steered us through the throng. Everyone looked a little too bleary-eyed to even notice who was passing, much less comment on us.

My plan was simple enough. Get Duke out of here so he could continue the story. In the now-missing scene, the Duke was supposed to spy on Edith King at the Bathtub, then follow her to the Lombard Hotel near Montrose Beach. All I had to do was send Duke to the hotel to catch up with Edith.

We reached the hat shop on the main floor. I scooped Koshka into my arms, cradling him to my chest as we made our slow way through the dark hat shop. Mannequin heads in fedoras and trilbies and bowlers seemed to stare at us as we passed.

"Odd, isn't it? All these mannequin heads?" Duke whispered. "Makes one feel like you're—"

"Being watched?" a man's voice asked.

We froze.

The overhead lights came on suddenly, making it impossible to hide. Then the man stepped into our path. I recognized that stony face, those cold marble eyes. He, too, was dressed for Gangland Chicago in a fedora and black overcoat with a fur collar. And yes, he did, as Duke said, look like a man whose mother had never once kissed him good night.

"X," I said.

"Hello, Rainy March," the man said. "We meet again."

He didn't smile, but I could tell he was enjoying himself.

"That's the blighter who got the drop on me," Duke said, as he interposed his body between X and me. "Shall I thrash him for you? Do say yes."

Duke's voice was steady, brash, unafraid. Classic male bravado. While set in the 1930s, Duke's early books had been written and published in the late 1940s and '50s, during the height of the noir craze. Noir was a reaction to the societal tumult wrought by World War II, industrialization, women leaving home for the big cities and getting jobs. Noir detectives were their own breed, devils on the side of the angels, fighting a losing battle against evil but knowing no life other than the fight. That was part of the reason I'd fallen in love with Duke as a teenager—we'd both chosen the fighting life.

"She'll say nothing if she knows what's good for her," X said as he pulled a gleaming, period-appropriate pistol from his jacket. "Now stay still. Time to burn the trash."

"Trash? Are you speaking to *moi*?" Duke said.

X shrugged. "What can I say? I don't like your kind."

"My kind? What is my kind?" Duke demanded. "Do you hate the English? If you're Indian, Irish, or French, I'll accept that answer but otherwise—"

"Shut up," X said.

For the first time since meeting X, Duke's charm faltered. "Do whatever you want with me," he said, "but let the girl and her cat go."

"That's no girl. That's a witch." X pointed the gun in my direction before aiming it back at Duke.

"Those things are hardly mutually exclusive," Duke said. "And if you hurt her, I will kill you. I might even do it if you don't hurt her—"

"Yeah, sorry, no," I said. "You can't protect me. I'm supposed to be protecting you. Excuse me, please. Can you scooch back a bit, Duke? Thank you."

I held my breath, took a step sideways, and moved into the gap between X's gun and Duke's noble heart.

"I'm not comfortable being defended," Duke said.

"Get used to it," I said. "I know what I'm doing. The pen is mightier than the sword."

"True," Duke said, "but he has a gun, darling, and you don't have a pen *or* a sword."

Technically true, but I didn't have to admit it.

"X," I began, "what's the plan here?"

"Same plan as always," he said as he bent down and lifted a small can of gasoline. He set it on the table by him and patted it like an obedient dog. "I'm going to burn this world down."

It was as bad as I'd feared. When someone in the real world burns a single copy of a book, all they've done is make a mess. The book still exists in other copies, other formats. But when a Burner enters a story and burns it from the inside, the story itself will turn to ash and all copies in all formats in all the world will cease to exist. Even in the memories of readers. It will be as if the book had never been published, never been read, never even been written.

"You can't—" I paused and turned to Duke. "Can you cover your ears, please?"

"Why?"

"She doesn't want you finding out you're a fictional character in a book series," X said, feigning shock. "Oh, dear. Did I say that?"

"Someone's publishing stories about me?" Duke asked. "They must not be very good, because I haven't seen them for sale anywhere."

X waved the gun around the room. "This—all of this—is a book. We're inside it right now. I thought you were supposed to be some sort of hotshot sleuth?"

Duke looked to me for help. "Do you know what this berk's going on about?"

I wanted to lie, to tell him anything but the truth, but I couldn't.

"We're midway through the second book in your series," I said. "It's how I knew how to find you. You weren't supposed to be tied up—that wasn't part of the story. When I said I was a witch? I'm not the pointy-hat kind with the broom and all that. I'm a Book Witch. I'm here to set the story straight."

"None of this is real, you're saying."

"Some of us are," X interjected. "Just not you."

Duke nodded. "Now *I* seem to be having an existential crisis."

"It'll have to wait," I told him, then turned my attention back to X. "Why? Why this book series? Why the Duke?"

"Because it's garbage," X said. "Drivel. Poorly written hack work."

"If you don't like the Duke of Chicago books, don't read them," I said. "But leave them for the rest of us."

"I'm sparing you from your own bad taste," X said. "When we're finished with our work, there won't be any books like this left in the world. Only the true classics. *The Odyssey. The Iliad. The Aeneid.* Shakespeare. Chaucer." He smiled. "When the right people read good books once again, the world will be perfect."

"Perfect? You know Chaucer's *Canterbury Tales* were written during the Black Plague."

"Perfection is a state of mind. The world fell apart when people turned their backs on great literature. When we're done, all the garbage will be taken out and only the classics shall remain. Starting here and now."

He pulled a paperback book from his coat pocket and held it up.

"Is that . . . about me?" Duke asked.

"*Empty Graves,* the Duke of Chicago book two," X said. He tossed the book to me, and I caught it awkwardly. "Soon we'll call it *Empty Pages.*"

Pages eighty-six and eighty-seven were now blank.

Koshka hissed, and I swore violently.

"Rainy, darling," Duke said, scandalized. "Where did you learn that word? Down the docks? Wherever it was . . . say it again."

With a casual wave of his hand, X knocked the can of gasoline onto the floor, where the liquid swiftly spread.

"X," Duke pleaded, "I'll stay if the girl and her cat can go."

"They can go," X said. "I'm not stopping them, only you."

"Koshka, run for it," I ordered. "Find another witch. There has to be one somewhere in this town. Maybe the one who cursed the Cubs."

But Koshka stayed and so did I.

"Noble, if misguided," X said. "There might be stories worth dying for but not this historically inaccurate and poorly written nonsense." He gave the can a kick and more gas splashed out.

Our eyes watered from the stench. Koshka gave a soft cry of distress. I tried tucking his head into my coat to protect him from the fumes, but I would never be able to shield him from the flames.

"Duke, I need you to do me a favor," I said through my tears. "I need you to knock the gun out of his hand—which we both know you can do—then get to the Lombard Hotel by Montrose Beach and catch up with Edith King."

"That's two favors, actually," Duke said, ducking his head into his collar. "And I'm not leaving you behind."

"We'll be fine," I said, although I wasn't sure if it was true.

"No, they won't," X said, patting his pockets. "Now where's my lighter?"

The fumes were making me cough, but I forced myself to speak.

"Ignore him, Duke. You have to go. Now. You have to finish the story. Listen," I said. "I'm nobody. But you . . . you're the Duke of Chicago. Even decades after your books came out, they're inspiring people, entertaining them, comforting them. And I know because I'm one of them, all right? I fell in love with your books when I was sixteen, and I still love them. It's why he hates you," I said, pointing to X, "and when people like that hate you, you know you're doing something right. Please . . . I'm begging you, finish your story."

I met his eyes, imploring him, willing him to leave me behind and get his story back on track.

He looked at me and a strange expression crossed his face, one even his own author might have struggled to describe, but it seemed as if some kind of seismic shift happened behind his dark eyes.

The floor began to quiver under my feet. The windows rattled in their frames. Hats fell from their mannequin heads.

A different four-letter word escaped my lips. Duke's too. Then X's.

"What is happening?" X said as dust filled the air.

"You're the one who told the Duke he was fictional. Now he's self-aware, and he's taking over the book," I said. I'd heard of this happening. Writers had complained about it for centuries, about characters taking control of the story, but I'd never seen it in action.

"I am?" Duke yelled.

"Yes! And you need to stop it!" I told him, lurching sideways. Koshka jumped out of my arms and ran for cover in the doorway.

"I can't!"

A ceiling tile crashed near X, who jumped away from the falling debris. That gave Duke the chance he needed to grab the gun from the Burner's hand. Duke raised it, planning to coldcock X.

"*Si vis pachem, para bellum,*" X chanted. He flicked a silver lighter on and disappeared into a puff of smoke.

"Damn," Duke said. "I was hoping to crack his skull. Rainy, what do I do?"

The earthquake grew stronger. I fell to my knees as the hat shop crumbled around us.

"What do you want to do?" I called out. "To move a story forward, fictional characters need to want something. Have a goal! A purpose! Will it into being!"

Duke pulled me to him, covering my head with his arms as more of the ceiling crashed down around us.

"I want us to be safe somewhere together!"

And suddenly, just like magic, we were.

CHAPTER FOUR

It happened that fast, like someone had clicked a button on a slideshow. One second we were in the hat shop and *click*—we were somewhere else entirely.

Duke, Koshka, and I were in the middle of an office. What office? I couldn't tell. The only light in the room came from a gas streetlamp burning outside the window.

Duke walked over to a desk and switched on a brass lamp with a green shade.

"How are you, darling? All in one piece?"

I gasped, slapping a hand over my mouth when I saw the door. It had a panel of frosted glass with a name painted on it in gold letters. And although the letters were backward, I knew what they said.

I lowered my hand. "This is your office. This is the Duke of Chicago's office."

"You're far more impressed by that than you should be. Perhaps if we were in my bedroom . . ." he said with a wink. Then he shrugged off his coat and hung it on the rack. In his pin-stripe vest and shirtsleeves, he looked slightly less intimidating but even more handsome.

He came behind me and helped me off with my coat, which I enjoyed much too much. He hung it up next to his on the rack. Our coats, side by side. I'd had dreams like this . . .

"Where did our friend go? And what on earth was he saying?" Duke asked while I tried to calm my racing heart.

"X? He's back in the real world," I said.

"How on earth—"

"It was a spell," I said. "For some reason people tend to think Latin works better for magic." While we Book Witches used umbrellas to delicately and carefully go in and out of stories, Burners used lighters to burn holes in and out. Another thing to repair once I got back home.

"So he's gone away? We're safe?"

In the lamplight, I gave myself a once-over. My suit was pin neat, not a speck of dust to be seen. Koshka leapt onto the desk and began to groom his paws. But that was only force of habit. He was fine too.

"Gone for good, I hope, but at least for now. You scared him off with that earthquake stunt."

"Thank God," Duke said. "I was dying to be alone with you. And you, comrade." He bent and gave Koshka a little pat on his head, then rose up and looked around. "How the devil are we in my office? Did you do this with your"—he wiggled his fingers in the air—"*book* witchcraft?"

"I have some interesting abilities, but this kind of scene change is not one of them," I said. "Burners can destroy stories and Book Witches can restore them, but only a fictional character can take over a plot from the inside and change it like you did. Which I appreciate. I really did not want to be burned again."

"Again?" He spun and faced me.

"Oh, I was burned in a story once. Didn't enjoy it. Don't recommend it. Zero out of five stars."

"Were you injured?"

"A little," I said and pulled up my sleeve. "Not much."

The burn scar was about the size of a playing card, pink and smooth and not very pretty.

His eyes widened. "Rainy, that's an enormous scar."

"We don't call them Burners for nothing," I said and started to roll my sleeve back down. Duke caught my hand and held it.

"May I?" he asked.

"If you want."

He pulled my sleeve back again and touched the scar tissue. A third-degree burn, it had left me with no sensation. A shame. I would've enjoyed feeling his gentle caress.

"Nobody burns *The Grapes of Wrath* on my watch," I said, trying to sound bold and brassy. "Or the Duke of Chicago."

He kissed the back of my hand and whispered, "My hero."

That was, of course, when Koshka bit my ankle.

"Ow!" I shouted. Duke started. I looked down at Koshka at my feet. "You were supposed to bite *him* when he got flirty, not me."

He didn't apologize, but that's no surprise. In *The Last Unicorn,* the legendary fantasy author Peter S. Beagle writes, "No cat anywhere ever gave anyone a straight answer." Well, no cat anywhere ever gave anyone an apology either.

Duke only laughed softly and released my hand.

"Have a seat. Can I offer you a drink?" he asked.

Most noir detectives had drinking problems. It comes with the territory. Duke was a rare exception. He drank but not heavily and rarely on the job.

"It's Prohibition," I teased, as I sat in the chair facing his desk.

"Your point?" He dropped into his office chair and threw his feet on top of his desk, crossed at the ankles.

"The truth is, I can't drink." I petted Koshka, who was handling this shift of scene far better than I was. "Or eat. Or sleep. I could be stuck here if I did."

"Oh no," he said, feigning shock and horror. "Anything but that."

"You're flirting again."

"You're hardly one to talk after that speech you gave about being in love with me."

"No, no, I didn't say that. I said I was in love with your *books*. That's different."

He nodded. "So you weren't in love with me?"

"Well, I didn't say that either."

He laughed softly. "I knew it."

"I had a teenage crush on you a long, long, long time ago."

"Did you ever . . ." Duke wiggled his fingers again, as if performing a magic spell.

"Did I ever what?"

"Visit me before?" he asked. "Lurk in the shadows, blow kisses at my back?"

"Oh, no, never," I said. "That's completely against the rules. We can't go into a book unless we're on a mission."

"But you were tempted, yes?"

"Every single day."

He laughed his warm, delectable male laugh, a laugh that could make a nun break her habits.

"So tell me how this works, darling," he said. "Your magic. Are you Book Witches born or did you sell your soul to someone? Do you cast spells? Own a cauldron? Can I see your wand or should I buy you dinner first?"

"You really want to know?" I asked.

He took his feet off the desk and faced me.

"I want to know everything about you," he said. From any other man that would've sounded like a line, a pickup. But I could tell Duke meant it. I knew I should be getting Duke back on the plot, but I couldn't tear myself away from this conversation. Not yet. This was a teenage dream come true.

"Some Book Witches are born into it, like me," I said. "Witchcraft often runs in families. Otherwise, we put enchanted recruitment posters up in libraries and bookstores and coffee shops. To normal people, the posters look like someone's selling gently used tractor tires. To anyone with latent magical ability, it says we're hiring people to protect and defend stories."

"Fascinating. So no soul selling? That's all anti-witch propaganda, I assume?"

"We don't sell our souls to anyone, although we do, usually, owe our entire paychecks to the local bookstore. To get in and out of stories, we use little spells. No cauldron, but I do have a coffee mug in the shape of a cauldron. And my wand, so to speak, is in the alley outside the Bathtub."

"How did you know that Burner person had infiltrated my world? Magic, I assume?"

"We have a whole coven that monitors books for damage. Someone discovered a blank page in your book. X had you tied up in a basement so you couldn't finish the plot, and the story started to die."

"Die?" He sounded aghast.

"You pull a plant from the ground, it'll eventually wilt and die. It's kind of like that. But I rescued you so he decided to—"

"Eighty-six me on page eighty-six?"

I nodded. "But now that X knows I'm watching your books, he likely won't try it again for a long time. And once you get back to your mission with Edith King, and I leave, the story will go back to the way it was, the way your author intended it."

"And if I don't finish the mission?"

"You saw the blank pages," I said. "That blankness will spread through the rest of *Empty Graves,* then all copies of *Empty Graves,* and then finally . . . people who read the book will forget it ever existed."

"Dastardly. Well, we shan't let that happen," he said, lifting his glass to salute me.

"You're handling this well," I said. "Finding out you're a fictional character would do a number on most people."

"It's good news in a way, really," Duke said.

"How so?" I asked.

"My brothers," he said. "You can never die if you've never lived, yes?"

I knew his backstory as well as he did, but listened as he recounted his brothers' fates. His oldest brother, David, died in the Great War. Charles, the second-oldest, caught typhus in the trenches two years later. Edmund died by suicide.

"Eddie had been suffering from shell shock," Duke said, his voice soft. "Poor lad. But you say this is a novel, yes? Then it didn't happen, did it? My brothers didn't go to war. They didn't witness horrors. They didn't die for naught and in vain. It was all just lines in a book. I find that strangely comforting."

While Duke was reciting the litany of his tragedies, Koshka had trotted over to him and pounced into his lap.

"This," he said, stroking Koshka under the chin, "is also strangely comforting. I wish my writer had given me a cat. No, no, I'm not bothered at all to learn I'm pure fiction. It explains so much."

"Does it?"

"I don't seem to age. Time passes very slowly. If I get shot—which I do more than I should, I think—I tend to heal completely by my next case. Always seemed slightly suspicious to me. I solve every case I take on. And I'm tragically unattached. You'd think a duke would at least have a steady girl."

I couldn't help but laugh. "Fictional detectives are almost always single."

"Surely not."

"Miss Marple? Single. Poirot? Single. Sherlock? Sam Spade? Easy Rawlins—he's after your time—he was married but got divorced."

"Glad to know it's not anything I'm doing wrong," he said.

"You do everything right," I told him. Then blushed. "I mean . . . your character does all the right things. Like focusing on solving cases instead of dating. That's what I mean."

"Edith King again?" he asked.

"You do really need to finish your story."

"But I'm having so much fun with you, Rainy. You . . . you're not fictional, are you? You're real. You're more real than anyone I've ever met."

"How can you tell?" I asked.

"The same way I can tell a diamond from a story about a diamond."

My face turned hot. He smiled at me.

"This is why I was in love with you in high school," I said.

"And now?"

"No, no, and no," I said, and perhaps the lady was protesting too much. "Look, hypothetically, even if we did fall in love, we couldn't ever be together. Rule Number Seven—Real people belong in the real world. Fictional characters belong in works of fiction."

His brow furrowed and he sat up. "Whose rules?"

"The Book Witches'."

He shook his head. "Thought witches were a bit freer with their affections than all that. More propaganda, I see."

"Nope, never dated the devil," I said. "Or any demons. I had a brief fling with a mildly wicked Coastie, but it wasn't serious."

"A Coastie?"

"Coast Guard," I said. "If you live in Fort Meriwether, Oregon, you are legally required to date a Coastie at some point in your twenties."

"How about fictional detectives?"

"No, sorry. Strictly verboten."

"You're breaking my heart."

"Don't worry. When I leave, I'll put a spell on you to make you forget this ever happened."

"I won't allow it."

"You don't have any choice."

"Outrageous," he said. "I should not be treated like a second-class citizen simply because I don't exist. Next you'll be telling me I can't vote in elections."

He couldn't vote in elections—not because he was fictional, but because he was English.

"I don't make the rules," I said, holding up my hands. "I just follow them so I won't get into trouble."

"Rainy . . . what's your last name?"

"March," I said.

"Rainy March, I want you to listen to me. And you should listen to me because I'm very wealthy, handsome, and highborn, which foolish people mistake for wisdom and authority. But I want you to make that mistake as well, so you'll bend to my will."

I was trying very hard not to laugh at him.

"I'm listening," I said.

"A person who breaks one rule is a rule breaker. A person who breaks all the rules is a *rebel.*" He stroked Koshka's back like a comic book villain. "Come be a rebel with me, Rainy."

I crossed my arms and sat up ramrod straight. "No. And give me my cat back. You're a bad influence."

He held Koshka to his shoulder like a baby. "Come and get him."

I exhaled heavily and reached out my arms across Duke's desk. "Please? Finish the case?"

"A few more minutes, Rainy. It's all I ask. You said I'd forget all of this once you're gone."

"Yes, once I do the spell."

"Give me one more hour," he said, "then I'll do anything you want. *Anything.*"

"It's against protocol but since you did save our lives . . ." I glanced at the mantel clock. In Duke's world, it was eleven. We'd have to be gone by midnight. "One hour? You promise?"

"On my honor, whatever I have left. Then you may scramble my brain all you wish."

"It won't feel like scrambling," I explained. "You'll just remember this all like a dream."

"Feels like a dream already," he said. "Probably why I'm, as you say, handling it so well."

"Also, it's in your character," I explained. "The Duke of Chicago is famously unflappable and imperturbable."

"Perhaps, but not now. I'm feeling both flapped and perturbed."

"Imagine how I feel," I said. "I'm in your office, sitting in this chair in front of your desk. I dreamed about this place. I imagined what it looked like all my life, and now I'm here." Something caught my eye, and I rose from my chair, walking over to the fireplace as if pulled by invisible hands. I pointed. "That's your actual ducal coronet on the bust of General Cincinnatus. You like to put it on and shout orders out the window to the 'peasants' below."

"I only did that once. And it was my birthday."

"There's a running gag in your books about how you keep trying to hire a secretary, but every time one shows up for the interview and when you explain the job to them—solving murders and kidnappings while also doing all the typing and filing—they run for the door. When I was seventeen, I had this long-running *very* elaborate fantasy that I'd apply for the job, and you'd try to scare me off, but you couldn't. And then, of course when you realized how brilliant I was, you'd make me your partner, and we'd fall madly in love."

He laughed. "Very sweet, but I don't believe in child labor or cradle robbing."

I picked Duke's magnifying glass up off the mantel and peered through it at him. "In my teenage fantasies, I was older, I promise."

"Thank goodness. I'm glad to know I wasn't a cad even in your dreams."

Koshka bumped his head against Duke's chin.

"I said 'cad,' not 'cat,' young man."

"Something's not right," I said and grabbed the copy of *Empty Graves* that X had left behind. "This isn't the right painting."

I flipped to the first chapter of the book, where Edith King's husband hires Duke to find her after she's been kidnapped.

"What do you mean?"

Another running joke in the series had Duke constantly changing the painting that hung in his office. Every book he had something different, and it always reflected Duke's mental state or the theme of the book. The painting in *Empty Graves* was one of girlish innocence, reflecting Edith King's flight from her violent husband into a new life of peace and safety.

"It says right here that the painting is supposed to be *Autumn Leaves* by John Everett Millais." I read straight from the book, page nine. "*On the canvas above the mantel, four young girls built a pile of fall leaves in a twilight garden. Innocent happy girls and not a man in sight.*" I jabbed my finger at the new painting. "So what is this?"

Now, hanging over the fireplace was a very different image.

"I believe that's *Circe* by John Collier," Duke said. "Don't like her? She is a witch."

"She's a naked witch. A naked witch with a cat."

Technically a naked witch and two big cats, but still . . .

Duke tried and failed to look angelic. "Can't blame a man for accidentally manifesting his subconscious longings, can you?"

"I can. Now put it back." I said.

He took a breath and when I glanced over the mantel again, the correct painting, *Autumn Leaves,* had been restored to its rightful place.

"Better," I said, then turned back to Duke. "Speaking of paintings, can I ask you something I've always wanted to know?"

"Anything, darling."

"Back at your penthouse," I said, "you have a safe, right? A wall safe behind a mirror?"

"I do. Why do you ask?"

"We have one, too, behind a painting."

"Mine's behind the mirror, but go on. I'm intrigued by this line of questioning."

"I've always wanted to know what you keep in it. I'm not being nosy."

He raised an eyebrow. "Really? Sounds rather nosy to me. Good thing I like your nose."

I laughed. "It's a literary question. Every Ducky has their theories about it. It's supposedly symbolic of—"

"Excuse me, what? Ducky?"

I blushed crimson. "Um . . . so, your readers have their own nickname. We call ourselves Duckies. Duke? Duck? Get it?"

It was worse than it sounded. When I was eighteen, I desperately wanted to get a Ducky tattoo on my shoulder until Pops reminded me that were I ever to hop into a Nathaniel Hawthorne novel or short story, there was a very good chance it would be considered a devil's mark, and I'd be hanged as a witch. So there went that idea.

"That is adorable, Ducky."

Still blushing, I cleared my throat. "As I was saying . . . One person says your wall safe symbolizes secrets that can't ever be told," I said. "Another said it's symbolic of, um . . . repressed sexuality."

"That would be my best guess." Duke nodded sagely.

"Or maybe it's your underwear drawer."

"What do you think is in there?" he asked. "What's your guess?"

"If we're speaking symbolically, I thought it might be . . . your grief."

"I keep my grief in a safe? Why do you say that?"

"I think that's where I keep mine—locked up. No father that I know of and my mother died when I was a baby. I . . . I sometimes want to talk about her, but I don't like upsetting my grandfather. So I hide it away. Part of the reason I think I identified with you. You'd lost most of your family, too, but you carry on anyway."

"I'm so sorry, Rainy."

"It's fine, promise."

He stood up, Koshka in his arms. "You want to know what's in the safe? I'll show you."

"You can't show me. We're in your office, not your—"

But in the blink of an eye—or the turn of a page?—we were in his penthouse apartment.

"I do like this power," Duke said, glancing around in approval. "Good, Nigel's gone to bed already. Don't need him around tonight asking questions. Drink? Oh, damn, right. You can't drink."

"Stand by." I held up my hand then dropped onto the sofa arm. "Having vertigo."

Being in Duke's office had been like visiting Santa Claus at the mall. Being in his penthouse was like getting to visit the North Pole. If the North Pole were a sumptuous bachelor's paradise that took up the entire top floor of a swanky Chicago hotel.

"What do you think?" Duke asked, leaning against a black marble fireplace mantel. Koshka lay curled at his feet as if he owned the place.

"This sofa is trying to seduce me," I said as I slid down the arm and onto the supple cushions.

"It's not the only one," Duke said. "Now come here, lass."

I struggled to get to my feet. Everything in this penthouse made a girl want to lie down and stay down. As I walked to the fireplace, I glanced over at a closed door. Duke's bedroom.

"I saw that," he said.

"You saw nothing."

Smiling, Duke reached up and started to take the mirror down from over the mantel, then paused and looked at me. "I want something in return for opening my safe for you."

"Oh, dear."

"Nothing salacious," he said.

Pity. I didn't say that out loud. "What do you want?"

"Your hat."

A glimpse into the Duke of Chicago's famous top secret safe . . . in exchange for my hat.

"I think you're lowballing yourself," I said, "but if you want it, it's yours."

I took off my hat and tossed it to him. He caught it midair and clutched it to his chest.

"Now why did you want my hat?"

"I didn't. I wanted to see you with your hair down."

He raised his hand to my hair, touched a strand that had fallen over my face, and pushed it behind my ear.

"That's all?" I asked. "My hair for your deepest secrets? Duke, you got suckered."

He shook his head as he went to work on the combination lock, spinning the knob this way and that.

"How wrong you are, Rainy March. That," he said as the safe door popped open, "was a steal."

CHAPTER FIVE

After the slightest of pauses—I think Duke was steeling himself—he reached in and removed a plain black hatbox. He carried it over to the sofa and set it in front of us on the coffee table.

"I had to hide everything I took," Duke said. "You know the saying . . . keep it under your hat."

He lifted the lid, and sure enough, a black silk top hat sat inside. When he took out the hat, I could see it was only a cover for an assortment of small things carefully wrapped in linen handkerchiefs.

Duke picked one up and unwrapped it.

"Davey's watch," Duke said. "A Cartier. He showed it off to everyone. They were still quite novel then. On men especially."

"Wristwatches were for women?"

"Back then," Duke said, "they were like bracelets with timepieces. Davey had his pocket watch stolen once, and when he bragged about how hard it would be to steal his watch later, I nicked it while he was sleeping."

"How old were you?"

"Ten," Duke said. "I gave it back the next day. A few years later, before he shipped out, he joked that I could have his watch if he got his head knocked off. I would rather have his head on than the watch, but beggars can't be choosers."

He wrapped the watch up again and returned it to the hatbox.

Koshka strolled over to the coffee table and eyed the treasures with curiosity.

Duke untied a piece of twine wrapped around a small brown paper rectangle. A book?

"*The Rose*," I said when Duke revealed the cover. "By W. B. Yeats."

"Charlie wanted to be a poet. He thought he'd be a poet-soldier, like Siegfried Sassoon." Duke glanced at me then back down at the pages. "He wrote poetry and love letters to another officer. I hope I haven't shocked you."

I smiled at him. "That's not shocking where I'm from."

"Where are you from?"

"The future," I said. He opened his mouth to ask a question and I raised my hand. "And no, I can't tell you about it."

He smiled, then turned a page in the Yeats book.

"Mother had all his papers burned when he died. A maid stole this from the bonfire for me."

"Did she think you might catch typhus from them?"

He thought about that question a moment before answering.

"Truly, I think she burned his poetry for the same reason everyone who burns books does—because it's less trouble than burning the people who wrote them."

He opened a page marked with a scarlet ribbon and read aloud:

When you are old and grey and full of sleep,
And nodding by the fire, take down this book,
And slowly read, and dream of the soft look
Your eyes had once, and of their shadows deep . . .

"Keep going," I begged.

Duke cleared his throat. "Better not. Let's see . . . what else have we here? Oh, yes, Eddie's toy horse."

"It's beautiful," I said, marveling at the intricate metalwork. It had tiny wheels on the hooves so a child could pull it on a string behind them.

Koshka stood on his back legs and lightly batted at the horse.

"No, buddy, be careful," I said. "That's not—"

"Let him play with it." Duke pushed it toward Koshka. "Eddie loved animals. He was always sneaking food to the cats in the stables. Father would catch him and whip him for it, telling him the cats wouldn't hunt mice if they weren't hungry. But Eddie didn't care. He'd do it again the very next day."

Koshka sniffed the horse, then batted at it again, then again, until he pushed the toy to the edge of the table.

I caught it as it fell and gave it back to Duke.

"Is my writer still alive, by any chance?" he asked me.

"Dead since 1969."

"Pity," Duke said. "I would've liked to have had a word with him. Was it really necessary to kill *all* of my brothers off?"

"Fictional detectives tend to have tragic backstories that make them obsessed with saving other people. Since you couldn't save your brothers, you try to save everyone else."

"I still say I'm owed compensation. A beautiful girl madly in love with me, at least," he said, as he wrapped the horse in its linen shroud and placed it back into the hatbox.

"If they're only characters in a book," Duke asked, "why do I love them so bloody much?"

"You can love fictional characters. At times, it's almost easier to love them than to love real people."

He smiled at me again.

"I was wrong," I said. "It's not your grief in your safe. It's your heart you keep locked up."

"I've only ever unlocked it for you."

"When you say things like that, I lose my ability to reply coherently," I teased him. "I'm worried I'll say the wrong thing."

He shook his head. "Say something true, even if you don't think it's the right thing to say. I like hearing your voice."

"What if I say I'm jealous?"

"Jealous? Really?" He didn't sound insulted, only intrigued.

"I have no idea who my father is, and I never got to know my mother. She was a legendary Book Witch. My boss tells me constantly how perfect she was. Saved dozens of stories, never broke a single rule. But when she died, the only thing she bequeathed to me was a Nancy Drew book—*The Secret of the Old Clock.*"

"Only one book?" Duke sounded horrified, which I appreciated. Sometimes I felt guilty for expecting more from my mother. She was gone, after all, and couldn't defend her decisions to me, although I liked to think she had her reasons.

"I assume it was her favorite? Must have been to leave it to me. I love the book, too, but I can't help but want more. An old toy from when she was a kid or a piece of clothing I could wear or a message?"

He stared at me and the moment grew heavy with waiting and meaning, though I couldn't say what this all meant, only that it meant something, maybe more than it should have.

"We should go," I said. "We've been here too long and you need to—"

"Finish the story, yes," he said. "I will, of course. I always do. I've never not solved a case, and I don't intend that to change. But I can't help but wonder . . . if I'm not real and Edith King's not real, what's the point of it all?" He asked this while petting Koshka, who had buried his head in the hatbox, sniffing for treats or more toys. "He's a real cat. Isn't it more important that I pet a real cat than help a fictional girl?"

I pulled the copy of *Empty Graves* from my pocket.

"Here's what happens at the end of the book," I told Duke. "You follow Edith King to the harbor, where she's going to get on a boat that will eventually sneak her into Canada. Her parents and husband told you she was kidnapped. But you finally put two and two together and realize she'd faked her kidnapping to get out of the country and away from her violent husband. You have your chance to catch her, but this happens instead . . ."

I cleared my throat and read the passage aloud to him.

Duke watched Edith watching him from the dock, waiting for him to make his move, nab her, drag her back home. If he ran, he could stop her. He didn't move.

"Go," he mouthed. "Now, Edith."

Even at a hundred yards, he could see her smile.

"Thank you," she might have said before she turned and ran across the boat ramp, aboard the ship waiting to take her away forever.

Few people are more despised than the soldier who deserts his unit or the wife who deserts her husband. But at that moment, they were the only people who made any sense to Duke. The war had never ended. Maybe it never would. Not until the world stopped sending its sons through the meat grinder of battle and selling its daughters off to brutes.

Tonight, however, the war ended for Edith. If Duke had ticker tape in his pocket, he would have thrown her a victory parade.

The boat pulled away from the dock. As it drifted from view, he thought he saw Edith crying, but no . . . she was laughing.

"Go and don't look back," he said to Edith, words he wished he could've said to Davey, to Charlie, to Eddie. "The world has corpses aplenty but not nearly enough laughing girls dancing the Lindy Hop on their own empty graves."

Edith King danced away.

Slowly, I closed the book.

"Those paragraphs are why *Empty Graves* has been banned or challenged in a dozen middle and high school libraries."

"Those Burners at it again?"

"Real people do it too. No magical powers required, just a fatal lack of imagination and compassion. They say this passage is 'anti-military' and 'anti-family.' That's not how other people read it, though. There was a march against domestic violence not long ago. I saw it on TV . . . which hasn't been invented yet. Imagine small movies inside your house."

"Very nice," Duke said.

"At this march, one woman wore a T-shirt that read, 'Dance, Edith, Dance.' Edith King came to symbolize every woman who escaped and started a new life. The Statue of Liberty isn't a real person either, but she means something, right? Something worth fighting for?"

Duke was silent for a moment, then stood up. "I'll finish the story tonight. And all my cases. I'll finish them all. If only for you."

I looked up at him. "Thank you," I breathed. "It's nearly midnight. We need to get back to the alley by the Bathtub—"

"I can take you. Let me get my coat." He stood and reached for the lid to the hatbox, then stopped and sat back down again. "Wait, please. One more thing."

"You're stalling," I said.

"Not stalling. I have a gift for you."

He took a small black velvet bag from the hatbox and untied the string. Into his palm dropped a ring. He held it out to me. A small gold ring, the band delicately engraved with vines. The setting was black enamel with a white flower, five petals, made of tiny seed pearls.

"When David died, my grandmother had this made for my mother. It's a mourning ring. That flower is a forget-me-not. There's a locket compartment on the back. She said Mother could take a strand of David's hair and put it in the locket."

Duke turned the ring over and with his thumbnail carefully popped open the tiny locket compartment. It was empty.

"Mother refused to wear it, said it was morbid and foolish, and we had best keep our chins up and carry on. I was so young at the time, it fit on my pinkie. So I kept it. Doesn't fit anymore. Will you take it and wear it?"

"Duke, I can't do that."

"Why not? You said you didn't have anything of your mother's to wear. And I have this whole box of treasures. I'm happy to share. What was your mother's name?"

"Ellery," I said. "Like Ellery Queen."

"Who?"

"Never mind."

Duke fished a little black notebook out of his pocket and scribbled something very, very small on the corner of a page. Then he tore it off and slipped it into the locket compartment of the ring.

"Now the ring has your mother's name in it. Wear that and when you look at it, you'll think of me giving that to you in honor of your mother."

"I'll think of her *and* you?"

"Two-for-one special," he said with a smile. "Be a good girl and put it on. Please, Rainy."

He meant it, I could tell. He wasn't trying to be nice. He wanted me to have this ring, and if I said no, he'd be heartbroken. And the younger me would never forgive the older me for breaking the heart of the Duke of Chicago.

"Thank you," I said. I reached for the ring, but he caught my hand and gently slipped it on my index finger. It wouldn't quite fit.

"Oh, dear," he said. "Let's try a different finger."

Then he put it on my ring finger.

"Made for you," he said, still holding my hand. "You'll simply have to wear it forever now."

"My boss would kill me if she found out I took a gift from a character."

"Break a rule or two. You might like it."

The ring did fit me perfectly, like my finger had been waiting for it. I touched the five pearl petals of the forget-me-not. "I have such good taste in books."

He caressed the back of my hand.

"Edith King," I reminded him. "Self-awareness is no excuse for not getting the job done."

"Yes, yes," he said. "Let's be off."

Instead of using his newfound magic, Duke simply drove us back to the Bathtub and parked by the alley.

"Can we drive?" I asked.

"I'll scout around," he said. "Stay put, you two."

He got out of the car and checked the street, the alley. I was seeing the Duke of Chicago in action, the investigator with eyes in the back of his head. He jogged back over to the car and opened my door. He took Koshka from my arms and, with his free hand, helped me out of the car.

"To the alley," he said. We slipped past the garbage piles and into the dank darkness. "Now what?"

"I hate to say it but you'll have to relinquish my cat."

"Never," Duke said. Even Koshka gave a little whine of protest.

"Boys," I said sternly.

"Be brave, comrade. Do as your mistress says," Duke said, giving Koshka another scratch. Reluctantly, he wriggled from Duke's arms and hopped lightly onto the ground.

I looked up to where my black umbrella hung a few inches above my head.

"How does that work?" Duke asked.

"That's our way in and out. Like a magic tunnel. I close my umbrella, say a little charm, and *poof,* we're gone."

"Fascinating," Duke breathed. "What else can you do? Dance across the notes on sheet music? Pop in and out of pictures?"

"Stories only," I said. "But we all have lots of special powers. If you're looking for a good book but don't know what to read, I can do a little charm and before you know it, the book you're longing for will make its way into your hands. And I can tell what someone's favorite book is and why. I can also mend broken spines. Book spines, not human spines, unfortunately. And I can—"

"Can you take me with you?" Duke asked softly.

"Duke," I said and nothing else.

"You can, can't you?"

I could, yes, but I didn't tell him that. If he asked me again, I might not be able to say no.

"Duke, right now, I'm supposed to perform that spell now, the one that will make you forget me."

"Don't," he said. "Please don't."

"It would be easier for you."

"Eden's doors are locked and guarded for a reason," he said. "There's no going back." He stared deeply into my eyes. "Please, Rainy? Don't make a duke beg."

How could I say no to the man who had saved my life? Or, at least, had given it meaning when nothing else could?

"All right, I won't do the spell, but you have to solve all your cases. And no more using your self-awareness to take over the stories. Okay? I don't want to lose my job."

It was going to be fun cleaning up the mess we'd already made—and by "fun" I meant "not fun."

"I'll be a good little detective, I promise," he said.

Duke lowered his head and brushed his lips against mine, then kissed me again, deeper. And of course I ruined it by saying against his mouth, "I am being kissed by the Duke of Chicago . . . This is the greatest single moment of my life."

"You realize you said that out loud?"

"Oops." I stepped back. "I'll miss you. Always."

"See you soon," he said.

"No, you won't."

"You know what they say—love laughs at locksmiths."

"What does that mean?"

"You'll find out."

He stepped back. I scooped up Koshka and reached for my umbrella. Once I had it in hand, I flicked the button to close it, whispered the words I used to escape stories—"Our revels now are ended"—and then, with a swirl of magic, we were home.

CHAPTER SIX

Mission accomplished. With a spell or two, I restored the text of *Empty Graves* to the original, removing any trace of damage wrought by X or by me overstaying my welcome. Pops was thrilled, of course. Dr. Fanshawe even smiled once. Commendations all around. But the victory was a hollow one. For a week after leaving Duke's world behind, all I could think about was him. I moped so much even Pops asked why I was down.

"You were right," I told him. "You should never meet your heroes."

"That bad?" he asked.

"That good."

Daydreams and night dreams and fantasies filled my hours. I'd wake up already pining for Duke. My days were spent longing for him, and then I'd fall asleep every night wishing and hoping and praying to see him again, until whoever the universe left in charge of hearts—my guess is St. Valentine—approved my request.

It only took eight days for the universe to grow tired of my nagging. "Anything to shut her up," St. Valentine likely muttered as he brought the rubber stamp down.

At least I'm guessing that's what happened, because how else can you explain that, eight mornings after I told Duke goodbye forever, I woke up from one of those dreams—the kind that leaves scorch marks on your pillow and smoke coming out of your ears and causes you to make very awkward eye contact with yourself in the bathroom mirror while fixing your hair—to find Duke sitting on the end of my bed with Koshka half-asleep on his lap and my mother's copy of *The Secret of the Old Clock* propped open with one hand.

Gasping, I sat up. "Duke?"

He smiled the smile of a man who'd never been told no in his life, even by the laws of the universe.

"Morning, darling. Ripping yarn, this book," he said. I'd been reading it the night before, something I only did these days when I was particularly lonely.

My brain took a long time to catch up with this new reality. Finally, I said the least interesting thing I could have said.

"You're here."

He closed the book, put Koshka down, and crawled across the bed to me. "I told you I'd see you soon. Can't fathom how I wound up here, but you shan't hear me complaining."

Against my better judgment, I let him take me into his arms.

"Did you miss me, darling?" he asked.

"Obviously," I said, nodding toward the tower of Duke books on my nightstand.

The books—of course. How could I have been so thoughtless? Once when I was a little girl, I'd accidentally dragged characters out of their story. Grandma had nearly passed out the night she'd come to my bedroom to tuck me in and read to me, only to find twenty-five very well-behaved babies in my room. I'd pulled an entire rabbit family out of *The Country Bunny and the Little Gold Shoes* by DuBose Heyward and Marjorie Flack and was having a tea party with them.

But I had never, ever pulled a character from their books by dreaming about them, longing for them. First time for everything, though.

"I missed you too," he said. "Obviously."

He bent to kiss me, and I stopped him with a hand on his chest.

"The rules," I told him, in a panic. A very pleasant panic but still, a definite panic. "Rule Seven: Fictional characters belong in story worlds. Real people belong in the real world. You have to go back in your books. Right now."

"Now?" He raised an eyebrow. "Or after?"

"After what?"

"You tell me," he said.

At that, I used all my strength to push up and flip Duke over onto his back, where I straddled him across the hips, held him down with one hand, and pointed my finger in his face with the other.

"I guess you told me," he said, grinning.

"No, we can't," I said in no uncertain terms.

"We can," he said, raising his hand to stroke my cheek with his fingertips. "We absolutely can."

"There's no way we can be together. None. Never. Never ever. We'll get caught. I'll get fired. Your books—"

"Rainy, darling, just because we don't know how to be together now doesn't mean we'll never know. It's a mystery. That's all. The mystery of us. And didn't you always want to solve a case with me?"

Better question . . . would I? Surely as long as Duke wasn't out of his books for more than an hour or two or three . . . but no, I shouldn't. Then again, there was his face to think of, his smile, his everything. If we were careful, nothing bad would happen. I looked down at Duke luxuriating on my pillow.

"We can try," I said. "But if we get caught—"

He pulled me down, and the last thing he said before he kissed me was . . .

"I promise, darling, you won't regret it."

Book Two

MYSTERY

CHAPTER SEVEN

Present Day

Reader, I regretted it.

Two years have now passed since I woke up to find Duke in my bed.

For one glorious year, he and I secretly dated. I'd visit him in his stories, or I'd pull him out to visit me in the real world—sometimes on purpose, sometimes simply by dreaming about him. He'd assist me with my missions, and occasionally I'd help with his cases. It was a passionate affair, clandestine, forbidden . . . and utterly doomed.

We got caught. Of course we got caught. And we got caught by the worst person who could possibly catch us—my boss, Dr. Fanshawe.

Duke and I were forbidden from seeing each other, which effectively broke us up without even a proper goodbye. Even worse, because I did have a bad habit of yanking Duke out of his stories by the sheer force of my love and longing for him, my Duke of Chicago books had been seized by Dr. Fanshawe like illegal contraband.

Bad enough to lose Duke, but to lose his stories as well?

I tried to move on, but it wasn't easy. Yes, I was living in Fort Meriwether with Pops, but I'd left my heart in Chicago.

Which brings us to the present. Even after a full year of penance, I was still in the doghouse with Dr. Fanshawe. So while the rest of Fort Meriwether was outdoors, enjoying what was probably the last sunny day before the winter doldrums set in, I was in my home library up to my eyeballs in Gothic romance novels. An army of young women in white nightgowns raced across fields and moors, fleeing bad men and burning castles. And it was my job to save them.

The books, I mean, not the girls in nightgowns. The ladies were on their own.

All these books had come out in the 1960s and '70s and had never been digitized. The only remaining copies were these decaying mass market paperbacks. My job was to magically heal the broken spines, mend the torn covers, and return the loose pages to the fold. When I'd finished with that, I had to not-so-magically catalog them so they wouldn't be entirely lost to the ravages of time.

Come to think of it, *The Ravages of Time* would have made a good Gothic romance title. In the stack of books I was currently working on, we had some banger titles. *The House of Doom. The Castle of Evil. The Mirror Never Lies.* And my personal favorite, *A Dark and Wicked Desire.*

That one . . . I might set aside to read in bed later.

True, the titles were a little melodramatic, and all the couples in the books needed marriage counseling, divorce lawyers, or restraining orders, but they were fun reads. Lust, corruption, sinister patriarchs guarding scandalous family secrets! Heady stuff wrapped up in moonlight and silk.

Plus, I identified with these heroines. I also felt like my life was one castle fire after another.

I couldn't help but think Dr. Fanshawe had an ulterior motive for assigning this particular genre to me, as each musty book was a vivid reminder that romance was more trouble than it was worth. After my seventh full-body sneeze, I was willing to entertain that possibility myself.

Every time Nixon-era dust shot up my nose, I reminded myself that I was helping to preserve the secret history of women warning other women that they shouldn't always trust the authority figures in their lives. And when all else fails, burn the evil castle to the cursed ground and run for it.

The library door opened and our housekeeper wheeled the tea tray in and parked it next to the reading table.

"Tea, Miss March," she said in a broad English accent rarely heard anymore except on old BBC shows. As usual, Mrs. Turner wore a gray dress with a white apron and had her hair tucked under a white bonnet. She was the very picture of Victorian respectability. Once, I'd offered to buy her some jeans and T-shirts to wear around the house, and she'd acted as if I'd told her to put on a bear costume to clean the bathroom.

"Oh, thanks, but you didn't have to do that," I said.

"I heard you sneezing your poor head off, Miss March," she said, tsk-tsking at me. "Tea's what the doctor ordered."

Although I was twenty-seven years old, Mrs. Turner tended to treat me like a weak and sickly child. I would've been offended, but she did the same thing to my late grandmother and to Pops. Two weeks ago, Pops had gotten a paper cut—occupational hazard. Mrs. Turner wrapped a Snoopy Band-Aid around his finger and ordered my eighty-two-year-old grandfather to take the rest of the day off from handling books to recover. He refused, and an hour later sliced another finger.

"Tea cures sneezing?" I asked her.

"Tea cures *everything.*"

She poured a cup of orange pekoe for me, added a single sugar cube, and set it next to my elbow on a saucer, a process that had taken her mere seconds. The woman was a tea-serving machine.

"Your biscuits, Master Koshka," she said. She set a saucer containing three cat treats on the floor in front of Koshka, who'd spent the past hour asleep in a sunbeam. He woke up at once, rubbed his cheek on Mrs. Turner's ankles, then ate his treats with feline gusto.

Mrs. Turner returned to the tea trolley. "Dinner for one tonight?"

"Dinner for one," I said. "Until Pops finally gets back."

Pops had left a week ago on some sort of secret mission, and I was more than ready for him to come home.

She shook her head. "Hope you don't mind me saying it, Miss March, but you're twenty-seven. If you're not married soon, you'll be a spinster. You don't want that now, do you?"

"More time to read," I said.

"Pretty girl like you already on the shelf." She sighed as she wheeled the trolley from the library. "Now drink your tea, Miss March, or I'll take you to hospital."

This was not an idle threat from Mrs. Turner. I drank the tea.

TEACUP IN HAND, I WANDERED TO THE FIREPLACE.

On the mantel in our library sat the only picture I had of my mother and me together. In the faded five-by-seven photograph, she's thirty years old, and though she's just given birth, she looks very thin and wan. She wears a white bathrobe with her long dark hair in a loose braid. I'm not in her arms, but in the cradle. She's reading to me from a hardcover. On the illustrated dust jacket, a teenage girl in a blue skirt suit and matching cloche hat carries an old carriage clock through the woods.

The Secret of the Old Clock, Nancy Drew book one. Published in 1930.

The book itself, the very one in the picture, sat inside the wall safe behind the portrait over the fireplace. When you lose a parent when a you're a baby, like I did, it's hard to believe that parent was ever real or alive. Sometimes I needed to hold her book in my hands to remind myself that once upon a time she was a real living breathing person with hopes and dreams for herself and for me.

I put my cup and saucer on the mantel, pulled over the ottoman, and climbed up. After removing the portrait, I typed in the combination and the door popped open.

There it was, my mother's book. I took it from the safe and grimaced at the sight. Although not a first edition, it was old and somehow between the last time I'd read it and now, it had developed yet another tear in the cover and one page seemed to be coming loose from the binding.

Of course, as a Book Witch, I could have charmed it, turned it into a new copy even, but I was worried if I made it too new, my mother's name and every trace of her fingerprints would disappear from the pages.

No, I would simply have to be more careful with it.

I sat at the reading table, opened the book, and began to read from the first chapter, entitled "The Lost Will."

"It would be a shame if all that money went to the Tophams! They will fly higher than ever!"

Nancy Drew, a pretty girl of sixteen, leaned over the library table and addressed her father, who sat reading a newspaper by the study lamp.

"I beg your pardon, Nancy. What were you saying about the Tophams?"

Carson Drew, a noted criminal and mystery-case lawyer, known far and wide for his work as a former district attorney, looked up from his evening paper and smiled indulgently upon his only daughter.

Every time I read those lines, I felt a stab of jealousy. Nancy and I had so much in common—we were both girls without mothers who had a penchant for getting ourselves into and out of scrapes. And while I'd had a wonderful childhood with my grandparents, Nancy had a father, Carson Drew. To an orphan, even an absentee or neglectful father sounded like the height of luxury, but Nancy had one who clearly adored her. I envied her like a twin sister who had gotten an extra Christmas present. According to *The Secret of the Old Clock,* Nancy's mother had died when she was ten. That meant she'd also gotten ten years with a mother in her life, and I'd only gotten a few months, months I didn't even remember.

Of course I'd asked my grandparents everything they knew about my mother, and they'd told me wonderful stories about her. Young Ellery March, like me, had been obsessed with books. First it was anything with unicorns, then sharks, then anything set in space, then Nancy Drew by the time she turned ten. Before me, she was the youngest Book Witch, joining the Ink and Paper Coven at only fifteen years old. She took on every assignment fearlessly, making her a legend by the age of twenty-one.

And then . . . something happened. At age twenty-nine, she disappeared for an entire year without a trace. And when she showed up on my grandparents' doorstep, she was eight months pregnant with me. She would answer no questions about where she'd been or say who my father was, not even to her own parents.

Pops said that shortly before she died, my mother had given him *The Secret of the Old Clock* and told him to pass it on to me when I turned eighteen or became a Book Witch myself, whichever came sooner. He'd always assumed she'd left a secret message in the book for me, a letter or something, but when Pops gave it to me the night of my initiation into the Ink and Paper Coven, the only note I found inside was her name on the title page written in peacock blue ink.

Ellery

There *was* a message in the book for me, however. And you didn't even need Nancy Drew's help to decipher it. It came through loud and clear. The book was about a girl growing up without a mother. Nancy Drew turned out fine, more than fine. She was clever, courageous, good-hearted, intelligent, strong-willed, and happy. So happy she barely even thought of her dead mother and certainly never grieved for her.

Be clever, courageous, and happy. Don't think too much about what you've lost, and you'll be all right. That was the unwritten message from my mother. In other words, be just like Nancy Drew.

When the red hotline phone on the desk suddenly rang, I dove for it like a drowning girl diving for a life preserver. The secure landline was for Coven business only.

"Hello? Rainy March at your service. Please."

"Hi, Rainy, it's Penny Nichols!"

Oh, joy. Penny. Penny, the pretty, perky apprentice Book Witch. Penny Nichols, the crown princess of exclamation points. She'd only been with Ink and Paper for about a month, and it seemed she'd spent that entire month trying to be my new best friend.

"Hi, Penny," I said and tried not to sigh audibly.

"How are you, Rainy? Doing anything fun today?"

"Having an allergy attack."

"Is that fun?" She sounded skeptical but open-minded. I couldn't help but like her, even if she did make me feel about fifty years old.

"Even less fun than it sounds."

"Would you like a break from having an allergy attack?"

"I would kill for one," I said. Was I finally out of the doghouse with Dr. Fanshawe?

"What's the situation?" I asked.

"Rogue main character. Burner set her free for some reason."

A runaway main character was an important assignment, much

more important than mending spines and making Excel spreadsheets of book titles and publication dates. *The Mark of Sin* and *Loving Lucifer* would have to wait their turn.

“Dr. Fanshawe says to meet her at the bookstore in African Cuisine in fifteen minutes.”

“I’ll be there in ten.”

CHAPTER EIGHT

No time to waste. I climbed onto the ottoman once more to retrieve my umbrella. Book Witches use umbrellas as wands, of course, but we also use them as umbrellas. Book Witches, not unlike certain vampires, spend a lot of time in the Pacific Northwest and out here umbrellas are a must-have. Summers are very nice, but the rest of the year? Rain. Endless, driving, pitiless, merciless rain. Biblical rain. End of the world rain. Name your daughter after the rain, because around here, the rain is in charge and it never hurts to suck up to the boss. That kind of rain.

I pulled my umbrella out of the safe. Pops had taken his with him on his top secret mission. I told myself he was likely tucked away in some eccentric billionaire's private library, being paid handsomely to catalog his collection of ancient occult tomes and magical cursed codices. He was Ink and Paper's go-to guy for that sort of thing. He was probably having the time of his life. Still, he was almost never gone this long, and I couldn't help but worry a little.

Into the safe I placed *The Secret of the Old Clock.* Before Duke, I'd always kept it in my bedside table in a locked drawer, but after learning what Duke kept in his safe—all the treasures from his brothers—I started storing the book in our wall safe too. Why? I don't know. Romantic silliness, really. Plus a touch of paranoia courtesy of Pops. For some reason, all my mother's papers and case notebooks had been seized when she died. Pops said the Coven's leaders took them for "reasons," and he worried they'd want to take the book too if they thought she'd left some sort of secret message behind in it.

If you asked me, there were too many secrets in this house.

The Secret of My Grandfather's Mysterious Mission.

The Secret of My Mother's Missing Year.

The Secret of The Secret of the Old Clock.

Not to mention the continuing saga of *The Secret of How to Get Back into My Boss's Good Graces.*

Hopefully if I handled this new mission skillfully enough, that would be one less mystery to solve.

I locked the safe, hung the portrait back in place, and stepped down off the ottoman.

"Come on, Koshka. We've got a job."

At once, he woke up from his deep sunbeam sleeping and was on all four feet. He might take a catnap every chance he got, but when there was work to be done, the boy was a consummate professional.

As I put on my gray trench coat, I called out to Mrs. Turner.

"Dinner for none tonight! We're working."

Mrs. Turner peeked her head out of the kitchen door at the end of the hallway. "You have to eat, Miss March."

"I'll get something in town."

She nodded as if agreeing. "I'll put something in the icebox for you."

Koshka and I left the house by the side door. Usually we'd walk to the Coven's bookstore, a mere six blocks away on Seventeenth Street, but it sounded like I was going to have to leave on my mission immediately. So we went to the garage. I hit a button on my key chain and the door yawned open, revealing a metallic gold VW Bug, vintage 1974, a.k.a. the Sun Buggy. Cute but about as sturdy as a soapbox derby car, so I always strapped Koshka into his safety harness and carrier, even if we were only going a few blocks. True, I was a Book Witch, and he was my magical familiar, but that didn't make us immortal. If only.

We drove to the bookstore down the quaint, quiet streets of Fort Meriwether. Nearly five o'clock in the evening, yet the sidewalks were mostly deserted but for a few people walking their dogs. The houses were all weather-beaten Victorians or craftsman bungalows that were listing a little. Our town was built on the side of a hill overlooking the Columbia River. Gorgeous view, but you needed to be sure your car's brakes were in good working order unless you wanted to pull a Thelma and Louise off the docks and nose-dive into the drink.

You might not know from looking at it, but Fort Meriwether is a veritable hub of literary magic. Fictional characters tend to be drawn to either charming small towns or dramatic coastal vistas, and we have both in spades. When a fictional character escapes the bounds of their book, they gravitate to settings similar to the story worlds they left behind. This is a port town, built on the junction of the Columbia River and the Pacific Ocean, and it is charming as heck, if slightly overpriced. Even better, from our little city, you can travel south and stop in at glorious beach after beach after beach. It's fictional character catnip, especially for female leads in emotional turmoil. I mean, look at every other cover of a women's fiction book or historical novel. What's on it? A woman looking at the ocean.

We parked on the street in front of a sky blue Queen Anne house with a sunshine yellow door, the home of Words, Words, Words, Fort Meriwether's only bookstore. The name came from Shakespeare's *Hamlet* Act Two, Scene Two.

POLONIUS:
What do you read, my lord?

HAMLET:
Words, words, words.

Classic.

The bookstore, as the white wooden yard sign explained, was owned and operated by mystery writer Medda Baker. She was our sole local celebrity, an author who had lived in our town all her adult life. She wasn't a Book Witch herself, but she was on our team in more ways than one. And she let the Ink and Paper Coven meet on the second floor.

Once inside the bookstore, I started for the cookbook section to rendezvous with my boss. I turned a corner, and right there in front me was the Duke of Chicago.

NOT LITERALLY. METAPHORICALLY. POETICALLY. HE WASN'T THERE in the flesh, but his books sat on a front table display with a sign.

With the publication of Edgar Allan Poe's short story "The Murders in the Rue Morgue" in 1841, detective fiction was born!

I didn't like that exclamation point, but I kept reading.

His character C. Auguste Dupin is literature's first fictional sleuth! On October 7, 1849, Poe would die under mysterious circumstances. In memory of his final mystery, read a work of detective fiction this October!

Two more exclamation points? Something needed to be done about this punctuation abuse.

On the table sat books featuring all the great fictional detectives in history—Agatha Christie's Miss Marple and Hercule Poirot; Dorothy Sayers's Lord Peter Wimsey; Walter Mosley's Easy Rawlins; Carolyn Keene's Nancy Drew (of course); and Tom Hightower's Duke of Chicago.

I couldn't help myself. I picked up a slim paperback copy of *The Velvet Coffin*, a Duke of Chicago novella that had been reprinted with the original 1949 pulp cover: Duke in a purple velvet-lined coffin, his eyes closed, playing dead.

Of course Duke didn't look quite like Duke. Fictional characters never look like the cover art, and no artist could adequately capture how handsome he was in the flesh.

"I miss you," I whispered, touching the cover.

"Rainy?"

At the sound of Dr. Fanshawe's voice, I hid the copy of Duke's book behind my back. If she knew that I was even within ten feet of a Duke of Chicago book, I might never get an assignment again.

"Dr. Fanshawe," I said, stepping away from the table like it was radioactive. A mistake as I was still holding *The Velvet Coffin.* I grabbed the nearest hardcover and hid Duke's book behind it. "I was on my way to African Cuisine, I swear."

"Hi, Rainy!" Penny Nichols jogged to me, grinning and waving as if she hadn't seen me in years. "And, hello, Koshka!"

I could hear the exclamation points in her voice.

Penny was one of those effortlessly stylish girls who I'd always mildly envied. She couldn't have been a day over twenty but dressed to the nines every day. She wore her hair in a chic dark bob and skipped around Fort Meriwether in kitten heels.

Dr. Fanshawe, however, looked like a librarian. Specifically, a librarian from the Library of Alexandria, and she was still furious about that fire. She scared me frankly, which is why I needed to distract her.

"Um, great sign, Penny," I said, nodding to the mystery display on the table. Both of them took the bait. They looked at the sign while I slipped the Duke of Chicago book I was hiding back onto the shelf. "Your work, I see."

"You're so clever!" Penny said. "How did you know I made it?"

All apprentices in our coven worked in the bookstore part-time. Truly, nothing prepares one better to battle evil than working retail.

"Call it a wild guess," I said. Then I noticed something I'd missed while I'd been panicking. "You're wearing bunny ears." The bunny ears were dark brown, almost the same color as her hair. "Are you seeing this, Dr. Fanshawe? Wait, you're wearing a crown. What is happening? Am I losing my mind? Again?"

"Apparently, it's Mad Hatter Day," Dr. Fanshawe said drily. "Penny is insisting we celebrate it."

"Good old Mad Hatter Day!" Penny said. "October sixth. Don't miss it!"

I blinked at her. Exclamation points tended to make my eyes water.

"This is a *real* holiday?" I asked.

"In *Alice in Wonderland,*" Penny began, "the book's famous illustrations by Sir John Tenniel feature a drawing of the Mad Hatter with a price tag in his hatband that reads 10/6. Ten shillings and six pence. And 10/6 is also October sixth, therefore . . . Happy Mad Hatter Day!"

"In England, they do the day before the month so we really should celebrate it on June tenth," I reminded her.

"But we're not in England. Here. I brought you these. We can be twins!"

She stepped forward and placed a pair of white bunny ears on my head.

"Koshka can be the Cheshire Cat," she said. "Would you like that, you handsome boy? I won't make you wear a hat. You don't even have a forehead!" She bent down and scratched Koshka under the chin. He was in heaven. I, however, was not.

"You know, I only celebrate one book holiday a week, and tomorrow," I said, nodding to the table display, "is the anniversary of Edgar Allan Poe's tragic unsolved death, which is a big day in the March household. So . . ."

"What is that?" Dr. Fanshawe demanded, eyes narrowed.

While I didn't say my favorite four-letter word at that moment, I thought it. Loudly.

"What is what?" I asked.

"Do you have a book behind your back?"

I gripped it tight, praying she didn't notice the slim paperback tucked inside.

"Uh . . . it's, uh . . . a Nancy Drew book. Book two. *The Hidden Staircase.*"

"And why do you have it?"

My bunny ears were forgotten as I scrambled to think of an excuse.

"Never read it," I said, sweating and stammering. "I read the first one a long time ago. Ages. I can't even remember the title."

"*The Secret of the Old Clock,*" Penny offered from the floor, where she had Koshka on his back while she stroked his gray belly.

"Yes, that was it. I thought it was time I should, you know, read book two."

"You can read them out of order," Penny offered helpfully, yet not helpfully.

"Great," I said. "Good to know."

She gave me an encouraging smile, as if suffering a little second-hand embarrassment on my behalf.

Meanwhile Dr. Fanshawe stared at me so hard I was surprised laser beams didn't shoot from her eyes into mine. (Thankfully not a magical skill Book Witches possess.) I stood still, sweating and praying she was buying this story. Dr. Fanshawe had personally confiscated my Duke of Chicago book series, every last copy, and my stomach still churned with the memory of being an adult having my books taken away from me, shamefaced as a child caught stealing money from her mother's purse.

"Put it down," she finally said. "You have more important things to do than read children's books."

"Right, right, the mission," I said and slid the book back onto the table, nearly fainting from relief. I hadn't gotten caught, not this time anyway.

"The file, Penny."

Penny rose off the floor and held out a small canvas book bag to me.

I peeked into the bottom of the bag and found a paperback copy of Jane Austen's *Pride and Prejudice*.

"Didn't expect her to go rogue," I said. "Bad news."

"Very bad," Penny agreed somberly, no exclamation points in sight.

Bad enough when a minor character escapes their book. A story can usually survive without them for at least a few weeks.

But when the hero gets out? We had three days tops before the book would be damaged almost beyond repair. This is why I never let Duke out of his books for more than a day. You can have a book without a hero, but would you really want to read it?

"What's the situation?" I asked, all business again.

"Two days ago, our M.C. landed in Portland, Oregon," Penny said, using Book Witch shorthand for "main character." "She joined a dragon boat team practice, had her first Thai food, went to Powell's City of Books, and came very close to pawning her engagement ring to buy the complete works of Charles Dickens."

"Well, that would be modern lit to her," I said.

"This morning she caught a bus to the coast," Dr. Fanshawe said. "We tracked her as far as Sunset Beach."

"Beach," I said, nodding. "Typical."

"I want her back in her book before sunset," Dr. Fanshawe said. "Can you do that?"

I knew what I had to do, and if she'd been gone two days already, we had no time to waste. "Come on, Koshka. Let's get Elizabeth Bennet to the church on time."

We started toward the door. Had I gotten away with it? Was I home free? I hadn't been caught with Duke again?

"Rainy?" Dr. Fanshawe's voice stopped me in my tracks.

I slowly turned to face her, feeling doomed.

"You're still wearing the bunny ears."

"Oops."

I took them off, tossed them in the tote bag, and went to work.

CHAPTER NINE

According to the case notes, a Burner had yanked Elizabeth Bennet out of her book right before her wedding to Mr. Darcy, hoping to thwart one of the happiest endings in all of Romancelandia. Turned out, Elizabeth enjoyed modern life a little too much and had gone on the lam.

And it was my job to put her back where she belonged before every copy of *Pride and Prejudice* turned into a blank book.

Luckily Sunset Beach wasn't far from Fort Meriwether. Koshka and I headed out of town and took Highway 101 south. The 101 is a famously scenic highway but not so much the stretch I was on. We passed Best Buy, Walmart, the grocery store . . . hardly the stuff of postcards. At least the sun valiantly still shone at the edge of the sky, though clouds threatened and the light seemed gray and tired.

I put my foot on the accelerator. Five minutes later, we were going slightly above the speed limit. "Good thing you're cute," I said to my sluggish, elderly car, which was also something I said to Koshka at least once a day.

The sun dropped even lower as I made a right turn off the highway. This was an unusual street. It appeared to be like any other West Coast country lane. A few weather-beaten houses. A few small businesses. A trailer park. Then . . . sand. A little sand at first and then piles of it appeared on either side of the road. The farther west I drove, the more sand we saw. You got the feeling that if you kept going, you'd drive off the edge of the world.

And you would be right about that.

I pulled off the side of the road at the entrance to Sunset Beach. With the little binoculars I kept in the glove box, I scanned for Elizabeth Bennet. No luck. Had she sensed me coming and run for it?

Ah, got her. In the distance I spied a head of dark hair bobbing through the dunes. I knew at once it was her. She gave off pure main character energy. I could confront her right now, but I worried she'd run off. I'd wait for her to reach the edge of the water where she'd have nowhere to run or hide.

Koshka meowed loudly, a distress signal.

"What is it, comrade?" I asked, but then I saw what had upset him.

On the side of the road sat a Little Free Library designed to look like a miniature beach house. The shelves were empty, and the glass in the doors was broken.

Ninety percent of the time when a community library or a free library is empty, it's because someone took all the books without putting any back. Annoying, but human. But the other ten percent? Sabotage.

"Don't worry, buddy," I told Koshka. "I've got this."

The people on this route lived miles away from the nearest bookstore or library. This wasn't some ritzy beach community. Seasonal workers made their homes in the trailer park we'd passed, eking out a living on tourist tips. Maybe this little broken box was their only easy access to books.

I had about two minutes until Elizabeth Bennet reached the beach. Plenty of time. Inside my trunk I found the box labeled EMERGENCY USE ONLY.

I grabbed one copy of Kurt Vonnegut's antiwar novel *Slaughterhouse-Five,* named for the actual slaughterhouse he'd taken shelter in during the Allied firebombing of Dresden when he'd served in the U.S. Army in World War II. Then a copy of Maya Angelou's powerful and poetic memoir, *I Know Why the Caged Bird Sings.* In honor of Oregon's native son, Ken Kesey, I also grabbed *One Flew Over the Cuckoo's Nest,* and for Portland's favorite daughter, Ursula K. Le Guin's *The Lathe of Heaven.* Ray Bradbury's *Fahrenheit 451,* of course, Margaret Atwood's *The Hand-*

maid's Tale, The Invisible Man by Ralph Ellison, and also *The Invisible Man* by H. G. Wells. For the kids living nearby, I threw in *A Wrinkle in Time* by Madeleine L'Engle, because are you ever too young to start fighting the cosmic battle against evil? Finally, I added a couple classic picture books—*Where the Wild Things Are* by Maurice Sendak, Nikki Giovanni's *Rosa,* and Dr. Seuss's *The Lorax.*

An even dozen. Not much, but better than nothing.

After placing the books in the box, I shut the door and latched it, then cast a quick charm that would help protect the books from weather damage until we could replace the broken glass.

Then I reached into my pocket and drew out a small bag of what looked like blue sand but was in fact a bit of magic in pure physical form. When sprinkled on a library (or box or bag or anything you like really), it would act to draw in books. Not just any books. The books people coming to this library needed without even knowing they needed them. Maybe a romance novel that could make a woman realize she deserved better in life than her current cruel or callous boyfriend. A bio-thriller with a scientist hero who inspires a college student to go to medical school. A silly happy funny book about a pigeon or a squid or Bigfoot that helps a child who's lost her mother laugh out loud for the first time in months. Whatever book anyone who used this box needed would eventually make its way to these little shelves.

I sprinkled the dust over the box right as a gust of wind blew up from the ocean. Half got onto the box and half landed all over my face.

Well, if you're going to accidentally cast a spell on yourself, the book-you-really-really-need charm is the one you want.

Now safely enchanted, this little library would never find itself empty of books ever again.

Work completed, I returned to the car and wiped the dust off my face.

"Not sure who busted up that library," I said to Koshka as I started the car, "but stay on your toes. All eighteen of them. Let's go."

Soon the sand completely covered the asphalt. "Brace yourself," I warned Koshka. My Sun Buggy was vintage, adorable, in mint condition . . . but wasn't designed for off-roading. A 1974 VW Bug?

Let's be honest, it was barely designed for on-roading. But I didn't want to lose our lady. Just ahead, the road ended. I drove past the dunes and right onto the beach (which, let the record show, is legal). As the sun began to fall, I spied a set of petite shoe prints in the wet sand.

Got you, Bennet.

KOSHKA AND I FOLLOWED THE FOOTSTEPS PAST A FEW OTHER cars parked on the beach, locals or tourists hoping to catch a rare October sunset unmarred by cloud cover. A few hundred yards down the wash, I spotted her standing at the edge of the ocean staring at the gray waves, your classic fictional heroine in emotional turmoil.

Elizabeth Bennet had gone Oregon native. She was wearing gray leggings, a white tank top, and a North Face backpack over a black rain jacket. Her thick chestnut hair was tied back in a decidedly un-Regency-like messy bun. Probably the first time in her buttoned-up, straitlaced, prissy, proper, rigidly ordered, ladylike life she'd ever even worn trousers.

Slowly, I approached her, smiling so she would know we meant her no harm. She stiffened slightly as I stopped by her side, but she didn't make a run for it. I had a feeling she knew why I was there and had, in fact, been expecting me.

"I have that same jacket in red," I said.

A slight smile crossed her face, but she said nothing.

"This is Koshka, and I'm Rainy March, Book Witch," I said. "And yes, the name is a pun and a weather forecast. You're probably wondering why I'm here . . . or not?"

She sighed the gentlest of sighs as she gazed out on waters she'd never seen before and would certainly never see again.

"Look, if it's cold feet," I said, "I get it. Marriage is a big commitment. But you need to get back into your book, all right? Books without heroes wither and die, and you probably noticed while you were at Powell's, your book is pretty popular."

"Me? A hero?"

"You don't know you're a hero? When Mr. Darcy proposed to you the first time, what was he offering you?"

"Marriage," she said in her elegant English accent.

"More than that. Marriage to Darcy meant money and power and status. And what does everyone in the world want? Money. Power. Status. But Mr. Darcy was incredibly rude to you, rude to your entire family, and even broke up Jane and Mr. Bingley. You picked loyalty to your sister over money, power, and status. That was an act of true heroism and decency. And the world needs books about heroism and decency right now."

Waves rolled in, waves rolled out. She watched the ocean as if it had the answers she sought, and if she kept her vigil long enough, it would whisper them to her through the music of the wind and the water.

"Your book helps people," I said. "Your book helped me."

She glanced my way a moment, surprise in her fine, dark eyes, before turning back to the water.

I continued, "For a few months . . . I dated a duke."

She looked at me again, her lips parted in shock.

"Yeah, I knew that would get a reaction," I said. "But Duke—that's what I call him—he's not a real duke. Wait, no, he is a real duke. He's not a real *person.* He's fictional, like you. And fictional characters and real people can't be together, no matter how badly we want to be. If he left his book series, his books would die. If I moved into his books . . . Well, I can't. It's against the rules. If we were in a romance novel, our trope would be forbidden love. We tried to make it work, of course. I'd sneak him out of his books for a few stolen hours. Then several days later, I'd hop into his books for a few more stolen hours. This went on for a year. A perfect, painful, beautiful, agonizing year."

"What happened?" she asked.

"I stayed a little too long in one of his books," I said, "and the story started to change. Suddenly I showed up in a sentence. One sentence but it was a real doozy of a sentence."

And that doozy of a sentence?

Rainy March had the sort of face that made a man square his shoulders, straighten his tie, and see that his affairs were in order, because he'd either marry her or die trying.

"When I came back to the real world," I told Elizabeth Bennet, "my boss was waiting for me. I was caught. She reminded me, in no uncertain terms, that if I didn't end things with Duke, I was risking permanent damage to his book series. I had to choose between him and his stories. As much as I wanted to be with him, I knew I had to do the right thing and end it. And there are a lot of perks to being married to a duke."

"I should think so," Elizabeth said.

"When I broke up with Duke, I thought about you turning down Darcy's first proposal. I thought if you could do it, I could do it."

"I said yes the second time," she reminded me.

"True, but by then Darcy had learned his lesson, cleaned up his act, and proven himself worthy of you."

"He had, yes," she said with a little grin. "But you see . . . yesterday I met a young woman with violet hair. And tattoos like a sailor."

"That's Portland for you," I said.

"She took me for Thai food."

"Incredible, right? But I'm sure English food is . . . Never mind. But there are so many reasons to go back to your home. Your father. Jane. You do want to see Jane again, don't you? If I had a sister like Jane, I'd want to see her—"

"The woman was a university student," Elizabeth said in wonder. "Can you imagine? And she thought nothing of it."

"You want to go to college?" I asked her.

"I . . . would've liked . . . I would have liked the chance." She straightened her shoulders. "But I suppose that's not my story."

"If it helps, your book is taught in colleges. In that way, you're in college, if you think about it."

She glanced up at the sky, at the sun beginning its slow long drop behind the horizon.

"I always planned to return home," she said.

"Did you? Good, that was easy enough. Thank you. I need a win here."

"It's only . . . Oh, isn't it beautiful?" She waved her hand to the Pacific Ocean.

Unshed tears gleamed in her eyes, hovering but not falling. From now until the end of time, it would be nothing but dinner parties and luncheons and card parties and neighborhood balls. She'd get to London once a year perhaps, but otherwise, she'd probably never travel farther than fifty miles from her home. And even if she and Darcy took a grand tour of Europe, she would never again lay eyes on the Pacific Ocean or the rocky, windy, wild Oregon Coast.

"What are men to rocks, mountains, and oceans?" she said. She gave me a little conspiratorial smile. "Don't tell Mr. Darcy, but this is even prettier than Pemberley."

"Your secret's safe with me."

"Is there time to watch the sun set?" she asked. "I've come so far."

"I'm supposed to put you back before sunset but . . . how can I say no to the legendary Elizabeth Bennet?"

"Lizzy, please," she said.

"Lizzy," I repeated, flattered to be on a first-name basis already. "Call me Rainy."

Together we watched the sun turn crimson red as it seemingly fell toward the earth.

While she watched it fall, I took the book from the canvas bag and opened it to the scene that came right before the blank pages.

When the last of the red faded over the horizon, Lizzy turned to me and said, "If you must."

"I must," I said, then looked her up and down.

"Oh, yes, of course." She shrugged out of her jacket and pulled a gown from her backpack, putting it back on over her tank top and leggings.

As she dressed in her real clothes, I read softly from the book, working the necessary storycraft to return her to the safety of her own world, where she and Mr. Darcy would live happily ever after for all eternity.

Next to being married, a girl likes to be crossed in love a little now and then. It is something to think of and gives her a sort of distinction among her companions.

The sun gone, Lizzy turned to me.

"Thank you," she said with a most ladylike curtsy. "But please, Rainy, the next time a duke offers marriage . . . say yes."

"Promise," I said, and though it broke my heart to take this all away from her, I whispered the charm that would make her forget her little Oregon adventure.

When I closed the book, the sun was down, and I was alone except for a cat using the beach as a litter box and one set of petite women's footprints in the sand, which the very next wave washed away.

CHAPTER TEN

When Koshka and I returned to the bookstore, it was about half an hour before closing time. Koshka meowed insistently at me once we were through the doors.

"Oh, fine. Go play in the teen section if you want, but don't let anyone adopt you this time, please."

Koshka trotted off toward a rainbow-painted door that read TEENS ONLY. He loved being adored and spoiled, and teen girls especially lost their minds over him. He'd been catnapped from the bookstore more than once. But that was fine. He was microchipped. And he always came home by dinner.

Alone, I took the stairs up one level. There was an extra pep in my step, the pride of a job successfully completed.

The stockroom of the bookstore looked like an innocent, friendly, slightly shabby yet charming office. It had a few antique desks, a floral love seat, and a red Moroccan rug. If you pulled back the large rug, you'd find a large rectangle painted on the hardwood floor for the rare occasions when we had to summon fictional characters into the real world (books are rectangular, which is why we use that shape for magic, not pentagrams). We also had an altar in the stockroom, of course, which was actually just a big bookshelf covered in papers, books, and electric candles. Real candles are nicer and spookier, but Book Witches do not mess around with fire.

Mentally, I prepared my report. Quickly and efficiently, I'd gotten Elizabeth Bennet back into her book. I'd also performed a spell on the story to make sure she'd forget her brief adventure in reality. Otherwise she would make a run for it again in a week or two, whenever she next was forced to be in the same room with the Bingley sisters, probably. A job well done. I was certain I'd be greeted with cheers, champagne, at least a pat on the back.

Unfortunately, I was *very* wrong.

"You're late," Dr. Fanshawe said when she finally deigned to notice me.

"What?" I demanded. "Late how?"

Confused, I glanced around, hoping someone could explain what I'd done wrong. Penny stood up from her chair and shrugged. Poor old Professor Dodsworth also looked terribly confused, but maybe that was because he wore gray Dormouse ears. Even he was celebrating Mad Hatter Day, likely under duress.

"You promised you would have her in her book by the time the sun had set. You didn't." Dr. Fanshawe tapped a hardcover copy of *Pride and Prejudice* with a long, sharp fingernail.

"You were watching me?"

"Monitoring you," she said and held up the book. "I felt it the moment Elizabeth Bennet was returned to her story, and it was two minutes after the sun had set."

"Lizzy said—"

"You call her Lizzy?"

"She told me to," I answered as I stood in the middle of the floor like a schoolgirl called upon the carpet. "But the book is back to normal. Check it."

I held out the Words, Words, Words tote bag. Dr. Fanshawe wouldn't take it, but Penny did.

"Elizabeth Bennet politely requested to watch the sunset," I said. "It's all she asked. Was that so wrong?"

"Yes," Dr. Fanshawe said. "She is a fictional character. Fictional characters belong in books and nowhere else."

"So I'm supposed to treat her like an escaped zoo animal?"

"Precisely. For her sake if not for the book's. She could have been killed, drowned—"

"We weren't swimming," I said. "Believe it or not, I know what I'm doing. I've been a Book Witch for over a decade, and I've never lost a character yet."

"I think she did a very good job," Penny said. "The book is already fully restored."

She brandished the copy of *Pride and Prejudice* from the tote bag, demonstrating that the blank pages now bore all the original text.

"See?" I said, pointing to the pages. "Who cares if I got her in two minutes late? She's back where she belongs."

"I care," Dr. Fanshawe said, then held out her hand. "Give me your umbrella."

"What?" I asked. I looked at Professor Dodsworth, but he only shrugged.

Penny stood up for me, however. "That seems *quite* unfair!"

"It's only for the time being," Dr. Fanshawe said. "Only until I'm certain you won't be using it to attend Mr. Darcy's wedding. Or planning your own."

"What? I would never—"

She raised her eyebrow. "Never? We both know better than that."

I opened my mouth, then closed it again, shamed into silence.

"If I have told you once, I have told you a thousand times, Rainy March, that fictional characters belong in stories and real people belong in the real world. But for some reason you think the rules don't apply to you. Your mother never once gave the Coven any cause for concern. Ellery did her work perfectly every single time. I had hoped you'd turn out to be a Book Witch of her caliber, but I'm beginning to doubt that."

"Yeah, well," I said, as I surrendered my umbrella to her, "you're not the only one."

After I'd retrieved Koshka from the lap of a tween girl who'd inexplicably renamed him Fuzzypants McGee, we headed to my car.

As I was unlocking it, Penny ran out the front door, waving to me to stop.

"Rainy," she said a little breathless. "I'm sorry. I tried to argue with her but—"

"It's not your fault. Thanks for trying anyway."

"Are you all right?"

"Fine, fine. Fine and dandy even," I lied, straight to her face. I was neither fine nor dandy. I was, in fact, furious, frustrated, scheming, bitter, and a little bit grumpy. Not that I was going to dump all that on sweet, young Penny.

"No offense, Rainy, but you don't seem dandy. I'm off work now. Do you want to get some coffee with me or some dinner? We could talk about it."

"I better get home. Mrs. Turner said she'd save dinner for me. But thanks for backing me up in there."

"Anytime," Penny said.

Koshka jumped into his carrier, and I shut the door, then waved at Penny through the window.

But when I turned the key, my car only sputtered, refusing to start.

Could this day get any worse?

Which is exactly what I said when I opened my car door.

"Don't say that," Penny warned me. "Sometimes the universe answers yes."

"Maybe I shouldn't have driven a fifty-year-old car onto Sunset Beach," I said as I got out. "Engine's flooded. It needs to sit for a couple hours. Come on, buddy," I said to Koshka. "We'll walk home."

"Let me get my coat," Penny said. "I'll walk with you."

"You're the sort of girl who rescues worms off hot sidewalks, aren't you?"

"You're not a worm, Rainy. Unless you mean a bookworm. Although if you were a *worm* worm, I'd put you back in the grass and then add a little leaf on top of you like an umbrella," she said, miming the act of putting a leaf over my head. "And you would do the same for me, wouldn't you?"

"Let's not talk about me."

"We could," she said. "While I walk you home."

"You'll regret it," I said.

"How far away do you live?"

"Six blocks."

She grinned broadly. "I can most certainly walk six blocks."

Five minutes later . . .

Penny sighed heavily. "You were right, Rainy. I regret it!"

"It's only six blocks," I reminded her, panting slightly myself. "Just . . . six blocks uphill."

Fort Meriwether is a hilly town, so hilly that sometimes you'll look out your window and see your neighbor's house has shifted a few feet closer to the Columbia River. And while a map may make it look like our house was an easy stroll from the bookstore, you need good calves, a funicular railroad, or a ski lift to get there.

"I'm still getting used to living on the side of a cliff," Penny said. "It's much flatter where I'm from, practically two-dimensional."

"Can I suggest sensible shoes in the future?" I teased her. "You're in Oregon now, kid. Practicality trumps fashion around here. See?"

I held out my foot for her to admire my waterproof hiking boots.

"Do those come in mauve?" she asked.

"No."

"I'll stick to my Mary Janes."

"If you want, I could carry Koshka," I offered. "Might help."

"I like carrying him," Penny said, giving Koshka a small scritch under his chin. "He doesn't weigh much."

Koshka, like his mistress, was mostly an indoor cat. He could've walked all the way home, but when Penny had volunteered to carry him? Well, Koshka never did say no to being lugged around by a pretty girl.

"You have a familiar, Penny?" I asked, trying to steer the conversation to harmless topics.

"I'll get a dog eventually."

"Where did you come from?"

"Oh," she said breezily, "pretty little river town in the Midwest. Can't even find it on a map."

"What brings you out to the Pacific Northwest?"

"I have family out here. And I heard this was a very literary town with an active coven. I've only been here a month, but I like it!"

"I can tell," I said flatly. "Have you met Medda Baker yet? The owner of the bookstore?"

"Not yet," Penny said. Then she stopped and faced me.

"What?"

"I need to be very rude for a moment," Penny said.

"Rude? You?"

"What did all that mean when you told Dr. Fanshawe you'd never use your umbrella to go to Elizabeth Bennet's wedding or your own? I was so confused."

"Long stupid story," I said, toying with the ring on my left hand. "You know the Duke of Chicago?"

"Not personally," she said. "But I know of his books."

"So . . . he and I kind of had a thing."

She didn't bat an eyelash. "He is very charming!" she exclaimed.

"Very! I mean, *very.*"

"What did you do? Go on a date or two?"

"Worse. We fell in love."

She gave a dreamy smile. "Sounds lovely."

"There's nothing better in this world or any world than dating a fictional detective," I said. "They always solve their cases. Every last one of them. So no matter what goes wrong . . . they can fix it. Being with Duke made me feel like no matter how bad my problems were . . ."

"He could solve them?"

I nodded. "Exactly."

"There's no way for you two to be—"

"You know the Black and Whites," I said. "Stories are for fictional characters. The real world is for real people. My own fault for falling in love with a man made out of ink and dreams."

Penny glanced left, then glanced right.

"You did break the rule," she said. "However"—she leaned in and whispered—"it is a very stupid rule."

I laughed. "Thanks. I needed that."

We turned and started walking up the hill again.

"Have you lived here all your life?" she asked.

"I had my own apartment after college in Portland," I said, "but moved back in with Pops when my grandmother died two years ago."

"That was nice of you."

I pointed my thumb to the house on the left. "It wasn't a sacrifice."

"Oh my," she said as we stood at the end of the walkway that led to our porch. "How pretty!"

It is a nice house, I won't pretend otherwise, which is why I didn't begrudge her that last exclamation point in her voice. A three-story Victorian, one of Fort Meriwether's famous "painted ladies." The house itself was smoky gray, but the shutters, gingerbread, fence, and flower boxes were all painted bright colors—lilac, rose pink, and lime green. The front double-doors were oak with large stained-glass panels.

"Does it have a name?" Penny asked.

"Pilcrow House."

"Pilcrow House?"

"You know, a pilcrow is that little backward capital P symbol, but it has two vertical lines instead of one."

I opened my case notebook and drew one on the inside cover.

"Oh, yes, I see it now!" she said. "The 'insert new paragraph' symbol. I knew what it was, but I never knew it had a name!"

A drizzle began to fall, and we hurried down the pathway to take shelter on the porch. A cold wind was blowing off the Columbia. Penny was wearing a very chic double-breasted wool coat in wildly impractical white. She pulled it around Koshka, tucking him against her for more warmth.

On the porch, Penny raised her hand to trace the symbol embedded in the stained-glass panels. "Why a pilcrow?"

"When medieval monks were copying manuscripts, they used the pilcrow to indicate a new thought or new idea. A fresh start, sort of. It's a house of new beginnings. Pops moved here when he and Grandma got married."

"Is it only you and your grandfather then?" she said, then turned to Koshka inside her coat. "And you, of course."

"At the moment, it's only me and our housekeeper, Mrs. Turner. Pops went on assignment over a week ago. He hasn't been in touch."

"Really? I never heard about an assignment for him. And I keep the assignment books!"

"Wait . . . He's not on assignment?"

"He could be," she said. "But if he is, it's off the books."

Off the books? That didn't sound like Pops at all. The man lived and breathed paperwork. A lump filled my throat like I'd tried to swallow a rock but couldn't get it down. If he wasn't on an official assignment for the Coven . . . what was he doing? A private commission?

"Guess so," I said, trying not to betray how worried I was. "Well, we better go."

"Busy?"

"It's, um . . . Cary Grant movie night with Koshka."

This was a ruse. I needed to be alone to figure out what was going on with Pops. Also, anyone who knows me knows that Cary Grant movie night with Koshka is Sunday, not Friday.

"Of course. Movie night with your familiar is important." She opened her coat and Koshka leapt out. Penny smiled kindly, but I could tell I'd hurt her feelings. "Have fun, you two crazy kids."

Penny started to walk away, but before I could head inside, she turned back.

"Rainy?"

"Yes?"

"Dr. Fanshawe shouldn't have said that you aren't living up to your mother's example. That was cruel of her."

"She's right—"

"You don't know that. Perhaps your mother would've been very proud of you for being so kind to Elizabeth Bennet, letting her see the sunset over the Pacific like you did."

"I'll never know," I said.

"And she should not have taken your umbrella," Penny said, who could have done with an umbrella at the moment as the drizzle began to fall harder. "But if it makes you feel any better, she put me on sticker removal duty last week for being five minutes late to a meeting."

"Brutal," I said.

"I can smell Goo Gone in my dreams," she said, then shook her head. "Your poor umbrella. It makes me sad thinking about it sitting in the supply closet all alone. Hope I remembered to lock the back door at the shop? I'm sure I did! Or not . . ."

I peered at her through the misty rain. Surely she wasn't suggesting what I thought . . . no. Not Penny. Sweet, angelic, positively perfect Penny.

"Oh, I almost forgot something." Penny took the tote bag off her shoulder and held it out to me.

"What is it?"

She smiled. "A little gift. Since you were eyeing it earlier."

"You didn't have to do that."

Without looking in the tote bag, I knew what it was—*The Hidden Staircase.*

"I used my employee discount," she said. "A going-away gift too, I suppose."

"Going away?"

"Going home for a visit," she said. "But we'll see each other soon!"

No wonder she wanted to hang out tonight. She was leaving town.

"Thanks again, Penny. For the book and, well, for everything."

She opened her mouth like she wanted to say something else, but nothing came out.

"Good night, Rainy," she finally said. "Until we meet again!"

"Have a nice trip home."

Penny turned away and walked swiftly into the dark.

Koshka pressed against me, purring softly.

I looked down at him. "I know, buddy. I like her, too, even if she does speak in exclamation points. Should I go get her?"

Before I could finish the sentence, Mrs. Turner swung open the front double-doors.

"Miss March," she said breathlessly. "Thank goodness you're here."

"What's wrong?"

Just when I thought I'd escaped exclamation points, Mrs. Turner exclaimed, "We've been robbed!"

CHAPTER ELEVEN

The safe door hung open, as if the thief had been interrupted in the middle of the burglary. They hadn't taken the time to close it, let alone rehang the portrait to cover it. There'd only been one thing in that safe . . . and that one thing was now missing.

"It's gone," I said absently, staring into the empty safe above the fireplace. "My mother's book is gone."

Koshka rubbed against my leg, and I picked him up, holding him against me.

"I had to run to the shop for sugar," Mrs. Turner said, rubbing her hands together nervously. "I'd locked the house up as always, and the double-doors were still locked when I returned. After I saw the state of the library, I went round and checked every room but only the safe was cracked. I'm afraid whoever did this is long gone."

"At least you're all right," I said.

"And you and Master Koshka," she said, shaking her head. "Nothing to do but call Scotland Yard and put the kettle on."

She strode from the library before I could remind her we didn't have Scotland Yard in Oregon.

I put Koshka down, then dropped my trench coat and bag on the floor and collapsed into my grandfather's desk chair. Equal parts dread and confusion were brewing inside me. Why would anyone on earth bother to steal a copy of a book you could buy online for a few dollars?

The book was valuable—invaluable, in fact . . . but only to me. Had the thief mistaken it for a rare edition? If so, they were going to have an unwelcome surprise when they tried to pawn it.

Mrs. Turner came back to the library. When she saw my things on the floor, she immediately picked them up, tsk-tsking the entire time. I wasn't usually this helpless, but it was my first time being robbed and all.

"The police will send someone round when they have a moment. And if the thief returns, send him my way," she said as she grabbed the fireplace poker and carried it out of the library.

For the thief's sake, I prayed they didn't come back for more. Mrs. Turner had a very nineteenth-century concept of justice.

I sank deeper into the chair. Koshka jumped onto my lap, purring to comfort me. I wish I could say it helped.

The one and only gift my mother had left me . . . gone. My stomach churned, knotting itself up in anger and sorrow. I would have let a thief take anything else in the house. Any or all of it. Every single book and painting and stick of furniture . . .

And Pops would have too.

Aching with loneliness, I plucked a framed photograph off Pops's desk. This was my favorite photo ever taken of us together. Pops and Grandma had taken me to a park somewhere with all sorts of storybook and fairy-tale exhibits. Grandma had taken the photo, I remembered. Pops, his beard still mostly brown back then, held me in his arms as we posed inside the open mouth of a giant witch's head. The irony of two witches pretending to scream in fear of the "witch." It was obvious from our faces we were trying not to laugh the whole time.

I hardly remembered the day, but somewhere in the back of my mind, I felt that old happiness, that old sense of safety. But also . . . I remembered that even back then I was aware that I was with my grandparents and not my mom or dad, and I hoped no other kids there would notice and think there was something different about me.

If only Pops were here now. Instead, he'd run off on some off-the-books assignment. Or had he?

"Duke . . ." I whispered his name softly like a charm. Duke could solve this crime in under twenty-four hours. He worked quickly, partly because his books never broke fifty thousand words and partly because he was just that damn good. In many of his stories, he was working against the clock. Take *The Velvet Coffin,* for instance. A dead man and his coffin go missing the day before the funeral. Who does the widow call? Duke, of course, who solves the case before the first mourners arrived. I was there for the climax—turns out it wasn't the man's body the thieves had been after but the coffin. Someone had hidden a fortune in the velvet lining. That's all I'll say, in case you're planning to read it for yourself (which you totally should).

I loved being there for Duke's big reveals, when he explained the who and how and why of the crime. When I snuck into Duke's books, usually on the last page, he and I could spend a little time together. At the end of *The Velvet Coffin,* for instance, I dressed in mourning black, hopped into the last page, and joined the other funeral guests. The second that coffin was buried, Duke and I hit the town.

That's the thing about fictional characters, a thing anyone who's ever fallen in love with one knows . . . their "lives" go on even when the story's over. THE END is never the end. You never see a fictional character going to the bathroom, after all. And they do, especially after drinking a few glasses of bathtub gin.

Oh yes, fictional characters, the ones we love anyway, the ones who steal our hearts and capture our imaginations, do take on lives of their own. And that was the life Duke and I had together, a secret, off-the-pages, between-the-lines, written-in-the-margins sort of romance, in that sweet and dreaming place between the end of one story and the beginning of the next . . .

Duke was a wonderful dancer. Back in his penthouse suite that overlooked the whole city, we slow-danced cheek to cheek as Glen Gray's "Blue Moon" played on the Victrola. I could still feel his five o'clock shadow rubbing gently against my neck every time he kissed me.

I had started to hum the song when I heard a loud knock at the front door.

I went down the hallway to the double front doors. I was generally fond of those old front doors with their stained-glass panels, but they made it very hard to see who was out there on the porch after dark. As soon as I turned the knob, a gust of wind blew the door open so hard I gasped.

A man stood in the shadows on the porch, silhouetted by the streetlight at his back. With the porch lights off, I couldn't see his face but could make the outline of his suit. Would they send a detective over to take an incident report on the theft of a single book? Well, it was a small town. Our police didn't have much to do most days.

"Hello?" I said.

He didn't respond.

"Hello?" I said again. "Are you here about the robbery?"

"It was a dark and stormy night," the man finally said in a posh English accent I recognized instantly and would recognize in this world or any other.

He stumbled and caught himself on the banister. I rushed forward to help steady him before he fell. He clung to me, and I half dragged, half carried him into the house and propped him against the wall while I pushed the door shut.

Door shut and locked, I turned around, and there he was.

Tall. Black hair, wet and yet somehow still perfectly coiffed. Three-piece suit tailored to the nines.

Handsome. Far too handsome. Desperately handsome. Cary Grant's eyes and Gary Cooper's face handsome.

"Duke!"

MY HEART MIGHT'VE STOPPED AT THE SIGHT OF HIM. IT MIGHT'VE skipped a beat or two. Any cardiac event was possible when the Duke of Chicago walked, or in this case stumbled, into a room.

He put an arm around me, clinging to me as hard as I clung to him. It wasn't easy, but I managed to steer him into the foyer and set him down on the staircase.

I knelt in front of him, checking for injuries. Head seemed fine. No fever. No cuts or bruises. But he was ice-cold to the touch.

"Duke? Are you all right? What were you doing out in the cold rain?"

His chocolate brown eyes fluttered open. He gazed around the room as if seeing it for the first time. "*I was a newborn vampire, weeping at the beauty of the night.*"

"No, no, you weren't, Duke. Listen to me. That's Louis de Pointe du Lac from *Interview with the Vampire*. You're Duke, the Duke of Chicago. Do you remember?"

He blinked and looked around, brow furrowed.

"*Midway upon the journey of our life / I found myself within a forest dark, / For the straightforward pathway had been lost.*"

"That's the *Divine Comedy*. Are you in Hell?"

He blinked again, leaned close, and smiled at me drunkenly. "Never with you, darling. Never with you."

Without warning, he slumped sideways, and I grabbed him and pushed him upright.

"Duke, listen, you're having a massive traumatic displacement. Do you understand?"

He didn't reply, nor could he. A "traumatic displacement" happens on rare occasions when a fictional character is wrenched too violently from their story and into the real world. I've been told characters who go through it find themselves lost in the woods, and everywhere they look, they see stories. This had never happened to Duke before and I wasn't sure why it was happening now. Some rougher magic was at work than just my own.

"Duke, can you walk? I need to get you to the library."

"Through the dark forest?"

"Yes, I'm right here. Even if you can't see me, I'm right here." We slowly made our way down the hall, Duke stumbling over his feet.

At the sound of Duke's voice, Koshka ran to us.

"Big bad wolf," Duke whispered.

"Small good cat," I said. Koshka didn't take it personally. He was a Book Witch's familiar, so he'd seen this before.

"Koshka, get Mrs. Turner, please." Koshka ran to the kitchen. "Duke, keep going. You can do it."

His head started to droop again. He sagged against the wall. I grabbed his arm before he passed out. When I caught him, he met my eyes.

"*All that we see or seem / Is but a dream within a dream . . .*" he whispered in horror.

"Edgar Allan Poe," I said. "It's only a poem. You're all right."

He moved close to me, so close our lips nearly touched.

"*A woman has to live her life, or live to repent not having lived it,*" he whispered, and a shiver ran through my entire body from my head to my toes and back again.

"Oh no, not *Lady Chatterley's Lover,*" I said. "We broke up, remember?" Apparently, he did *not* remember, because he brought his mouth to my ear and quoted another line from *Lady Chatterley* that had certainly contributed to it being banned in the U.S., Canada, Australia, India, and Japan. Somehow, in his posh English accent, he still managed to make it sound like a proper activity for a Sunday afternoon.

Not that I was complaining.

It wouldn't be accurate to say I dragged him to the library, but it wouldn't be wholly inaccurate either. However it happened, I finally got him to the couch. Where was Mrs. Turner?

He collapsed, laying his head on the sofa arm, eyes closed. "*We know what we are but know not what we may be,*" he mumbled.

I knelt in front of him. His eyes fluttered open and met mine.

He whispered, "*Thou art tied to me by cords woven of my heart-strings.*"

"Are you trying to seduce me with *Moby-Dick*?" I teased.

But he shook his head as if I hadn't understood the message he was trying to give me, as if we were speaking different languages.

"*Give sorrow words,*" he whispered. "*The grief that does not speak knits up the o-er wrought heart and bids it break.*"

Shakespeare. *Macbeth,* if I remembered correctly, and, as a Book Witch, I usually did.

"Duke?" No answer.

Mrs. Turner entered the library pushing a tea trolley. "Master Koshka tells me we have a guest."

"Unfortunately. Duke just showed up out of nowhere."

Mrs. Turner glanced down at the rug. "His Grace has tracked water on my floors."

"Not his fault," I told her. "He's had a traumatic reentry. His body is in this world, and his spirit is trying to catch up with it."

"No excuse for untidiness, especially in the Quality."

"Let's try some tea. That might help."

"First sensible thing you've said all evening, Miss March."

She poured the tea into a white cup and saucer. "Milk? Sugar?"

"Black," I said. "This is business, not pleasure."

She passed me the cup, and I held it to Duke's nose and let the steam waft into his nostrils. For a moment, his eyes cleared.

"Drink this," I ordered.

Duke took a single sip of the tea. His eyes began to clear and focus like he'd found his way out of the shadows and into the light of day.

"Rainy, darling . . ." he breathed.

"I'm here, Duke. Right here."

He smiled at me. "I'm not."

Then he closed his eyes and passed out yet again.

"Duke?" No answer. "Out like a light," I said with a sigh. "Mrs. Turner?"

"Shall I make up the guest room?" she asked.

"No, he can't stay. It's breaking the rules. Wait. How did Duke even get here? Did any books come in the mail while I was gone today?"

"Of course. Today's mail is on the reading table as usual."

Duke was snoring soundly now, so I went to the table and tore open the packages.

Two books. More Gothic romances to catalog—*Legacy of Secrets* and *Child of Mystery.*

"You don't read the Duke of Chicago books, do you?" I asked Mrs. Turner.

"No, Miss March. Only the Bible. Oh, and *Good Housekeeping.*"

"Okay, okay," I panted. "Good. Maybe it's not me. Maybe I didn't bring him here. Maybe someone else dragged Duke out of his books, and he somehow found his way to the house. I mean . . . I didn't do any spells to bring him out, right? I mean, I held his book at the bookstore, but I didn't do magic. Or did I?"

I was talking to myself, but Mrs. Turner answered.

"I believe I did overhear you whispering his name with a deep and profound sense of longing."

"All right, so I did. But I can't magically wish him here. I need a book to work the spell. That's why Fanshawe took all of Duke's books from this house. They swept every room. So that means . . . it came today. But it didn't. So it wasn't me. If not me, then who? Wait." I growled. "Penny."

Earlier, Mrs. Turner had picked my things off the floor to hang them up. I ran down the hall to the coatrack to find the tote bag Penny had given me.

The first thing I pulled out was a pair of rabbit ears. Of course she'd given those to me. I stuck them on the small bust of Shakespeare on the pedestal.

Also in the bag? A book. A small, slim rectangle wrapped in brown paper and string. I ripped the bow open and tore off the paper.

Lo and behold . . .

The Velvet Coffin, the Duke of Chicago novella I'd been mooning over at the bookstore before Dr. Fanshawe had shown up. I'd fooled her, but I hadn't fooled Penny.

Mrs. Turner had followed me into the hallway and was watching me with curiosity. I glared at the paperback book in my hands.

"This is not a Nancy Drew book," I said. "This is supposed to be a Nancy Drew book! Now she's got me doing it!"

"Doing what, Miss March?"

"Exclaiming!"

Mrs. Turner peered at me. "Are you aware you have blue glitter in your hair, Miss March?"

"What?"

I ran to the hall mirror and looked at myself.

Sure enough, my hair glinted with shimmery blue powder. When I'd charmed the free beach library to attract the books people needed in their heart of hearts, I'd gotten some on myself. The next thing I knew, the book I'd wanted in my heart of hearts had found its way into my hands . . . and as a result the duke I wanted in my heart of hearts was now on my sofa.

Penny hadn't done this to me.

I had done this to me.

"This," I said to myself in the mirror, "is why I can't have nice things."

CHAPTER TWELVE

Although the cat—Duke—was already out of the bag—the book—I went upstairs and washed my face and hair to get the remainder of the dust off me. The dust had worked its magic already and was now powerless. Unfortunately, that power had been spent on one of Duke's books and not on the book that I needed now—the book that had been stolen.

When I returned to the library, Duke remained sound asleep on the sofa. But he had company now. Koshka lay curled on his chest, his small gray head tucked under Duke's chin.

Intellectually, I knew having Duke here was a huge mistake, and if I didn't get him back in his book soon, I could be in even more trouble than I was already. Once he was awake, I'd send him home, where he belonged. But for a long moment I watched Duke and Koshka, letting myself luxuriate in the simple, stupid joy of being in the same room again with the only man I'd ever loved.

And my cat.

"My boys," I said softly, smiling.

Koshka briefly lifted his head and looked at me.

"Don't wake him up," I whispered as I sat on the floor in front of the fireplace to air-dry my hair. "I know you missed him. But don't get used to him because he's leaving as soon as he wakes up."

To that, Koshka hissed at me, then put his head down again, closed his moss green eyes, and fell asleep.

At some point, I must've fallen asleep too, because a few hours later, I woke with a start.

Disoriented, I looked around and found myself in a bed. My bed? I switched on the little lamp on the side table.

Yes, my bed in my room that overlooked the garden. In the mornings, silvery light poured in through the windows, but now the windows were dark. Pale blue walls and built-in bookcases painted white. A queen-size bed, more than big enough for me and Koshka, who somehow took up half the bed every night even though he only weighed nine pounds. A glass door led to the balcony and the little secret garden I made up there of potted plants and hand-painted fairy houses.

It was all so familiar, so peaceful, that for one moment I thought that maybe I'd dreamed the whole crazy evening. I dreamed about Duke all the time anyway. If it had all been a dream, that meant Duke wasn't really in the house, which meant I wasn't about to get on Dr. Fanshawe's bad side for all eternity and be expelled from the Ink and Paper Coven—and possibly from the International Order as well.

I threw off the covers and called for Koshka. He usually slept with me, glued to my side or curled up between my feet. I checked my bedside clock. Nearly three in the morning. Breakfast was hours away so she should've been there.

"Koshka?" I called a little louder. Mrs. Turner had hung my bathrobe on the back of the closet door. I put it on and crept out of my room, heart pounding.

Silently, I made my way down the dark stairs to the library. Peeking in, I saw . . . nothing. I inched inside and turned on the table lamp.

By lamplight, the Pilcrow House library looked like a professor's secret reading room—the sort of shadowy place where one is compelled to study alchemy, the transmigration of souls, or how to slay vampires. In other words, it looked perfectly normal to me. Maybe I *had* dreamed the whole thing.

As I was about to let out a sigh of relief, Duke waltzed through the door with a teacup in one hand and a piece of cake in the other.

"Duke!"

"Hello, darling," he said as he strolled over to the fireplace. "Glad you finally woke up. Now I can kiss you properly." He bent and brushed his lips against mine, then smiled. "There. That's better. How was your nap? Shouldn't you still be asleep, love? It's barely the witching hour."

The old carriage clock on the mantel chimed three A.M.

"I . . ." I stared at him for a long time and for multiple reasons.

Reason one—he looked incredible. Sometime while I'd been asleep, he'd woken up and changed into a new suit. A pin-stripe charcoal gray three-piece with a light blue button-down shirt. He wasn't wearing the jacket or a tie now, so his collar was open at the throat, and I admit most of my staring was concentrated on that area.

But mainly I was staring at him because he was there, in my house.

Duke waved his hand, beckoning me to continue my sentence.

"You were saying, my love?" he asked.

"You *are* here. I didn't dream it."

"Yes and no. I am here. But you were dreaming about me. And it must have been a good one, the way you said my name in your sleep." He sipped more tea. "I came to shortly after midnight, and you were asleep right there." He pointed to the rug that lay in front of the fireplace.

"How did I get into my bed?"

"I carried you," he said as if it were the most ridiculous question he'd ever been asked. "Mrs. Turner found a fresh suit for me in the attic—"

"You carried me to bed?"

He gave me that wicked grin of his.

"Can't fathom why you're so surprised. It wasn't the first time I've carried you off to bed. Won't be the last either, I hope. Right now if you'd like?" He finished his cake with one final bite.

"No, no, we're not doing this," I said. "You can't be here."

"I am here, so clearly I can be here. You might think I shouldn't be here, but that's another matter entirely, love."

"No love. No darling. None of that. No sugar, sweetness, angel, poppet, pet."

"I have never once called you 'poppet.' I will, however, upon request."

"Duke," I said, putting my hands on his shoulders.

"Ah, this is more like it." He wrapped his large hands around my waist and leaned down for another kiss.

"Halt." I put my hand over his mouth. "You have to go home immediately."

He took my right wrist into his hand—very gently, I might add, maddeningly gently—and then kissed the center of my palm, making intimate and downright knee-buckling eye contact the entire time.

He lifted his head and sighed. "I have missed you ordering me around like a lapdog," he said, "almost as much as I've missed ignoring those orders."

"You can't—"

Mrs. Turner entered then, wheeling the tea trolley. She bobbed a curtsy to Duke. This was the dark side of having a very English, very Victorian housekeeper. Duke's merest wish was her command.

"More tea and cake, Your Grace," she said.

"I do love these black-and-white cakes." Duke took one off the trolley and devoured it in two bites. "My compliments to the chef."

"Those are Little Debbie Zebra Cakes from the grocery store," Rainy said.

"I don't know this Little Debbie," Duke said. "But she is a giant in my eyes. Thank you, Mrs. Turner. That will be all."

She curtsied again and left us alone in the library.

Duke poured another cuppa for himself. "Tea?" he offered.

"How can you drink tea at a time like this?"

"Darling, I drank tea during the zeppelin raids of 1915. A proper English gentleman can drink tea under any circumstances."

"Your author was American."

His dark eyes widened. "No need to be insulting." He pulled out a chair at the reading table and faced me. "Come, sit on our lap and tell us what's troubling you."

"For starters, you are here, and you shouldn't be. That's troubling me. Second, I am not sitting on your lap. We broke up."

"Did we? I thought all that was only for show? Keeping the bosses happy when really you were biding your time, waiting for a chance to be with me again. And voilà." He gestured to himself before stretching out his long legs, crossing them at the ankle, and then clasping his hands behind his head, the very picture of arrogant entitlement.

"Stop being gorgeous," I ordered him, pointing at his face.

"You first."

"You cannot be here. Okay? I hate to speak in small words, but you have to leave. Right. Now. Yes?"

"No."

"No is the wrong answer. You have failed this test. You are now expelled."

I started from the library and went to the kitchen, where Mrs. Turner was fussing over the next round of tea and cakes. "Duke is cut off," I told her. "No more tea and absolutely *no* cakes. Not even a cookie."

"Very sorry, Miss March, but a duke outranks a mere commoner."

"Are you calling me a commoner?"

"I am not calling you a commoner, Miss March. You simply *are* a commoner."

"Good help is so hard to find!"

I jogged back to the library, where "His Grace" was holding my cat in his arms like a baby and staring up at the portrait over the fireplace.

"Rainy, who is that man above your mantel? He's new, isn't he? Never seen him before, and I'm intimidated by his striking good looks."

"Pops gave me that painting for Christmas. His name is LeVar Burton, and he hosted a television show called *Reading Rainbow.* He's basically the patron saint of Book Witches."

I gave Mr. Burton the traditional salute—palms together and then opening them as if my hands were a book or butterfly wings.

"Should I be jealous?" Duke asked.

"He's married, and you're leaving. *Now.*"

"You're being quite hasty, darling," Duke said. "You hired me, after all."

"No, I didn't."

"But I did," Mrs. Turner said, carrying in another tray of Zebra Cakes.

I looked at him. I looked at Mrs. Turner.

To both, I said, "You're fired."

THEY IGNORED THIS NEWS, OF COURSE.

Mrs. Turner poured two cups of tea. Duke took one graciously. I took the other one far less graciously.

"Hello, I fired you both, remember? No offense. Either I fire you both or I get fired, and I really don't want to get fired. I'm a Book Witch. There's no other job in the world that calls for the only skill set I have."

"Allow me to remind you," Duke said, "I never quit a case once I start it, and I've never failed to solve a mystery. So you could do worse than me."

He was right. You could no more stop a fictional detective from working a case than you could knock the moon out of orbit with a peashooter. The odds of me solving the mystery increased exponentially with a fictional detective on the case.

However . . .

"No," I said. "Absolutely not. Do you know how much trouble you got me into?"

"Not nearly enough," he said, grinning behind his teacup.

"I had my umbrella confiscated tonight," I told him. "Because of you."

"Me? I wasn't even here."

"It's called 'consequences.' My boss doesn't trust me anymore, and this is exactly why." I pointed at his chest, then poked him over the heart. "Dr. Fanshawe is convinced you and I are still involved and obviously, she's right."

"Miss March, your mother's book has been stolen from the safe," Mrs. Turner reminded me. "Someone needs to find it, yes? And with your grandfather away, we could use the assistance—"

"Your grandfather's away?" Duke repeated. "Where?"

I didn't answer at first. Then I had to say it. "Some off-the-books mission. But he's been gone a week, and he's almost never gone that long."

"You mean your grandfather is missing?"

"I don't know, but I have a bad feeling."

"First, your grandfather's gone off to whereabouts unknown and now your book? Rainy," Duke said, "that isn't simply a case anymore. That's what we in the business call a *big* case."

"Mrs. Turner?" I said.

"Yes, Miss March?"

"Can you leave us alone for the next few minutes. I don't want any witnesses."

"Of course," she said. "Come along, Master Koshka. I don't want you involved in a rumble." With a curtsy to Duke, she wheeled the tea trolley out of the library, Koshka at her heels, then shut the door behind her.

Duke looked at me. "Darling, you know you need my help."

"Entirely beside the point. You have to go. Now."

"Rainy," he said, looking me deep in the eyes. "Please, let me help you. Allow me—for once in my useless, imaginary life—to solve a real case. I've been in print for eighty years and never once had the chance to help a real person before. Please. For your grandfather's sake, if not mine."

My shoulders slumped. "Duke . . . your books help real people—"

"No, no they don't. They distract real people from their real problems. Or entertain them for a few hours. But I solve paper murders committed by paper criminals and mend paper hearts and restore paper justice. Do you understand what it would mean to me to solve a real crime?"

"Your books mended my paper heart," I said.

"You're being very kind."

"I'm not being kind. It's true. And you don't have to prove your worth as a detective."

"But I want to, love. Here. Look." He gestured to the portrait over the fireplace. "They went to the trouble of cracking the safe. The thief took only your mother's book when there are several dozen expensive first editions strewn about in plain sight."

Duke ran his fingers over the spines of a dozen rare books on a nearby shelf.

"You know what that means, don't you?" he continued. "It means that book is not simply a book."

"Then what is it? Because I've read the thing a few billion times, and there's nothing there except a fun little mystery where Nancy Drew and her father find a dead guy's missing will."

"Are you certain?" he asked.

I dropped down onto the sofa. "Trust me, we looked."

"Where? How?"

"Everywhere, I promise. In the words, on the endpapers, behind the endpapers, hidden between the lines, in a cipher, or in invisible ink. Pops even broke the rules and snuck into the story to ask if anyone knew Ellery March. Nobody had ever heard of her."

"Did he go missing before or after your book?"

"He left over a week ago saying he had to go on a top secret mission. That's all. Except Penny, the new apprentice, mentioned tonight she wasn't aware of any missions or assignments he'd been sent on. And it's her job to know," I said. "Not five minutes after she told me Pops wasn't on an assignment, I find out my mother's book has been stolen." I held up my hands, empty of answers. "Honestly, I'm more worried about Pops than I am about getting the book back."

"Unless they're related."

"What?"

"In my cases, two odd events that happen in proximity to each other are always related. *Always* and without fail."

"Yes, but your cases are fictional, and there are no coincidences in fiction. This is the real world."

Duke put his hand to his chin as he often did when thinking deeply about a case.

"Duke?"

"Tell me what your grandfather said when he left. Every single word."

"Actually . . . he didn't say anything to me directly. He left a goodbye note."

"Do you have that note?"

Good question. Recycling came every two weeks in Fort Meriwether. I went to the blue wastepaper basket and dug through the invoices and magazines and scrap paper.

I found it near the bottom, the note written on an index card.

"Here it is," I said, and read the note aloud to Duke.

Dear Raindrop,

I'm afraid I need to leave on a top secret mission.

I'll be incommunicado, but I'll think of you every second of every minute and I'll be watching the clock until I can come home again.

Love Always,
Pops

"His handwriting?" Duke asked.

"Definitely. And only he calls me Raindrop."

Duke nodded, and I knew he was committing all this information to his prodigious memory.

"Where did you find the note?"

"He left it propped up on the reading table against the lamp," I said, pointing to the brass reading lamp. "That's always where he leaves notes for me to find."

"Was anything out of place? Any signs of a struggle?"

My stomach dropped at this line of questioning. Did Duke think my grandfather had been kidnapped?

"Nothing like that. Everything was normal. And he does go on missions sometimes. He gets up at five in the morning most days, so he's often gone before I get up, and he leaves me notes like this. Should I be scared, Duke? Because I am."

"Not yet," he said, which didn't comfort me as much as I would've liked. "Has he ever been gone this long before?"

"Not quite this long. It's been"—I counted in my head—"eight days. Which I guess isn't a long time. Is it? Is eight days a long time to be gone when you're eighty years old?"

I was trying to talk myself out of terror, but it wasn't working.

"You said you gave up looking for the secret message in the book?"

"I did. Years ago."

Duke mulled this over a moment.

"Is it possible your grandfather still believed there was a message hidden in your mother's copy of *The Secret of the Old Clock?*"

I shrugged. "Maybe. A year or so ago I asked him to stop talking to me about it. I think he kept looking though."

Duke's brow furrowed. "Why did you ask him to stop talking to you about it?"

"Who knows?"

"I know," Duke said softly. "You wanted there to be a message, and yet there wasn't one. The wound couldn't heal as long as your grandfather kept picking at it."

"A disgusting yet apt metaphor," I told him.

"You said you believed your grandfather was still attempting to crack the code, so to speak?"

"Right. I think so."

"How do you know he carried on his work if he didn't tell you about it?"

"I'd catch him looking through the Nancy Drew book and writing in his case notebook. But he never said a word—"

"His case notebook? Tell me about that."

"Not much to tell. He keeps a case notebook. We all do," I said. In fact, anyone reading this story right now is reading *my* case notebook. "I think he took it with him."

"Are you sure?"

"He always kept it in his desk." I nodded toward the desk by the library windows. "And it's not there. I already looked."

Duke went to the desk and examined it thoroughly, pulling drawers, lifting objects, checking it top and bottom.

Despite my fear and extreme annoyance at having an unauthorized fictional character roaming around my house, I couldn't help but watch him work. This is why readers return to the same series over and over, even though the outcomes are always predetermined . . . Watching Sherlock or Miss Marple or Duke solve a crime is like watching a gymnast backflip or a sword fighter disarm an opponent with one glorious parry. It never gets old, watching someone being phenomenally good at their very difficult job.

"The bottom drawer is locked," Duke said, glancing up at me.

"Pops would have the key."

"I'll have to pick it," Duke said.

"Tried that already. It's an enchanted lock. It can only be opened with the key. See?"

I pulled the drawer handle, and pale orange electricity danced over my hands. But the drawer didn't budge.

"So you did have your suspicions?" Duke asked.

"I was being nosy," I admitted. "I wanted to know where he went."

He looked at me, eyes narrowed.

"He's lonely," I said. "With Grandma gone. I thought maybe he'd met someone and was going on a trip with her but was too embarrassed to tell me. I'm allowed to be nosy. He's the only family I have left."

"Let's see the note," Duke said. I handed him the card, and he read it aloud again. "*I'll think of you every second of every minute. I'll be watching the clock until I can come home again. . . .* Dramatic statement. Almost melodramatic."

"He does love me."

"Still, a bit of overkill," Duke said. "Miss you every second of every minute, *and* he'll be watching the clock?"

"What are you implying?"

"I am implying . . . it sounded like he wanted to send you a message."

"That is the message." I pointed at the card.

"A message . . . behind the message," Duke said. He turned around, scanning the library with laser-like focus. Then he walked straight over to the mantel, plucked the small carriage clock off the shelf, and shook it gently.

"What are you doing?"

He didn't answer, merely flipped the clock over and popped off the back to expose the inner workings.

"Voilà," he said and held up a small silver key.

"That . . . that's the key to the desk lock."

"Apparently there is more than one secret of the old clock. Now will you let me help you solve this case, darling?"

Slowly, I nodded my head, dazed and dazzled and delighted.

"You're hired."

CHAPTER THIRTEEN

"Thank you. I was already planning to solve this case, but now I'll do it *with* you instead of in spite of you," Duke said. "Makes things much more pleasant."

"But . . ."

"Darling, you know I hate when you start sentences with 'But'—"

"You can help me figure out where Pops went and help me find my book. *But* you have to be back in *your* book by midnight." I thought one day should be safe enough for him to be out of his stories.

"Midnight? Surely not—"

"In *The Velvet Coffin*, you solved the case in less than twenty-four hours."

He took a deep breath, then narrowed his eyes at me. "Challenge accepted. One day," he said. "If only because it means we might finally solve the mystery of how we can be together."

"And find out where Pops went."

"Right so. Priorities," he said. "Grandfather comes first. Book second. You and me third. A close third."

"All right, but if we're going to work together, even for a day, I need to set some ground rules."

"Ground rules?" he repeated. "I have a crown. Ground rules are for people who don't have crowns."

"It's a coronet, not a crown. And even dukes have to follow *some* rules."

"Tell that to the first Duke of Buckingham."

I began pacing. "Ground rule number one. No kissing me. Or me kissing you. Or anything more than kissing. Or even less."

"Less? I'm doing less than kissing you now."

"You know what I mean. No looking at me like you want to kiss me."

"So I should wear a blindfold? I could be persuaded." He grinned.

"Less," I shouted at him. "Less than that!"

"That's not a rule. That's torture."

"Ground rule number two—no declarations of love."

"I already told you I still love you," he said. "Didn't I? If not, I love you and always shall."

"Well, that's more than enough, and see that you don't do it again."

"You're adorable when you've lost your mind," he said.

"And finally, no asking to stay with me. No asking me to stay with you. It can't happen, won't happen, so don't even bring it up."

"My lips are sealed," he said. "May I start solving this case now?"

"Be my guest, please."

"Thank you, I shall."

Duke went straight back to the desk, and I followed him. He stuck the key in the lock of the bottom drawer.

It turned.

"Sometimes," he said, looking into my eyes in a way that I think I had forbidden, "I am so good at this I surprise even myself."

"Oh, open the drawer."

Duke opened it and removed a notebook, a small brown notebook with a cord wrapped around it.

"That's it," I said. "That's my grandfather's case notebook."

Duke opened the notebook and turned page after page.

"This is not a case notebook," he said, meeting my eyes. "Every single page is about *The Secret of the Old Clock*. Look."

He placed the notebook open on the desk. He pointed to a few entries, all standard fare.

August 30

I know my daughter. Ellery would not have left Rainy nothing but a book. Even her favorite book. There has to be something more.

September 2
New cipher failed. I won't give up yet.

September 20
Curiouser and curiouser.

A suggestion from an unexpected source has me thinking along new lines.

Pops had written the final entry a week ago, just before he left.

September 30
I think I understand the message now. Of course it was right there all along. But how could we have known? This changes everything we thought we knew about stories. And my Ellery did leave Rainy an inheritance of sorts, a richer one than I ever dared to dream. And poor Rainy and Duke, they'll be star-crossed no more.

But if I'm right, my God, if I'm right, then . . . Well, of course Ellery would've had to keep it all a secret. This is explosive information. People in charge will want to cover it up. I think . . . I think perhaps they already have? I must tell Rainy. Except how can I? No, I have to confirm the truth first, otherwise she'll be devastated. Yet if I'm right . . . she'll finally know the truth about her mother.

I can't believe it was staring us in the face the whole time.

For a few minutes I read and reread that final entry, tattooing every word onto my mind.

And my Ellery did leave Rainy an inheritance of sorts, a richer one than I ever dared to dream.

This changes everything . . .

"Rainy?" Duke said softly. "Are you all right, darling?"

"It wasn't just a book," I whispered. "She left me more than a book. An inheritance? That would make sense. The whole novel is about finding a lost will. Is that it? Could that be the thing that changes everything?"

My knees shook and I had to sit down. Gently, Duke put me into my grandfather's chair and knelt beside it.

"Breathe, Rainy. You're turning even paler than usual."

I met his eyes. "All this time, I thought I knew the message of the book. *Don't grieve me. Get on with your life and your adventures like Nancy Drew did.* But that's not it. There is more."

Duke nodded. "It seems there is much, much more. But I wouldn't start celebrating yet."

"Why not?"

He tapped my grandfather's notebook. "Your grandfather hid this and put an enchantment on the lock. I think he learned something so dangerous he was afraid to even write about it in his notebook. Which means either he *is* on a top secret mission investigating what he discovered . . . or someone learned he discovered this information and—"

"Don't say it. Please don't say it."

"I'm sorry, Rainy, but we have to accept the possibility he's been taken somewhere against his will."

My grandfather's old desk chair creaked as I sat back, my hand over my mouth in shock.

I shook my head. "No, he left me a note—"

"That he may have been forced to write," Duke said. "Which is why he had to write in code, to tell you where to find the key."

"He's been gone a week. What if he's—"

"Don't say it," Duke said. "We'll find him."

I threw my arms around his shoulders and he pulled me close.

"What about the ground rules, darling?" he asked.

"We'll get back to them in a minute."

I rested my chin on his strong shoulder. Relief coursed through me. I wasn't alone in this. Duke was going to help me. As I'd told Penny, fictional detectives could make you feel like they could solve all your problems, that everything would be okay if you just let them handle it.

I pulled back, and he smiled that irresistible smile of his.

Rules or no rules, I wanted to kiss him, and he certainly seemed amenable to the idea. When I leaned in, he leaned in closer.

But before our lips could touch, the phone rang. It wasn't my cell but the red landline on my grandfather's desk. Someone from the Coven was trying to get in touch.

"I have to get this," I told Duke.

"Let me listen."

I picked up the receiver, ten times as heavy as even the largest smartphones, and put the call on speaker.

"Hello? Rainy March here?"

Silence . . . a long silence, and then.

The line crackled and then someone spoke as if they were calling long-distance from another universe. "Rainy?"

"Pops! Where are you?" I jumped to my feet in excitement.

But the only answer was more static. Finally, he spoke, his words breaking up every few syllables.

". . . can't talk long," he said. "You found . . . notes?"

"What?" I shouted. "Yes, we found your notes! Are you safe?"

"Yes! I . . . right."

"You're all right?" I asked.

"He said he was right," Duke whispered, listening in and taking notes.

"Right? About what?"

"I know the message . . . book. What it means . . . changes everything . . . mother tried to tell . . . right about everything . . ."

"What's the message? And where are you?"

"I can't tell . . . wish I could . . ."

"Can't tell me? Why can't you? Is someone there?"

"Rain . . . need to . . ." The phone popped and crackled again.

"What, Pops? What is it?" I was practically screaming into the phone, willing my voice to find him and his voice to find me. My heart was pounding like a hammer on my ribs. "What do you need me to do? I'll do it!"

And then . . . suddenly, the line cleared and as if Pops were in the room with us, I heard him speak four strange words.

"Find the March Hare."

Then he hung up.

"FIND THE MARCH HARE?" I REPEATED. "WHAT DOES THAT MEAN?"

If there were a museum for lost and forgotten sounds, the dial tone of a landline phone would surely be a future exhibit. I listened to that sound for a full ten seconds before finally hanging up.

I looked at Duke, who was looking at me.

"What was that?" I asked.

"Good news," Duke said. "That was good news. We know your grandfather is safe. And right, apparently. He said he was right, he figured out the message from your mother."

"He's safe. He's alive. But where? And what does 'Find the March Hare' mean? Why couldn't he tell me?"

"Rainy, you're hyperventilating, so perhaps sit a moment while your brain reoxygenates itself."

"Right, right. Oxygen. Brain. Good." I slowly sank down into the desk chair again. I met Duke's eyes. "Any idea what he meant?"

"No clue," Duke said, sitting on the edge of the desk. "I was expecting a ransom call, not that."

"Ransom? Do you think . . . Duke, what if someone made him call me?"

"I didn't get that impression. He said he was safe. But he was speaking in a sort of code for a reason. Unless he *literally* meant we're to *literally* go into the *literal* story of the March Hare and have a *literal* chat with him."

"I can't think of any March Hare," I said, "except for the same March Hare in the other Alice book—*Through the Looking-Glass.*"

The March Hare, as all readers know, is a fictional character in Lewis Carroll's 1865 children's novel *Alice's Adventures in Wonderland.* Like every other denizen of Wonderland, the March Hare was mad. But that's all I knew about him. What else was there to know?

"This is crazy, Duke."

"Mad even," he said.

Suffused with nervous energy, I stood up and started to pace.

"Pops locked the drawer," I said. "Enchanted lock. He must have felt us breach the lock."

"He did leave us the key to find," Duke said. "Makes sense. And according to your grandfather's final entry in his notes . . ."

He paused, picked up Pops's notebook again, and read it out loud . . .

I think I understand the message now. Of course it was right there all along. But how could we have known? This changes everything we thought we knew about stories. And my Ellery did leave Rainy an inheritance of sorts, a richer one than I ever dared to dream. And poor Rainy and Duke, they'll be star-crossed no more.

But if I'm right, my God, if I'm right, then . . . Well, of course Ellery would've had to keep it all a secret. This is explosive information. People in charge will want to cover it up. I think . . . I think perhaps they already have? I must tell Rainy. Except how can I? No, I have to confirm the truth first, otherwise she'll be devastated. Yet if I'm right . . . she'll finally know the truth about her mother.

I can't believe it was staring us in the face the whole time.

I listened to every word, committing it to memory. I paced back to Duke and stood in front of him.

"Okay, let's go over this again now that I'm not freaking out. On the phone, Pops said he was right about everything. Which—according to that entry"—I said, tapping the page with my index finger—"means whatever secret message my mother hid in the book will change everything we know about stories. It says I supposedly have some kind of inheritance from her. And when I know it, I'll finally know my mother."

"Don't forget," Duke said, "it also says you and I could be together."

"It doesn't say that. It says we'll be star-crossed no more. That could mean we'll be together. Could mean we'll be *dead*."

"I'm thinking positively," Duke said with a grin. "And according to your grandfather, if we want to decipher this message, know the truth about your mother, find your inheritance, and perhaps even . . . uncross our stars? We must find the March Hare, odd as it sounds."

"Very odd," I said, still puzzling over the question of how a mentally ill leporid was supposed to help me solve the enduring mystery of my mother. "Seems almost too good to be true."

"Yes, so we should stay on our toes. And paws. Wait," Duke said, looking around the floor. "Where's Koshka?"

"Mrs. Turner took him away when she thought I was planning to murder you. Hold on."

I opened the library door, and Koshka sauntered in as if he'd been waiting for us to finish up our fight and get back to work.

While Duke paced, I filled Koshka in on everything that we'd discovered—the key, the notebook, the phone call from Pops.

"And now we have to find the March Hare," I told him. "Any ideas?"

At once, Koshka trotted to the bookshelf and meowed. Two shelves above his small gray head sat an old hardcover copy of *Alice's Adventures in Wonderland.*

"Koshka thinks Pops was being literal as well," Duke said.

I took the book off the shelf and brought it over to the reading table. Duke sat beside me, and Koshka jumped onto the table and sat in front of the book.

"You've read it?" I asked Duke.

"Donkey's years ago," he said.

Slowly I turned the pages so we could refresh our memories of the story and check for any damage. If someone was hiding my grandfather in a storybook, he might end up in the story somehow, as I had when I'd overstayed my welcome in one of Duke's books.

We began at chapter one. Little English girl Alice falls asleep on a sunny afternoon. She dreams she sees a White Rabbit and she follows him, eventually falling down a rabbit hole into Wonderland. She makes a journey through this strange dream world, meeting various odd characters.

"Here he is," Duke said, as we turned the page to reveal one of the more famous illustrations by Sir John Tenniel. The Mad Tea Party—at the tea table sat Alice, the Dormouse, the Mad Hatter, and, of course, the March Hare.

I read the chapter out loud to Duke and Koshka:

> *There was a table set out under a tree in front of the house, and the March Hare and the Hatter were having tea at it: a Dormouse was*

sitting between them, fast asleep, and the other two were using it as a cushion, resting their elbows on it, and talking over its head . . .

Alice sat down uninvited at one end of the table, much to the chagrin of the March Hare. The Hatter began speaking in riddles, which eventually caused the conversation to fall apart as nobody seemed to be buying his nonsense.

The Hatter was the first to break the silence. "What day of the month is it?" he said, turning to Alice: he had taken his watch out of his pocket, and was looking at it uneasily, shaking it every now and then, and holding it to his ear.

Alice considered a little, and then said, "The fourth."

"Two days wrong!" sighed the Hatter. "I told you butter wouldn't suit the works!" he added, looking angrily at the March Hare.

"It was the best butter," the March Hare meekly replied.

The chapter was only a few pages long, and I finished reading the rest quickly.

"What do you think?" Duke asked.

"I think they're all nuts," I said.

"That's patently obvious," Duke said. "What else?"

"There doesn't seem to be anything wrong with the book," I said. "Not even a comma out of place. If this March Hare were involved in some grand conspiracy against me or Pops . . . he's doing a good job of hiding it. I don't know. It doesn't make sense, does it?"

"No, but it is Wonderland, where they routinely try to fix broken watches with butter," Duke said. "Darling, I'm afraid we have no choice. We'll simply have to go and have a talk with the man. I mean, the Hare."

"Can't do it. Dr. Fanshawe took my umbrella, remember?"

"Do you know where it is?"

"Actually I do. Penny told me. And she said she might have left the back door unlocked."

"Penny, the new apprentice? Tell me about her."

"Not much to tell. She's a sweet kid, probably too sweet. For some reason, she let it slip that Dr. Fanshawe put my umbrella in the supply closet in Words, Words, Words."

"That's helpful. Very helpful. Remind me to send this Penny a thank-you note for the act of aiding and abetting." He stood up and glanced out the window behind the desk. "Good. The fog's rolled in. We'll need the cover. Ready?"

Duke held out his hand to me.

"Wait. Aiding and abetting?" I said, refusing him my hand. "Aiding and abetting what?"

"What else does one aid and abet? A crime."

"And what crime specifically?" I asked, although I already knew—and feared—the answer. I knew what. Of course, I knew. I just didn't want to know what I knew, you know?

"We're going to steal your umbrella back, you adorable fool."

I stared at his waiting hand. "That sounds like a bad idea."

"Oh, come on, love. A little felony never hurt anyone," he said. Then added, "When we find the March Hare, good chance we'll find your grandfather."

"Good point." I put my hand into his. "But if I end up in jail for this, I'm definitely firing you again." Then to Koshka, I said, "Come on, boy. Time to go commit crimes."

CHAPTER FOURTEEN

A bookstore by night is a different place than a bookstore by day, even if they share an address. A daytime bookstore is for real people with real problems seeking a few hours' escape into stories. It's awake, alive. But when a bookstore is closed, and the people are gone, it still doesn't sleep.

The books themselves work the night shift.

Every reader can recall a book that stayed with them for hours or days or even weeks after they'd closed the cover. They think about the book even when they're not reading it, not realizing that the book is also thinking about them.

Duke said that once he learned he was a fictional character, he became subtly aware of his readers. He felt their watchful eyes and sensed their quiet, gentle presence. He knew his stories were being read when the light had a certain warmer quality to it. And when the lights dimmed, he longed to be read again the way a plant with dry soil longs for rain.

Scientists have proven that reading fiction makes people more empathic, improves their disposition and emotional intelligence. People, in other words, need stories. But stories also need people. An unread book is a caged animal, trapped between paper walls. They want reading, need it. To open a book is to set a story free.

In a bookstore at night—or a library or a box of books left in the donation bin outside of your local Goodwill—you can feel the stories working their soft magic, singing a siren's song to draw readers to their pages.

Read me and I'll show you what passion looks like on paper . . .
Read me and breathe the rusted red air of Mars . . .
Read me and I'll reveal to you what really happened in that lonely cabin in the dark, dark woods . . .
Read me, for you think you're too old for unicorns and fairies, but in my pages, you'll learn you are a mere baby in the eyes of these ancient beings, and don't you want to feel like a child again?
Read me and remember . . .
Read me and forget . . .
Read me and hate . . .
Read me and fall in love . . .
Read me and learn the secrets you've been keeping from yourself . . .

When Duke, Koshka, and I reached Words, Words, Words at four in the morning, the air was heavy with this magic. Most people can't feel it directly. They simply wake up with an overpowering urge to go to the nearest bookstore and buy a new novel. But to a Book Witch, the spell is impossible to ignore. It surrounded the building like a heavy fog.

"The Burners and I agree on one thing only," I said, as the strange mist reached out toward us with tendrils of longing. "Books are dangerous."

Duke smiled and said, "I like a spot of danger myself."

We stood by my car, which I'd had to leave there earlier that evening when it wouldn't start. If anyone caught us, we had our lie ready, that we'd come back to retrieve my Sun Buggy.

"Are you all right, darling?" Duke asked.

I shivered in the cold. Koshka pressed his small body to my legs. He let me pick him up and tuck him inside my coat.

"The books are particularly wild tonight," I said. "Can you tell?"

He peered at the bookstore, shook his head no.

"Looks like a perfectly normal bookshop at night to me. A normal bookshop in an old, creaking Victorian house shrouded in fog and mist . . ."

"Books that don't have a home yet are always trying to seduce you," I explained. "That's why almost no one can go into a bookstore without buying something. At night, the books try to get into your head, into your dreams. For a Book Witch, it's like walking through a circus of ghosts . . . and they want me to run away and join their circus."

Duke stared at me agog. "A ghost circus? That . . . that is positively sinister, Rainy. I'm going to have nightmares now."

"It's not too bad. Unless you're in the horror section. Then it gets a little nightmarish. But it will be all right once I get my umbrella back. It'll shield me. Until then, stick close."

"Why don't you let me go it alone?" Duke asked. "I can nick your umbrella and bring it back to you."

"Bad idea," I said. "If Dr. Fanshawe notices it's gone, she'll know I stole it. We need to get in, use it while we're there, then put it back before morning."

"Noted," Duke said. "Penny said the back door was unlocked?"

"She said she thought she might have left it unlocked," I told him. "Do you have the book?"

"What book?" Duke asked.

"*Alice in Wonderland.*"

"I thought you had it," he said.

"Great. We're the worst criminals ever." I took a long breath. "Let's hope the bookstore has a copy of one of the Alice books in stock."

Koshka meowed.

"Right, boy, if we have to, we can use an ebook."

"What's an ebook?" Duke asked.

"Never mind. Let's go."

Duke took me by the hand. Together, we skulked through the shadows as we made our way to the back of the store.

As we neared it, my vision blurred.

"Rainy?"

"I'm okay. Keep going."

As we pressed deeper into the mist of stories, I saw shapes forming. Old friends. Old enemies.

A man with a handkerchief tied around his head and jaw glared at me, rattling chains forged of greed and regret.

Marley's ghost.

A Saint Bernard dog, enormous, rabid, barked silently at me, foam dripping from his mouth.

Cujo.

Three witches huddled together, stirring a cauldron of conspiracy and murder. One raised a gnarled, ancient hand and beckoned me to join them.

The Weird Sisters.

Yes, I should join their circle, shouldn't I?

"*Fair is foul, and foul is fair; / Hover through the fog and filthy air . . .*" I mumbled as I started toward them.

Then suddenly, as if someone had flipped a switch, they were gone.

"Rainy?" Duke held me by the upper arms and gently shook me. "Rainy, can you see me?"

I blinked once, twice, and my eyes cleared.

In my hands, I held my umbrella again. I clutched it to my chest like a very long, oddly cylindrical teddy bear.

"Oh my goodness, I missed you," I said and kissed it, which I know is odd behavior, and I make no excuses. "Did they hurt you?"

Duke hovered over me like a mother hen. "Rainy, you're talking to your umbrella."

"Don't judge. It's been a long day. Wait. What happened? Weren't we outside?"

My head throbbed, but my vision had cleared. No more ghosts or rabid dogs or wicked witches.

"I let go of your hand for thirty seconds to open the door and lock it behind us," he said, "and then you were gone. Koshka found you wandering in the fog muttering *Macbeth* quotes."

"The Weird Sisters got into my head and were trying to recruit me again."

"Again? I was content with the first part of the sentence, but when we got to the 'again,' I started to worry."

"No, no, it's okay. I'm okay. I know we don't have time to murder the king of Scotland tonight."

"Or any night, yes? Please say yes."

"Correct," I said and blinked a few more times to get the last of the cauldron smoke out of my eyes. "Sorry, Shakespeare is heady stuff." Koshka rubbed against my legs, then crawled into my lap. I gave him his favorite chin scritches. "I'm fine, comrade. Now let me up. We have work to do."

Koshka leapt off my lap and onto the nearest desk.

"Umbrella achieved," Duke said. "What's next?"

"Children's fiction." I found the steps that led from the stockroom to the main floor. Duke and Koshka followed behind me.

We passed through the stockroom door into the Indigenous room, where the bookstore kept a good collection of fiction, nonfiction, and craft and cookbooks about the native Clatsop people. The floor creaked mournfully with every careful step we took.

"I don't remember it being this loud during the day," I said quietly, wincing every time my toes touched the ground. "They can probably hear us stomping around next door."

"Carpeting," Duke whispered. "That's what we need. Thick wall-to-wall carpeting."

Meanwhile Koshka, who barely weighed ten pounds and was born with rubberized feet, trotted merrily along, not disturbing so much as an atom of the universe.

"Or we should be cats," I said.

"They are called cat burglars for a reason," Duke said, and the floor whined under his shoes.

It felt like an eternity passed before we'd made it to the children's book room. My hair was damp with flop sweat and terror.

Koshka found the book first on a shelf painted rainbow colors labeled as CLASSICS.

I pulled a hardcover unabridged copy of *Alice's Adventures in Wonderland* off the shelf with a sigh of relief. "Let's get this over with," I said and put the book on a tiny plastic table, open to the end of chapter six.

I pressed my hand to the page, reaching out with my magic to touch the story. Orange electric filaments crackled around my hand as they had when I tried to open my grandfather's locked desk drawer.

"Oh no," I gasped.

"What?" Duke asked.

"We have a problem."

"Two," he said.

"Two what?"

A light flashed through the shop window. Not headlights. A flashlight.

"Two problems," he mouthed.

Book in hand, the three of us raced back to the stockroom, where we ducked behind a book cart.

"Can you get us into the book now?" Duke whispered.

The front door of the bookshop whined open.

A stern male voice called out, "Anyone here? Police."

Eight or nine unprintable words passed through my mind.

"The book's locked," I whispered back to Duke.

"What do you mean it's locked?"

The policeman's heavy gait rattled the old window frames.

"Pick any book," Duke hissed.

That was an idea. I glanced around wildly, looking for a place to hide us.

A nearby cart carried special orders that hadn't been picked up by customers yet.

I grabbed at them.

Dante's *Inferno*? No, we were definitely not hiding out in Hell.

The Plague by Albert Camus.

Absolutely not.

The Parable of the Sower by Octavia Butler.

"Why is everybody reading depressing, scary books? Somebody order something happy," I muttered.

At the bottom of the pile, I found exactly what we needed. The footsteps grew louder.

"Hurry," Duke said.

There. Perfect. I opened the book to a random page and prayed for a safe chapter.

"Got it. Koshka."

He leapt into Duke's arms. Then I grabbed Duke's hand.

I quietly and quickly recited, "*Hic jacet Arthurus, Rex quondam, Rexque futurus.*"

With a flick of my fingers, I opened my black umbrella and the three of us fell through a hole in the fabric of reality, turning ourselves into the dot on a lowercase "i" in the word "*Hic.*"

DOWN, DOWN, WE WENT, SEEMINGLY FALLING FOREVER.

When we did finally land, it was slowly, like a balloon returning to earth. Our feet touched ground in a meadow of wildflowers. Duke stumbled to the side and caught hold of a tree trunk while I sank to my knees to catch my breath.

"Where . . . where are we?" Duke asked.

Panting, I glanced around, taking stock of our surroundings.

Snowy white wood anemones carpeted the edge of a wild forest.

And far in the distance, gleaming like a new and golden morning, stood a castle.

"You, a duke of the realm, don't recognize *that*?" I asked, pointing to the castle.

"No . . ." he breathed and stepped away from the tree. "Is that . . . ?"

"Welcome to Camelot, Duke."

There are no words for the moment a son of Britain sees Camelot for the first time. So we said nothing, merely soaked in the sunlight. And there is no sunlight like the sunlight of Arthurian England, though we all have seen it, of course. Remember your best day in the sun as a child. That's the light. The sunlight that shines only in a perfect memory.

"Rainy . . ." Duke said. "How did we get here?"

"Someone had special ordered *The Legends of King Arthur,*" I said. "Good place to hide for a few minutes, right?"

My black umbrella hovered overhead. I took it by the handle and moved it into the shadows cast by an oak tree. Merlin was afoot and he would definitely steal a magic umbrella if he ran across one. Who wouldn't?

"How long do we stay here?" Duke asked.

"Long enough for the police officer to see nobody's in the bookstore and leave."

"Good."

At that, Duke took off his suit jacket, then rolled up his sleeves.

Not that I was one to ever complain about seeing Duke's perfect forearms, but I had to ask . . .

"Duke, what are you—"

He laid down on his back among the wildflowers.

"I'm in Arthur's Britain, Rainy. Let me bask."

"Oh, well, bask away."

I sat down on the ground next to him and started pulling red clover, tying the stems together in a daisy chain. Meanwhile, Duke was making wildflower angels in the meadow.

"You're going to get grass stains on your suit," I said.

"Worth it." He abruptly sat up. "Can we meet him?"

"Arthur? No. We're not dressed right, and we'd probably accidentally change the story. Never meet your heroes, as Pops likes to remind me."

"You did." He winked at me.

"And you see how much trouble it got me into." I poked him in the shoulder. Duke smiled, then turned his bright, dark eyes upon Camelot again. It was a fairy-tale castle, with white turrets and towers, shining high on a hill. A castle made not of wood and stone but of longing and dreams.

"I had a Welsh nurse as a boy," Duke said, "who spoke of Arthur as if he were still alive. Edward was never her king. Arthur, he was her true and only king."

"*Hic jacet Arthurus, Rex quondam, Rexque futurus,*" I said, quoting the legendary writing on Arthur's grave. "Arthur, the once and future king."

"She made me believe he would come back to our world, our time," Duke said. "I can almost believe her now."

"I believe her," I said.

Duke sat up and eyed me. "You do not."

"Who was King Arthur?" I asked. "He was a story. The story of a man chosen by fate to attempt great and noble things for the good of others. And he did his best with a broken heart. A hero. A storybook hero. Sounds like someone I know."

"Who?"

"You," I said and placed the clover crown on his head.

He looked at me, eyes narrowed. "Don't be ridiculous, darling."

"King Arthur and his knights live on in you and every other hero out there trying to help us poor damsels in distress."

Duke took my hand and kissed the back of it.

"Ground rules," I said.

"Yes, of course." He dropped my hand. "I am not King Arthur reincarnated. Although I am trying to do the best I can with a broken heart."

"Is your heart broken now?"

"Not when I'm sitting by Rainy March in the shadow of Camelot."

I smiled, trying not to remember how much I loved him. Easier said than done.

"They say my mother came here once when she was a young Book Witch. Saved Sir Galahad from a whole legion of Burners who were trying to stop him from finding the Holy Grail."

The Quest for the Holy Grail is a foundational story. Any book with a noble hero trying to find a magical object owes a debt of gratitude to the Holy Grail myth.

"How did she do it?" Duke asked.

"Supposedly she put herself between Galahad and the Burners and dared them to kill her to get to him. They would've happily slaughtered a fictional character, but killing a real girl? Well, they backed down and Galahad was saved." I looked around as if I could spot my mother, young as me, maybe younger, peeking at us from behind one of the trees. "Can you imagine anyone that brave?"

"Of course." He took off the crown of clover and dropped it on my head. "You."

"Now you're being ridiculous."

"You stood between me and that ghastly Burner X, did you not? You practically dared him to kill you to get to me. You're more like your mother than you know."

"Thank you. I don't know if I believe you."

"You should never doubt me. Ever." He smiled.

"Don't look at me like that," I said. Then suddenly, I sat up. "Wait. Where's Koshka?"

"There," Duke pointed. "Hunting."

In a thick patch of clover, I spotted Koshka, stalking a tiny field mouse.

"Koshka," I scolded. "No eating the characters. Even the minor ones."

He started to trot over to me, then stopped, turned around, arched his back, and puffed up like a Halloween cat.

"Koshka?"

"Oh, dear," Duke said. "I'm afraid we have company."

He pointed to a rider in the distance astride a black horse.

"That's . . . not in the story," I said. "Duke, hide."

"Why?"

"It's a Burner and you're not supposed to be out of your books. Hide now."

"I'm not going to leave you alone with—"

"So help me, LeVar Burton, if you do not hide in the woods right now, I'm locking you into the Eighth Circle of Hell in Dante's *Inferno* and throwing away the key."

Duke blanched. "I won't hide . . . I will, however, conceal myself, and then leap out if you need me."

The ground shook as the horse's hooves beat on it, then its rider reined his mount to a halt in front of me. The rider wore a closed helmet, but when he lifted the visor, I recognized him at once.

X.

"Are you going to say 'We meet again,' or should I?" I asked him. My heart raced wildly, but I pretended I wasn't bothered by his sudden appearance.

He only smirked. "You should smile more," he said. "You'd look much prettier."

I bared my teeth at him and growled.

"I'm trying to do you a favor, March," he said.

"A favor? Attacking Arthurian legends is a favor?"

"Oh, I'm not here for King Arthur. I like this book, actually," he said, glancing around and nodding his approval. "Classic. Traditional. When men were men and women were—"

"Witches? Queens who had affairs with their husbands' best friends?"

"Ladies," he said. "Who dressed properly."

He eyed my outfit, my leggings, boots, and sweater.

"That's what you get out of the King Arthur stories? Fashion?" I asked.

"And good manners."

"Right, good manners. Violence, adultery, and incest. I'm starting to think you don't actually read the books you claim to love or hate. No, you wave them like flags in a war no one's fighting but you."

This was all bluster on my part, but I wanted to make X angry enough at me that he didn't even glance into the dark woods to see Duke hiding, I mean, concealing himself in the shadows.

"If you're going to be like that, I'll go," he said.

"Oh no. Anything but that."

"I'll go . . . before giving you the advice I came to give you."

"You came here to give me advice? How did you even know I was here?"

"You're being watched," he said. "I don't know who's watching or why, but someone is keeping a very close eye on you. Probably because they know what a troublemaker you are."

"I'm flattered to be so notorious." I waved my hand at him. "Come on, what's this 'advice' of yours? Let's get it over with."

I was pretty sure I knew what he would say.

Quit your job. Join the Burners. Eat my words and die. That sort of thing.

"You're trying to find the March Hare," he said.

Shocked, I said nothing.

"If you do, you won't like what you find."

I snorted a laugh, more bluster. "About hares?"

"About your mother."

My stomach sank into the fabled earth of Camelot.

"My mother?"

"Take it from me, March. Your mother wasn't the saint you think she was."

"What's that supposed to mean? My mother was a legend. Dr. Fanshawe said so herself, and she never gives out compliments."

"Find out at your own peril," X said. "But if I were you . . . I'd drop the whole thing."

"Good thing you're not me."

"Don't say I didn't warn you," he said, then with a jerk of the reins, he turned and rode away.

CHAPTER FIFTEEN

Duke emerged from behind the tree.

"Are you all right, darling?" he asked.

"I know you shouldn't hate people, but that guy? I hate. My mother wasn't the saint I thought she was? Why would he even say that? Why would he give me advice?"

I didn't like this, not one bit.

"This always happens to me in my books," Duke said. "When someone gives me quote 'friendly advice' to back off from my investigation, I know I'm on the right track. It's a good sign, truly."

"How was that a good sign?"

He put his arm around my back and made me face him. Clearly he could see how distressed I was. "If a Burner is trying to stop you, that means we're on the right track. Forget about him, love. Now, shall we get back to work?"

"Please. I need to find my grandfather so I can hug him, then shake him until he tells me what is going on."

"Lead the way," Duke said, handing me my umbrella.

The three of us stood together, holding hands and paws.

"Our revels now are ended!" I called out, quoting Shakespeare's *Tempest*. Quoting one book inside another book is the easiest way to get pushed out of a story. It's sort of the storycraft equivalent of thinking about kissing your ex while on a date with a new guy. Not that I would ever do that.

As if swept up in a miniature tornado, we breezed out of Arthur's Britain and landed back inside the stockroom of Words, Words, Words.

Duke reeled and caught himself on a bookshelf.

"I had forgotten," he said quietly, "how much I hate that part."

"Sorry," I whispered back. "Been too long since we story-hopped together." I snapped my umbrella closed with a satisfying whoosh and snick.

"Far too long. Now you two wait here. I'll check the shop."

Koshka and I huddled in the employees only restroom while Duke went on reconnaissance.

Two long minutes later, he returned and called out, "All clear."

We reconvened in the darkened stockroom.

"Shall we go?" Duke asked. "Wonderland awaits."

"We can't," I said. "Right before that cop got here, I checked the book." I held up the copy we'd nabbed from the children's section. "It won't let us in."

"Why not?" Duke asked.

"Because I'd completely forgotten that *Alice in Wonderland* is a Code Red Ink book."

"And that is?"

"Not good," I said. "For us anyway. You know that enchanted lock on my grandfather's desk? Code Reds are also kept under lock and key since they're considered V.I.T."

"V.I.T.? Do I want to know?"

"Very Important Titles."

"Of course. I should've guessed." He rolled his eyes.

"They're books that Burners are always trying to destroy for one stupid reason or another. *Alice in Wonderland* was the first major children's book that wasn't written to teach kids any moral lessons or anything like that. It was pure entertainment. Changed children's literature forever. Any book that turns kids into lifelong readers is going to be under constant threat from Burners."

"So we can't get into Wonderland to speak with the March Hare?"

"Without the right key, there's no way—"

"Nonsense," Duke said, empathically. "You ferried me to Camelot with a click of your heels. You can do anything."

"It was more a flick of my finger, but I get what you're saying."

"I'm saying that I know you can find us a way into Wonderland. Think. Use that gorgeous brain of yours. Is there a back door? Or . . . I don't know . . . a French translation?"

Koshka, resting his chin on my foot, raised his head and hissed.

"I meant a Russian translation," Duke said. Appeased, Koshka put his head back down again. "Or one of those, what did you call them? E . . . books?"

A back door into Wonderland? Another version of the book? A translation? I considered our options.

"Translations won't work. Or ebooks or audiobooks. The story is the story no matter what language or format it's in." I began pacing the stockroom floor. "Any version we go into will be monitored. Unless . . . wait. Wait one single second . . ."

"What?"

"Pops told me a story a long time ago," I said, "about the first case he worked after my mother died. A Burner had gotten into Ray Bradbury's novel *Something Wicked This Way Comes.* There are villains in the book, evil carnival performers who tempt you with your deepest desires. Pops's deepest desire back then was to have my mother back, of course. The evil carnival barker, Mr. Dark, cornered Pops in the town library."

"What did he do?" Duke asked.

"He realized he was in a library. A fictional library in a fictional town, but the books on the shelves had all the pages, all the words. So instead of escaping back to the real world, he escaped into a novel in the library!"

"He went into a book . . . in a book?"

"Exactly," I said. "Pops jumped into one of the library books. A copy of Hawthorne's *The House of the Seven Gables.* He hid out in one of the unused servants' rooms for an hour and then popped *back* into *Something Wicked This Way Comes.* Mr. Dark had given up by that point so Pops could finish his mission and come home."

"Would that work? Going into a novel with a fictional library and using a fictional copy of *Alice in Wonderland*?"

"It should," I said. "If it's a fictional copy in a fictional library, we wouldn't be able to change it in the real world. Neither can Burners. But we can go into it."

"What about that book your grandfather used—*Something Wicked*?"

"Too dangerous," I said. "The villains are soul stealers. We need a library in a book that's slightly less deadly. And one that isn't under a Code Red."

There were only a few dozen or so books under Code Red, most of them political, foundational to the canon, or beloved by children worldwide—the Alice books, of course, plus *1984, Fahrenheit 451, Don Quixote,* the *Odyssey, The Tale of Genji, Things Fall Apart, To Kill a Mockingbird, Beloved, Frankenstein,* the Lord of the Rings trilogy, and literally everything Shakespeare penned.

"A good library," Duke said. "A large, well-stocked library."

"And one that's not being used. A private library."

"So a library more for show than for reading. The private library of someone with money, someone showing off," he said. "An aristocrat. Or someone pretending to be . . ."

"And somewhere we can sneak in without anyone noticing us."

"We'd need a lot of people there," Duke continued. "A crowd we can join."

"A party?"

He nodded, smiling.

"The library of someone rich, someone showing off, someone who throws lots of house parties . . ." I said. "Are you thinking what I'm thinking?"

Together we said the most famous name in American fiction.

"Gatsby."

"PERFECT IDEA, DARLING," DUKE SAID, NODDING. "I'LL POP INTO the shop and find a copy—"

"Won't work. I can't go to a Gatsby party dressed like this. Even you look underdressed."

His mouth dropped open. He gestured at his suit. "This is Savile Row!"

"Sorry. It's not a tux. You need a tux and I need . . ." I looked down at myself. "Anything but leggings."

"I see the issue here. Best pop home."

"So much for sneaking my umbrella back into the supply closet. I'll have to take it with us and risk getting caught."

"Halt. I have a brilliant idea," Duke said. "Per usual."

He disappeared again. A moment later, he came back, holding another black umbrella in his hand.

"Lost and found box," he said.

"You are as brilliant as you are handsome."

"Yes, I know."

It wasn't exactly the same make and model, so to speak. Mine was wood and steel and this one had a plastic handle, but unless they looked too closely, no one should notice the difference.

Duke returned the fake umbrella to the supply closet, and we met Koshka at the back door.

"It's going to look very suspicious—a man in a suit, a woman with an umbrella not in the rain, and a cat sneaking out of a bookstore at dawn. So play it cool. Walk, don't run to my car," I told the boys.

Koshka whined in protest.

"Right, very short legs," I said. "You can run. If we see anybody, just smile and nod. Oh, and pray the car starts. I'd rather not walk home."

"Because we might get spotted?" Duke asked.

"No, because it's six blocks uphill."

Duke pushed the door open, and we slipped outside. He took me by the arm and escorted me through the fading mist of the story magic. As the sun slowly rose, the books fell silent, waiting like wallflowers at a ball for a new suitor to come and claim the next waltz.

No thieves, robbers, petty crooks, shoplifters, assassins, or pickpockets ever snuck away from the scene of the crime as sneakily as we snuck to my car. My head faced forward but my eyes ping-ponged in all directions to make sure we weren't being watched. We made a beeline for my Sun Buggy. If the car didn't start, Plan B was walking. There was also a Plan C, because I always have a Plan C.

Plan C is, of course, *crying*.

We got lucky. The car started. I could have Plan C–ed with relief, but I was in too much of a hurry to get us home and out of the cold and damp.

"Good job, team," I said as I drove us up the hill to Pilcrow House. "Well done. We didn't get arrested. Yet."

"*Gatsby* isn't a Code Red Ink book, is it?" Duke asked.

"It's not. Long story but Burners tend to leave it alone."

"And you do have a copy of the book at home, yes?"

I gave him a look, the one where you keep your lips in a perfectly straight line, the look that tells the person you're looking at that you're questioning either their intelligence or their sanity—or both.

"Right," Duke said. "Of course you do."

"Yes, a house of Book Witches has a copy of the most famous American novel of the twentieth century."

As famous as it is now, *The Great Gatsby* had been a poor seller, practically a flop when it came out. The story caught a second wind during World War II, however, when a nonprofit sent free books to soldiers. After the war the book became a staple on high school and college reading lists and hasn't left them since.

We made it home, and I'd rarely been so glad to stumble through the front doors of Pilcrow House. No time to rest, we headed straight up to the attic to dig through our costume closet.

Flapper dress? No, a bit too flashy for me. I found a black drop-waist cocktail dress, silk and sequins but blessedly free from ticklish fringe. I put my hair in a bun at the nape of my neck and added a sequined headband.

For Duke, there was my grandfather's old tuxedo, which I hoped would fit.

"Ready," I called out.

"Two minutes, love," Duke called back. "I might need braces. Or glue."

"Oh yeah, Pops has about twenty pounds on you."

I found a pair of black suspenders and handed them through the dressing room door.

"Earlier you said Burners leave *The Great Gatsby* alone. What's the story on that?" Duke asked from inside the room.

"Honestly, I think it's because they like the depressing ending, which tells people to never dream big. Gatsby takes a bullet for the woman he loves, and Daisy walks away scot-free and goes back to her husband. The title of the book could've been *Why Bother?*"

"Not the most cheerful of endings," Duke agreed.

"As usual, the Burners are missing the point if they really believe that's what the story means," I said while adjusting my stockings.

"Are they? What do you think it means?"

"*Gatsby* isn't about the death of the American dream," I said as I applied my lipstick in the mirror. "It's about a man who wants to write his own story, not let someone else write it for him."

"A lovely sentiment, my dear, but the man was a bootlegger," Duke said. "A nobody from Minnesota who wanted to cut the line and achieve greatness without actually doing great things."

"You're being very judgmental."

"I'm English. Of course I am. You only like him because he's handsome and he sacrificed his life for the woman he loved. Although, for the record, she did not deserve it."

Nick Carraway, the forlorn narrator of *The Great Gatsby,* has said as much himself. *They're a rotten crowd . . . You're worth the whole damn bunch put together.*

Then again, Nick Carraway was undoubtedly in love with Gatsby, which may have clouded his judgment.

"Not true," I said. "Actually, I like him because he tried to escape the life he was born into, and there is something noble about that. Sound familiar?"

"Surely you're not talking about moi?"

"I'm not talking about me, am I?" I said. "You were the one born into an aristocratic family. You didn't like it, and now you're in Chicago working as a detective. Sounds like you wrote your own story."

"Hardly, darling. If I were writing my own story, we would not be having this conversation."

"What would we be doing instead?"

"I have an extensive mental list, none of it fit for mixed company. Are you ready? Brace yourself. I look devastatingly handsome, and you might have a fit of the vapors."

"Hit me," I said.

He threw open the dressing room door.

While I looked like a modern gal playing dress-up in her great-grandmother's closet, Duke, who had the Roarin' Twenties in his fictional veins, looked like he was born to wear a tuxedo. He'd even slicked back his hair. He looked dapper, debonair, and ready to dance.

"Wow," I said. "I am vaporized."

"Rainy, love, you look absolutely beautiful."

He took my hand and spun me in a quick, dizzying circle.

"To the library, old sport," I said. We started down the stairs, which was not easy in high heels.

"Will we need to take Victorian clothes with us to change into?" Duke asked.

"It's Wonderland. The weirder we look, the more we'll fit in."

In that regard, it was not unlike Portland.

Koshka was waiting for us in the library, sitting on the reading table by the bookstand.

"Buddy, no, you can't go to Wonderland with us," I told him. "The Cheshire Cat is even weirder than you are."

He let out a whine pitiful enough to break the hardest heart.

"Darling, don't be cruel. Maybe he could come to the party?" Duke said. "Keep watch in the library?"

"You are a sucker," I told him. "A sucker. And that cat is a con artist."

Duke petted Koshka. "It never hurts to have backup."

"Fine," I told Koshka. "You can go to the Gatsby party, but you have to stay there. No Wonderland for you. Deal?" I held out my hand, and he put his paw in it. "Good. Let's go. Book me."

Duke handed me the hardcover copy of *The Great Gatsby.*

I flipped through the pages to an early scene where Nick Carraway and his date, Jordan Baker, are wandering through Jay Gatsby's mansion during a party. They enter his enormous library, where they meet a man looking through the books, utterly dazzled that Gatsby's books are real, not cardboard fakes. But the pages, he sees, are uncut, unread. It seems like a throwaway scene the first time you read it, a moment of comic relief, but to me it shows that Gatsby is a man of great potential never fulfilled.

I only hoped his library was as impressive and extensive as F. Scott Fitzgerald described.

Koshka didn't wriggle when I scooped him off the reading table. He was ready for a mission. I also didn't wriggle when Duke put his arms around me from behind, which sounds a little saucy, but if he'd held me from the front, he would've squished the cat.

"I'm enjoying this more than I should," Duke said.

"I can tell. Now hush, I need to find a place to land us."

Everyone remembers the last line of *The Great Gatsby,* but there are many other beautiful lines that go unnoticed. I only needed one to draw us into the story, but which one? I turned to a page from the party scene and found what I was looking for.

Quietly I whispered the words like an incantation. "*In his blue gardens men and girls came and went like moths among the whisperings and the champagne and the stars . . .*"

With a flick of my thumb, I opened my black umbrella over our heads and turned us into the dot in the first "i" in the word "whisperings."

Think of a moment when you slipped and fell and you saw your life flash before your eyes as you went down, stomach lurching, the sudden scream, learning in an instant that we are all gravity's prisoners . . .

We felt that, all three of us and all at once, and then the coldness of nothing, of leaving the solid rock of the real world for the mists and the fog of the ethereal, unreal realm of stories.

Like a swimmer knocked sideways by an ocean wave, I sought purchase only to find shifting sand under my feet. But then I felt a floor, a floor made of words, and I could stand on those words and see them, not for what they said but for what they meant—gleaming hardwood in a magnificent house by the bay built out of one man's impossible dream.

Gatsby's house in West Egg.

CHAPTER SIXTEEN

When the three of us arrived in the book, we were immediately swept up in the flow of the plot. We came to on a sofa in a side room, draped over each other like we'd had too much to drink and passed out.

Slowly, I sat up, rubbing my head.

"You all right, toots?" asked a man in a tuxedo who'd paused in the doorway to light a cigarette.

"I lushed too mush," I said, playing the part.

"Drink a little water, dame. You'll be kickin' up your heels in no time." He gave me a wink as he did a little Charleston into the next room. Or maybe a Lindy Hop. I've never learned the difference.

Champagne flutes, a dozen of them or more, sat on the tables around us. A roar came from close by—music and the stomping of feet that caused the whole house to subtly vibrate.

Next to me, Duke raised his head, blinking like a man waking from either a very long nap or a very brief coma. As soon as his eyes focused, he jumped to his feet and surveyed the room.

"We're here," he breathed. "We made it. Look at that wallpaper." Duke rubbed his hand along the walls. "It feels like . . . like wallpaper. Gatsby's wallpaper. Rainy, my love, I have missed this."

"You missed going on adventures with me?" I asked. Back before we broke up, Duke had accompanied me on several of my assignments.

"I missed going anywhere with you," he said, smiling. "And the boy, of course. Wait, where's our boy?"

I glanced around. "I'm going to have to put a bell on that cat if he doesn't learn to stay close."

"Anybody missing a pussy?" someone shouted from the next room over.

A man's voice called back, "Not me! I got too many already!"

"I think we know where Koshka is," Duke said. He gave a wolf whistle. In seconds a gray streak sped into the room and jumped on the sofa next to me.

"How many times have I told you not to wander off?" I scolded Koshka, pointing my finger at his nose. He licked my fingertip, which was not an apology. "Now, carefully . . . sneak out of here and find the library. Report back immediately. Go."

Koshka went into recon mode, tail down, belly close to the ground, as he slinked from the room.

"Shouldn't take him long," I said. "He can sniff out a book from a mile away. We better move my umbrella somewhere safe."

As long as the umbrella stayed open, we could mostly stay hidden in the book.

"Here we go," Duke said. My umbrella hovered like a bee in the corner of the room. Duke took the handle and hung it upside-down from the chandelier. "A magic umbrella is probably the least bizarre thing ever to hang from this chandelier."

A young girl dressed in a servant's uniform entered the room with a tray of champagne. "Anything for you two dolls?" she asked with a flirtatious smile at Duke.

He took a glass of champagne and gave the girl a little salute.

"None for me," I said. "I've had enough."

She glanced at the empty glasses. "Save some for the rest of us, kitten."

With a little kick of her heels, she shimmied out of the room.

"Can anyone walk normally here?" I asked. Then I looked at Duke. "Don't drink that."

"Not even a sip?"

"You might be stuck here forever. We're playing by fairyland rules."

"Hate to waste good champagne, but better safe than eternally trapped in a tragedy." He poured the champagne out the window. "Rainy, come here."

"What is it?" I joined him by the window. He pointed to a green light on a dock across the bay.

In *The Great Gatsby,* that green light on the dock belongs to Daisy Buchanan, with whom Jay Gatsby had a brief relationship years earlier. Although she is married and has a child, he's determined to win her heart back and so buys the house across the water from her and throws wild parties hoping against hope that one night, she'll show up, and they can find their old happiness again.

A foolish fantasy that ends in disillusionment and blood, but still, I felt something stir in my own heart when I looked out at the dock.

"The fabled green light," Duke said. "I can't believe I'm seeing it with my own eyes. No wonder you love your job."

"Everyone who ever read this book has pictured that green light in their minds," I said. Everyone has their own light that's just out of reach, the thing they long for, strive for, row toward even as the current pulls them away from it."

"What's your green light?" Duke asked.

"Being as good a Book Witch as my mother was, no matter the cost."

"The cost being me," he said. "Us. Us being us."

"You're fictional, Duke. I'm real. It can't happen, no matter how much we wish it could."

"Do I get a say in this?" he asked. "In my own destiny?"

"Not really." I winked and elbowed him gently in the side. "What about you? Do you have a green light? Or is that not in your character?"

"Every case is a new green light," he said. "Every time I'm on a job, I can't rest until the mystery is solved. But now . . . maybe it's because I'm not in my books, but it doesn't feel like enough. The light's too dim. There are brighter lights so much closer."

He met my eyes, a beautiful moment interrupted by a small meow.

"Koshka," I said. "Did you find the library?" He started for the doorway, and we followed him, but then we saw which way he was headed . . .

. . . straight through a mass of inebriated partygoers dancing like it was the end of days.

"We can't walk through there," I said. "We'll have to dance. Can you do that?"

"Darling, you know I can cut a rug like ten pairs of scissors with a sharp sword to boot." He took me by the waist and practically tossed me onto the dance floor.

I laughed as we whirled through the wildly gyrating bodies, waltzing at triple speed while everyone else kicked and dipped and twirled.

"This working?" he asked with a wide smile.

"Works for me!" I shouted over the din of "Sweet Georgia Brown" played by a live twenty-piece ragtime band. "More to the left!"

We boogied and/or woogied to the left, where Koshka's small face peered around the darkened doorway. Almost there.

Duke spun me around, and for a split second, I saw a painfully handsome man in a perfectly tailored suit standing alone at a window with a cocktail in his hand, staring at the same green light that had so captured our eye.

"Gatsby," I whispered, but Duke didn't hear me. That was good. It's easy to get starstruck in a book this legendary, but I knew better than to talk to a tragic hero when we were trying to fly under the radar.

The song ended and we pushed through the dancers to the hallway. There was Koshka waiting for us. He meowed, and we followed him down the long hall toward a set of closed double-doors. Duke looked around quickly before opening them, then all three of us disappeared inside.

We entered the library like pilgrims at a shrine, in reverent silence. When Duke closed the doors behind us, the music of the raucous party faded to nothing. The hush that fell over the room was so profound even my footsteps sounded offensive to my own ears.

Gatsby's library . . . if anything, Fitzgerald's description hadn't done it justice. It looked almost medieval, as if, as the story said, the entire magnificent room had been imported from a castle in Europe and put back together here on fictionalized Long Island.

I coveted the dark wood paneling, the floor-to-ceiling bookshelves, and the chandelier throwing golden light over every surface. At random, I chose a book off a shelf and opened it.

David Copperfield by Charles Dickens.

Moby-Dick by Herman Melville.

Jane Eyre. Wuthering Heights. The Count of Monte Cristo. The Three Musketeers. All of them exquisite antiques, maybe even first editions.

"Rainy?" Duke asked. "You all right, love? You look like you're about to cry."

I turned a slow circle inside the library.

"Let me bask," I said. "This is my Camelot."

AFTER A FEW MOMENTS OF SILENTLY BASKING IN THE GLOW OF the world's most beautiful private library, we got down to business. "Split up," I said, "and find that book."

Duke and I searched the shelves with our eyes, while Koshka made a slow circuit of the room, sniffing out *Wonderland.*

"I take back my previous assessment," Duke said. "This library is annoyingly extensive."

"I know. I think Gatsby has every book in the world in here."

"Wonder if he has my books? Or is popular detective fiction not good enough for the bootlegger?" he asked.

"*Gatsby* was before your time," I said, scanning the bottom shelves. "It came out in 1925, remember? The first Duke of Chicago book didn't come out until '45, when cozy crime fiction turned into noir."

"But it's 1930 at home," he said, running his fingers over book spines as he worked his way to the corner where his wall met mine. "Isn't it? I could've sworn—"

"In your stories, it's always 1930. But your books came out between 1945 and 1966. Twelve novels, three novellas, and twenty-one short stories. Supposedly your writer left an unfinished book of yours behind."

"Wait a moment. Remind me what year this is again?" Duke asked.

"In the real world or Gatsby's?"

"The real world."

"It's 2025," I said.

"So if I was 'born' in 1945, and it's 2025 . . . I'm fifteen years younger than I thought. I'm only eighty, not ninety-two. No wonder I look so good for my age." He gave a triumphant little laugh.

"Still too old for me," I said, but gave him a little wink to soften the blow.

"Don't wink unless you want me to kiss you," he said as we both reached the same corner.

"I can wink if I want." I winked again.

"That's it. You're getting kissed. Brace yourself."

It was against the rules, but they were my rules and so I supposed I could break them if I wanted.

Duke bent to kiss me.

Suddenly, the door flew open.

A young woman in a flapper dress burst in.

"Come on, gals and pals! It's champagne o'clock!" she cried out. Then she took a look at Duke. "I've got a whole bottle for you, guv."

She shook the bottle at him.

"Out," I ordered her.

"Someone's feisty. But I get it, honey. He's a dish and a half," she sang. Then she spun around and dashed away.

I closed the door behind her and put a chair under the knob. It wouldn't stop anyone who really wanted to come in, but it would slow them down.

"Now," I said, turning around, "where were we?"

"About to passionately kiss like we hadn't a care in the world," Duke said.

"I do have cares, though," I reminded him. "Pops."

"Very well. We'll find your grandfather, *then* I'll kiss you."

Koshka let out a high-pitched whine, the one he usually reserves for when he'd cornered a toy mouse and wanted me to praise him for his hunting prowess.

"What is it?" I asked him.

Koshka stood on his back paws and stretched himself to his full height of two and a half feet, then batted at a book.

"Victory!" Duke said as he pulled out the book. He held it up. "*Alice's Adventures in Wonderland,* complete with illustrations by Sir John Tenniel. Good man. You're officially the world's smallest librarian. And the most distinguished."

He gave Koshka an exuberance of pets and scritches.

"Thank you, Jay Gatsby," I said, taking the book from Duke's hands.

Thankfully the pages were uncut and as I flipped through them, I could tell it was the full text, words, pictures, and all. Even better, when I tested its magic, it started to give a little. This copy wasn't locked because this copy wasn't real.

"Perfect," I said. "Well done, comrade. You earned your tuna today."

"Shall we?" Duke asked. "Wonderland awaits."

My elation at having found the book disappeared immediately when I remembered step two of our brilliant plan was actually going into Wonderland.

"We shall," I said. "But brace yourself. It's going to be weird."

"I eat weird for breakfast, love. We go in, ask the March Hare a few questions, and get out. Easy as pie."

"Easy as extremely strange and difficult pie," I said. "Remember, don't eat anything, drink anything, or smoke anything. And if you see the Queen of Hearts, run."

"Anything else?" he asked.

"If I start to go mad, you have permission to slap some sense into me," I said.

"I'd never slap a woman. Perhaps a light pinching, however . . ."

"And if you go mad, I'll—" I reached under his tuxedo jacket and snapped his suspenders.

Duke cried out and laughed. He rubbed his chest.

"My nipples may never recover," he said.

"Trust me, it's better than going mad." To Koshka I said, "Keep watch, buddy. Don't let anyone reshelve us."

I placed the book on a side table open to the page before the famous Mad Tea Party chapter when Alice meets the March Hare.

"Okay, let's go, Chicago," I said.

"I have missed you calling me that." He wrapped his arms around me and held me close. "Now what? Do you need your umbrella?"

"I suppose not. We need to keep it open here. I've never attempted a book within book immersion before, so let's hope the umbrella keeps us covered for both stories."

"I have no idea what that means," Duke said, "but I trust your judgment implicitly."

"It might go easier if you help me. I'll say Alice's lines," I said, pointing to the open page, "and you say the Cheshire Cat's. Try to believe you're a part of the story, try to believe the words."

Duke smiled a little sheepishly. "Never gone undercover as a talking cat before, but I'll do my best."

And his best, it turned out, was very good. When he spoke, he did sound almost mad.

"*In that direction . . . lives a Hatter,*" he began, "*and in that direction, lives a March Hare. Visit either if you like: they're both mad.*"

"*But I don't want to go among mad people,*" I said.

"*Oh, you can't help that . . . we're all mad here. I'm mad. You're mad!*"

The magic was working. Our voices warped and slowed like someone playing a record album on the wrong speed. The outlines of our bodies wavered and faded. And if you want to know what it looks like when a Book Witch enters a story, it's almost exactly like the Cheshire Cat vanishing, as it says in the book, *quite slowly, beginning with the end of the tail, and ending with the grin . . .*

"*How do you know I'm mad?*" I read aloud.

"*You must be,*" Duke said, his voice distant and distorted, "*or you wouldn't have come here . . .*"

And as we faded away, leaving one mad party for another, I whispered a final warning to Duke.

"By the way," I said, "I hate Wonderland."

"Why?"

"You'll see."

We faded out of one story and faded slowly into another, finding ourselves standing underneath a tree in a strange wood. Sunlight streamed through the branches from all angles, because nonsense reigned here, not logic. I stared at the shadows, the light, the shadows again . . . I felt unmoored, faint, not like I was dreaming but like someone was dreaming me.

And hovering in that tree we saw something—not a cat without a grin, but a grin without a cat.

"That's why."

CHAPTER SEVENTEEN

"Rainy?" Duke asked, his voice rousing me from my reverie. "Do you see what I see?"

"Yes," I whispered, clutching Duke's hand with scared and sweating palms. "That is the Cheshire Cat. He's disappearing. Let him disappear please."

"How is this a book for children?" he whispered back.

"I'm sure it's a very nice cat."

Duke said, "I am not. At all. Can we run away? Quickly?"

The smile still hung above the tree branch like a crescent moon by day. And then, softly, somewhere, we heard a cat chuckling.

"Yes," I said.

We took off running. A path lay ahead, half in light and half in shadow. Every step took us from the darkness into the light, like we were climbing a ladder.

The worn footpath led us out of the woods and up a gently sloping hill.

"Can I say something, darling?" Duke asked.

"Of course. Anything."

"I also hate Wonderland."

"Pops brought me here on one of his missions years ago. I swore then I'd never come back. It's even weirder than I remember," I said. "And that's saying something."

"When you're a child," Duke said, "a talking cat is a sweet little fantasy. When you are an adult, a talking cat is a waking nightmare. And that sharp-toothed grin floating in midair and nothing attached to it? And it was laughing at us? I'll take Al Capone over *that* any day."

"In its defense," I said, because Book Witches are always defending books, "the book has inspired some amazing art and music and movies and theme park rides and other writers and—"

Duke glanced back at the woods where we'd seen the grinning nothing.

"Not worth it," he said.

"Aw, Chicago, I'm so sorry," I teased. "Do you need a hug?"

"I'll take a kiss *and* a hug. And an apology from Lewis Carroll. And a few sessions with Dr. Freud. And a stiff drink."

I put a hand on his shoulder, rose on my tiptoes, and kissed him lightly on the cheek before pulling away.

"That's all?" he asked. "I didn't even get my drink."

"You do not want to drink anything in this story. You'll end up ten inches tall."

"Right, of course. Now what?"

After surveying the area, I got my bearings. "We need to head up that hill."

"What fresh horrors await us there?"

"That should be where the March Hare's house is," I said. "Can you handle it?"

"For you, yes. Only you."

"All right, this way."

We followed a path that passed through a small garden. Daffodils and daisies, all nice and normal. I decided not to remind Duke that the flowers could likely talk too.

"This is better," he said, taking a deep breath. "This . . . this is my childhood. Summers in the country with my grandparents. Long before the War. Before I even knew there was such a thing as war. I can't tell you how disappointed I was with the real world when you brought me into it the first time, and I discovered the Great War wasn't merely something awful that had happened in my books."

"Unfortunately not," I said.

He turned his face from the sun and met my eyes. "Do you ever wish you could stay here?"

"In Wonderland? No, it's terrifying. Giant talking animals are only cute in theory—"

"Not Wonderland, of course. I mean . . . in a book? Do you ever wish you could stay in a story? Hop in like we have, but never hop out?"

"Like one of your books?" I teased. "That's what got us into trouble last time."

"Not mine," he said. "A book without wars. Without suffering. A book with sunlit meadows and no darkness?"

"Sometimes," I admitted. "But I can't think of a single book worth reading where nothing bad happens. Even in Wonderland, a mad queen threatens to chop off heads every other page."

"I suppose you're right," Duke said. "It seems different in books somehow. In stories the suffering leads somewhere, it means something. Remember when you took me to meet your friend Edmond Dantès?"

"I wouldn't say the Count of Monte Cristo and I are friends," I said. "But only because I'm afraid of him."

The year Duke and I were together, he tagged along with me on my mission to get a Burner out of French author Alexandre Dumas's masterpiece of revenge, *The Count of Monte Cristo.* For the Burner's own sake, actually. Anyone who's read the book knows you do not want to get on the Count's bad side.

"Well, that's neither here nor there," Duke said. "My point is the Count spends ten years in a hellish prison, escapes, finds a massive treasure, and gets poetic revenge on his betrayers. In the real world, a man who spends years in prison for a crime he didn't commit gets . . . what?"

"Traumatized," I said.

"Precisely. In your world, suffering means nothing. Nothing good comes from it," Duke said. "One thing fiction has over real life."

I stopped and looked at him.

"Of course good things come from suffering in the real world. You know what good comes out of suffering?"

"What?" he asked, clearly skeptical.

"Stories," I said. "Art. Songs. The Duke of Chicago books. That's the good that comes from suffering. Years before we met, you were helping me get through the loneliest days of my life. Doesn't that mean something?"

He raised his hand to my face and stroked my cheek. "I'd kiss you for the next ten hours, but I think I've spotted a house with rabbit ears."

WHEN DUKE SAID THE HOUSE HAD RABBIT EARS, HE WASN'T REferring to a television antenna or anything so logical or normal. No, the enormous house had a thatched roof, and the thatching had been stacked to resemble two large actual rabbit ears.

"Mad as a March Hare," I said, staring at the bizarre dwelling.

"Let's hope he's in a good mood today," Duke said.

We found our way to the front of the house, where a long table under a tree was laid out for a tea party. There were seats for a dozen people—or whatever you wanted to call the citizens of Wonderland—but I saw no guests at all. Not even the Mad Hatter or the March Hare. The table was empty.

"That can't be right," I said, leaning close to Duke. "The mad tea party never ends."

"Never?"

"The Mad Hatter's watch is broken, stuck at six o'clock, forever teatime."

"That is entirely too much tea even for me," Duke concluded.

"Yeah, well, welcome to Wonderland," I said with a shrug.

Together we approached the tea table. Carefully I lifted the tablecloth on the off chance the partygoers had passed out from too much mad revelry. Nothing under there but the abandoned chairs and the soft green grass.

"Anything?" Duke asked.

"Nothing," I said. "And no one." We met eyes across the table. "The tea party that never ends has ended. Makes no sense. I mean, even less sense than Wonderland usually does."

"Did a Burner do this?" Duke asked.

"Maybe. But this feels different. I've been in stories where Burners have tried this. In one book they succeeded. It's not like this. It's not empty. Not . . . blank."

"What is it like?"

"They left the bodies for the Witches to find."

"Rainy . . ." Duke said. "You never told me that."

"Why would I? The history books say Charles Dickens didn't finish his last novel, *The Mystery of Edwin Drood.* He did though. The reason everyone thinks it's unfinished is because the Burners got to it before we did."

"This isn't the Burners then?"

"I don't believe so. This feels like . . . a set. A theater set but no actors."

Duke walked along the tea table. It was a disaster. Empty cups. Empty pots. Plates covered in crumbs and jam.

And there in the middle of the table, at the only place with a clean plate and cup, a name card.

"Seems you were expected, love," Duke said.

In swooping cursive, the place card read *Rainy March.*

"A woman's handwriting," Duke said. "Let's hope it wasn't a trap."

"Should I sit down?" I asked, picking up the card.

"No, let me," he said.

"Duke—"

"Rainy, I am the detective here. Let me detect."

"Please be very careful."

He pulled out the chair and sat down. Nothing happened.

"Now what?" he said, speaking to himself.

"Listen to me," I said.

"I always do, love."

"Look," I said and held out the place card to him. On the front was my name. On the back in that same handwriting it read *Listen to me.*

"Listen to what?" Duke asked.

"In the book, Alice finds food and bottles that say 'Eat me' and 'Drink me.' This one says, 'Listen to me.' So there has to be something to listen to. Try the teapot?"

"The teapot? You want me to listen to . . . a teapot? Darling, have you gone mad? I'm ready and willing to pinch you if I must. Even if I don't, I'm willing—"

"Let me try," I said. But Duke held up his hand to stop me.

"I feel absolutely mad doing this," he said, "but I suppose that's the point." He put the spout to his ear. His eyes suddenly widened.

"What did it say?" I asked.

"You listen," he said.

He passed me the teapot, and I put it to my ear.

This is what happens when you spend more than five minutes in Wonderland. You'll put teapots to your ear to listen for secret messages. And sometimes you'll hear them.

A voice, like the whooshing echo from a seashell, whispered to me, "Wrong March Hare . . ."

"Wrong March Hare?" I repeated, then took the lid off the teapot and shouted into it. "What do you mean, 'Wrong March Hare'? There's only one March Hare in literature, and he's supposed to be hare! I mean, *here*!"

No answer.

"It is an English teapot," Duke said delicately, as if speaking to someone defusing a bomb. "Perhaps try using your manners. If you have any?"

Infuriated but also desperate, I put the spout to my lips and said with feigned politeness, "Ever so sorry for losing my temper, but could you please elaborate, my dear teapot? If it's not this March Hare, pray tell, what March Hare is it?"

"Not sure that was much better," Duke muttered.

Ignoring him, I put the spout back to my ear like we were playing telephone.

The teapot replied, "The answer is staring you in the face . . ."

"What the heck's that supposed to mean?" I shouted back into the lid.

But the teapot started to make a strange sound, a low, faintly annoying, yet instantly recognizable, buzzing.

A dial tone. A teapot had hung up on me.

"Tea is the worst hot beverage!" I said, which wasn't true but it felt good to shout.

"An infuriating piece of crockery," Duke said, nodding.

"Did I mention I hated Wonderland?"

CHAPTER EIGHTEEN

So we had the wrong March Hare, apparently. Not the one in Lewis Carroll's Alice books but a different March Hare that was somehow more obvious—staring us in the face, the teapot had said—yet less obvious because, well, I had no clue where to find another March Hare.

Nothing to do but go home and keep looking.

Usually when escaping a story, I chant, "*Our revels now are ended.*" It worked as a charm, popping me out of the story like popping a champagne cork. But since we weren't going home but back to Gatsby's library, I tried a different charm this time: "*I like large parties. They're so intimate. At small parties there isn't any privacy.*"

Jordan Baker's famous line about parties did the trick. One moment Duke and I were walking swiftly away from the home of the March Hare, and the next, we were tumbling into Gatsby's library.

"Did we make it?" Duke asked, still groggy from the leap.

"Maybe?" Prying my eyes open, I looked around, saw books, bookshelves, dark paneling, and Koshka, of course, who was half-asleep on top of the open pages. "We made it."

Luckily, we'd landed on the sofa together, Duke mostly on the bottom. I tried to get up, but admittedly I didn't try very hard. A wave of dizziness hit me, and I had to close my eyes again and rest my head on Duke's chest.

"I hate Wonderland. Did I mention that?"

"You mentioned it several times," he said. "Now I understand why. That was . . . troubling."

"Talking teapots are only cute in cartoons."

Duke stroked my back. "I'm sorry we didn't find your Hare. We'll keep looking."

"It's staring me in the face, apparently. But the only thing staring me in the face right now is you. Are you the March Hare?"

"I am neither March nor Hare," he said, then winced.

"What's wrong?"

"Something is digging into my hip. Hold on." He wrapped his arm around my back, twisted us both to the side, and yanked a champagne bottle out from under one of the sofa cushions.

I took the bottle and set it on the floor. "Everyone in this book needs a liver biopsy."

"They're fictional," Duke reminded me. "They've been partying here a hundred years."

"Then they *really* need liver biopsies." I rested my chin on my hands and looked up at him. "That's a joke, by the way. I know they're fictional and therefore immortal, more or less. Lucky them."

"Immortality is overrated." Duke brought his hand to my neck, stroking it. "I'd far rather be able to grow old."

"Really? Why?"

"If I can't grow old, I can't grow old with you."

Ever have anyone say something so violently sweet to you that it felt like a punch in the stomach?

"Stop being wonderful," I said. "You're making it worse."

"Would it make it better or worse if I kissed you?"

"Ground rules," I said.

"Very well," he sighed.

He did kiss me then, but only on my forehead. It was exactly what I needed. I laid my head on his chest again and let him hold me.

"I know this is stupid," I said, "but I thought it would be easy. Jump into the story. Interrogate the March Hare until he spilled the beans about where Pops had been taken and where my book was and all that. Now that I think about it, that really would have been too easy. Too literal."

"Don't give up. We did learn we have the wrong March Hare. Therefore there is a right March Hare. We just need to find him. And, if it comforts you, in my cases, I never get it right the first time."

"No offense, but your cases are fictional. If you got it right the first time, the book would be very short."

"Longer story, more time with you," he said.

I lifted my head. "Thanks. I couldn't do this without you."

"You could, but I won't let you."

Koshka jumped off the book and trotted over to us. Very reluctantly, I pulled away from Duke's arms and stood up.

Koshka let out a soft *mrrwrp,* which I knew meant "*Breakfast*?"

"Right, boy. We're going, I promise. We need my umbrella."

"I'll get it," Duke said. "Stand by."

He slipped out the door, Koshka following.

My head was still spinning, but I had to check the book.

I picked Gatsby's copy of *Alice's Adventures in Wonderland* up from the table and flipped through the pages from beginning to end.

Good. Although our tea party was abandoned, in the book all the characters were present and accounted for. We'd done the book no harm with our excursion. Wonderland was as bizarre, troubling, trippy, and unnerving as always. Perfect.

Duke returned holding my umbrella open over his shoulder.

He gave it a little spin before returning it to me.

"Luckily no one vomited in it," Duke said. "I checked."

"Excellent. Koshka, let's go." He jumped onto the table and into my arms. Duke put his arms around me and held us both tight.

"Our revels now are ended!" I said, clicking my umbrella closed.

We tumbled through time and space—the time it takes to read a sentence and the space between one word and the next—and finally landed on the rug in the Pilcrow House library.

I groaned.

Duke groaned.

Koshka squeaked like a child had squeezed him too hard.

"Duke? You alive?" I asked.

"Barely, darling, but give us a moment. Right as rain soon. Or I'll pass away. Fifty-fifty chance."

I turned to my familiar. "Koshka?"

He let out another pathetic squeak.

"What about you, love?" Duke asked. "You're alive, I hope?"

"More or less," I said, leaving out the grim details. Everything hurt. Arms, legs, chest, heart, lungs, even teeth and eyelashes. "Book within a book? Let's never do that again."

Koshka yawned so wide his entire small body shook. Yawning suddenly felt like a great idea, so I let one out as well. "What time is it?"

Duke glanced up at the clock on the mantel. "Nearly eight in the morning."

"No wonder I'm exhausted. We've been awake all night."

"You should sleep," he said as he got off the floor and slipped out of his tuxedo jacket.

"Aren't you sleepy too?"

"Never, darling. A fictional detective is indefatigable until he solves the case," Duke boasted. "We have drive. We have determination. We have—"

"Cocaine," I said. "I mean, if you're Sherlock Holmes."

"And I am not," he said. "You go and sleep."

"I can't. We have too much work to do. Pops told us—"

"Your grandfather is safe and alive, but you are dead on your feet. I'll stay up and work on the case, figure out this pesky March Hare of yours. How does that sound?"

It sounded awful, honestly, not that I told him that. Duke would leave at midnight, case solved or not, which meant we only had sixteen hours left together. Yes, I had to get a little sleep or I'd be useless, but I didn't want us spending any time apart when this was literally our last day on earth together.

"Actually," I said, "I have a better idea."

TECHNICALLY, WE DIDN'T BREAK ANY OF THE GROUND RULES.

After getting Koshka his breakfast, I put on my pajamas—an oversize, gloriously hideously purple Friends of the Fort Meriwether Library T-shirt and sleep shorts—and Duke took off his shoes and tie. I lay down on my pillow while Duke sat propped up against my headboard to continue working on the case.

Koshka, an excellent chaperone, stretched out between us and fell fast asleep.

Sleep hit me like a sneaker wave, pulling me under the surface into strange but sweet dreams. I dreamed Duke and I were getting married in a library I'd never seen before with tall arched windows and a fireplace so big you could step into it. Pops was there, holding my hand. And for some reason, I had bunny ears on with my white dress, but hey, that's a dream for you.

In the dream, Pops squeezed my hand. *Almost time.*

I wish Mom were here, I said. *She could give me away.*

Don't worry. Your father will be here soon. He told me he was on his way.

In the dream, a door started to open, and I knew it was my father. He'd made it just in time.

And I felt that sort of relief mingled with full-body joy that you only experience in dreams when your brain plays such a good trick on you that you think it's real, that you and the person you love will be together, and you do have a father and he is coming to your wedding and everything is fine now and always will be forever and ever . . .

Then I woke up.

It felt like I'd slept for days, but when I opened my eyes and checked the bedside clock, only three hours had passed.

With a groan, I rolled over toward Duke.

"Morning, sunshine," he said with a smile. "How'd you sleep?"

"Like a baby. Or not. Babies don't usually sleep that well, do they?"

"I slept like a baby when I was a baby," Duke said. "But that might have been from the opium in our cough syrup."

I felt a warm, empty spot on the bed. "Where's Koshka?"

"Having a fit of feline insanity," Duke said. As if on cue, I heard tiny feet galloping up and down the stairs like someone had let a Shetland pony loose in the house.

"Zoomies. He might be a familiar, but he is still a cat."

Duke didn't answer, merely turned a page in whatever book he was reading.

I sat up and eyed it. "Where did you get that?" I asked.

He had a copy of *The Secret of the Old Clock* in his hand, the same 1930 version as my mother's book, except his was a brand-new copy.

"The bookshop," he said. "Don't worry. I paid for it. Left a dollar bill on the till."

"Books cost a little more now than they did during the Great Depression, Duke."

"I'll mail them a cheque for the difference."

I almost told him the bookstore also did not take checks, but I decided to let it go. I would buy the book. It was nice to have a copy back in the house, even if it wasn't my mother's copy.

"Haven't you read this before?" I asked him.

"I seem to recall starting it . . . but never finishing it. Can't remember what happened. Oh, yes, someone interrupted me. Who was it? And what was she doing?"

He stared out the window, rubbing his chin.

"Oh, you remember. We *both* remember."

"Ah, yes," he said, giving me a look to burn paper. "It's coming back to me now."

"Stop looking at me that way. Ground rules."

He buried his face in the pages of the book. His voice muffled, he replied, "Sorry, love. I'll behave and read my book."

I pulled the book away from his face.

"You're being ridiculous," I said.

"No, I swear, I'm invested. This Nancy Drew character is quite the young spitfire."

I sat up next to him, back to the headboard, leaning in to read over his shoulder. "What do you think of Nancy's skills? Detective on detective?"

He turned another page and ran his fingers over the nearly hundred-year-old words.

"For a girl of sixteen, she's doing quite well," Duke said. "She's incredibly determined. Simple stubborn refusal to quit is half the battle. Good instincts too. And she's on the case for the right reasons. She cares very deeply about helping the poor and disadvantaged. She even defends a falsely accused shopgirl about to lose her job. And she's quite a good driver. Ready and willing to eavesdrop, sneak into places, steal evidence . . . Feisty lass."

"Too feisty. Did you know that in the 1960s, they rewrote the original Nancy Drew books and re-released them? The original books had blue tweed covers and the new versions were yellow. They also were shorter and made Nancy older and better behaved. I like bad blue tweed Nancy better personally."

Duke pondered that a moment.

"How would that work?" he asked. "Two different versions of the same character? Do you think the two Nancys ever swap places?"

"I've never thought of that. You think there're two Nancy Drews? The original *and* the rebooted Nancy Drew?"

That was an intriguing thought, that if you rebooted a book series, you created a clone or a new version of the original character. Would they know each other? The 1930s blue tweed Nancy Drew, my mother's Nancy Drew, and the yellow 1960s Nancy Drew? I could only imagine the shenanigans not one but two Nancy Drews would get into . . .

"Wonder if my books will ever get a reboot," Duke said, then shook his head. "No, I'm already perfect."

"They tried to turn you into a TV series, but it only lasted one season."

"I still don't quite comprehend what television is, but I'm deeply offended." He turned another page in the Nancy Drew book. "It's interesting. She mentions her dead mother a few times, but never thinks much about her, never grieves."

"She is from the Midwest."

"I'm from England. Even Midwesterners look at the English and say, 'Let it out a little.'"

"Trust me," I said, "it's for Nancy's own good. If you let it out, what if you can't put it back?"

"The grief?" Duke asked.

I nodded. "Or maybe she's happy to be a daddy's girl."

"I do like this Mr. Drew," he said, tapping the first page. "Treats his daughter like an equal and gives her enormous freedom and latitude. Very unusual for his time." He paused, then corrected himself: "*My* time."

"You'd be a father like Carson Drew," I said. "You'd adore your daughters and let them get away with murder."

"As long as it's not literal murder. That I would frown upon." He closed the book and held it against his chest. "I admit I like the sound of that."

"Murder?"

"Having a daughter." He glanced at me, then away. "But I suppose that's not meant to be. Not in the cards for me. Not part of my story."

"Maybe not. But maybe?"

"You've read all my books. I never get married. I never have children."

"Your series only covers about a year of your life. Look at you, though. There's so much more to you than what's between the pages of your books."

"True. There's so much left unsaid. Nancy Drew, after all, never goes to the toilet," he said, holding up *The Secret of the Old Clock*. "And she's a tea drinker. She would go. Often."

I took the book from him and opened it to a random page. I touched the white space around the black letters.

"The margins," I said. "The places between scenes and chapters. Between the lines. What do you fictional characters get up to between the lines? Or after the final page? After THE END? Maybe getting married and having children?"

"The problem there, you see . . . the only girl I want to marry is you. And I don't want you in the margins. I want you on every page in black and white and bold print with your face on the cover."

My heart pounded so hard I was surprised Duke couldn't hear it. "Why do you love me so much? You're one of the most famous fictional detectives ever written, and I'm . . . not."

Duke looked at me for a very long time.

"You want to know why I love you?"

"I wouldn't mind."

"I had a case once at an orphanage. Someone had kidnapped one of the orphans, which was very strange. Who would kidnap a child when that very same child was already available for adoption?"

I recognized the case he was talking about from book five in the Duke of Chicago series, *The Devil's Children.*

He continued, "After we recovered the boy safely, the children at the orphanage didn't want me to leave. So I stayed all evening reading them stories until they fell asleep."

That was from the book. One paragraph, buried in a scene, easy to skim over but not for someone like me, who sought out and treasured every little personal detail Duke's author gave us readers. His favorite tea—orange pekoe. His favorite song—"Ain't Misbehavin'." His ability to flirt with literally anyone if it would get him the answers he needed.

And this passage I remembered for its sweetness and the longing it inspired in me to be in that moment with him.

And since the children wouldn't let him leave, Duke sat in a chair by the fire and read stories to them for hours. And even then, he found he could not make his feet find their way to the door until every last one of them had fallen asleep . . .

"One of the books I read to the children has stayed with me ever since," Duke said. "*The Velveteen Rabbit.* Do you know it?"

"I do, but it's been a long time since I read it."

"There's a little toy rabbit in the story, made of velveteen," Duke said, "who is teased by the other toys in the nursery—the mechanical toys—for being too old-fashioned. The oldest toy in the nursery, the wise and shabby Skin Horse, comforts the rabbit by telling him that if he's loved enough by the boy, he could become real. The rabbit asks the horse what this 'real' jazz means—my own words. And the horse replies . . ."

Duke took a breath and furrowed his brow. As a fictional detective, he had a phenomenal, almost supernatural memory.

"Real isn't how you are made . . . It's a thing that happens to you. When a child loves you for a long, long time, not just to play with, but REALLY loves you, then you become Real."

"Does it hurt?" asked the Rabbit.

"Sometimes," said the Skin Horse, for he was always truthful. "When you are Real, you don't mind being hurt."

Duke met my eyes.

"That's beautiful," I whispered, because whispering is always the right response when in the presence of beauty.

"So that's why," Duke said.

"Why what?" I'd been so entranced by the story I'd forgotten the question I'd asked him.

"That's why I love you, Rainy March. Because when I'm with you, I'm real."

When the man you love says something like that to you, there's only one correct response.

"Kiss me," I said.

"What about the ground rules?"

"We're in bed," I reminded him. "Not on the ground."

"I haven't finished my book yet," he said.

I should've known he'd play hard to get.

I took the book from his hand, closed it, and then lightly tossed it onto the floor.

"How dare you. That was your mother's favorite story," he said in a scolding tone even as he took me into his arms and pressed me onto my back.

"You're my favorite story."

CHAPTER NINETEEN

An hour later, I was lying on Duke's bare chest in my bed, exhausted but smiling.

"I don't think you're a detective at all," I said, yawning luxuriously under the covers. "I think you escaped a romance novel."

"*The Witch and the Duke*?" he asked.

"*The Wicked Witch*," I corrected, "*and the Dashing Duke*. Don't forget your adjectives."

"I won't argue with the dashing part, but you're hardly wicked, my love. Well, you were twenty minutes ago but not generally speaking."

He rolled over so that we lay face-to-face, eye to eye. Duke looked resplendent in his suits, perfectly coiffed, and impeccably put together. How lucky was I that I got to see him like this—naked, dark hair mussed, five o'clock shadow before lunch. As he said . . . *real*. A real man with a heart of flesh and blood beating steadily under my palm.

"If Dr. Fanshawe saw me now, I'd never step foot in another book again," I said.

"If Dr. Fanshawe saw you now, we'd have her arrested for breaking and entering and voyeurism. So there."

"We probably shouldn't have done this. It'll only make saying goodbye harder."

"Then let's not say goodbye," Duke said. "Let's stay together, rules be damned."

"Duke, I can't—"

"You *can*," he said. "You won't."

"If you leave your book series, your books will cease to exist. You get that, right?"

"I'll still be here in this world, won't I? I'll join your reality and live and grow old and die here."

"Exactly. You hear the problem with that? The grow old and die part? The no books anymore part?"

"I'll be with you. I'll have a life with you. Isn't that worth a few books?"

He was talking as if it were nothing to him, as if he were simply moving from Chicago to Oregon and not leaving the realm of imagination for the stone-cold world of rock-hard reality.

I opened my mouth to make another argument but knew I couldn't win, not this way.

"You want tea?" I asked, changing tactics.

"Always and forever."

"Stay here and put on your pants."

"I will do one of those two things."

I got out of bed, put on my bathrobe, and went out to the top of the stairs. "Mrs. Turner?" I called.

She appeared at once at the bottom of the stairs. "Yes, Miss March?"

"Duke wants tea. Do you mind serving it up here?"

"In your bedroom?"

"Yes, please."

"Unorthodox, but anything for His Grace."

I returned to the bedroom, where Duke was at the mirror, tying his tie. Fictional detectives did seem to have a miraculous ability to get dressed in mere seconds.

"Where would you like to get married?" Duke asked. "Here or in Chicago?"

"You've actually never been to Chicago," I reminded him. "*Real* Chicago."

I went into the bathroom and started running hot water in the tub.

"We'll do it here, then," he said when I came back into the bedroom. "June wedding in the Pilcrow House garden?"

Mrs. Turner knocked discreetly on the bedroom door.

"Come in," I said.

Mrs. Turner, with Koshka at her heels, entered holding the tea tray. She set it on my desk and poured.

"Thank you, Mrs. Turner," Duke said. "You are a saint. Rainy and I are discussing marriage. What do you think of a June wedding in the garden?"

"Only heathens get married outside of the Church. But whatever you prefer, Your Grace."

She gave Duke his cup first, of course, then served me mine. "Is that all, miss? I'll be going out if so."

"That's all," I said. She started to leave, but then I launched my offensive.

"Wait, Mrs. Turner, can I ask you something?" I said. "Who did you work for before me and Pops, back when you were in London? Can you remind me?"

She blinked, then cocked her head to the side as if trying to recall an ancient time shrouded in the mists.

"Two boys," she said. "Long, long time ago."

"Rainy," Duke said to me, his tone chiding.

I ignored him. "Go on, Mrs. Turner. Two boys in London?"

"Brothers? I think. One was very clever, and one was . . . very kind. Clever and kind. And brave. Yes, two boys. Always getting into scrapes." She sighed. "Then they grew up and didn't need me. John and . . . hmm . . . something that starts with an 'S.' Been too long. Yes, troublemakers but good lads."

"Would you like to go back?" I asked her. "To your old job, I mean?"

"Oh, dear me, no. I'm too old to work with rambunctious boys. I wouldn't say no to a change of scenery, however. I do miss the big city. I miss . . . I miss the way it used to be. Sometimes it feels like I don't quite belong here. Can't say why . . . I'm being silly, I suppose." She smiled to herself, possibly the first time I'd ever seen the woman smile. Then she composed her face and shook her head. "But not until you've grown, Miss March."

"I'm twenty-seven, you know."

"Age is only a number. Now I must be off. I'll save your lunch for later."

She left then, and a deep uncomfortable silence filled my bedroom.

I looked at Duke. He didn't look at me.

"Well?" I finally said.

"That was uncalled for, Rainy. I know perfectly well who and what Mrs. Turner is."

"Then you should know *that* is your future if you stay here."

"That is *not* my future. And you're being unfair."

"Sherlock Holmes. She couldn't even remember Sherlock's name. People all over the world know who Sherlock is, but in her addled mind, he's a kid she used to babysit a million years ago."

Duke turned away and stared out the window, down to the garden, where we would never have a June wedding.

I'd made a devastating counterattack. Mrs. Turner, as Duke knew, was a fictional character herself. Or had been. Once upon a time, Sherlock Holmes and John Watson had a housekeeper at 221B Baker Street named Mrs. Turner. But somehow—perhaps it was a Burner, perhaps she simply wandered off in a London fog and got lost—Mrs. Turner escaped her story, and by the time a Book Witch found her, it was too late. She'd been replaced in almost all the Sherlock stories with a character named Mrs. Hudson. Over the years, various Book Witches had taken her in, given her a place to live, a job to do. She was a housekeeping machine. Because all her character had ever done was make tea and tend house, all she could do now was make tea and tend house. She was living proof of what could happen to a fictional character who stayed out of their story too long.

"She wants to be back in a story," I said. "You can tell how much she misses her old life. But it's too late. There's no place for her in those books now."

"That would never happen to me," Duke said, sounding as if he were trying to convince himself.

"You don't know that. And I'm not the only reader in the world in love with you."

"But you're the only one I love back."

"I know," I said. "But I don't want you to stop being the Duke of

Chicago. The Duke of Fort Meriwether doesn't have the same ring to it," I teased, trying to make him smile.

"The only case I've never been able to solve," he said. "How you and I can be together."

"Maybe some mysteries," I said, "aren't meant to be solved. So let's focus on the one we *can* solve, all right?"

It wasn't all right. I could tell that from his face, but he also knew when to drop it, if only for the moment.

"If you insist," Duke said. "I do have some questions for you." He picked up his notebook and flipped through the pages.

"Fine," I said. "You can interrogate me in the bath."

"HAVE YOU EVER OWNED A HARE OR EVEN A TROUBLED-LOOKING rabbit?" Duke called out. He sat at my desk outside the bathroom door while I soaked the soreness out of my muscles.

"Not a one. We Marches have always been cat people."

"Hare statues? Hare artwork? Painting? Tapestry? Anything that could be in the house that is a hare belonging to the March family?"

"Nope."

"I recall," Duke went on, "that hares have some meaning in mythology. When I was a boy, our groundskeeper was a rather half-mad, half-pagan Irishman named Oisín. He always warned us boys that when we were out stalking to never lay a finger on a hare."

"Why not?"

"If you followed one through the mists, you might find yourself in the Otherworld," Duke continued. "One myth tells the story of a hunter who wounded a hare in the leg, then followed the hare through a magical door into another kingdom. There he found a beautiful young woman on a throne with a wound in her leg."

"You're saying we shouldn't follow hares?" I asked as I washed the back of my neck.

"Well, you simply don't know where they'll lead you."

"Interesting, but not helpful," I said.

"Did your mother ever have a case involving a hare? Stop that. I'm trying to take notes and this is not helping."

I couldn't see what was going on, but I could guess. "Is Koshka eating your pencil?"

"This is an outrage. Desist, feral beast."

"Use a pen. He never eats pens."

I heard Duke drop the pencil into my pen cup and pull out a pen. "Now back to my question."

"Not that I know of. Her case notebooks were taken by the coven when she died."

"Yes, you mentioned that. Is that normal practice?" he asked.

"I don't know. Maybe?"

"Who took them? Did your grandfather say?"

"Dr. Fanshawe. She had just been put in charge of the Ink and Paper Coven."

"She took your umbrella. She took your mother's notebooks."

"Almost twenty-seven years apart," I said. "This is so frustrating. I really do feel like the answer is staring us in the face, but I can't see it. Why couldn't the teapot have been a little more helpful?"

"I'd say it's because the story would end too quickly," Duke said, "but we're not in one of my stories."

"Feels like it," I grumbled.

Duke was quiet a moment, then I heard my desk chair squeak. He stood in the doorway with a hand over his eyes, a pointless courtesy considering what had been going on less than an hour ago.

"What's the bubble situation?" he asked.

I moved my arms through the warm bubbles covering me like the lightest of blankets. "I'm at full rolling boil."

"Then I'm coming in. Brace yourself."

Duke dropped his hand, then sighed. "My kingdom for a snorkel."

I popped one bubble with my fingertip.

Duke raised his eyebrow as he took a towel from the rack and dropped it on the floor. Then he went onto his knees by the side of the bathtub and faced me.

He furrowed his brow. "Are you reading a novel?"

"What? This?" I glanced at the paperback in my hand as if I hadn't realized I'd been holding it. "It's against the law to take a bath without a book."

He plucked the book out of my hand and examined it. The title was *Out with a Bang!*, and the cover featured an old-fashioned prop gun with a flag hanging from the barrel that read, BANG!

"You're cheating on me with another detective," Duke said. He sounded positively aghast.

"It's Medda Baker's new book. She's the writer who owns the bookstore. And don't be jealous. Her fictional detective isn't my type. John Odin is a seventy-five-year-old psychic."

"Too old for you?"

"I don't trust psychics. Now why are you in my bathroom?"

"You said yourself it feels like we're inside one of my stories. Yes?"

I sat up a little in the tub. "I did. If only because everything seems harder and more complicated than it needs to be. Why wouldn't Pops tell me what he meant? Why be so mysterious? Why all the false leads and red herrings and inscrutable clues?"

"Why so mysterious, indeed?" Duke repeated. "One has to wonder, doesn't one?"

"What is one wondering?" I asked him.

"Rainy . . . what if we *are* in a story?"

"I'm a Book Witch, Duke. I know the difference between the real world and story worlds."

"Yes, of course, but what if . . . what if someone, whoever is behind all this, wants us to *feel* like we're in a story? A mystery story? I don't know, a mystery reader or perhaps even an author?"

"An author. You think an *author* is behind all this? Have you met authors, Duke? They aren't criminal masterminds. Authors are anemic agoraphobes who sit in dark rooms and hallucinate. They're more like moths than people."

"But think about it, darling. Only a fictional story"—he brandished the paperback of *Out with a Bang!* at me like a prosecutor holding up Exhibit A—"would be this purposefully and annoyingly difficult to solve. And the one clue we have—'Find the March Hare'—that's straight out of a novel. No real criminal would be so elaborate and difficult. *And* literary."

He wasn't wrong. One of the great comforts of mystery fiction is the inherent cleverness of the villains. Intelligent criminals, driven by powerful motives to commit crimes they considered perfectly justified. We all want to believe crime happens for a reason, don't we? Better than the alternative—that crime is meaningless, arbitrary, and utterly random.

"I did sort of accidentally get magic book powder all over myself yesterday," I said. "I was performing a charm on a Little Free Library. It's supposed to bring the book you most need into your possession. And the next thing I know . . . someone gave me a copy of *your* book, which led to me unwittingly pulling you out of it. So clearly the universe thought I needed your help. A fictional detective for a fictional crime."

"Exactly. Precisely. Indubitably."

My heart raced with excitement. It felt like we were on to something here.

"I like this. This is good," I said, nodding. "But why would a writer want to put me through all this? And why drag Pops into it? Any theories?"

"I'm afraid I can't answer as to their motive," Duke said, "but the means seem quite clear. Whoever is doing this to you is putting you through the wringer of a mystery plot."

Medda Baker was staring back at me from the back of her book. While I didn't know her very well, Pops and Medda were old friends. She wouldn't be the one to put me through the wringer like this, but—

"Rainy?" Duke said.

"I was just thinking," I said. "Koshka loves Cary Grant films."

"Koshka does, does he?" Duke asked, raising his eyebrow.

"There's this famous story about the Cary Grant film *North by Northwest*—after your time," I said before he could ask. "The screenwriter, Ernest Lehman, and the director, Alfred Hitchcock, hit a snag in the screenplay. They had written most of it but couldn't figure out the ending. So Hitchcock being Hitchcock, said no worries. They would get Patricia Highsmith to come in, read their script, and tell them how it should end."

"Who?"

"Also after your time," I said. "Patricia Highsmith was a famous mystery writer, she wrote *Strangers on a Train* and *The Talented Mr. Ripley.*

Hitchcock's thinking was . . . who better to solve a fictional mystery than a mystery writer, right?"

"Did it work?"

"They ended up figuring it out for themselves, but . . . I mean, it's worth a shot."

"Then let's pay this Medda Baker person a call and hope she's home," Duke said.

"Hope she's home? Have you ever met a writer?"

After shooing Duke from the bathroom, I dried off and dressed as quickly as I could.

I knew Medda Baker's address, of course. Everyone did. You don't even need to know the house number or the street. You wanted the woman who wrote murder mystery novels . . . you found the house that looked most like the setting of a murder mystery novel.

She lived on the opposite side of the town, high on the hill and overlooking the bay in a cottage painted black with white trim and two stone gargoyles standing guard on either side of her arched front door, which was painted a garish blood red. I parked the Sun Buggy on the street, and Duke peered at the house through the car window.

"She lives in a black house?" He was mildly aghast. "Did it used to be a funeral home?"

"It's a storybook cottage."

"It's black," he said again.

"Well, she writes very dark storybooks. Ready?"

Duke, Koshka, and I strolled nervously up the cobblestone path to her front door.

"What about the boy?" Duke asked.

"You mean my cat? Again . . . have you ever met—"

"A writer? Right. Yes. Understood. What about me? Cover story?"

"I'll tell her you're my friend Nick."

"Of course," he said. "You ring though. I'm too nervous."

"You're scared of Medda Baker?"

"She kills people," he said.

"Only in books."

"Yes, in books, where I *live*," he reminded me.

"I'll protect you from the big bad writer," I said, patting him on the back.

I rang the doorbell twice and waited.

After a few tense seconds, we heard steps and the floor creaking and a lock unlocking.

The door slowly opened to reveal a woman, approximately five feet tall and eighty years old. She looked like the platonic ideal of a grandmother. Cut her and she would bleed doilies and Werther's Originals.

"Rainy March, is that you?" She perched her reading glasses on the tip of her nose.

"Hi, Ms. Baker. I was hoping you could help me with something story-related."

"Of course, of course, come right in." She shuffled back and held the door open for us. "Who's your handsome friend?"

"This is Koshka, my cat, and this is, um . . ."

"Nick," Duke said. "Nick Baron. Ma'am. Madam. Miss . . . tress. Mistress ma'am. Milady."

Medda looked at me.

"He's nervous that you'll murder him," I explained. "Since you kill people on paper."

She laughed and held her hand out to him.

"Little ole me?" she said with a sweet grandmotherly smile. "Don't you worry about that, young man. I'd never murder the Duke of Chicago."

We stared at her, shocked, jaws scraping the porch.

"Oh, don't look at me like that," Medda said to me. "Of course I know who he is. I'm a Ducky too."

CHAPTER TWENTY

Medda led us through her house and down a hall that led to her office.

Inside, the cottage looked like . . . well, imagine a cottage. There. That's it. Floral wallpaper in shades of pale green, pink, and yellow. Some cozy old furniture and rugs, a fireplace, and some family photos on the side tables. Neat and sweet.

The office was a different story, however. Pure literary chaos. Floor-to-ceiling bookcases. Towers of books on the floor. Boxes of books. Bags of books. Even a laundry basket of books. A desk was somewhere under the rubble. Koshka charged straight in and leapt onto the windowsill while Duke and I moved books off the chairs, a necessary maneuver before we could sit down.

Medda wandered about turning on the lamps.

"So . . . you like to read?" Duke asked, and I was impressed that he could keep a straight face.

She gazed around the office and nodded. "When buying books, I always tell myself, 'Medda, it could be worse. It could be amphetamines and male escorts.'"

"The male escorts," Duke said, "could help you organize the books. The amphetamines too, come to think of it."

"You're writing a new book?" I asked, nodding toward the piles upon piles of papers.

"Retired," she said. "*Out With a Bang!* was my last Odin novel. Hence the title," she said as she shifted book stacks around, perhaps hoping to actually find her desk under all the mess.

"I suppose you're a Book Witch, as well?" Duke asked. "As you know about me and weren't nearly as surprised and amazed to meet me as I would've liked."

"Not a Book Witch," she said. "But I don't know a writer alive who'd be surprised to learn fictional characters have a reality of their own. Plus, I've even consulted on a few of the Coven's cases. I assume you're here for the same reason?"

"Actually, no," I said. "There's a strong possibility Duke and I are in a story. A mystery story. Sort of. Kind of. We need an expert opinion."

"Really?" Medda said, eyes wide with astonishment. "How do you figure that?"

I opened my mouth to answer, but Duke raised his hand.

"Yes, Duke?" Medda said.

"Not to interrupt, but is tea an option?"

Medda looked at me. "He's never met a writer before, has he?"

Ten minutes later . . .

"Tea is served," Medda said, carrying a tray into the office with mugs for us all, including catnip tea for Koshka.

"You keep catnip tea on hand?" I asked as I put the mug on the floor for the boy.

"I had some left from my last cat, Velma. Thought I'd thrown it all out, but I found some in the back of the pantry."

My stomach clenched in sympathy. "I'm so sorry. Your cat died?"

"Six months back. She was twenty and had a good long life. I've missed having a cat in the house. Never gone this long without one." She gave Koshka a pat between his ears. He bopped his head into her hand, a sure sign he liked her.

Laughing softly, she took her seat behind the desk, sipped her tea, and said, "Story time."

Duke raised his hand again.

"What now?" she asked him, not unkindly.

He lifted his teacup. "It's not poisoned, is it?"

"Not yet," she said in a singsong warning.

Cowed, Duke drank his tea.

"Now," Medda said, "tell me everything."

Over the next half hour, I told the story from the very beginning. My mother's odd disappearing act and death when I was a baby. Her case files being taken. My grandfather leaving a week ago under very mysterious circumstances. The theft of my Nancy Drew book. The bizarre phone call from Pops. Stealing my umbrella. The Gatsby party. Our failures in Wonderland, the teapot, and the clue about the answer staring us in the face.

"And then," I concluded, "Duke realized this whole thing feels exactly like one of his mystery novels, so we thought maybe a mystery novelist could help us figure out what's going on?"

She mulled this over a moment before answering. "If you want my professional opinion, it does sound like someone is attempting to drag you through the Rube Goldberg machine that is a fictional mystery plot. And if you are in a whodunit, question number one is . . . Who's doing it? Any theories?"

I shrugged. "I don't recall ever crossing a novelist in my entire life. In fact, novelists should love me. I put their books back to rights. And, no offense, but your kind doesn't seem to get out very often."

"Very true," Medda said. "Another Book Witch perhaps?"

I shrugged. "Maybe."

"A Burner with a grudge?" she said.

"X does hate me, but he's not this clever."

"What about a fictional character who's in the mood to torture you for some reason?" Medda suggested.

I looked at Duke. "That's a possibility."

He gave me an innocent look. "I would never torture you," he said, "except in the most pleasant of ways."

"Behave," I said to him.

"Rainy," Duke said, "in all seriousness, you did break my heart when you put me back into my books and said goodbye. Is it possible you broke any other fictional hearts?"

"A good theory," Medda added. "Maybe there's a character who wants to give you a taste of your own medicine? See how you like being stuck in a story with no idea what comes next?"

A fair question. I considered it. "I have wrangled lots of fictional characters back into their books, but none who seemed genuinely upset about it. Other than Duke. Especially since we charm them into forgetting the real world. Sorry, I really have no idea whodunit or why they're doing it."

"Based on the 'plot' so far," Duke said, "could you give us any idea how we could move things along?" With his hands, he mimed wheels rapidly spinning.

Medda said, "You want me to help you skip to the end? Let you peek at the last page? Cheat, in other words?"

"What? No!" Then I thought about it for a minute. "Well, yes, actually."

I opened *The Secret of the Old Clock,* the new copy Duke had inadvertently shoplifted from Words, Words, Words.

"Look at this," I said, holding up the book to chapter twenty-five. "The final chapter is called 'A Reward' and it sums up the whole mystery. The cruel Tophams are disinherited. Nancy's lawyer dad helps the poverty-stricken friends and relatives get the money they were promised. And Nancy gets the old clock to keep as a reward. Everything is tied together with a neat little bow. Would it be possible to get one of those epilogues where the writer says, 'Six months later and everything was back to normal'? Too much to ask?"

"Afraid so," Medda said. "In a story, you must earn your own ending. But I might be able to point you in the right direction."

"I'll take any help you can give us," I said. "Whatever we do, we end up hitting a wall." While I didn't say it out loud, I couldn't help but think that my mother would have solved this mystery hours ago.

"I know it feels like that," she said. "But, really, you're gathering pieces of the puzzle. Once you have all the pieces, you'll see every wall you hit gave you a clue you needed. Let me show you something. Duke, could you hand me that file next to you?"

He retrieved a manila file off a bookshelf and gave it to her.

Medda opened it and took out a sheet of paper with a chart drawn on it—a single line trending upward until it reached a peak before dropping straight down.

"This is what a book plot looks like," she said. She picked up a red pencil and drew a circle at the beginning of the line. "This is where you started. In your ordinary life. Then something happens, shakes things up. A knock on the door. A phone call out of nowhere. A body hits the floor."

"My mother's book was stolen," I said. "Yesterday evening when I was on a case."

"Then what's that?" Medda asked, pointing to *The Secret of the Old Clock* clutched in my hands like a lucky charm.

Duke winced. "I may have inadvertently nicked that from your shop last night," he confessed. "Apparently books cost more than a dollar these days. Highway robbery if you ask me."

"I'll spot you this one time," Medda said with a wink. "The mysterious theft of a book full of secrets is a good way to start a story. That's what we call your 'inciting incident.' Now the ball of the plot is rolling. But it's rolling uphill," she said, pointing to the graph, which did in fact look like a hill with a very steep cliff at the end. "The climax is here, at the highest point, right before the end. In a mystery, the climax is the final confrontation between the antagonist and our detective. But it sounds like you're not there yet. Maybe here? The midpoint?"

She tapped the center of the line.

"What happens there?" I asked her.

"The midpoint is often where the characters take a little rest before their final sprint to the climax. A breather so to speak. And if there's a romantic couple in a story? The midpoint is usually when they hop into bed together."

"Accurate," Duke said.

"Duke!"

"Darling, we're trying to solve a case. No time to be coy."

"Fine," I admitted. "An hour ago."

"That means we're about at the midpoint then. No wonder you came to me. Midpoints often involve a new setting, a new character, or a plot event that turns the story in a new direction. Ideally, all three."

"You're a new 'character,'" I said. "And your house is a new setting. What's our new plot event?"

"I'm no expert," Medda said, "but I think I can guess. Can you hand me that book?"

I passed Medda the new copy of *The Secret of the Old Clock.*

She opened the front cover, turned one page, then the next, then smiled.

"Thought so," she said and held the book up to display the title page.

Under the title in peacock blue ink was one word. One name.

Ellery

"WHAT ON EARTH?" I SAID, PRACTICALLY LEAPING ONTO MEDDA'S desk to retrieve the book. "This is my mother's! But it can't be. It's a new copy." It was brand-new, in fact. Fresh new cover, crisp white pages, even had that new book smell.

"Can't you Book Witches bedazzle an old book into a new book?" Medda asked, miming waving a magic wand over the cover.

"We don't call it 'bedazzling,' but yes, we can. But how . . ."

Duke took the book from me.

"Rainy, darling, I swear I got this off the shelf in the children's section. The spine wasn't even cracked."

" 'The Purloined Letter,' " Medda said.

"The Edgar Allan Poe short story?" I asked, hands still shaking with shock, joy, and more than a little confusion. "What about it?"

"In the story," Medda began, "the detective Dupin is hired to find a letter that has been stolen from the queen. The man who stole it is blackmailing her with it. The police have searched the suspect's home high and low, but the brilliant Dupin finds it sitting out in the open with the suspect's other mail."

"Hiding in plain sight," Duke said.

"Exactly," Medda said. "Someone wanted to hide this book but in such a way that you could find it and no one else," Medda said.

"Fiendishly clever." Duke nodded. "Who else would immediately buy this book except someone who'd just lost their copy?" He pointed at Medda. "You are *very* good."

She crossed her arms and smiled. "Three Edgar Awards can't be wrong."

"Thank you," I said, tenderly holding the book to my chest. "If only finding Pops were that easy, but I'll take what I can get. What do you think this means? A Book Witch is behind all this? They stole my book? Then why get it back to me?"

"We know you have a secret enemy," Medda said. "Maybe you also have a secret ally? But don't ask me who."

"I'll ask you this, Lady Edgar," Duke said, leaning in to meet Medda's eyes. "Who is the March Hare?"

"Ah, well, you see, this is where you figure that out," she said, tapping her pencil tip on the graph, distressingly far away from the midpoint. "You have to get closer to the climax for that."

"What about Dr. Fanshawe? Could she be the March Hare? She did confiscate my umbrella."

"I'd guess she is involved somehow, but I can't see her as being the key to all of this. Can you?"

"Not really," I said. "She's not a March and she has nothing hare-like about her."

"Better keep looking," Medda said, crumpling her plot graph into a ball and tossing it over her shoulder. "The midpoint is a bit too early to figure it all out anyway. But you're well on your way."

"I hope you're right. Supposedly when we find the March Hare, we'll know what my mother was trying to tell me. And hopefully we'll find Pops too."

"And we'll know how to be together," Duke said, looking at me.

"That would be a happy ending, wouldn't it?" Medda said.

We'd gotten all we could get from her—tea and information and my book back.

She led us to her front door.

"Thank you again," I said, still holding my book. "For this anyway. Can I pay you back? Maybe hop into your new book with you so you can tell John Odin goodbye?"

She furrowed her brow. "An author meeting her own main character . . . now that's an idea. Let me think about it."

"You know where to find me," I said and gave her a hug. She patted my back, then let me go.

"Wish I could solve this case for you, Rainy, but that's not how it works. Every story, in one way or another, is a journey of self-discovery."

"I'm not giving up yet," I said. "No rest until Pops is home."

"Good girl," she said. "And tell him to come visit me the minute he's back."

She opened the door, and we stepped out into the silver light of early afternoon. Duke, Koshka, and I stood on the porch while she leaned against the doorframe.

"It was nice to meet you," Duke said. "Thank you for not murdering me."

"You know, I met your writer once," she said.

"You did?" Duke asked, visibly shocked.

"Tom Hightower. Met him at a book signing in New York when I was a teenager. He lost his brother in the Great War, liberating Belgium. He said he came up with the idea for your books by imagining a young man who said 'No, thank you' to all that, and found a way to make the world a safer, better place without picking up a gun. Which you did."

"Not this world," he demurred. "Only a fictional version of it."

"Oh, yes, this world," she said. "Did you know that when Hightower died, he left an unfinished manuscript for the thirteenth Duke of Chicago mystery?"

"Does anyone know what happened to it?" Duke asked.

"I know exactly what happened to it," Medda said. "About twenty years ago, his estate asked me to finish writing it."

"What?" I said. "Are you kidding?"

She shook her head. "I gave it a try, but there was nothing to go on except the first chapter and half a page of notes. I couldn't do it. Like a kid trying to color inside the lines of a Picasso. One of my few regrets in life is not finishing the book. The estate dropped the idea after I gave up."

"Maybe you'll try it again?" I asked.

"Yes, and put a love interest named Rainy March in it for me," Duke said. "I'll be forever in your debt."

"I'll keep that in mind, handsome."

Duke caught her hand in his, raised it to his lips, and kissed the back of it.

"Charming devil. Your writer knew what he was doing."

A question occurred to me then that I was a little afraid to ask, but with time running out, I asked it anyway. "In a mystery, what comes after the midpoint?"

"Things will seemingly get better. Something will jump out at you, give you a brand-new idea. But then things will get much, much worse. In a murder mystery, another body would hit the floor."

"Someone will die?" I asked, horrified.

"In my stories, yes. In your story? I imagine it's only a metaphorical body. A failure or a false lead. Still, watch your back."

Always good advice.

"But don't you worry. Eventually you'll figure it all out," she told us. Then she gasped.

"What?" I asked, hoping she'd thought of something wildly helpful.

"Wait here." She went back into her house and returned a minute later, holding a book and a pen. "Would it be gauche of me to ask for a signature?"

Medda held the book out to Duke—it was *Kiss Me Once, Kill Me Twice,* the Duke of Chicago book ten. On the vintage painted cover, a man kisses a woman who holds a gleaming silver knife behind her back.

"I'm having an existential crisis again," Duke said. "I've never been asked to autograph one of my cases before. People died."

"I suppose it is a bit offensive to ask—" Medda began.

"Not at all." Duke eagerly reached for the book and pen. "They were bad people."

Medda half laughed, half coughed at that. She took the book back from Duke and held it tight to her chest. "You two run along. I have to clean my office, and you have a March Hare to find."

"If you think of anything else, let us know," I said.

She tapped her chin in deep thought, then she pointed at me. "I can tell you this much. Writers, critics, and scholars squabble all the time about how many types of stories there are in the world. One says there are two—comedy and tragedy. Another says there are seven—quest, voyage and return, et cetera, et cetera. But I firmly believe there is only one type of story in all the world through all the ages. Every story is a mystery story if you don't know where it's going. Or, in other words . . ." she said, lowering her voice dramatically, "things are never what they seem."

CHAPTER TWENTY-ONE

We returned to my car. Duke stood by my side, staring at Medda's house while I buckled Koshka into his carrier.

"I really hope Medda was kidding when she said someone was going to die before this story is over. Pops is eighty-two, you know," I said, unable to imagine life without my grandfather. No mother, no father, no grandmother, and Duke would have to leave by midnight. I didn't want to be the only character in this story. I petted Koshka. At least I had him.

"It's not your grandfather," Duke said as I stood up and turned to face him.

"How do you know?"

He lowered his voice, then nodded toward the cottage. "Medda was talking about herself."

"What? How do you know that?"

"I may not know writers, but I know cat people," he said. "She lost her cat months ago and hasn't adopted another one? She knows she doesn't have long and doesn't want to leave a cat without a home."

"Maybe she's not ready."

"She said she'd never gone so long without a cat. Her fingers were swollen, and I could smell her tea. Ours was Irish breakfast. Hers was lemon and honey. Classic treatment for a cough. Those book piles had little sticky papers on them—"

"Post-it notes?"

"She's sorting her books to give them away. And boxes of manuscripts for a university. She's preparing her papers to donate. And one of the books on her desk was a Last Will and Testament preparation kit. It also had those sticky notes in it."

"And she told me to tell Pops to come see her in a hurry. Oh, I wish you hadn't told me that."

"I'm sorry, love. I can't help but notice these things."

"You're a detective. You detect." I let out a long breath. "Like she said, things aren't what they seem."

"Things seem hopeless," Duke said, looking at me. "So let's hope she's right."

"Let's go home. I want to put the book somewhere safe," I said, patting my bag just to reassure myself it was still there. "Other than the safe, I mean. Maybe I should keep it with me? What do you think?"

Duke started around the back of the car to the passenger side but stopped, staring at the trunk. He didn't answer.

"Duke?"

"Medda said something would jump out at us, give us a brand-new idea," Duke said, studying my license plate for some reason. "Rainy, what does that mean?"

My car was fifty years old, and with my vintage car came a vintage license plate. Back in the day, all Oregon cars were given dark blue license plates with yellow printing and the state motto.

And what is the state motto of Oregon?

Pacific Wonderland.

There it was, right in front of me.

"That's it!" I said. "We're in Wonderland already. That's what people call the Pacific Northwest."

"This entire state is Wonderland?" Duke asked, looking around.

"We were told the answer was staring us in the face, right? Well, here it is, staring us in the face, the state of Oregon."

"It is, my love, but it's quite a large area. A hare could be anywhere—"

"Get in the car," I said. "Hurry!"

"Where are we going?"

"Pilcrow House. I need to check something."

We raced—okay, no we didn't race, but we definitely *chugged* up the hill to my house.

Inside the library, I grabbed a photograph of me with my grandfather off his desk.

"Here," I said, shoving it into Duke's hands. "My grandma took this picture of me and Pops there when I was a kid."

It was the picture of Pops and me standing in the wide-open mouth of a storybook wicked witch, pretending to scream in terror. Two real witches pretending to be afraid of a fictional witch.

"Aww," Duke said, smiling. "Weren't you a rather odd-looking small child . . ."

I grabbed the photo back from him. "Not my fault my head grew before the rest of my body. This," I said, tapping the glass over the picture, "is a park somewhere east of here."

"I assume," Duke said, "were it west of here, it would be in the ocean."

"I don't remember the name, but I remember this park had tons of exhibits of different fairy tales and storybooks. I think I remember seeing the Mad Tea Party scene from *Alice in Wonderland*."

I put the photograph down and dug out my phone. Smartphones weren't to be trusted with Book Witch business, as Dr. Fanshawe always stressed. Our enemies were numerous, and they were technologically savvy. Our main tools were analog—print books, landlines, magic, and the ability to concentrate on one thing for more than five minutes at a time. But all Book Witches had smartphones. Even magical beings need to google sometimes.

"Yes, yes, yes," I said, my heart racing with excitement. "This is it. The Enchanted Forest Park. Right off I-5. Has an attraction called Storybook Lane with these life-size exhibits of famous children's storybook characters. Little Red Riding Hood, the Three Little Pigs, Miss Muffet . . ."

I showed him the pictures on the park's website. It seemed like every fairy tale, every famous kids' story got an exhibit on Storybook Lane.

"The Mad Tea Party," I said, spotting a photo of a brightly painted tableau. "That's the March Hare."

"Do you think this is it?" Duke asked.

"You meet informants all over Chicago. Fancy restaurants, dark alleys, speakeasies. Why not meet our informant at a park?"

"It's definitely a lead worth following. Shall we go?"

"Yes! No," I said, reading the park's hours online. "The schedule online says it's already closed for the season. Oh, and no animals except service animals allowed."

"Rainy, I'm the Duke of Chicago, remember? I've hopped trains, streetcars, hot-air balloons, and airships. I've broken into bank vaults, hotel suites, the mayor's office, and even the governor's mansion in pursuit of justice. I can get us into one little park, and I could do it with my eyes closed."

"You're very handsome when you're being you. Let's hit it."

LUCKILY, BREAKING INTO THE ENCHANTED FOREST ENDED UP NOT being that difficult. Built on the side of a hill and nestled among trees, it wasn't much more than a rather grandiose roadside attraction.

As we drove inland, the hard rain turned to a light drizzle, and by the time we parked on a private side road, even the drizzle had turned to a faint mist. Duke and I, both in hiking pants, boots, and raincoats, trudged through the brush and trees until we reached the wooden fence at the edge of the park.

"All right," Duke finally said. "I don't see any security guards anywhere. I think the coast is clear. Up and over."

He gave me a boost over the wooden fence, then he followed right behind me.

We walked a bit, getting our bearings. Everywhere we looked, we saw closed attractions—a haunted house, miniature storybook cottages, even a roller coaster. "Shall we split up?" he asked.

The park, as I'd read online, was about twenty acres. Not big but with all the trees and winding paths, I knew I'd get lost immediately. "Let's stick together for now."

"Very well," he said, "but if we get separated for any reason, let's meet at the carousel." He pointed to the merry-go-round a few yards away.

"It's called a merry-go-round."

"Then we'll meet at the bloody merry-go-round."

I grinned. Annoying Duke was one of my favorite pastimes that didn't involve reading.

"Hope we're alone," I said as he scanned our surroundings again.

"Fingers and toes crossed there's no security on duty. But if so, let me do the talking."

"Let you do the talking? Are we sure about that?" I asked.

He thought it over for a second, then his eyes lit up. "Give us your ring."

"My ring? The ring you gave me?"

"That one."

"But I never take it off."

"It's for the greater good, love."

It felt like going naked to take the forget-me-not ring off my finger, but I gave it to him anyway.

"What are you going to do with my ring?"

"That's for me to know and you to find out. Now let's go."

We crept around corners, snuck past Wild West shacks, pausing only at a park map.

"Storybook Lane is down here," he said, pointing to a bend in the path.

The park was either the work of a truly dedicated artist or a madman or . . . both. Probably both. But the best kind of madman, who loved stories enough to create a monument to them. Everywhere we looked, we found life-size sculptures made of concrete painted in bright colors.

The Three Little Pigs fended off the Big Bad Wolf.

Miss Muffet sat on her tuffet (whatever a tuffet is) as a spider with a weirdly human face crept down behind her.

Snow White had her seven captors—I mean, "dwarfs."

"This place is . . ." I said, my voice trailing off.

Duke nodded. "It certainly is."

"Enough said?"

"Enough said."

On a warm summer's day, the park would've been charming, but breaking into it on a cloudy day in October when we were the only souls walking the winding paths . . . it was positively unnerving. Almost as bad as Wonderland.

In my peripheral vision, I saw movement, then heard a rustle of leaves.

Duke and I ducked into a dark artificial cave, which turned out to be the mine where the seven dwarfs dug up colorful jewels.

"Security guard?" I said to Duke as he peeked out.

"Better. And worse." He pointed down the walkway.

An elk. A massive male elk with antlers tall enough to scrape the bottom branches of the trees. He walked the path as if he owned it and perhaps he did. This forest had been home to his kind far longer than it was home to ours.

We watched in awe as he ambled past us to the wooden fence, effortlessly leapt over it, and disappeared into his true forest.

A magnificent beast, three times the size of even the biggest deer I'd ever seen.

"Wow," I breathed. "Glad we left Koshka at home. He'd try to ride him."

"You don't see that in Chicago every day," Duke said. "Come along."

As fast as we could, we made our way down Storybook Lane.

"There," Duke said, pointing to the Wonderland exhibit.

We ran to the Mad Tea Party, made of concrete and painted garish colors, which were chipped and fading.

"Yeah, that's the March Hare," I said, leaning against the exhibit fence. "Now what?"

"We didn't think that far ahead," Duke answered.

For a moment, we both stared at the scene—the table, the teacups, the Mad Hatter, the March Hare, and the Dormouse. What were we waiting for? Like Duke said, we hadn't really thought this far ahead, obsessed as we were with finding the right March Hare. But now that we'd found what was certainly the only March Hare in all of Oregon . . . what did we do?

"I'm going to do something stupid," I said.

"Full steam ahead."

"Hello!" I shouted. Shouted? Bellowed? One of those I did. "This is Rainy March, and I'm looking for the March Hare! You there, Hare?"

Duke winced and covered his ears. I was probably bellowing more than shouting now that I think back.

He lowered his hands from his ears. "Anything?"

"No answer."

"My turn to do something stupid now," he said.

"Go for it."

He went over the barrier fence with a quick, athletic leap.

Inside, Duke walked around the statues, peering over and under the table, examining every inch of the exhibit.

"Nothing," he said. "No notes. No sign anyone's been here recently. Dead end."

He stopped and stared into the face of the March Hare statue. It looked like every other statue. Cute. Whimsical. Brightly painted concrete. Empty eyes that held no secrets.

"Wrong March Hare again?" I asked.

"Perhaps so, love. Still . . ." He stood up and looked around. "Any chance there's another hare around here? Or even a rabbit?"

"Maybe? I have to confess I don't exactly know the difference between a rabbit and a hare. Color? Size?"

"They're different species entirely," Duke said. "Easiest way to tell them apart is that rabbits are charming and hares are slightly terrifying. They're also larger, have longer ears, longer bodies, and stronger back legs."

If it sounds like Duke was reading from a book, he probably was in his mind. This was another of his fictional detective superpowers—the ability to remember obscure facts and recall them on command.

"Do they come in white?" I asked.

"Arctic hares do. Hares with albinism . . ."

"Follow me."

We jogged back up Storybook Lane and took the path to the merry-go-round.

"Is this a hare?" I asked, standing next to the large white creature with the long, long ears and—

"Very troubled eyes," Duke said. "Thousand-yard stare. Perhaps he served in the Great War."

"It looks mad as a March Hare, but the question is . . . is it *the* March Hare?"

I patted it on the nose.

It said nothing. It did nothing. It offered us no answers.

"Guess not," I said.

Duke leaned back against a small pony and crossed his arms. "I'm afraid I'm out of ideas. Shall we go?"

I hated to leave without trying everything.

"Maybe if I rode it? If I'm on the hare, then it's Rainy March's hare . . . And you could follow it? I'm grasping at straws."

"Why not try?" he asked.

Duke went to the controls while I slung my leg over the hare's saddle.

I screamed.

"Rainy! You all right?"

"Sorry, sorry. It's just . . . it's wet. I have a wet butt. A cold wet butt, and I don't like it."

Duke put his hand on his heart. "I thought you'd been electrocuted."

And that's when we heard the man's voice shouting.

"Don't move!"

CHAPTER TWENTY-TWO

Anton Chekhov, the legendary Russian short story writer and playwright, had a famous dictum about plotting. *One must never place a loaded rifle on the stage if it isn't going to go off. It's wrong to make promises you don't mean to keep.*

This is known as Chekhov's Gun or, in our case, Chekhov's Security Guard. Duke had brought up the possibility of security guards, and lo and behold, here one was, like we'd summoned him.

"Not moving," Duke said to the guard.

"I'm definitely not moving," I added. "The ride's not on."

The security guard, a lean, tall man with intelligent but wary eyes, strode up to us.

He stood about ten feet away from Duke, still standing at the ride's controls, and I stayed on my hare, hands tight on the pole. And yes, I did feel unbelievably stupid about the whole thing.

"You two have permission to be here?" the guard demanded.

"Define 'permission,'" I said.

The guard looked at me. "Someone said you could be here?"

"Well, no. We don't have permission, then," I replied.

Duke lifted his hand slightly in my direction, the universal signal of a man telling a woman to let him handle this. Well, good luck, Chicago. If there was a way to get out of this guy calling the cops on us, I didn't see it.

Then again, I wasn't Duke.

"Look, old chap, I'm terribly sorry. This is all my doing," Duke began. He put his hands back into his jacket pockets and shrugged. "Her father brought her mother here on their first date years ago. And I brought her here on our first date. My work is about to transfer me to the East Coast, so I wanted to see the old place one last time. Romance and all that. She didn't even know what I'd planned."

The security guard was unarmed, it appeared. No gun in sight. He might have had pepper spray on him, but it was his walkie-talkie that worried me. All he had to do was radio the authorities, and we would be dragged out in handcuffs. And when they tried to book Duke and found out he had no identification on him? Disaster.

"That's all? Why don't I believe you?" the guard asked us.

His hand began to lift toward his walkie-talkie.

"Well, to be perfectly honest with you . . . it's not all," Duke said. He glanced over his shoulder at me and grinned. "I didn't want to do it like this, but it seems fate had other plans."

Duke pulled his hand from his pocket and showed my ring to the security guard.

"Do you mind?" he asked the guard. "Before you lock us up and throw away the key?"

The guard was a half-step ahead of me; I was still trying to figure out why Duke had told the guy my parents had come here on their first date.

Then the guard broke into a smile, and when I saw that ear-to-ear, *can't-wait-to-tell-the-guys-about-this grin,* I knew what was happening.

"Go for it," the guard said. "I'll take pics."

Duke walked over to me and got down on one knee.

"Rainy, my darling . . . If you were a book, I would read every page of you in one sitting and then when it was over, I'd start back at page one and read you again. If our life together was a story, I'd want it to be a million pages long, a billion pages. I hope there are scenes in the book of our love that burn holes in the paper. I hope the happy chapters are the longest and the saddest chapters are barely a page. And I hope and pray that however our story ends, it ends with us together and the last word of the story of our life is 'forever.' Will you, Rainy March, please do me the honor of letting me become your husband?"

I didn't know what to say, so I said nothing. "Well?" the guard said. "Don't leave the poor guy hanging. Yes or no?"

"Sorry, I'm in shock," I said. "I never imagined I'd get proposed to while I was sitting on a giant hare. But yes. Yes, I will marry you. And, um . . . thanks for asking."

Duke took my left hand and put the ring on my ring finger, where it belonged and always would belong.

Before I could say anything, he stood up, leaned in close, and tenderly kissed me.

"This is great," the guard said, laughing and waving his phone at us. "I took a bunch of pictures. I'll text them to you. A couple breaking in to get engaged on the carousel was not on my bingo card." He laughed again.

Duke chortled in triumph. "Told you it was a carousel."

And that's how we managed to escape arrest. Because it turns out the security guard was a hopeless romantic. Lucky us.

After we'd posed for the last picture—Duke standing on the carousel next to me while I held up my left hand in the classic Envy me, for now I am an *engaged* woman pose—the guard said he would need to escort us out before we got him fired.

And so Adam—that was the guard's name—led us to the main gate, chatting the whole time about how excited he was to witness the proposal, that the other guards would be jealous.

"Usually when something weird shows up on the security cams," Adam said, "it's two elk making baby elk by the ice cream shop."

"Who doesn't like ice cream?" I said.

We reached the entrance.

"Thank you for being so understanding, Adam," Duke said at the gate.

"You betcha," he said. "I hope you two are very happy together for a long time. Come back and show me wedding pictures. But let's wait until the park's open next time, all right?"

"We absolutely will," I said. "Promise."

Duke held out his hand to Adam.

When the guard took Duke's hand to shake it, a strange look came over his face.

"You . . ." he whispered to Duke. "Do I know you?"

ADAM'S EYES WIDENED, AND HE FROZE AS IF UNDER A SPELL. THIS happens sometimes when a reader of a story meets a character face-to-face. Like all Book Witches, I possessed a special power, and I used it right then. Narrowing my eyes, I reached out to see Adam and Duke's past together . . .

I saw a sleek leather sofa in a starkly minimalist apartment in Portland. I saw a man in sweatpants, the beginnings of a beard on his face and the start of a drinking problem showing around his red-rimmed eyes. A case of toilet paper sat by the front door, and bottles of hand sanitizer lined the coffee table like dominoes.

And I saw it was Adam on that sofa, staring at his phone, scrolling, scrolling, scrolling his life away. Unshowered. Unshaven. Unhappy. Alone.

And then, as if it were my own phone in front of my eyes, I saw what he was seeing.

A friend he follows has posted a book review. A Duke of Chicago book. The post's caption reads, *Latest five-star read. I loved these books when I was a kid. Glad to see they hold up. And man, it was nice to escape 2021 for a day.*

This post reminds Adam of something, that he, too, loved the Duke of Chicago books when he was a kid.

And, God, does he want to escape 2021 . . .

So he closes whatever social media app it was that was sucking his soul from his body through his eyes and opens his library app.

Quick thumbs pull up what he wants, and in an instant, Adam has downloaded the very first Duke of Chicago book.

He begins to read . . .

In the first chapter of the first book, the Duke stands by the graves of his three brothers in the rain. He's just inherited a title he never coveted and an estate so large it feels like a millstone around his neck.

The sight of his brothers in the ground reminds him of Ebenezer Scrooge being shown his own lonely grave by the Ghost of Christmas Yet to Come. In a moment of clarity, he realizes he is next. Even if he doesn't die physically, even if the wars and diseases and disasters spare him, he will die another way. His dreams will die, and like a failing heart or brain, they will take the rest of him with them.

His mother, the dowager duchess, stands next to him and coldly says, "It's all yours now, my son."

And in a moment of quiet rebellion the Duke speaks a line that became a kind of protest anthem for fans of the books, akin to Bartleby the Scrivener's famous *I would prefer not to.*

Duke simply says to her . . .

"No, thank you."

Then he turns on his heel and walks away. By the next chapter, he's in Chicago, starting his new life as a private detective whose only qualifications are that he's rich, charming, and handsome, which, unsurprisingly, turns out to be his superpower.

Duke's effect on Adam's life flashed before my eyes. Adam Nguyen read that book on the sofa of his sleek apartment during a long Covid lockdown when the only things keeping him from losing his mind were the books and movies that distracted him from the relentless bad news in the real world. Something about that moment, that line, rang a bell deep inside his heart.

His boss had offered him a promotion—twice the money but triple the work, and Adam had never liked the job anyway. He wasn't even sure what they did sometimes or why they did it. Most days felt like a game of Monopoly, moving play money around a game board, killing time, helping no one.

His parents would be thrilled when he told them about the job offer and the raise. So many people struggling? Yet here he was being offered a promotion?

But what he wanted, what he dreamed when he let himself dare to dream . . . was to go back to school to become a teacher. A sixth-grade teacher, because that's when the kids got to read really good books like *A Wrinkle in Time, The Giver,* and his personal favorite, Louis Sachar's *Holes.*

And it's when they start learning interesting history like the sinking of the *Titanic* and World War II.

His own sixth-grade literature teacher, Mr. Jordan, had been his favorite. When he'd asked Adam what he wanted to be when he grew up, Adam had said a teacher, not an "Assistant VP of Data and Analytics."

But he can't be a teacher. It would pay almost nothing compared to what he was making. It would take him years to get his teaching certification. He'd be thirty-five by the time he could have his own classroom, even if he started the next day. And he'd have to work part-time to pay the bills while going to school. Nights and weekends. Huge sacrifice, and all for what? Useless joy? Wasteful happiness? Selfish personal fulfillment?

Personal fulfillment, after all, wouldn't pay the bills.

So of course, he would take the promotion and the money.

But he could finish the book. And he did. Then he read the next Duke of Chicago book, then the next.

Shot, stabbed, chased, falsely accused of terrible crimes . . . No matter what happened to Duke, he stayed endlessly polite, endlessly charming, endlessly hopeful. He never gave up, never gave in. His mother was furious at him. His peers, the aristocracy, thought he'd gone mad. He'd given up the promotion, the money, the respect of his family and countrymen . . .

And all for what? Happiness. Purpose. All because he'd had the courage to say those three words. Those three magical words . . .

Maybe if it worked for Duke, it would work for him?

After finishing the third Duke of Chicago book, Adam wrote his boss back an email of three little words: "No thank you."

The next day he showered, shaved, and enrolled in Western Oregon University's online teaching program.

To pay for it, he worked two jobs, including the weekend security guard job at the Enchanted Forest Park.

He quit drinking, quit doom-scrolling. Now that he was taking care of his dreams, he'd somehow, almost by accident, started taking care of himself.

"Magic" isn't a strong enough word for that. This goes way beyond your average storycraft. No, this is alchemy, turning base things into gold.

It had happened to me too. It happens to most of us if we're lucky enough. The fictional characters we love stamp their names on our hearts. They show us how to fight our battles, how to change, how to make it to page three hundred a different person than we were on page one.

But because they're fictional, there's no way to ever thank them for the good turn they did for us, for showing us when we needed it most what a hero looks like.

Except in these rare moments when a reader meets his hero on a misty autumn day in a strange Enchanted Forest.

I reached out, took Duke's other hand in mine, and let the vision of Adam's past flow from me into him. Duke saw what I had seen, the change he'd wrought in this young man's life. Real change from a fictional detective.

"Have we . . ." Adam asked, brow furrowing. "Have we met before?"

"Unfortunately not," Duke said. "I'd remember meeting a good man like you."

"Oh, sure. I could've sworn . . ."

Duke patted him on the shoulder, and Adam finally released his hand.

We started to leave through the front gates, and Duke turned back one more time.

"Thank you again," he said to Adam, who still wore a look of awe and wonder in his eyes.

Then Adam said to Duke's face what every reader who ever loved a storybook hero wanted to say to their hero's face.

"No," Adam said, still dazed and dazzled by his brush with magic, "thank *you*."

Duke and I walked away.

"*Now* you understand how important your books are to the world?" I asked him.

Too moved to speak, he merely nodded.

"And that," I said, glancing back at Adam, "is why I'm a Book Witch."

CHAPTER TWENTY-THREE

Sadly, the high of that touching moment had worn off by the time we got back to my car.

"I know you're disappointed, love," Duke said, "but Medda did warn us we'd probably suffer another defeat before we figured it all out."

"But we wasted so much time," I said and slammed the door of the Sun Buggy closed behind me. "We drove all this way and found the only March Hare in this, the Pacific Wonderland, and it was all for nothing. I'm almost glad my mother isn't here to see how badly I'm screwing this up."

"Don't say that, darling. I know you're frustrated, but it's not all for nothing. Like Medda said, we're gathering puzzle pieces. And we did get engaged," Duke reminded me as he put on his seatbelt. "Surely that counts for something."

Because I can multitask, I was able to glare at Duke while putting on my own seatbelt.

"What was that sourpuss look for?" he asked.

"We are *not* engaged," I told him.

"I'll ask Adam to be my best man," he said. "Surely that lass Penny would be your maid of honor."

"Need I remind you—and clearly I do need to remind you—that you are a fictional character who lives on a completely separate plane of existence than I do?"

"You could live with me, couldn't you?" he asked. "In my world? Even if only part-time?"

I can't begin to describe how tempting it was to say yes, yes, a thousand times yes.

"It's against the rules." I started to put my key into the ignition.

"Sod the rules, love. I need a duchess."

Before the key went in, I stopped, looked at Duke. "The Black and Whites exist to protect the— Wait, did you say 'duchess'?"

He grinned at me. "I did. I did say 'duchess.' I'll even say it again. Duchess. You can have your own coronet. We'll wear them around the house and nothing else."

"Duke."

"Listen," he said, and the teasing in his tone had vanished. "Rainy. They're *my* books. Do you understand that? My author is gone, dead. That's sad. It is. I would've liked to have met the man—"

"That might have killed him on the spot."

"True, but still . . . the point is . . . for better or worse I know what I am now. I'm not a puppet anymore. There's no one left to pull my strings but me. I want you in my world, Rainy. If we can't be together out here . . . why can't we be together on paper?"

"This is why fictional characters aren't allowed free will," I said.

"I'll still solve my cases. Only this time, with you by my side. The Duke and Duchess of Chicago? How does that sound?"

It sounded against the rules.

It sounded very, very against the rules.

But it also sounded like something I'd read.

"I'll think about it," I said, which I shouldn't have said and knew I shouldn't have said, but I said it anyway.

"You will? You mean it? What about your precious 'Black and Whites'?"

"It does seem unfair that you don't get a say in your own stories."

He placed the back of his hand across my temple.

"No fever," he said. "Are you the real Rainy March or have you been replaced with an impostor?"

Playing along, I glanced at myself in the rearview mirror.

"Looks like me," I said. "But that's exactly what an impostor would say . . . Wait."

Sometimes that's all it takes. A word. A glance. Two things that seemingly have nothing to do with each other and then—click. And the moment I glanced at myself in the mirror, I heard the click.

"Duke, here's a riddle for you—"

"You know I hate riddles as much as you hate puns. They're for children and the shiftless."

"You'll like this one. Remember, the answer is staring us in the face? Well, what stares you in the face every single day of your life?"

"Impending doom?"

"Your own face in the mirror."

His eyes widened. He glanced at the side mirror, then at me.

"Another word for a mirror . . ." he said.

"Looking-glass, Duke. Looking-glass. The March Hare's in *Through the Looking-Glass.* The sequel to *Alice in Wonderland.* Of course!"

"But, darling," Duke said, "I thought you said it's the same March Hare in both books. We ruled it out."

"I'm ruling it back in again. It's the only thing that makes sense. A mirror stares me in the face. 'Mirror' is another word for 'looking-glass.' And the March Hare in *Through the Looking-Glass* goes by a different name. *Haigha,* which is pronounced to rhyme with 'mayor.' "

"Why?"

"Who knows? Lewis Carroll was a weird guy. What do you think?"

Duke took a breath.

"You know I'll go anywhere with you," he said. "Lead the way. But please don't be disappointed if we . . . well, if our rabbit hunt turns into a wild-goose chase."

From my bag, I pulled out *The Secret of the Old Clock,* staring at the cover, Nancy Drew in blue running through the woods with a clock under her arm, like she was trying to stop time. If only that worked. Our own clock was ticking. The afternoon was fading into evening, and by the time we were home, it would be dark.

"I have to try," I told Duke. "For Pops."

"Then let's go through the looking-glass, love."

"We'll need to go back into Gatsby's library," I said. "Since both Alice books are Code Reds. Gotta be a library around here somewhere . . ."

We would need a library, but when I'd scrolled through my phone, I couldn't find any libraries still open. And the nearest bookstore was a thirty-minute drive away. Doing immersions in a bookstore wasn't a good idea anyway. You always ran the risk of an employee reshelving your book, which can make escaping much, much harder. And if someone bought the book, when we escaped we could end up anywhere.

"We'll have to hurry home," I said. "Buckle up. I'm going to floor it."

Fifteen minutes later, we'd gotten up to the speed limit.

"By floor it," I explained to Duke, "I meant not floor it."

"Of course."

The sun had nearly set by the time we rolled up in front of Pilcrow House. When we opened the door, Koshka came mewing and mrrwping all the way down the stairs, then bounded into my arms. For all of two seconds, before he launched off my chest and into Duke's arms.

"Greetings, comrade," Duke said. "We missed you too."

"Library," I said. "Not a moment to waste!"

Even now the sky was darkening. Midnight would be here before we knew it. Midnight was the deadline I'd set, the hour I would have to tell Duke goodbye again and forever.

"Surely there's time for tea," Duke said, setting Koshka down. "I'll pop in the kitchen and see if Mrs. Turner—"

I spun on my heel and stalked back to him, took his tie in my hand, and dragged him bodily down the hallway.

"Tea can wait, Chicago. Now come on."

This sounds violent, but when I glanced in the hallway mirror, I saw that while my mirror twin was scowling, Duke's mirror twin was grinning, clearly enjoying the manhandling more than he probably should.

Then I let go of Duke's tie.

"Why did you stop, darling? And why is Shakespeare wearing rabbit ears?" he asked, nodding toward the bust of the Bard where I'd placed the bunny ears Penny had given me yesterday.

"Rainy?" Duke said again.

I ignored the question, ignored everything but my own reflection in the mirror.

"Rainy? Darling?" Duke said again. He sounded worried now. "What is it?"

"I saw something in there," I said, pointing to the glass.

"What?"

"My twin."

"Of course you saw your twin in the mirror. Who were you expecting?"

I put my hand on the glass.

And then I . . .

. . . FELL THROUGH THE LOOKING-GLASS.

Book Three

FANTASY

CHAPTER TWENTY-FOUR

I found myself standing in a long, seemingly endless hallway. And along the walls hung mirrors of different sizes and shapes. Some with plain wooden frames. Some with ornate gilt carvings fit for a princess. Some big. Some small. On one white and dainty dressing table sat a hand mirror. Next to it, a mirrored wall, like you'd find in a gym or dance studio.

I'd fallen through the looking-glass and found . . . infinite looking-glasses.

Shaking slightly, I stepped to the nearest mirror, which hung over a river stone fireplace that was cold and smelled as if it had been cold for a long time. A fireplace for show, not warmth. I climbed onto the hearth and put my hands on the mantel, hoping it would show me Duke, Koshka, and Pilcrow House, but instead I saw a room I'd never seen before.

A young woman with red hair lay on a sofa reading something, brow furrowed in concentration.

Beside her lay her phone. It rang. She looked at the screen, winced, then silenced the call and went back to reading.

My kind of girl.

"Who are you?" I whispered. I knew I'd never seen this woman before in my life.

"That's a good question," said a voice from behind me. I whirled to face the source and saw a woman standing in the shadows. "Better question, however—who are *you*?"

"I know who I am," I said. "Rainy March. Who are you?"

"You already know. But I don't think you want to know."

"That sounds ominous. Are you trying to be ominous? If so, congratulations. If not, please find a new way of being because you are freaking me out."

I couldn't see the woman, but I heard her laugh. From nowhere, a light flickered on. A gas streetlamp, like something out of a Sherlock story. And a pretty brunette in a trench coat leaning against the post.

"Recognize me?" she asked.

"No. Although . . . you do seem kind of familiar?"

"This is how I used to look back in the day. I didn't routinely lean against gas lamps in the dark, but I wanted to. Maybe you'll recognize me . . . this way."

She stepped out of the circle of lamplight, and when she came closer I saw soft white hair, a face gently wrinkled. If you cut her open, doilies and Werther's Originals candies would fall out . . .

"Medda?" I asked. "Medda Baker? How did you get here?"

"Not Medda Baker," she said. "But close. Maxine Blake. We have met before, in a way."

"Okay, enough dancing around answers," I said. "Tell me who you are and what's going on?"

"Soon, very soon. Call it . . . suspense," the old woman—Maxine, apparently—said, stepping closer. "I like suspense. Keeps readers on the edge of their seats."

"Can I not get a straight answer, please?" I begged.

"The shortest distance between two points is a straight answer," Maxine said. "But the distance between the self and self-discovery is a very long story."

"I'm starting to dislike you. A lot."

Maxine Blake, whoever she was, only smiled. "Here, this will help. You think of a number between one and infinity, and I'll tell you what you're thinking."

"Fine," I said and immediately thought of an impossible-to-guess number—19,325.

"Nineteen thousand, three hundred twenty-five," she said.

I stared at her. She raised her hands as if to say, *Told you so.*

"How did you . . . never mind," I said. "Let's do it again."

I thought of the number eight.

She said, "Eight."

I thought of the number eight again.

She said, "Eight. Again."

I thought of the number one hundred billion . . . and two.

"One hundred billion . . . and two," she said. "Also, your favorite color is fog gray, not only because you like the fog, but because it's the same color as Koshka's fur."

It was. She was right. But how? I thought of Koshka at home, his fog-colored fur and how soft it was. But then, I thought of his eyes, his glimmering fern green eyes, which were an even more beautiful color.

"Wrong," she said. "Now your favorite color is fern green for his eyes. You tell people your favorite movie is *The Red Shoes,* but that's only your second favorite movie. Your first favorite movie is—let's see . . ."

She paused as if in deep thought.

"How about *The Wizard of Oz*?" she continued. "Although you hate the ending of the film, where it was all a dream. They should've stuck to the book's ending, where the magical world is real."

Suddenly . . . I felt something shift in me. Yes, I did love *The Red Shoes,* that glorious Technicolor spectacle about the ballet dancer torn between worlds—heart versus art, but now . . . now . . . yes, *The Wizard of Oz* had moved to number one in my heart. But why did they have to make Oz a dream?

"How do you know that?" I demanded. "Can you read minds?"

"I'm not reading your mind. More like . . . writing your mind."

"You're scaring me," I said, taking a few steps back.

"It's going to get worse before it gets better." Just then a small round table appeared covered in the classic red-and-white checkered tablecloth. On the table sat a cup of tea and a black-and-white Little Debbie Zebra Cake.

"Which would you prefer first? Tea or cake?" she asked. "And no, they are not poisoned."

"I can't eat in a story world. It's too dangerous."

"You're not in a story world," she said.

For some reason, I believed her. "Guess I'll have cake then?"

"Good choice." She held out the cake on a dessert plate. On top, someone had written in dark icing, *Eat me.*

I took a bite, and it was delicious as usual. Pure sweetness.

In a flash, I shrunk to the size of a doll. I shouted up to Maxine, "You said it wasn't dangerous!"

"Don't be afraid," Medda/Maxine said. "Just proving a point. Here's your tea."

She set the teacup down in front of me, and it was the size of a hot tub. On the side of the white cup in elegant cursive were the words *Drink Me.*

I climbed onto the rim of the saucer and leaned over, drinking from it like Koshka with his water bowl.

Instantly I was myself again. My size, my height.

"Why did you do that to me?" I demanded.

"So you'll believe me when I say I know you better than you know yourself. I know you're in love with Duke, but you can't bring yourself to ask him to stay with you since you know his book series would cease to exist. And a little part of you is afraid that if he stopped being fictional, you might not love him as much since he wouldn't be the hero of story and legend anymore but an ordinary man taking the garbage out every Thursday night and forgetting to put his dirty socks in the hamper. You'd rather live in his world, helping him with his cases . . . but you can't leave your grandfather. You'd feel too guilty."

I only stared at her, speechless.

She took a deep breath. "One more," the woman said.

From behind her back she pulled a book, a hardcover.

The dust jacket was white with a black umbrella in the center.

Two words were printed on the jacket.

READ ME.

I hesitated.

"Go on. If you're afraid to read a book, it's probably because you know it has something to say to you that you don't want to hear."

Slowly, I opened the cover to the title page.

THE MARCH HARE MYSTERY

The Book Case Files of Rainy March, Book Witch

by Maxine Blake

Then I turned to the first chapter, first page.

"Out loud," she said.

My voice was steady when I began but broke and shook as I read the following words out loud.

All stories are love stories if you love stories.

And I do love stories. As a Book Witch, you kind of have to love them. It's on our recruitment posters, after all.

My name is Rainy March, and yes, it's a bad pun and also a weather forecast, and no, sorry, I can't change it now. It's already embroidered into my underwear and printed on my bookplates.

The book fell out of my hands.

"You know now, Rainy?" she asked gently.

I nodded.

"I know," I said. "You're a writer. You're . . . my writer."

"And who are you?" she asked.

"I'm Rainy March," I said. "I'm a fictional character and always have been."

"I did try to warn you," she said. "Things are never what they seem."

"DO YOU WANT TO FAINT?" MAXINE ASKED.

"If you don't mind."

"Go for it," she said. "Fictional characters do tend to faint more than the general population."

"Thanks. I appreciate it. Back soon."

My knees buckled, the world went black, and I was out like a light, like a fictional light in a hallway made of words, paper, and pure imagination.

When I came to, I lay on a soft shag rug that hadn't been there before I fainted. "Sorry about that," I said as I blinked at the ceiling. There was also a mirror up there, but I didn't look too deeply in it.

"Don't mention it," she said. "Want some more tea? Water? I can conjure some up for you if you'd like. Or would you prefer bourbon?"

"Bourbon? I don't drink bourbon. Or do I?"

"You're having a mild existential crisis. Bourbon might help."

She reached out her hand to me. I took it, and she helped pull me upright. We sat cross-legged on the rug facing each other, like two little girls about to play patty-cake on the playground.

"One shot won't kill me, right?" I asked.

"Not on my watch," she said. She reached behind her, and suddenly there was a picnic basket. She put it on the rug, which had become a red-check picnic blanket, and opened the lid.

"Here we go," she said. "I picked up a bottle of this in Kentucky on my last book tour."

She set a bottle of bourbon on the rug between us and two shot glasses. On the label was a picture of a woman in a cowboy hat holding a scythe.

"Should I be drinking something with a scythe on it?" I asked as she poured a shot for me, then one for herself. "Don't answer that. I'm going to do it anyway."

She picked up her shot glass, lifted it, then said, "Bottoms up until you're facedown."

She drank. I drank.

She didn't cough. I coughed.

"You all right, Rainy?" she asked, and I could tell she was trying not to laugh at me although she wasn't trying very hard.

"I feel like I got punched in the throat."

"Hate it?"

"I don't *not* hate it." I took another sip. "Wow."

"Feeling better?" she asked.

"Not yet." I finished my shot, counted to five, felt a warm fire crawling up my brain stem. "Okay, now I feel better." I held out the shot glass to her.

"Another?" she asked.

"Bury it in the ground," I said. "Please."

She took the glass from me and placed it back in the picnic basket along with her glass and the bottle too.

"So you said your name is . . . Maxine?"

"Maxine Blake," she said. "Not Medda Baker. I wrote myself into the story because . . . I was being meta."

"Never liked metafiction."

"Me neither, but it's my last book, so I thought I'd pull out all the stops. And as I won't be reading the reviews . . ." she said with a strange expression on her face. "Well, are you feeling better now?"

"Do you really care? No offense, but if you really are my writer, you've ruined my life."

"Fighting words," Maxine said, though she didn't sound particularly offended.

"You killed my mother." I lifted my fists. Generally, I don't believe in violence toward authors, but for my own author, I felt at least a hard slap was justified.

She winced. "I did, didn't I? I'd apologize, but . . . Well, you know, it made a better story."

"Also, the man I love and I can't be together. I have a missing inheritance apparently. Oh, and my grandfather has vanished, maybe disappeared. Explain yourself, please."

"What was I supposed to do?" she asked. "I'm writing a story, not a recipe. Stories thrive on conflict. You do realize the fairy tale 'Little Red Riding Hood' without the Big Bad Wolf is nothing but a brief paragraph about an uneventful food delivery."

"Fine. Bad things have to happen in stories, but can you please tell me what's going on? Why am I here? With you? We're not supposed to meet, right?"

"It's a long story, so get comfortable."

"We're sitting on a rug on the floor of a Hall of Mirrors. Nothing is comfortable about this situation."

"I can help with that," she said. "Stand by."

Chairs appeared. Cozy armchairs, the kind you sit down in and then require help—physical and mental—to get back up again. They had a distinctly hideous floral pattern.

"That's more like it," she said and patted the back of one of the armchairs. "We had a chair in the library where I grew up like this one. The Storytime chair. We kids would sit on the rug, and library volunteers would read to us. I dreamed of the day I would be the one sitting in that chair, telling stories."

She sat down, and I took the chair opposite her. We were still in a bizarre Hall of Mirrors that made no sense, but at least the seating arrangement had improved.

"Better now?" she asked.

"I'm more physically comfortable but psychologically? I'm a wreck."

"I'd imagine you into being a little more accepting of the whole thing, but I know you too well for that."

"Imagine me? Is that where we are?" I pointed to the mirrors, the strange dark hall, the gas streetlight that came from nowhere and might to nowhere return.

"That's right," she said. "My imagination. I'm fantasizing this whole conversation. This is where you live until I put you on paper. Which is why I can do anything I want here."

"So you can imagine me tiny or ten feet tall, and you can know what number I'm thinking of because . . . we are literally inside your brain."

"Don't worry," she said. "This is the nice neighborhood in my brain."

"Is there a bad neighborhood?"

She pointed to a black door with smoke billowing out from under it. I stood and went to the door and peeked inside. Behind it lurked monsters—anger, doubt, guilt, regret, and a weird erotic fascination with the late actor Christopher Plummer.

"Yikes," I said and slammed the door shut.

"Warned you," Maxine replied.

"I hope you're in therapy for some of that."

"Too late now," she said with a shrug. "Have a seat."

I returned to the armchair. "Is this my real body or an imagined version of me?"

"You don't have a body. You have no physical reality."

That was a gut punch to my nonexistent gut. "And Koshka? And Duke?"

"They aren't real in the physical sense either. You are all figments of my imagination that I put onto paper and turned into books."

I sat back in the chair. "All this time, I thought I was real, and Duke was fictional. Wait, if we're both fictional, we can be together. Can you put us together? You can do anything in a book. We could get married on the moon if you wrote it."

"Wish I could, Rainy," she said. "But . . . ah, we'll get to that. You want to know where you come from, yes?"

"You know I do," I said. "I do because you're pulling my strings. Playing God with me."

"No strings. And no playing God. Just . . . playing," she said with real tenderness in her voice. "You and I have known each other a long, long time. Any writer will tell you that their characters, especially ones they've written for decades, will take on a life of their own. Yes, you're in my mind, but even I can't imagine you burning books and kicking puppies."

"That's some comfort, I guess. All right. Tell me everything."

"Good. Well . . . Let's be old-fashioned and begin at the beginning. You were born on January twenty-first, 1975, the day your first book was released."

"Hold on," I said. "It's 2025 so . . . I'm fifty? Are you serious?"

She calmly nodded. I glanced at the nearest mirror on the wall.

"I am aging *very* well," I said. "Not a single gray hair."

"You're welcome. Shall I continue?"

"Please."

"Back then," she continued, "I was a secretary at a gravel supply company. Most boring job in the history of the world, but I had access to a typewriter and a boss who was never in the office. I'd get all my work done in two hours and spend the rest of the day pretending to work while I wrote."

"What were you trying to write?"

"I wanted, more than anything, to write something like the Nancy Drew books, a mystery series for girls. I'd loved Nancy so much as a kid. She was so brave, so spunky, so smart. I would've given my right arm for a spin in her little blue roadster."

"You could've given me a little blue roadster, you know. But no, I had to have a Sun Buggy, which is as lethal as it is cute."

"You have a VW 1974 Sun Bug because that was my dream car

when I was in my twenties, and I couldn't afford it. And you live in a giant Victorian house in Astoria, Oregon, because I wanted to live there and couldn't. And you—"

"I live in Fort Meriwether."

"Doesn't exist," she said, waving her hand as if magically making my entire hometown disappear. "I based it on Astoria, Oregon, but I wanted to fictionalize it so I could take liberties with the geography and that sort of thing."

"Great, thanks. I don't exist. My town doesn't exist. My cat doesn't exist. Does anything exist?"

"Yes," she said. "All of these exist . . ."

CHAPTER TWENTY-FIVE

A cardboard box appeared on the table, slightly bigger than a breadbox. Maxine took a book from the box—a slim hardcover with a picture on the front of a young woman holding a black umbrella over her head in the rain, a dark Victorian house behind her in the distance, and the unmistakable shadow of a vampire falling onto her path. She handed it to me.

"*The Children of the Night,*" I read aloud in astonishment. "By Maxine Blake."

"The first of the Book Witch stories," she said. "Dracula escapes the prison of his pages, and only Book Witch Rainy March, with the help of Dr. Van Helsing, can catch him and return him to his story. First edition, first printing."

"The cover is insane," I said. "Could it be any more Gothic?"

She leaned forward and snatched the book from my hands. "Everyone's a critic. It was the seventies." Maxine held the book up. "This edition is worth a small fortune, I'll have you know. No series title, no number. By the second printing, my publisher knew it was going to be a hit and added the series title—The Book Case Files of Rainy March, Book Witch—and put a number one on the spine."

"Is that supposed to be a pun? Book Case Files . . . *like a bookcase*?"

"It wasn't my idea," she said. "I didn't like it either. So I've been mocking puns in your books ever since as payback."

She began to pull other books from the box.

A Pleasure to Burn. That was about my mission into *Fahrenheit 451* when the Burners attacked the most important novel ever published on book burning.

"Book fifteen," she said. "We had to get permission from Mr. Bradbury to use his book, but he was more than happy to sign off on it. His editor's daughter was a fan of your series. And this is book twenty-nine."

This Deplorable Folly. My mission into Poe's "The House of Usher." It still gave me the chills to remember that vile house, the scent of death and rot in the walls.

She pulled another from the box. "This one was fun. I didn't usually send you into children's novels since my series was technically for adults, but Jack Masterson's editor arranged for a crossover event."

Do Clocks Wish for the End of Time? My assignment on Clock Island, where I helped the famous Mastermind grant a child's wish to meet her hero, Lucy Maud Montgomery.

"And my personal favorite," Maxine said. "But don't tell anyone writers play favorites. Book thirty-five."

The Dragon Gate. My mission with the Count of Monte Cristo, the title coming from the famous quote, was technically for adults. *I don't think man was meant to attain happiness so easily. Happiness is like those palaces in fairy tales whose gates are guarded by dragons: we must fight in order to conquer it.*

"My goal was to write thirty-six," she said. "And I did before I had to retire."

"Had to? Why?"

"We'll get to that," she said.

She put the books back into the box, and the second she shut the lid, it disappeared.

"Wow. Magic."

"Fiction," she said. "I think it, it happens. At least in here."

"Really? Can you bring Duke here?"

"It would be better if I didn't. We have important things to discuss, and we both can concentrate better without him around being handsome and overprotective. But . . . how about . . . that?"

She glanced down the hallway where a small form moved through the shadows, trotting toward us—a streak of fog-colored fur.

"Koshka!" I cried out. He ran straight to me and jumped onto my lap. "Oh, buddy, I missed you." I cupped his small face in my hands and kissed him between the ears on that flat part of his head I called his landing pad. His warm, small body purred against me.

"Thank you, Maxine. This doesn't make up for all the horrible things you've done to me over the years, but I appreciate it."

"My pleasure," she said. Koshka leapt lightly from my arms and jumped into her lap. She scratched him between the ears. "*What greater gift than the love of a cat?* Charles Dickens supposedly said that. Of course, you and I both know—"

"—it's a misattribution."

"Exactly," she said, stroking Koshka's back. "You know because I know."

"I know because you . . ." My voice trailed off as the enormity of what she was saying dawned on me. I didn't know everything she knew; I only knew what she wanted me to know. But now we were face-to-face, and I had questions . . . and she, almost certainly, had all the answers I was owed.

"You know the identity of the March Hare," I said. "I mean, I have a theory but—"

"We're getting to that. I told you, no skipping to the last page. We have more story to get through first."

"Fine, go on. But I'm starting to dislike you again," I said. "Which, come to think of it, is weird, if you're in charge of everything I do and feel and say."

"No one is more self-loathing than an artist," she said with a laugh. "And I don't really blame you, kiddo. When I say I feel your pain, I mean it literally. I lost my family too. I think I wrote you as an orphan because . . . I didn't know how else to write you. They say writers should write what they know. That's what I knew."

"I'm sorry," I said, and I was. "Is that why you liked Nancy Drew so much? No mother?"

"Oh, that was part of the reason. Really, I wanted to be her best friend, wanted that more than anything. When I was a girl, I wrote my own Nancy Drew stories. Childish fan fiction before there was even a term for it. Then I grew up and tried to create my own Nancy in her honor. A teen girl detective, Rainy, that's who you were supposed to be. Maybe a little more modern, a little hipper. But I wrote and I wrote and I wrote, and nothing worked. Everything I wrote was Nancy Drew Lite. Derivative drivel. Eventually, I simply gave up."

"You quit?"

"I decided to stop wasting the office's paper supply on pages that always ended up in the wastebasket. I'd killed enough trees already. And that's when it happened."

"What happened?" I leaned forward in my chair.

"I would always bring a book to read during lunch, but I'd accidentally left mine on the bus. Bored, I read the newspaper instead. November sixteenth, 1973 . . . On the third page, there was an article about a school board in North Dakota. They'd ordered thirty-six copies of Kurt Vonnegut's *Slaughterhouse-Five* burned."

"Burned?" I asked. "Literally burned? In a fire?"

"Burned. And the order had been followed. The custodian threw them in the school's incinerator." She met my eyes, and I saw the pain in them. Fifty-year-old pain that had never healed. "They were burning books in Chile too. The military was, I mean. The fascist military. And in North Dakota, America. I couldn't believe it."

I sat back in my chair, stunned.

"There are Burners in the real world?" I asked.

"Like X? No. But people who burn books out of ignorance and fear? Yes, I'm afraid so," Maxine said.

Was this how Duke felt when he learned World War I had been real? "It came out that most of the school board hadn't even read the book, only a few paragraphs taken out of context. Some of the kids tried to hide their copies, but their lockers were searched, their books confiscated. Some lied and said they'd lost their copies. Some offered to buy the books from the school. I couldn't get those kids out of my mind. The ones who'd put up such a valiant fight to save a book. To save their own homework. Can you imagine?" She raised her hands and shook her head. "The adults in town either couldn't or wouldn't help them. I realized then that kids didn't need another kid hero book. Kids weren't the problem. It was the adults. I needed to write to the adults. So I created the champion those kids needed. Someone, a grown-up, who would fight the burners for them. Someone who would dedicate her life to protecting stories, guarding stories, saving stories. A traveling angel character. Instead of solving crimes in books, like Nancy Drew, she would solve crimes *against* books. In other words, Rainy March . . . *you*."

HOW LONG DID I SIT THERE, LETTING HER WORDS SINK IN? MAYBE a minute. Maybe an hour. Did time have any meaning in this place anyway?

"Me?" I finally said.

"You. Now are you still mad at me?" she asked.

"Less mad. You did call me an angel, which was very nice of you."

She laughed softly. "Traveling angel," she said. "It's not a compliment. It's a literary term for a certain type of fictional character who exists to help people solve their problems. You're in good company, Rainy. Sherlock Holmes. Nancy Drew, of course. Even Jack Reacher."

"I'm like Jack Reacher? Hasn't he used the same toothbrush for almost thirty books?"

"You'd have to ask Lee Child," she said. "But I'll put it this way—if fictional characters unionized, you two would be in the same trade union. Traveling angels go from place to place helping people, changing lives for the better, but you yourself, you don't change. In fact, you can't change, Rainy. You wouldn't be you if you changed. Sherlock's never going to become a schoolteacher instead of a detective. Jack Reacher will never retire to the country and keep bees. Nancy Drew will never give up sleuthing to become a lawyer like her father and marry Ned. Thank God. She can do so much better. For fifty years and thirty-six books . . . you haven't changed, and that's how it is, kid. Or was. Until now. Now things have to change, especially if you want to solve the mystery of the March Hare."

"Why do things have to change now?"

She lowered her head, then lifted it slowly. "You know why, Rainy."

Maxine gestured to a delicate white vanity table with a stool and a mirror.

I got up, sat on the stool, and peered deeply into the glass.

At first, I saw nothing, not even my own reflection. But then mist swirled in the glass and as it cleared, I could see into a bedroom.

A room suffused with gold and red light, sunset. Stucco walls. A nightstand covered in pill bottles and water cups. A breathing machine. And nearly hidden under the white quilt, a thin, frail figure nearly the same color as the sheets. White hair, ashen waxy skin, a thin chest rising and falling slowly, slowly, far too slowly.

A man with white hair sitting at her side, head down as if in prayer or exhaustion or both.

"Duke was right," I said. "You're dying."

From behind me, I heard her sigh.

"*If my doctor told me I had only six minutes to live, I wouldn't brood. I'd type a little faster,*" she said and smiled. "Isaac Asimov said that, bless him. I really wanted to write a Foundation book with you, but we couldn't get the rights. I think Kubrick had them tied up. Or was it Spielberg?"

I walked back and sat down in my chair opposite her. "You are dying, aren't you?"

"Pencils down," she said.

"Pencils down?"

Maxine smiled. "When I'd finish writing one of your books, I'd send it to my editor. We'd go back and forth for weeks trying to get the story right. And then when I did, I'd get a two-word email from him. *Pencils down.* That meant my work was done. Those were my favorite emails."

I looked around at the interior of Maxine Blake's imagination, the long hallway, infinite. She could be thinking of anything here and yet she'd conjured me to sit in the fantasy chair opposite her.

"You're dying, and you're thinking of me? Why?"

"Because I need you," she said.

"For what?"

"Book thirty-seven. *The March Hare Mystery.*"

"What about it?"

"Look."

Suddenly the book was in my hands again, the one that said *Read Me* on the cover.

"Turn to the last page," Maxine said. "Read it for me."

As instructed, I turned to the very last page in the book and read aloud . . .

"Why did you stop, darling? And why is Shakespeare wearing rabbit ears?" he asked, nodding toward the bust of the Bard where I'd placed the bunny ears Penny had given me yesterday.

I ignored the question, ignored everything but my own reflection in the mirror.

"Darling?" Duke said again. He sounded worried now. "What is it?"

"I saw something in there," I said, pointing to the glass.

"What?"

"My twin."

"Of course you saw your twin in the mirror. Who were you expecting?"

I put my hand on the glass.

And then I . . .

"I what?" I demanded, turning to Maxine. "What did I do?"

"I don't know. I never finished writing your book . . . and I never will."

"You're dying with the book unfinished?"

"When I started it, I'd been retired for five years. Heart trouble," she said. "But about a year ago, I had an idea, an idea I couldn't let go of. Now I'll never finish it. Which brings us to why I brought you here. Your mission, if you choose to accept it . . ."

"My mission?"

She led me to the mirror over the stone fireplace, the one I'd first looked into and spied the red-haired woman on her sofa. Koshka jumped lightly onto the rug. Maxine stood up and sighed happily, then laughed at herself.

"Word of advice, kid—enjoy your young knees while you have them."

Side by side we stood on the hearth to peer through the mirror.

The redheaded woman had finished reading the book, which I knew now wasn't really a book but an unfinished, incomplete manuscript. I watched her toss it onto a glass coffee table. Even though the words were backward on the front cover, I could make out what they said.

Read Me.

"That's my book, my last book," I said. "*The March Hare Mystery.* Why does she have it? Wait, is she the March Hare?"

"No, Rainy. Her name is Jessa," Maxine said. "She's the March *Heir.*"

"Heir," I said in disbelief, pronouncing it like "air."

She looked at me and nodded sheepishly.

"You know how I feel about puns," I said, narrowing my eyes at her in fury.

"Couldn't help myself," she said.

"That young woman is a mystery writer," Maxine said. "She's the one I've chosen to carry on the series, to be the new me. My handpicked heir."

The writer, Jessa Something, picked up the book again and lightly slammed it against her head, as if that could somehow shake the ideas loose. Luckily for her, my books weren't massive doorstops. She would have had to hit herself with a box set to do any real damage.

"Will she do it?"

"She feels inadequate to the task," Maxine said. "Ridiculous girl. She can write circles around me, but she idolizes me for some foolish reason."

"But if she doesn't finish the book, I'll never solve the mystery. I'll never go home again. I'll never see Pops or Duke or Koshka or . . . She has to finish the book!"

"Exactly," Maxine said, nodding. "And it's all there. All the clues. All the hints. Quite frankly, I probably made it a little too obvious. Any mystery writer worth her salt can put the pieces together. But she's the one I want."

"So what do I do?" I asked.

"Go out into the real world and convince her to finish the story."

CHAPTER TWENTY-SIX

"The real world?" I repeated.

"The *real* real world," Maxine said.

"But how? How do I get from here to there?" I gazed at the world on the other side of the mirrors, the so-called *real* real world.

"Magic, of course."

"Okay," I said, taking a deep breath. "How do I get back after I finish the job?"

I had a feeling chanting "Our revels now are ended" wouldn't work quite as well in the real world.

"Once your new writer starts writing you, you'll be back in your book," Maxine said.

"But while I'm out there . . . I'll be alive?"

"So alive that if you fail in your mission, well . . . I hope you like Santa Barbara, California, as much as I did, because you'll be living there."

"I'm not opposed, but I'd rather be home with Duke and Koshka—" I looked around. "Wait, where is Koshka? He was right here."

"Oh, damn." Maxine shook her fist in frustration. "Why did I ever give you a cat? Do you know how hard it is to keep up with a non-speaking character in a scene? He's back home at Pilcrow House. Or will be if you complete your mission."

"And you're sure a new writer will know how to solve my mystery?

Find the real March Hare? Get Pops back? Figure out what my mother was trying to tell me?"

"Absolutely. Especially that one," Maxine said, pointing to the mirror containing the redheaded writer. "She'll find every clue I laid out."

"That's a relief. Glad someone knows what the heck's going on."

"She will. She's already angry at herself because she knows how it's supposed to end but can't bring herself to write it. But once you have a word with her, she'll change her mind."

I was barely listening by this point. My heart raced at the thought of my heart racing. Real body. Real life. Real beating heart in a real world. One thing kept repeating over and over in my head: *I'm going to be alive. I'm going to be alive. I'm going to be—*

"I'm going to be alive," I said aloud. "Happy birthday to me." I looked to Maxine. "How do I get there?"

"Pick a mirror," she said. She walked from mirror to mirror. "That one leads to my living room. And that one there will take you to the changing room at the public beach near my house if you want to get your bearings first. Lots of options. Pick one and go."

"I can pick any mirror?"

"They all lead to somewhere I know and love."

I went to the wall and walked along the ones close by. One looked into Maxine's bathroom, another into her hallway, another her office . . . then I found one that seemed familiar. Not that I'd been there, but I'd been to places like it before.

"I just go?" I asked her, glancing over my shoulder. "Just like that. Just . . . *whoosh*."

"Whoosh," she repeated, then snapped her fingers and pointed.

"And after I whoosh? Then what?"

"Find my husband, Anthony. You'll need his help."

I took another breath. "Okay," I said. Go to the Real World. Find Anthony. Talk a recalcitrant redhead into finishing my book. I can do that. Should I run? Like a running start?"

"I won't stop you. But before you go . . . a parting gift." She reached behind her and pulled out a familiar black umbrella. "In case it rains."

"My umbrella," I said, taking it from her hand. "Thank you."

I felt more like myself again.

"Remember . . . once you're through the mirror, that umbrella is just an umbrella. You won't be able to work any of your usual storycraft. There is magic in the real world. It's not as flashy or showy, and it's easy to miss if you aren't looking for it, so I'd suggest looking for it."

Being real sounded like a lot of work.

I clung tight to my umbrella and started forward. Then I stopped and turned to her.

"I've never been real before. Any advice?"

Her eyes softened. "Advice on being alive? I'd be a fool to think I could tell anyone how to live their life. But you can always count on Shakespeare. *Hamlet* Act 1, Scene Three. *To thine own self be true.*"

I smiled back at her. "Good advice."

"You should also know . . . by the time you get there, I'll already be gone."

"Oh. I wanted to say goodbye."

"Then we'll say goodbye here," she said.

Her eyes filled with tears that she seemed too proud to shed. I stepped forward to hug her, but she held up her hand to stop me. If I held her, I realized, she might not be able to let go.

"I'm still mad at you about my mother," I said instead. "But I really appreciate you giving me a cat and Duke and Pops and a nice house and even the stupid car. And a very cool job. Thank you for everything."

"My pleasure. And thank you for giving me something I could give the world."

"You're welcome."

"All right. Bye, kid."

I took a step toward the mirror I'd chosen.

"Rainy?"

"Yes, Maxine?" I said.

"There's a scene in *Through the Looking-Glass* where Alice meets the old, feeble White Knight."

"I know that scene."

"You know, I always thought of *Alice in Wonderland* as a comedy about how silly and nonsensical it is to be a child. But *Looking-Glass*? It's a tragedy because as crazy and confusing as it is to be a kid . . . it's better than getting old and dying." She held up her trembling hands and looked at them. I sensed I was losing her.

"Why are you telling me this, Maxine?" I asked gently.

"Sorry, mind wandering. Getting foggy up here." She tapped her temples. "Time for me to go through my Looking Glass. Too bad. I was enjoying this life." She took a breath and seemed to pull herself together. "Sorry, where was I?"

"The White Knight and Alice."

"Right. The White Knight escorts Alice to the end of his move. Then he gathers his horse's reins, and as he's about to leave her, he says, '*You'll wait and wave your handkerchief when I get to that turn in the road? I think it'll encourage me, you see.*' And she does. Alice waves at him and thinks maybe she did encourage him a little." Maxine laughed at herself, dashing her tears away with her thumbs. "Maybe you'll wave at me when you go? I think it'll encourage me. I mean . . . you've never lived before, and I've never died before."

"Let's wave at each other then," I said.

"Good idea. You always had such good ideas."

"Great minds think alike."

I started again toward the mirror I'd chosen, walking sedately. I'd given up on the idea of making a running start and leaping through the mirror. The risk of cutting myself seemed too great. And really, honestly, I wasn't quite ready to leave Maxine yet.

When I reached it, I turned back around.

"Did you love me?" I asked her. "I know that's a stupid question but—"

"I wouldn't have written all those books about you if I didn't love you. I did want to shoot you out of a cannon every now and then, but only when the writer's block hit."

I laughed.

"Thanks again," I said. "For everything. Literally everything."

"It's been a pleasure working with you," she said.

She raised her hand and waved at me. I waved back. It did seem to work. I was encouraged, and I think she was too.

"Tell Anthony . . . Well, you know what to tell Anthony," she said, and in her last moments, she imparted into my mind and heart exactly the words she wanted me to say when the time came.

"Got it," I said. "Bye, Maxine."

A standing mirror suddenly appeared at Maxine's side. A bright and beckoning light poured from it. "Here we go," she said, "the next chapter."

She stepped through the mirror and was gone.

And for the second time that day . . .

. . . RAINY MARCH FELL THROUGH A LOOKING-GLASS.

Book Four

NONFICTION

CHAPTER TWENTY-SEVEN

Rainy stepped through the mirror into a women's restroom and immediately slipped on the recently mopped floor, landing hard on her hands and knees.

"Shit," she said, then slapped her hand over her mouth. Had she sworn out loud? Why did that feel so strange to her? Surely she'd cursed before. Or had she? Had Maxine simply written "Rainy swore" in her books without ever actually letting her say the words?

"Shit," she said again, marveling at the feeling of relief that washed over her. "Curses! Damn the torpedoes! What the hecking hell? Oh, this *is* fun."

She got to her feet before someone walked in and found her on the floor swearing at nothing and cackling. Luckily, no bones were broken, but the palms of her hands stung like fire, and her knees were definitely bruised. She waited for the pain to disappear, but it didn't. It subsided to a dull ache, but even after she washed her hands in soothing cold water, the pain wasn't quite gone.

What had Duke said the first time they'd met? When he learned he was fictional?

If I get shot—which I do more than I should, I think—I tend to heal completely by my next case.

She'd been thrown from runaway carriages, stabbed in sword fights, blasted by alien lasers, and had gone back to work the very next day.

Other than her burn scar that she wore like a badge of honor, all her other injuries healed almost immediately.

But not here.

Life, she was quickly learning, *hurt*.

Her poor umbrella was already broken. Well, not broken but bent. Rainy had landed on it hard enough that two of its metal ribs were twisted sideways. That had also never happened before.

Actions had consequences here.

"Well, damn, darn, and blast," she said, "I don't like this *at all*."

Bruised knees and a broken umbrella aside, Rainy had a mission, and she needed to complete it before she got herself killed.

After a steadying breath, she peered deep into the mirror, first to see if she could see the Hall of Mirrors behind the glass—she couldn't—and then to see if she looked like herself—she did.

She wasn't sure what she'd been expecting. Maybe if she were real, she'd look different. More vibrant somehow? Taller? Stronger? But no, her own face and body greeted her.

Same dark hair. Same gray eyes. Same nose and lips. And her clothes, too, were her usual uniform of black leggings, black-and-white striped sweater, and rain boots.

She straightened her sweater and squared her shoulders. She had a mystery writer to find.

"Let's get to it, March," she told herself. "Self-awareness is no excuse for not getting the job done."

First, she took stock of her surroundings. Even on the other side of the glass, she'd recognized this place as a library bathroom. Posters on the beige, green, and brown tile walls advertised book drives, clothing drives, and reminders about upcoming classes, clubs, and events. No posters recruiting new Book Witches or selling gently used tractor tires, of course. In this world, there were no Book Witches. Maxine had said there wasn't even magic, at least not like the storycraft she was used to. She examined the logo at the bottom of one of the posters. The Santa Barbara Public Library. California, if it was the same Santa Barbara as in her world. So what was happening here that Maxine's imagination had created a portal into it?

A woman entered the bathroom and stopped in her tracks. She

looked older than Rainy, maybe thirtysomething, and was dressed all in black. It was clear from the streak of eyeliner and the redness in her eyes that she'd been crying, but her face brightened at the sight of Rainy.

"Oh my gosh," the woman in black said, then laughed. "You look amazing. Just like her."

"Who?" Rainy asked.

"Rainy March?" she said, her voice teasing as if Rainy should've known. "Incredible cosplay."

"Oh, this is how I always—" Rainy began, then realized what the woman was saying. "My . . . costume. Thank you." Then, not knowing what else to do, she curtsied.

Luckily, the woman in black didn't notice the curtsy. She was busy rummaging through her handbag at the sink. She pulled a concealer stick out and began to repair her makeup.

"Are you all right?" Rainy asked. She'd cried in library bathrooms before, but only when she'd snuck into mystery sections to visit the Duke of Chicago books after hers had been confiscated. Was this woman also carrying a torch for a fictional character? Seemed the most logical explanation.

"Oh, guess I got a little weepy looking at the books and the memorabilia out there. With Maxine Blake gone, it feels like a part of my childhood died too. I was reading those books long after my friends switched to romances."

"All stories are love stories if you love stories."

The woman looked at her. "Good point."

"Do you have an umbrella tattooed on your arm?" Rainy asked.

The woman held out her right arm, palm up. An umbrella was indeed tattooed inside her wrist. "Reminds me that when the going gets tough, it's probably time to escape into a book."

Rainy laughed.

"We better get out there," the woman said. "It's already standing room only. But if you prefer to sit, they have a big screen up in the gallery next door."

"I . . . I'll stand?"

"Are *you* all right?" the woman asked.

"I'm fine, great. A little nervous. To go out there." Rainy hoped this was a reasonable response.

"Introvert? Same. Crowds are not my favorite either. You take your time. I'll save you a spot."

"Great, great. Which way do I go?"

"By the fireplace. The big windows. Can't miss it."

"I'll be right out," Rainy said. "I, um . . . I need to fix my umbrella."

The woman glanced at it and saw the bent ribs. "How did that happen?"

"I tripped over the mirror."

The woman narrowed her eyes in confusion.

"Over *by* the mirror," Rainy corrected.

"Here, I can fix it." The woman held out her hand and Rainy passed her the umbrella. "I used to live in Boston, and once a year at least, those winds would try to blow me to Oz."

Quickly but carefully, the woman bent the metal ribs back into place, then opened and closed the umbrella, testing it out. "That should work. If not, steal somebody else's. There're a million out there." The woman winked at her, then headed out of the bathroom.

Rainy stared at the now-repaired umbrella in her hands. Hot tears of gratitude filled her eyes as she clutched her umbrella to her chest.

Was this the magic of the real world Maxine had told her about? This subtle, quiet magic of a stranger helping another stranger fix her broken umbrella in a public bathroom?

She almost liked this magic better than her own.

EXITING THE BATHROOM, RAINY FOUND HERSELF IN A LOBBY AREA filled with large posters on easels.

The first poster made her breath hitch.

Maxine. Rainy knew her like she knew her own face in the mirror. Maxine looked thirty or forty years old. She wore slim jeans and a chunky white sweater. Her hair was in a soft bob, and the large tabby cat in her arms looked magnificently grumpy yet blissfully content in that way only well-loved and terribly spoiled cats do.

Rainy tore herself away from the poster and went to the next one.

She also recognized it—the very Gothic cover of the first Rainy March novel. Under it, a caption read,

Published January 21, 1975, Lion House Books. While commonplace now, the Book Witch series was one of the first cozy mystery series to utilize paranormal elements. Since 1975, the Book Witch series has sold forty million copies and has been translated into over thirty-five languages. Publishers coined the term "Book Witch effect" to describe the surge in sales of older classic titles that accompanied every new Rainy March novel. After the release of book nine, for example, Dead Men Don't Bite, *sales of* Treasure Island *surged, and the book briefly appeared on the* New York Times *Best Sellers List. Manhattan bookseller Petra Locke recalls, "I remember the month we couldn't keep* Beowulf *in stock.* Beowulf! *And it wasn't students buying it for a class. It wasn't even homework. Rainy March had one of her adventures in the epic poem, aiding Beowulf in his hour of need after another character has deserted him. We sold a hundred copies or more in one week. That's bestseller numbers for a book that was written in the tenth century. That's the Book Witch effect in action."*

"Good for me," Rainy said and would've patted herself on the back if she'd been alone.

The next poster displayed a timeline of the series from the first book in 1975 to the final book, published five years ago. Thirty-six books in total before Maxine was forced to retire from writing because of ill health. The last book, it said, was called *The World Was Being Watched.* It was set inside H. G. Wells's classic science fiction thriller, *The War of the Worlds.* Rainy remembered this case well, because in her mind it had happened only a year ago. The main character had been captured by aliens, thus altering the ending of the story. It had been up to Rainy to rescue him. How could that have been five years ago? Book time, of course. Book time passed very differently than real time.

One date in particular stood out from the rest. October 1999. As the poster explained, *In The Book Case Files of Rainy March, Book Witch #21,* An Unreasonable Amount of Trouble, *Maxine Blake introduced a love interest for Rainy in the form of the fictional Duke of Chicago. Sales, which had been lagging in the late nineties, rebounded, and the Duke soon became a regularly occurring character in the Book Witch series.*

Rainy's heart gave a little jump against her rib cage when she read Duke's name. But the date? 1999?

"We've been in love for over twenty-five years? Well, it's about time we got engaged, I guess." She touched her ring, glad to find it had survived its trip into reality.

A young librarian in a polo shirt and khakis passed by pushing a book cart, then stopped to whisper, "They're about to start, by the way."

Rainy pointed to the poster. "Do you have any Duke of Chicago books?" She lowered her voice and whispered, "I'm a Ducky."

"Oh . . . um . . . well, we carry all the Book Witch books. They're checked out right now, though—"

"No, I mean the mystery series. The Duke of Chicago series."

Understanding dawned on the young librarian's face. "Ah, no. The Duke of Chicago is fictional. Maxine Blake made him up for the Book Witch series. There are no actual Duke of Chicago books."

Rainy met her eyes. "Are you serious?"

"Sorry."

"If Maxine Blake weren't dead, I'd kill her."

The librarian blinked at her.

"I didn't mean that literally," Rainy said.

"It's okay," the librarian said. "I feel your pain. It should be a felony to introduce fictional books in novels and then not let readers read them."

The librarian pushed their cart along to the next room, and Rainy jogged down past more posters detailing her own life, ignoring the temptation to stop and read them all.

But one caught her eye and she paused to look at it.

It was a single-panel cartoon in black and white, like the ones in *The New Yorker.* A figure who was very clearly supposed to be her stood on a small hill by a single tombstone with the name *Maxine Blake* carved on it. The cartoon Rainy's black umbrella was open and rested on her shoulder. Her head was bowed in mourning. A bundle of forget-me-nots lay atop the gravestone.

The caption simply read, *No words.*

Rainy swallowed a lump in her throat as she read the description above the cartoon: "A tribute from children's book illustrator and Clock Island cover artist Hugo Rees ran in over five hundred newspapers two days after the death of Maxine Blake."

No words? She still had plenty of words. Three of them for that recalcitrant redheaded mystery writer, whoever she was.

CHAPTER TWENTY-EIGHT

Rainy walked through the library, following the sound of piano music. Under one of the floor-to-ceiling arched windows, a man sat at a baby grand playing a piece she instantly recognized from the score to *The Red Shoes;* it was called "Vicky's Last Dance."

She had a feeling Maxine had chosen the music herself.

Rainy looked up from the piano player and saw that the woman in the bathroom had been right—it was standing room only in here.

Hundreds of people filled the atrium. Most sat in folding chairs, but some sat on the floor, others on the stairs, and many more stood by the walls. A dais sat in front of an enormous fireplace, and on it was a speaker's podium.

When Rainy reached the main floor, the woman she'd met in the bathroom saw her and waved.

"I found us seats," she whispered as Rainy slid in beside her.

"Thanks," Rainy whispered. "I never got your name."

"Frankie. What's yours?"

"Ra . . . chel. Rachel."

"Hi, Rachel."

The music changed to a song Rainy didn't recognize, but a woman with gray hair sitting in front of them clearly knew it because as soon as the notes hit the melody, she laughed.

"What is this song?" Rainy whispered to her.

"It's the Beatles. 'Paperback Writer.' You're so young," the woman said, shaking her head.

"I'm fifty," Rainy whispered, but the woman didn't hear her. Everyone who was seated stood as three people walked out a side door and onto the dais.

Two women and one man. The man had white hair. Rainy recognized him from the mirror on Maxine's bedside. Anthony. Her husband. No, not her husband. Her widower. And what did that make Rainy? An orphan? Again?

The other woman, the older one, Rainy didn't recognize. But the younger one? The younger woman had red hair. The redheaded March Heir.

"Who is that?" Rainy asked, pointing out the redhead.

"That's Jessa Charming, the mystery writer," Frankie said. "She's giving one of the eulogies."

Eulogy? So that's what this was—Maxine's funeral. Held not in a church or a temple or a mosque, but on the sacred ground of all writers—the public library.

The woman with white hair nodded toward the pianist, who let the music trail off gently. She stood at the podium and adjusted the microphone. Silence filled the atrium, silence broken only by the sounds of people quietly crying or trying valiantly not to cry.

The white-haired woman coughed once, then smiled at the hundreds of people gathered there. "You know already Maxine Blake was a very special woman," she began, "to get this many introverts to leave their houses."

At the punch line, the crowd laughed, and the heavy blanket of sorrow seemed to momentarily lift.

"It's good to see so many faces here today," the woman continued. "Thank you all for coming. My name is Nancy Kendell, and I've been director here for seventeen years. And yes, if you're wondering, I was named for Nancy Drew. A show of hands, please . . . Do we have any Rainys in the room?"

Rainy didn't hold up her hand, but she saw three other hands go up.

"Mama was a Book Witch reader," Ms. Kendell said. Lots of head nods, more laughter. "Although this is a sad occasion that brings us together, let's all remember that in the midst of our sadness, we are here also to celebrate Maxine Blake and her stories. Before I turn the mic over to our special guests, I want to share some numbers with you. And don't be afraid. These are not math problems."

Ms. Kendell pulled a piece of paper from her pocket, then placed her reading glasses on her nose.

"The numbers are . . . one hundred seventy-two, ninety-six, seventy-eight, one hundred eighty-eight. Those," she continued, "are the numbers of holds on the first four Book Witch novels at this branch of the library. Almost five hundred total holds in our community. For books that are fifty years old. That tells me two things. One—we need to order more copies of those books." More laughter rippled through the atrium. "And two—Luigi Pirandello was right in his play *Six Characters in Search of an Author* when he wrote, *The writer, the man, the instrument of the creation will die, but his creation does not die.*"

No one laughed then. Not even a giggle.

"Now let me introduce our first guest. And I know many of you are big fans of her books too, so if you need to applaud, go ahead. Nothing would be more fitting. It is my great honor to introduce the Edgar Award–winning author of the Skulls & Skullduggery series, Jessa Charming."

The crowd applauded, a few even cheered, and Rainy joined in. The woman came to the podium and shook Ms. Kendell's hand.

Rainy studied her. Dressed up, Jessa Charming was pretty in a bookish way, although she didn't look particularly comfortable in her dark gray pantsuit and high heels.

"Don't be fooled by the outfit," Jessa Charming said. "I had to buy this since I was told yoga pants were unacceptable attire for a funeral."

The crowd laughed again.

"Although, considering it's a writer's funeral, maybe it would've been all right? Anthony?" Jessa glanced over at him, pale and silent in his somber black suit.

"Too formal. Try sweatpants," he called back. Another soft ripple of laughter.

Even from the back of the atrium, Rainy could see that despite the joke, Anthony was struggling. He sat stiffly and his clothes looked large on him, like he'd lost too much weight too quickly. But still, he carried on, sitting up straight and doing his best to keep it together, though, she imagined, he was ready to fall apart.

Jessa continued her eulogy.

"Some of you know I dedicated my first book to Rainy March," she said. "When I turned fifteen, I was going through a hard time. My grandmother, who was always trying to get me off my phone, gave me a book called *My Buttered Toast Waits for Nobody.* If you haven't read it, it's about Rainy March's adventures in *The Woman in White,* the famous mystery novel by Wilkie Collins. Maybe because it rained—a gift from Rainy?—that weekend and I had a cold, I was bored enough to try reading the stupid book, if only to make my sweet grandmother happy. And a funny thing happened. I enjoyed the book—a lot. A lot more than I expected to. I blinked and I was already on page one hundred. But then . . . when I finished the book, I realized I kind of wanted to read *The Woman in White.* Women kidnapped and forced into asylums? A ghostly figure walking around in all white? Sign me up. I told Grandma I was a little curious about it, and she gleefully ordered a copy to be delivered to my house. And so two days later, a brick landed on my doorstep."

Another laugh, which Rainy didn't understand. *The Woman in White* was nearly eight hundred pages long. Calling it a brick wasn't a joke at all but a fair and accurate description.

"I was this close to returning it," Jessa said. "Or keeping it and reading the Spark Notes. But Rainy March had whetted my appetite. I started reading it. Try to imagine convincing any fifteen-year-old to read an eight-hundred-page novel published in 1860. Miracle, right? But Rainy March had done it. And the crazy thing was . . . I read the whole book. Took a week, but I did it. And I loved it. My first Gothic mystery novel. Now I write them. Maxine Blake created Rainy March, but Rainy March created Jessa Charming. Literally, I mean, and I'm using 'literally' literally since I have a feeling Maxine is listening. My pen name, Charming, is an anagram of Marching."

A soft ripple of delight passed through the crowd.

"For her entire career, Maxine was a fierce advocate for books and the freedom to read. She said many times that those who loved books and those who wanted to ban them have one single thing in common—we all believe reading a book can change you. It's only that the book banners consider this a bug, and Maxine—and likely everyone in this room—sees it as a feature."

After another round of applause, Jessa continued.

"I'm sure nearly everyone here was changed by one of Maxine's books. Did anyone here, like me, become a writer because you were inspired by a Book Witch story? Raise your hand, please."

Rainy was astonished when six hands shot up.

"Wow," Jessa said. "Let's try another. If you became a librarian or an English teacher because of the Book Witch series . . . please raise your hand."

Fifty hands or more shot into the air. Rainy gasped softly to herself.

"Amazing," Jessa breathed. "Okay, hands down. Let's do one more. And let's get loud. If you read a book you were too scared to read until Rainy March convinced you to try it . . . please stand up."

Everyone, all three hundred or more people gathered in that library, stood. When everyone standing realized everyone else was standing, they all applauded, cheered, laughed.

Jessa gazed out onto the assembly and nodded her approval.

"I hope you're seeing this, Maxine," she said, glancing up to the heavens. "I hope you're seeing this, Rainy."

Rainy whispered, "I am."

JESSA CHARMING FINISHED HER EULOGY, AND THEN NANCY KENdell returned to the podium.

"Thank you, Jessa. Now, before our last speaker, I have a special announcement. Before her passing, Maxine Blake and her husband, Anthony, began work on a very special project, called the Pilcrow House for Young Writers. Currently under construction, Pilcrow House will be a haven for underrepresented writers of fiction from diverse backgrounds to live and work in community. The residencies will range from one to six months, and all writers will receive full stipends to cover all living expenses. Pilcrow House will open to its first writers in May of 2026."

Rainy clapped along with the crowd, though her stomach sank at the thought of all those guests in her house. She made a mental note to warn Mrs. Turner they were going to need more towels, when she suddenly remembered . . . they weren't actually talking about her Pilcrow House. Her house didn't exist here.

Ms. Kendell raised her hands to bring silence and order back to the assembly.

"I'm very grateful . . . deeply, deeply grateful," she said, putting her hand over her heart, "to have, as our final speaker today, Anthony Blake. Anthony," she said, turning her head to address him directly while still speaking into the microphone. "I do not envy you this task."

The assembly applauded again.

"For those who don't know, Anthony and Maxine had been married for over forty years at the time of her passing. In a 2000 interview in *Writers & Poets* magazine, Maxine said of Anthony, '*Behind every writer is someone reminding her that she can't live on coffee and Oreos and maybe it's time to stand up and stretch, and while she's at it, take a shower. But Anthony isn't just my husband, he's my muse. Listen to him talk for five words and you'll know exactly where the Duke of Chicago came from. Except Anthony's even more romantic and handsomer. But don't tell him I said that.*' Oops," Nancy said to soft laughter. "I guess we were supposed to keep that a secret from you, Anthony."

Nancy stepped back as Maxine's husband rose slowly from his chair. The atrium echoed with the deep and pregnant silence of several hundred people trying not to cough or sneeze as a man, pale and fragile in his grief, walked to the podium.

Rainy looked for Duke in his features. They were both tall with broad shoulders, but other than that, she didn't see much of a resemblance.

"Thank you so very much for being here today," Anthony began. There it was. He and Duke spoke in the same voice, the same rather proper English accent. "Maxine and I were afforded the rare luxury of a long and gentle passing into the next chapter, as my wife called dying. We had time to make plans, and the first thing she told me was that she wanted her funeral held at the library. This was a sacred place to her, a home to all books, holy and unholy. That was her first request. Her second was to be cremated. She said some of the greatest stories ever told had been consigned to fires—Savonarola's *Bonfire of the Vanities* in 1497, Hitler's purges of supposedly subversive art and books in the 1930s, the burning of comic books in the 1940s and '50s, not to mention the burning of the Library of Alexandria in 48 B.C.—and she wished to share their fate."

His voice trailed off. Rainy caught herself holding her breath.

"Friends and family will gather at Santa Barbara Cemetery to inter her ashes at sunset this evening. Starting tomorrow, tributes may be left at her final resting place."

Rainy forced herself to exhale. Surely that was the end of his remarks. His voice shook with emotion and his shoulders were hunched. But somehow, he dug deep into himself and found the strength to go on. He took a breath, stood up straight, and in a steady voice said, "I'd like to tell you a story Maxine told me once, a story I will tell now and never again.

"Maxine liked to call herself a classic orphan," Anthony began, and the crowd laughed again, but quietly, nervously. Where was this going?

"A good old-fashioned orphan of the Dickensian persuasion. She was born in a small town near Chicago—"

Chicago. Rainy thought of Duke. That's where he came from . . . from Maxine's childhood.

"And her father, who worked on the railroad, died in a work-related accident. An explosion. That happened a lot back then. Her mother died a few years later of complications from pneumonia. Which . . . also happened a lot back then. No family stepped forward to take her, so Maxine, age nine, was sent to an orphanage in Chicago. St. Sophia's Home for Girls. It was a crowded, dank warehouse sort of place. I've seen the pictures. Six girls to a room. Harsh discipline. Inadequate nutrition. But at least the place had a small library."

He paused, then lifted his head. "The girls were mostly shell-shocked, angry, traumatized, violent. Some were orphans like her. Some had been taken away from parents who'd hurt them. Maxine was a quiet child, frightened all the time, not good at talking. She told me her loneliness was like a black hole. Only books could fill it because books were infinite. She could imagine herself on an infinite number of adventures with Nancy Drew or the Bobbsey Twins or Dorothy in Oz or Alice in Wonderland. She said she was lucky that place had a library. If it hadn't had books, she would've had nothing to live for. Some days she only ate the slop they served because the more obedient she was, the more library time she was given."

Anthony cleared his throat, then began to speak again.

"It's hard to think about her in that place," he said. He took a breath, then went on. "Maxine would often hide under her bed with her school notebook. She'd write stories where she and Nancy Drew solved crimes together, or she was invited to move in with the Bobbsey family and spend Christmas with them. It was her school notebook, a plain black composition notebook, so everyone assumed she was doing homework, not writing stories. All her life she used those notebooks for her books. I used to find them stuffed between the couch cushions."

He paused again, cleared his throat again.

"Very sorry," he said, then, like the good Englishman he was, kept calm and carried on. "One day, one of the little girls at St. Sophia's came home from school with a fever and a rash. Chicken pox, they thought, but no. It was scarlet fever. The girl, Rosa, was given antibiotics and quarantined in a room of her own far from the other girls. A nurse would check on her twice a day, but otherwise she was left completely alone. She'd never been alone in her life. Maxine said she'd wake up to the sound of the girl crying for her mama, her papa, her sister, her dog. Maxine didn't even know if she'd ever had a dog or if she was delirious and dreaming of her perfect life. All the girls were forbidden from going anywhere near the child. Understandably, but still Maxine would lie awake listening to Rosa's cries."

Anthony paused again, squaring his shoulders.

"Three nights into her illness, Maxine said the rumors started that Rosa wasn't going to make it. One girl said she'd overheard from another girl that Rosa would beg the nurse to read her a story every time she came in, but the nurse wouldn't stay a second longer than she had to, the disease was so contagious and deadly. The girls went to sleep, all except for Maxine." Anthony sniffed, wiped his nose. "Finally, Maxine couldn't stand it anymore. She got out of bed. She always kept a

Nancy Drew book under her pillow for emergencies. 'Where are you going?' one of the girls asked as Maxine opened the door. 'Bathroom,' she said. 'With a book?' the girl asked. And Maxine said, 'It's number two.' "

The crowd's laughter rose, then faded, and Anthony continued on.

"But she didn't go to the bathroom. Maxine took her Nancy Drew book down the hall and snuck into Rosa's bedroom. The girl was barely recognizable under the horrific red rash that covered her face. She looked like she'd been stung by a thousand bees or rubbed with sandpaper. But under the redness, the child looked gray, almost ashen. Rosa opened her eyes and asked, 'Who are you?' And Maxine answered, 'Special story hour.' The book was *The Moonstone Castle Mystery.* Maxine started at chapter one and read to the girl all night, read to her even after Rosa went still with sleep, even after Maxine realized she wasn't sleeping. Good company in a final hour, I think," he said. "Nancy Drew and Maxine Blake. Of course, Maxine caught Rosa's illness. She was sick for nearly a month as scarlet fever became rheumatic fever, which caused permanent damage to her heart. Maxine might still be alive today if she hadn't gone into that child's sickroom and stayed long enough to read half a Nancy Drew book to her. But then Maxine Blake wouldn't be Maxine Blake if she hadn't read that last bedtime story to a dying child."

He took another labored breath, then smiled at them all.

"Maxine's favorite poet was the great Emily Dickinson. I will give Emily the final words . . . *If I can stop one Heart from breaking / I shall not—*"

His voice broke and he couldn't finish the sentence.

"Forgive me," he rasped, then tried again. "*If I can stop one Heart from breaking / I shall not . . .*"

Rainy raised her voice and completed the quotation for him.

"*. . . live in vain.*"

CHAPTER TWENTY-NINE

The pianist began to play again, a piece everyone in the room—and the world—recognized. A slow, contemplative version of "Over the Rainbow" from *The Wizard of Oz*.

Tears flowed freely when four librarians gathered in front, not in mourning black but in their cardigans and T-shirts or polo shirts with the Santa Barbara Public Library orange poppy logo. They said nothing, made no announcements, but everyone at once seemed to understand who they were and why they were there.

For Maxine Blake, there would be no elegant men in dark suits to act as pallbearers. Not her style. Librarians in their everyday work clothes and comfortable sneakers and eyeglasses that needed a good cleaning . . . they would be her pallbearers.

Since she had been cremated, there was only the urn, which was actually just a plain wooden box that a male librarian held somberly in front of him. The three other honorary pallbearers carried other things. One librarian had a photo of Maxine from her younger years, proudly holding a copy of her first published book and kissing the spine. Another librarian had a stack of Maxine's books. The final librarian carried a composition notebook and a pen.

The four stood by the stage, silently bearing symbols of Maxine Blake's life's work.

The crowd was allowed to file past the four librarians. As Rainy walked by, she could see that the objects they held weren't symbolic but, in fact, very real. The photograph wasn't a copy but a faded original in a cheap frame, likely the only one Maxine could afford in her early days as a writer. The books weren't published copies but printed and bound manuscripts covered in editor's marks, including penciled-in pilcrows, since Maxine had a terrible tendency toward too-long paragraphs.

The notebook too had yellowed pages. They'd laid it open to the middle, displaying Maxine's own handwriting, and the pen was a simple pink plastic ballpoint from a local bank with the clip broken off.

Someone touched the pages tentatively, as if fearing they'd be scolded, but it was allowed. And then everyone after her touched Maxine's handwriting.

"Hurry," Frankie whispered into Rainy's ear. "Grab your umbrella."

Rainy did as she was told, though she didn't understand why. All the gathered filed quickly and quietly out of the atrium and walked swiftly through the library.

"This way," the woman said. "We're on the left."

Again Rainy did as she was told, still not knowing why, but it seemed a procession was being formed. She followed Frankie into an open courtyard alongside the library, where two groups of mourners, one on the left and one on the right, created a center path to the waiting limousine.

A woman who seemed to be the ringleader ran up and down the path, whispering orders. "Wait until the doors open and they all come out," Rainy heard the woman say. "Go at the whistle."

Moments later, a couple of wide-eyed library pages opened the double front doors.

The pallbearers came out in a line, followed by the library director, then Jessa Charming, then finally Anthony.

The funeral party started forward.

Someone blew a whistle.

At that signal, hundreds of black umbrellas all opened at once. The whoosh and click were nearly deafening, a crashing ocean wave of sound.

Rainy, caught off-guard, could only watch in silent awe. Frankie nudged her gently. Finally, she opened her own umbrella and raised it over her head.

Anthony stared at the tribute, his hand on his heart.

Then he nodded his gratitude. He and the funeral party walked down the path of the honor guard to the waiting limousine.

As Anthony passed Rainy, she smiled at him. He glanced at her, then started slightly.

As if Maxine had written the right words into her DNA, Rainy whispered to him, "She told me to tell you that you were her favorite story."

The shock on his face passed quickly.

"Better come with me," he said.

Rainy whispered a quick goodbye to Frankie, then stepped out of the line and followed him to the limousine.

She closed her umbrella as he opened the door for her.

At the car, he paused and turned to face the crowd. "If you all care to honor Maxine . . . find someone who needs a story and read it to them."

Then he got inside, and the driver shut the door behind him.

When they were alone in the back of the limousine, Anthony looked at her. She sat on the bench seat opposite him, her back to the closed partition.

"So . . ." he said. "It's you."

"It's me," she said. "Hi."

He took a deep breath. "It worked, I see."

"It worked."

He reached across the small space and held out his hand.

"Pleasure to finally meet you," he said. "The other woman."

She laughed and shook his hand.

"She loved you more," Rainy said.

"How do you know?"

"Her last thoughts were of you."

"Were they?" He sounded doubtful.

"I was there," Rainy said. "You were her happy ever after."

He laughed softly and sat back in his seat.

Something almost like a smile passed across his face.

"How long have you been here?" he asked.

"I arrived right before the funeral started."

"The first character to ever attend her author's funeral," he said. "I assume."

He laughed again, but quickly the laugh turned to a single sob.

"Sorry," he whispered, coughing.

"Don't be," Rainy said. "I'm glad I came. It was wonderful to see how loved she was. To me, all this time, she's been this invisible tormentor. I might want to smack her around, but her readers obviously loved her."

"There were a few dozen people in that entire place who'd actually met Maxine in person, only five or six who could call her a friend. You understand that, don't you? All those people weren't there because they loved Maxine, Rainy. They wouldn't be able to pick her out of a police lineup. It's *you* they love."

AS THEY DROVE TO THE CEMETERY, RAINY WATCHED THE WORLD pass outside. She didn't want to intrude on Anthony's grief, though she still had a thousand questions to ask him. Lost as he was in his own suffering, she was shocked when he spoke up again.

"It's very strange," he said, "not knowing what you're thinking."

"What do you mean?" Rainy asked.

"I know you only in the first person. Thirty-six Book Witch novels times three hundred pages each equals . . ."

"Don't ask me to do math."

"Over ten thousand pages of your thoughts and hopes and dreams and fears. Now you're . . . a blank page," he said.

"Imagine how I feel," she said.

"How do you feel?"

"Warm and dry, for starters. There's so much sunlight here. Do you ever get used to it?"

"Yes," he said. "I'll take it over London in February any day."

"Or Fort Meriwether," she said, smiling. "I mean . . . *Astoria.*" She scoffed. "Ridiculous name."

"Don't complain. They host a Rainy March Book Fair every March in your honor."

"Really?" She blushed. "A book fair for me?"

"We used to go there every year when Maxine was feeling up to it. We would've lived there except Maxine's health was too fragile for those brutal winters."

"So why did she set my stories there then?"

"She'd visited once when she was younger. In the off-season. March. She didn't realize how wet it would be, but she said it was the best trip of her life. She stayed inside and read the whole time. A weather reporter said something on the radio about it being a particularly 'rainy March.' And that's where your name came from."

"I knew it! I *was* named after a weather report!" She winced and looked at him. "Sorry. Got excited there."

He gave a little laugh. "I'm sitting in the back of a limousine with a fictional character."

"I'm sitting in the back of a limousine with the husband of my writer," she said. "Crazy. Any theories on how this is happening?"

"I have one, but you might not believe me," he said.

"Anthony," she said, pursing her lips at him, "I fought Dracula."

"All right, perhaps you will believe me." He took a long breath. "Once, Maxine did a good deed. A deed so good, so brave, so self-sacrificial that the entire universe took notice."

"Rosa," Rainy said. "Reading the Nancy Drew book to Rosa when she was dying."

"That was only the first part of the story. There's more."

He took a ragged breath and Rainy almost stopped him. Talking about Maxine was so clearly agony for him, like walking on glass, the broken glass that had once been their life together.

"If you don't want to talk about her—"

"I've seen people lose loved ones before," he said. "The day will come when I'll want to talk about her, and no one will be willing to listen. If you'll listen, I'll tell you."

"I'll listen."

He sat back in his seat and glanced out the window, as if it were easier to speak without making eye contact.

"Maxine was sick for weeks. What was worse, of course, was . . . Well, you've read *The Velveteen Rabbit*. You know what happens when a child has scarlet fever, what happens to their toys, their clothes . . . their books."

"They burned her books?" Rainy asked.

Anthony nodded. "They had to. She stood at the window and watched them make a bonfire in a bin in the back garden. In went her clothes. In went her sheets. In went Nancy Drew and *The Secret of the Old Clock.* In went her composition notebook and all the little stories Maxine had written starring her and Nancy Drew together."

"No wonder Maxine was so upset by book burnings. It had happened to her."

"I think it took some of her will to live. She got much, much worse after that. They finally took her to the hospital. The girls at St. Sophia's pooled their few nickels and pennies and bought her a get-well gift. A used, falling-apart copy of *The Secret of the Old Clock.* You would've thought it was a teddy bear. Maxine slept with it under her pillow."

He cleared his throat.

"One night," he continued, "Maxine woke up. A girl with blond hair wearing a blue dress with a matching hat stood by her bed."

"Nancy Drew?" Rainy breathed.

"The very one. Maxine's hero, her favorite character, her best friend. She told Maxine she had a surprise for her. She worked a little magic, and suddenly the used copy of the book became a nice brand-new copy. She told Maxine to get better so they could share more adventures together. It worked. Maxine got better. When she told me that, I thought she'd dreamed it but . . . well, now I think that Maxine simply loved Nancy Drew into existence."

"I always thought only Book Witches could do that," Rainy said. "Was Maxine a Book Witch?"

"I would say so," Anthony said. "In her own way. As much as Maxine loved Nancy, Nancy loved her back. As you know . . . that does happen sometimes."

Rainy thought of Duke in Pilcrow House, waiting between the end of one chapter and the beginning of the next, waiting for her forever.

Anthony started to say something else to her, but the limousine suddenly slowed. It turned into a parking lot and then onto a winding path through the cemetery.

"There will be people here who knew Maxine," Anthony said. "I'll tell them you're my niece, if they ask. But you better come up with a fake name."

"Right," she said. "Of course. I'll be Sunny August."

He glared at her.

"Joking," Rainy said.

"You get that from her, you know?"

"The resilience to smile in the face of tragedy?"

"An obnoxious sense of humor."

"Jessa Charming will be there, won't she?" Rainy asked.

"She will."

"Good, I need to have a little chat with her."

The driver parked and opened the door. Anthony got out first and then helped Rainy out of the low-slung limo. He took a ragged breath. "Let's get this over with."

A few men and women in dark suits waited for them at the top of a gentle hill. Anthony didn't seem to be in any hurry to reach them. They walked up the sloping path to a marble monument with two small doors, side by side. One had Maxine's name on it, and the other was blank, though in time, it would bear Anthony's name. Rainy noted that on other graves there were crosses or Stars of David or crescents and stars. But Maxine had chosen the pilcrow symbol.

Death, she seemed to be saying, was only another new beginning.

Two of the men in suits wore name tags indicating they worked for the cemetery. Everyone else—a dozen or so men and women—greeted Anthony with careful hugs and firm handshakes, hearty pats on the back, and promises of "anything you need, please let us know."

One of the men with a name tag spoke softly but clearly. "Ms. Blake didn't want formalities at her graveside service. If anyone would like to say anything before the interment, please feel free."

"Please," Anthony said. "Anyone but me."

A long, tense silence followed. Everyone was too grief-stricken or scared to speak.

Even Jessa Charming opened her mouth, then closed it again.

But Rainy knew exactly how to say goodbye.

She looked at the little mausoleum, smiled, and said Maxine's two favorite words.

"Pencils down."

CHAPTER THIRTY

After the men in suits placed the wooden box holding Maxine's ashes in the marble chamber, Rainy and the other mourners drifted away to let Anthony have a moment alone at his wife's final resting place.

Rainy couldn't imagine a lovelier place to spend eternity. The cemetery overlooked the ocean. She walked right to the edge of a cliff and saw the beach below and then the endless expanse of sea and sky. The sun had started to set, turning blood red as it sank lazily toward the horizon.

And there, at the fence that overlooked the beach, stood Jessa Charming, all alone, like the heroine of a women's novel searching the water for answers to questions she didn't even know how to ask yet.

Game time.

Rainy took a deep breath, then walked over.

Jessa's eyes widened as Rainy approached.

"Good cosplay," Jessa said as she wiped her face with a wad of tissues.

"It's not a costume," Rainy said. "This is how I dress."

"You dress just like Rainy March?"

"I *am* Rainy March."

Jessa turned to her, took a step back, and nearly tripped, but Rainy caught her by the arm and righted her.

"Finish the story," Rainy said. The words came out a little harsher than she'd intended, so she quickly added, "Please?"

Jessa looked at Rainy's hand on her arm, then her face. She pulled away, her mouth open.

"It *is* you. How?"

Rainy grimaced. "Can we skip all the explaining? It's magic. The end."

"At least tell me why you're here before I pass out."

"Maxine sent me. She wants you to finish the book. *The March Hare Mystery.* And don't pass out. I need you to get me back to Duke."

"You know about the book?"

"Know it? I lived it. And I'd like to know the ending, but I won't until you write it."

"I . . . can't."

"Can't? Or won't?"

"Both?" Jessa offered, wincing.

"Not good enough. Get to writing, please. Maybe I have some paper on me." Rainy dug around in her pockets. "No paper. Darn. You have a phone. Start writing on your phone."

"That's not how it works," Jessa said.

"Writing doesn't work by . . . writing?"

"Okay, fine, it does," Jessa admitted. "But you don't understand. I loved your books. I loved Maxine. I've been reading them since I was fifteen years old. I've read every story at least three times."

"Great. You sound supremely qualified to finish the book."

Jessa shook her head, turned her gaze back to the ocean. "I think I'm hallucinating, but I'm going to go with it for the time being."

Rainy nodded. "That's the spirit. Now tell me why you can't finish my book."

"When I was fifteen, sixteen . . . I wanted to be you. When I was eighteen, nineteen, twenty . . . I wanted to be Maxine."

"You wanted to be a writer."

"No, I wanted to be Maxine Blake. I wanted to be the author of *your* books."

"Now's your chance. Really, Jessa, I'm not seeing the problem here."

"I can't," she said again. "Don't you get it? Maxine is my hero, my idol. How could I begin to fill shoes that big?"

"Oh, please, she wore a size seven. Your feet are at least nines."

Jessa looked down at her shoes. "I'm tall, okay. I need a larger surface area for balance."

"And there's no reason to idolize Maxine. I met her. She wasn't perfect. She loved her husband but neglected her marriage to write. She doubted herself constantly. She probably sped up her own death by taking up writing again after she was supposed to retire and rest. She put on her granny pants one leg at a time, trust me."

"You're one to talk. You think your mother was the perfect Book Witch."

"She was."

"Ha," Jessa said.

"Ha?" Rainy asked.

"Ha!" Jessa exclaimed.

"Why are you ha-ing at me?"

"You really are clueless if you haven't put two and two together about your mother," Jessa said. "And if you didn't idolize her so much and think she was flawless, you wouldn't even need me to finish the book. You would have figured it out by the end of Act One."

"I don't even know when that is! Do you think I see the act breaks floating in the air like confused bumblebees?" Rainy waved her hand to indicate little word clouds dancing above her eyes. "It doesn't work like that, Jessa."

"It's after the 'Find the March Hare' phone call from your grandfather."

"You obviously know how the story ends. You know more than I do. I have a fairly good idea who the March Hare is, although what that has to do with my mother, I still don't know."

"I can tell you," Jessa said. "I can tell you everything."

Rainy narrowed her eyes at her and said slowly, threateningly, and in no uncertain terms, "Write . . . it . . . down."

"You are so annoying," Jessa said. "I can't believe I wanted to be you."

"I hop in and out of books and hang out with fictional characters.

I've been to Narnia. I've been to Middle-earth. I've been to Camelot. I've been to Mars, *sweetheart.* The last time I was on a beach looking at the ocean was with Elizabeth Freaking Bennet, okay? Everybody should want to be me." Rainy paused, rethought a few things. "Apart from the dead mother. Nobody wants that. Almost nobody, I mean. I've read *Carrie.*"

"My mother's alive," Jessa said.

"No need to rub it in."

"But my parents divorced when I was a freshman in high school."

Rainy's heart dropped. "Oh, Jessa, I'm sorry. That's the hard time you mentioned in your speech?"

"'Hard time' was a euphemism for 'the worst time of my entire life.' Probably why I wanted to be you. I was metaphorically living in books while you were literally living in books." Jessa looked up at the sky. "And now I'm arguing with you at Maxine Blake's funeral. I am having a nervous breakdown."

"Later. Finish the book first."

Jessa laughed. She shook her head and sighed. "I'm not Maxine," she said to Rainy. "I'll never be her."

"Good, because she's gone. And you're here. And here always beats not here. Jessa, I need you. I need a writer. I'm not saying you have to write a trillion more of my books, but at least finish this one so I know . . . I know what my mother was trying to tell me."

Jessa sighed. "Her message to you is pretty good."

"Maybe if we went down to the beach, you could write on the sand," Rainy suggested.

Jessa pulled her hands through her red hair and shook her head. "I don't know, Rainy . . . I mean, I don't even know if I believe this is actually happening."

Rainy felt her happy ending beginning to slip away.

What could she say to make Jessa understand how much she needed her?

"There's a fun scene in *Through the Looking-Glass,*" Rainy said, "where Alice meets the unicorn. You know it?"

"Of course I know it."

"Alice is shocked because she didn't believe in unicorns, and the unicorn is shocked because he never believed in little girls. So the unicorn says to Alice . . . '*Well, now that we have seen each other, . . . if you'll believe in me, I'll believe in you.*' So, Jessa Charming . . . if you believe in me, I'll believe in you. Deal?"

"Rainy March believes in me?"

"I believe in you."

Jessa lowered her chin to her chest and took a breath. "A week before she died, Maxine called me, asked me again to consider carrying on the series after she was gone. You know what I told her?"

"Whatever you said, it probably killed her."

Jessa glared at her. "I said, only if Rainy March herself shows up and tells me to do it. And you know what she said?"

"She said don't be surprised if I show up."

"How did you know?"

"I guess you could say we shared a brain. I don't know everything about her, but I know this much—she believed in you too. Otherwise she wouldn't have asked."

"It's a big ask," Jessa said.

"Come on, don't make me employ Plan C."

"Plan C? Oh, right. Crying." Jessa took a deep breath. "What if I finish the book, and it's bad?"

"Let me ask you this. Would you rather have bad pizza or no pizza at all? Or bad coffee or no coffee at all? Or . . ." Rainy waved her hand toward the cemetery, all the graves, not empty but occupied. "Would you rather have a bad day or no more days at all?"

Jessa pointed at Rainy. "You fight dirty."

"I fight to win. Come on, Charming, it's not Shakespeare. Slap a happy ending on it and call it a day."

"Slap a happy ending on it? Do you think that's how it works?"

"You're the writer, not me." Rainy put her hands on Jessa's shoulders. "Have you seen Duke in person?"

"No, of course not."

"I have. And whatever you're imagining . . . it's even better."

Rainy hoped this line of argument would work. She was running out of ways to beg.

Jessa nodded. "It was fun to finally read how you and Duke met," she said. "Maxine had been teasing readers with that story for sixteen books. Shame if no one else gets to read it."

Rainy started. "Wait a minute. My case files are my stories?"

"Is that a bad thing?" Jessa asked.

"A little, yeah. Those case files are my journals! Do you want people reading *your* journals? I wrote them for posterity, to record the glorious history of the Book Witches, not for public consumption."

"First of all, *no*," Jessa said as if she were talking to a child. "You didn't write them. You only think you wrote them. Maxine Blake wrote them. And second of all . . . there is no second point. You are a fictional character. Your journals are published works of fiction. Get used to it."

"It's a little embarrassing. There's personal stuff in there."

"I would never embarrass you."

Rainy narrowed her eyes at Jessa. "You mean . . . when you're writing my book?"

Jessa threw her hands in the air. "Fine! I'll do it!"

Rainy exhaled with relief, then held out her right hand to shake. Jessa took it, held it.

"Thank you. Please start right now," Rainy said.

"If we were in your story world, you could look into my heart with your magic and see how much your books meant to me over the years. I won't pretend they saved my life, but they did help me find myself."

"I don't need to see in your heart," Rainy said.

"You can see it in my eyes?"

"You're holding my hand so tight I'm losing circulation."

Jessa laughed. "How about a hug?"

"I can do a hug."

Rainy stepped in and embraced Jessa gently. "Don't forget to feed Koshka," Rainy told her. "Maxine said she was always forgetting to write him into scenes."

"I won't forget." Jessa let go first and stepped back, took a breath and nodded. "Is this where we say goodbye?"

"I don't say goodbye," Rainy said. "I say, 'Our revels now are ended.' Now please write the ending of my book. I need my grandfather back, and I want to see if my hunch was right."

"I do have a notebook with me. I always do."

"Thank you, Jessa. I'll never forget you. Oh, wait. I will forget you. Won't I?"

"You'll definitely forget me," Jessa said. "I'll make sure of it."

"That's disappointing. I was hoping to remember I was a fictional character when I'm back in my book. It would help with my stress levels."

"Oh, don't worry about that," she said with a mysterious grin. Then she sighed. "I won't forget you, Rainy. Ever."

Rainy took one last long look around. "Nice world you have here. I like mine better, though. So let's, you know . . ." She wiggled her fingers in the air, miming fast typing.

"I'm doing it. I'm doing it," Jessa said. "Wish me luck."

But Rainy didn't wish her luck. Instead she said, "Pencils up."

Rainy walked over to Anthony, who was waiting by the limousine. She gave him a big thumbs-up.

"She said yes?" Anthony asked. "That's a relief. For you at least."

"You all right with her finishing the story?"

He paused before answering. "Your books took her away from me. But then again, they bought our house."

Rainy took his hand, squeezed it gently before letting go.

"I'm at peace with it," he said. "It's what Maxine wanted."

Rainy rose on her tiptoes and kissed Anthony on the cheek. "Thanks for taking such good care of my writer."

"It was odd to meet you but rather nice," he said. "I'm glad Maxine was able to bring you here."

"Me too," she said. Jessa had her steno pad out of her bag, ready to begin writing. "But do you ever wonder . . . I mean, how do *you* know you're not in a . . ."

Rainy stopped speaking as a black SUV pulled up. A strikingly handsome man carrying a bouquet of roses got out, glanced around furtively, then approached Maxine's grave. Rainy recognized him at once from the portrait in the Pilcrow House library.

"LeVar Burton!" she shouted.

He turned to wave at her—

BUT RAINY MARCH WAS ALREADY GONE.

Book Five

YOUNG ADULT & HORROR

CHAPTER THIRTY-ONE

"Rainy!"

Duke's voice cut through the fog, pulling me back to reality.

Blinking, I turned away from the mirror and looked up at him. He had me in his arms. Fear gleamed in his dark eyes.

"Oh, thank goodness," he breathed. "I nearly lost you."

"What? What happened?" I asked. I couldn't remember anything from the last few minutes, other than a terrible sense of vertigo, almost as if I'd left the world for a moment.

"You looked at yourself so long in the mirror, you started to fall through it."

"Fall through it?" I looked back into the mirror.

"Literally. Your hand disappeared into it. How did you do that?"

"Lingering side effect of Wonderland, probably. What was I saying?"

"You saw your twin?"

"My twin? Yes! My twin." I grabbed the bunny ears off the marble head of William Shakespeare and perched them on my own head.

"It's Penny," I said. "Penny gave me the white ears. Hers were brown. It was Penny all along."

"Penny?"

I faced Duke. "Yesterday was Mad Hatter Day so she was dressing us all up like characters from *Alice in Wonderland*. Penny was wearing bunny ears. She gave me bunny ears. She joked we were twins. But we're not twins. If my ears are white, and hers are brown, then I'm the White Rabbit, and she's the—"

"—March Hare! Rainy, you did it!"

"*We* did it," I said. "We found her. She's been staring me in the face ever since she arrived. Trying to be my friend. Trying to help me. I don't know how or why, but it's her. Penny Nichols."

Duke's beautiful mouth opened slightly. I grabbed his face and kissed him.

He didn't kiss back.

"What's wrong?" I asked.

"Her name is Penny *Nichols*? That can't be her real name, can it? Poor girl. Anyway, carrying on. We know who our March Hare is finally, but where do we find her?"

"She said she was going back home for a while."

"Where's home then?"

"Uh . . ." I began to pace, trying to piece together every clue she'd given me about her life before she'd moved to Fort Meriwether. "She said she was from the Midwest, a pretty little river town not even on the map."

"That's nonsense. Every town is on the map. Unless . . ."

Duke fell silent and his eyes glazed over. This happened sometimes when he was doing higher-level mystery solving. If I had X-ray vision, I could have probably seen equations and maps and other strange visions floating through his brain as he mentally pieced the puzzle together. I left him in his trance for as long as I could stand it.

"Duke?" I said, snapping my fingers to no avail. "Come back to me. Only one of us gets to go into a fugue state a day."

Koshka nosed his way under Duke's pant leg and gave him a nip in the soft tissue under the ankle bone.

Duke yelped, then blurted out, "Penny isn't the March Hare."

"Yes, she is. She has to be."

"She is, yes, but Penny's not Penny," he said. "Penny Nichols isn't her real name, thank goodness. And yes, the answer has been staring you in the face for years, darling. Years!"

Duke picked up my mother's copy of *The Secret of the Old Clock* and held it in front of my face. I studied the cover I'd been looking at my entire life for some clue as to what Duke was going on about. If Penny wasn't Penny . . . could she be . . .

"Impossible . . ." I breathed.

"Penny said she's from a pretty little Midwest river town not on any map," Duke said. "What town isn't on any map?"

"A town that doesn't exist," I said. "But they don't look anything alike—then again . . ."

"I look nothing like my book covers either."

"I need my umbrella, stat!"

Duke grabbed my umbrella from the coatrack, then scooped Koshka off the floor.

Flipping to chapter one, I found a good sentence: *There was something about a mystery which aroused Nancy's interest, and she was never content until it was solved.*

I grabbed Duke's hand, and then, with a flick of my thumb, we disappeared into the book, becoming the dot on the "i" in the word "which."

IT WAS NIGHT IN RIVER HEIGHTS, U.S.A., WHERE NANCY DREW lived with her father, the noted criminal lawyer Carson Drew.

Duke and I stood on a sidewalk outside a lovely house with white wooden siding and a wraparound porch. A warm golden light glowed from a downstairs window that looked into a living room where a man read his newspaper.

The air smelled like road dust, cut grass, and summer. Fireflies flashed under the trees and across the manicured lawn. Crickets chirped. A cool breeze blew, and the garden roses swayed.

A storybook house in a storybook city in a storybook September.

And once upon a time in that house . . . a storybook romance?

"I should probably go knock on the door," I said, hanging my open umbrella in the branches of the nearest tree, like a giant Christmas ornament.

"We'll wait here," Duke said, hefting Koshka onto his shoulder. "Go on."

"You don't mind?"

"Not at all," he said and kissed my cheek as I patted Koshka's back. "Good luck."

Steeling myself, I walked up to the front door and knocked.

"I'll get it, Dad!" a girl's voice called out.

Then, a few seconds later, the front door opened.

A girl with bobbed blond hair dressed in blue.

"You don't look like your cover picture, Penny," I chided her.

She shrugged. "We both know characters never look like they do on the cover. Cover artists, am I right? Come in, please, Rainy. And from now on . . . unless I'm undercover, call me Nancy."

Once we were inside, Penny, who was, of course, actually Nancy Drew herself, put a finger over her lips to warn me to keep quiet for the time being.

"Who is it, Nancy?" a man's voice called from another room.

"A friend, Dad," Nancy called back. "Be there in a minute!"

She waved her hand at me to follow her into the kitchen. She turned a switch, and a gas light slowly began to brighten overhead.

"Pie?" she said. "It's cherry."

"I'm not supposed to eat in books," I said, which was a completely inane thing to say while standing in Nancy Drew's house and having a mild out-of-body experience.

She grinned broadly as she cut two slices. "I think *you*, of all people, can bend the rules," she said.

She set a big slice of cherry pie in front of me, and it did look tempting.

"What do you know?" Nancy asked me as she took a bite of her pie. "Then I can tell you what you don't know."

"I think . . . I think I know this is where my mother was during that year she was missing."

Nancy nodded. "Yes, she was. Keep going."

"And if she was here and she came home pregnant with me . . ."

"So close," Nancy said, grinning madly, eyes wide. "It's staring you in the face again."

I kept going as the answer dawned on me. ". . . and she left me your book and nothing but your book for a reason . . ."

"Go on, say it, Rainy."

It sounded laughable in my own head. Impossible. Unbelievable.

Though my heart was beating in my throat, I whispered the question.

"Are you . . . are you my sister?"

She grinned and leaned forward. "About time you figured that out."

"And your father is my . . . I'm going to faint."

"Don't faint," Nancy said. "The pie will go to waste. Go on. Eat some. You'll feel better."

It's almost impossible to say no to Nancy Drew. So I picked up my fork, chopped off the triangle tip of the pie slice, and took a bite.

Pure sweetness and heaven. I swallowed and the dizziness cleared and my eyes focused and all the tension left my body.

"I do feel better," I said. "They tell us not to eat here. It's fairy-tale rules."

"That rule is for people," she said. "Humans in fairylands. Even if this is a fairyland . . . you're half fairy." She winked at me and took another bite of her own pie.

"So my mother . . . and your father? How did that happen?" My mouth fell open at the very idea of it. And since my mouth was already conveniently open, I shoved more pie into it.

"Oh, it was an adventure," she said with gleaming eyes. "I was out driving in my blue roadster when a strange man started pursuing me, even hitting my back bumper. He wanted to make me crash. I didn't know at the time who or what he was, but now I know he was a Burner. Then it seemed like this woman appeared out of nowhere. Literally winked into existence to help me. In the rearview mirror, I saw her run into the road to stop him. He swerved, and she jumped out of the way, but she landed so hard, she was knocked unconscious."

"My mother jumped in front of a car? Sounds like her."

"You can imagine my surprise," Nancy said. "The marshal arrived, but the driver had vanished into thin air, it seemed. They brought your mother to our house so the doctor could see to her. Hannah, that's our housekeeper—"

"I know who Hannah is," I said. "Who doesn't?"

"Hannah gave your mother some water."

"Oh, no."

"And when she woke up . . . she had no idea how she'd gotten there. We assumed it was amnesia from her head injury, not because—"

"She drank fairyland water," I said.

Nancy nodded.

"We nursed her back to health for the next month. She was weak after her injury, but she could talk. I sat by her bedside for hours, reading with her and telling her about our life, trying to help her remember hers. She only knew her name—Ellery March—because it was on her library card in her pocket. Otherwise . . . she was a mystery."

"And Nancy Drew can't resist a mystery."

"Never! And, it turned out, my father couldn't resist your mother. The longer she stayed with us, the closer they grew. Of course they fell in love." She sighed as if recalling one of her happiest memories. "They were married on the lawn. I was maid of honor. Then I had to go and ruin it."

"How?"

"I'm a fictional sleuth," Nancy said. "We always solve every mystery. Eventually, I put the pieces together and realized, well, everything. Your mother was real. We were fictional. This was a story we were in, not the real world. I even found her umbrella still in the woods, open, so no one had spotted her in my story. When I told her everything I'd discovered, it all came rushing back. But by then, she was eight months pregnant with you."

"That's why she finally left? Because she remembered who she was?"

"It was only supposed to be a short visit," Nancy said. "She needed to see her parents and let them know she was safe and happy. She promised she would come back in a day or two. She told Dad she was going on a quick shopping trip to the big city for baby things."

"But she never came back," I said.

Nancy put her fork down and glanced away, and for a split second I could see all the grief and loneliness and sorrow that was so deep and wounding that even her authors had hidden it from readers. For one year, she'd had a stepmother who loved her, whom she had loved, and a new sibling on the way.

"No," she said. "She never came back."

CHAPTER THIRTY-TWO

Nancy put on a brave face and carried on. "When your mother left us to go visit her parents," she continued, "she warned me to be on the lookout for a Book Witch who might appear and charm us into forgetting she ever existed. Sure enough, shortly after she left, a woman appeared."

"What did she look like?"

"Like a young Dr. Fanshawe."

My stomach clenched. "I knew it. No, I didn't know it, but I knew she didn't like me."

"Like you or not, she's terrified of you," Nancy said. "Of what you represent. Why do you think she lied all this time about what a perfect, ideal, rule-following toady of a Book Witch your mother was? So you would never ever for even a single second entertain the possibility that you're the daughter of a fictional character."

My mother . . . she hadn't broken one rule. She'd broken all the rules. She hadn't been a follower, but, like Duke had said, a rebel.

"Why is that so terrifying to her?" I asked.

"Because she loves rules, and if you're half-fictional, that means the rules don't apply to you."

I gasped softly. She was right. If Dr. Fanshawe had said it once, she'd said it a thousand times—fictional characters belong in stories and real people belong in the real world.

"I *am* half-fictional, which means I . . . I do belong in books."

"Precisely," Nancy said. "Which means you can stay in any story you want—no rules broken. Which means you can change any story you want. If you want you could even change this one, and no one could stop you."

I could change stories . . . even this one? To test the premise, I glanced in the mirror and suddenly . . . my dark hair turned blond.

With a wink it went from long and straight to short and bobbed.

"Now we're twins," I said, laughing.

"Adorable," Nancy said. "But—"

"One more," I said. I rolled up my sleeve and looked down at the ugly pink burn scar on my forearm. I imagined it gone, and just like that, it was. My forearm looked like it had never been touched by fire.

"Wow," I said. "I *am* dangerous."

"It's nice," Nancy said, "but I like you just the way you are."

"So do I. Just because I can change things in stories doesn't mean I should," I said.

The scar was back and so was my dark hair.

"Unbelievable," I breathed, then looked at Nancy. "But why didn't my mother tell me all this? Leave me a note?"

Nancy smiled sadly at me.

"She tried, didn't she?" I said. "Of course she did. The book itself was the note. Right? Except Pops did hop into the book back then. He told me he did. He looked around to see if my mother had left a secret message for me, but he didn't find anything."

"I was gone on a case," Nancy said. "He only spoke to Hannah and Dad, and they'd already been charmed to forget your mother. If I'd seen him, I would have told him—"

"No," I said. "It was supposed to be me. My mother wanted *me* to come into the story and meet you. I could've figured this out years ago, but I was so angry at her for leaving me nothing but a book . . ."

"It's not your fault you misunderstood—"

"It *is* my fault. I'm as bad as the Burners, angry at a book when it was my own failure of imagination to understand what it was trying to tell me."

Nancy took my hand, squeezed it. "Come upstairs. I want to show you something. It'll make you feel better."

Upstairs was Nancy's bedroom—pin-neat, of course. Pretty floral wallpaper and a brass bed with a white quilt. A few books. Fresh flowers in a vase. White lace curtains. The dream bedroom of your average 1930s gal.

But also . . . under the bed, an old suitcase. Nancy knelt down and pulled it out. Together we hefted it onto the bed.

She opened it and revealed some clothes neatly packed away in tissue paper—dresses, shoes, gloves, hats. A few books with *Ellery* written on the title pages.

"My mother's things," I said. "How?"

I pored over every little treasure.

"I was more than ready when Dr. Fanshawe showed up at our house. I had a plan in place to make sure she didn't charm me as well. I hid all your mother's things away. You can hide anything in a book, you know. Tuck it between the lines, and no one but the most astute reader will notice it . . ."

She pulled a handkerchief from the suitcase and ran her fingers over the initials embroidered at the corner.

E.V.D.

Ellery Viola Drew.

She pressed it to her chest over her heart, then held it out to me.

"You should have this," she said. "I made this for her. A wedding gift. She carried it every day."

My hand trembled as I took it from her.

"A handkerchief embroidered for my mother by Nancy Drew," I said. "For her wedding to Carson Drew . . ."

"I never knew my mother's name," Nancy said softly, as if afraid of her own heartbreak. "Did you know that? In all the books, the authors never gave her a name."

"I know. I'm sorry."

"I think that's why I liked embroidering your mother's name so much. Because I knew it."

Lifting the handkerchief to my nose, I inhaled the faint scent of something.

"It smells like . . . chrysanthemums?"

Nancy held up a pressed flower. "They had a private wedding that autumn in our garden. Hannah and I made her a wedding bouquet of all pink and yellow mums. That's what I called her after they were married, as a little joke—Mums."

"Mums," I repeated. "She died long before I learned how to talk. I don't know what I would've called her. Mom? Mommy? I like Mums."

Nancy fell quiet, then spoke again.

"I waited a month before I started investigating. But time gets a little fuzzy in books," she said. "What felt like a month to me . . . the time between my case in *The Secret of the Old Clock* and my case in *The Clue of the Velvet Mask* was over twenty years in the real world. When I finally escaped to find out what happened to Mums, to you . . . she'd been dead for years and you were all grown up."

"But I have to ask . . . if you found me, why all this mystery?" I waved my hands in the air. "If you'd knocked on my door and told me you were my sister, I would've believed you."

"I tried that! Again and again I tried to tell you. The words wouldn't come out."

"You didn't know how to tell me, you mean?"

"I mean the words *literally* would not come out of my mouth."

I remembered how yesterday she had tried to say something but then didn't. Or couldn't.

"I don't understand."

"Rainy," she said, clutching my hand, "you're a fictional character. Half-fictional, which is more than enough. You can't simply tell a fictional character something life-changing about themselves. They must go on a journey of self-discovery. It's the only way."

"So you created a whole mystery for me to solve?"

"Exactly!" she exclaimed. "When I realized that Mums was never coming back, I escaped. See?" Nancy raced to her closet, opened the door, and pulled out a plain black umbrella. "She'd made me my own charmed umbrella to use in case of emergency. And what bigger emergency than a missing mother and sibling?"

She hung the umbrella back in her closet, then came to the bed and sat down on the covers facing me.

"It wasn't a happy day when I learned what had happened," Nancy said. "Mums was gone and had been gone for a long time. But you . . ." She smiled broadly. "You were alive and a Book Witch too. Believe me, I tried everything. The day we met, I tried writing you a note telling you the whole story, but the words disappeared off the page. I tried calling your phone number, but no one ever answered. Finally, it dawned on me that I couldn't tell you the truth about who you were . . . I could only arrange for you to discover it for yourself. So I threw you a mystery!"

"Who knows more about mysteries than Nancy Drew?" I said.

"No one!" she exclaimed. Then she leaned in, whispering conspiratorially. "I waited for my chance—Mad Hatter Day. I gave you the clues you needed. Then I had your grandfather make that admittedly annoyingly mysterious phone call. Since you're half-fictional, like any fictional character, you'd do the most obvious thing first. Someone tells you to find the March Hare, you go to Wonderland. So I set up the tea party for you. I even tipped off a Burner you had history with to add a little tension to the story."

"You tipped off X?"

"Rainy, a story has to have conflict. You know that!"

"I guess you're right. Who was it who said, the story 'Little Red Riding Hood' without the Big Bad Wolf is nothing but a brief paragraph about an uneventful food delivery?"

"I don't know," Nancy said, "but they're right. I had to make things difficult enough for you that it would feel like a real mystery. And I did! It was very clever of me."

"You're very proud of yourself," I said. "But that was pretty dangerous and reckless of you."

"Dangerous and Reckless is my middle name!" she proclaimed. "Nancy Dangerous and Reckless Drew."

"Have fun embroidering that on a bookmark," I said. Hopefully this was the last time I needed to learn something about myself. I was mentally and emotionally exhausted. Being a fictional sleuth was no joke.

Nancy reached out and took my hand in hers. "My baby sister . . ."

". . . who is older than you, remember?"

"Older *and* younger," Nancy said. "I'm sixteen, but I've been sixteen for nearly a century."

I rubbed my temples. "This is all very weird."

"Let's pretend we're twins," she said. "How's that?"

I liked the sound of that. "Twins," I said. My face hurt from smiling, but then my smile faded as reality set in. "Wait, I'll have to go on a journey of self-discovery every time I need to improve or change my life?"

She wrinkled her nose and nodded. "Yes. But there are upsides!"

"They better be good," I grumbled.

"You can stay young a very, very long time if you want." Smiling, she tossed her blond bob and batted her eyelashes. Nancy Drew, eternally a teenager. "And you're a fictional character without a book of your own. So I suppose you can simply pick one."

"What if I pick this one? What will happen?"

"I'd like that," she said. "But if I have a sister in this book . . . Well, there are a lot of Nancy Drew books that came after this one. Over six hundred."

"You mean, if I stay here and live with you and your . . . *our* father, over six hundred books will change?"

She nodded, wincing.

"No wonder Dr. Fanshawe didn't want me figuring out who I am," I said. "She freaks out if a single sentence changes in a single book. But a new character in six hundred books? Maybe I shouldn't live here. Your books mean so much to so many people. Changing them might hurt readers who need these stories."

"You're my sister," Nancy said. "You're welcome to stay, whatever the consequences."

"Wish I could stay, but I still need to find Pops. Any idea where he is now?"

"I was wondering when you'd ask."

"POPS!"

If there was ever a moment to use an exclamation point, it was now.

I ran to him where he stood in the doorway and threw my arms around him.

"Hello, Raindrop," he said. "Long time no see." He squeezed me tight and slapped me a few dozen times on the back. Hugs were an extreme sport with my grandfather.

I pulled back and glared at him. "Where have you been?"

"Where do you think?" he asked.

Whirling, I faced Nancy Drew, who was watching us with a little smile on her face.

"He was here all this time and you didn't tell me?"

"Don't get cross with poor Nancy," Pops said. "I'm just as guilty."

"Confess," I said. "Immediately."

"When I finally figured out what your mother had been trying to tell us all this time, that *The Secret of the Old Clock* wasn't simply a book she loved but the answer to all our questions . . . Well, I had to be sure before I said anything to you. I'd always wondered why Fanshawe had confiscated all your mother's case notebooks and papers when she died. What were they trying to cover up?"

"Me," I said. "That a real person had a child with a fictional character."

"Incendiary stuff," Pops said. "But more important . . . I couldn't risk telling you that you had a father and a sister without making sure I was right. I pretended I was leaving on a top secret mission to whereabouts unknown, hopped into the book, and was finally able to confirm my hunch."

"Why didn't you come back sooner?" I demanded. "It's not safe for you to stay in a book that long. What if you'd forgotten who you were? Is everyone a rule-breaker in this family but me?"

Pops only shrugged. "Even if I spent a year in a book, Raindrop, I'd never forget I'm your grandfather. And in fairness, I tried to come back sooner. Mrs. Turner put the book in the safe."

"Oh, no," I groaned. "That woman is too tidy for our own good."

"When I tried to get out, I did a bit of damage to the book." The tears in the cover. The loose pages. That was all because Pops had tried to escape a closed book. Then he smiled. "But Nancy here snuck into the house and got the book out—"

I pointed an accusing finger at Nancy Drew's innocent face. "*You* stole my book? You sneaky, thieving . . . Ah, you'll be stealing my clothes next, won't you?"

"Rainy," she said matter-of-factly, "whose name is on the cover of the book? And on literally every page? Face it, it was *my* book. Also I'm better dressed than you are. You'll be stealing my outfits long before I steal yours."

"Hurtful, but true," I said.

"She wasn't stealing the book," Pops reminded me. "She was helping me escape from it."

"So you did get free and yet you didn't come home? Do you know how scared I was?" I demanded. "Very scared. Very, very, very. In italics *very.*"

"I know, I know. I'm sorry. But I had a marvelous time getting to know Nancy here."

"So you were in on this mystery the whole time?" I demanded.

"Had to be done, Raindrop. Oh, and I promise we'll fix that Little Free Library we sabotaged."

"You did that? Why?"

"So you'd charm it with book powder," Nancy said. "Then when I gave you the Duke of Chicago book, you'd assume it was because you accidentally charmed yourself, not because I was setting you up with Duke to solve a mystery."

"I can't believe it. My own sister and grandfather, plotting against me."

"Plotting? Yes, but *for* you," Nancy said, "not against you."

"And it worked, because here you are." Pops smiled a little wistfully and looked around the house. "Your true home, I suppose."

"Can you believe it? I'm fictional."

He took my face in his dear old hands.

"Please don't run away into a book and never come home to us. All I ask, Raindrop."

I kissed his cheek, and he hugged me again.

When I turned my head against his shoulder, I saw Nancy grinning at both of us.

"Thank you," I mouthed.

"Anything for my sister," she said.

"Nancy Drew is my sister," I said. "And I'm . . . I'm Carson Drew's daughter. I'll never get used to that."

"And I have a new granddaughter," Pops said as Nancy rushed to join me in his arms.

For one beautiful moment, the length of a single sentence in a story, we three held on to each other. If this were the ending of my story, it would've been a happy one.

But we weren't to THE END quite yet.

I pulled away first and looked at them. "We have to go, don't we?" I asked Pops. "Before we damage Nancy's books by being here?"

"No," Nancy pleaded. "Don't go yet. I promise, we'll put everything to rights soon. You want to meet Dad, don't you?"

I did, more than anything. But . . .

"Will he even know who I am?" I asked, afraid I already knew the answer.

"No," Pops said. "Fanshawe's charm got him. He thinks I'm a traveling encyclopedia salesman. We can remove the spell, but Nancy and I decided to leave that up to you."

"We remove the spell," I said, "and he'll know who I am, but he'll also remember losing his second wife. I don't know if I can do that to him."

"You don't have to decide tonight," Nancy said. "We've been here ninety-five years. We're not going anywhere."

"I would like to meet him."

"I promise, you'll like him," she said. "Ready?"

A moment later we stood outside the door of the living room, where Carson Drew sat in his armchair. He had dark hair, like mine, and with his horn-rimmed glasses he looked like a handsome, intelligent college professor more than the criminal lawyer of legend.

"He's not that much older than I am now," I whispered.

"He's been thirty-nine for almost a hundred years," Nancy said.

"What do I even say?"

"The truth. Say, 'Hello, it's very nice to meet you.'"

"All right. Let's go." We started forward, but then I stopped her. "Duke's waiting outside with Koshka."

"I'll fetch them for you."

Nancy started to leave. "Stop," I whispered.

She turned back around at the door.

"How did you escape being charmed by Dr. Fanshawe?" I asked.

"Oh, that," she said, grinning broadly. "You know there are two Nancy Drew series, right? The original blue covers and the reboot with yellow covers?"

"Right . . ."

"Two timelines means . . . two Nancies," she said. "So me and the other Nancy switched places!"

I knew it.

Nancy left to bring Duke inside. While she was gone I hid in the shadows and watched Carson Drew chatting amiably with Pops.

My father. He didn't know who I was, but that was okay for now. What mattered was that he was here, immortal in that way all beloved stories are and living people never can be. His creator was dead. His writer was dead. Probably every girl who'd read and loved this book the year it had come out was long gone. But he lived on. The time would come when I could quietly reveal myself to him, but I didn't need that yet. I only needed one thing from my father tonight.

The front door opened. Nancy, Duke, and Koshka came quietly into the house.

Duke took my hand.

"I'll let Dad know you're here," Nancy said.

"What will you tell him?" I asked. "About me and Duke?"

"Oh, I'll tell him the truth, more or less—that you're Rainy, a new friend who's like a sister to me. And you," she said to Duke, "you're her boyfriend—"

"Fiancé," Duke said.

"Fine, her fiancé, a famous private detective from Chicago who wants to meet local legend Carson Drew."

She gave me a wink, then went into the living room. "Dad? We have company."

"Anyone we know, dear?" Carson asked.

Out in the hallway, Duke leaned in and whispered in my ear, "What am I supposed to do here?"

I nodded toward Carson Drew, then looked up at Duke.

"I want my father to shake hands with the man I love."

Koshka *mrwwp*-ed.

"Right. And shake paws with my cat."

CHAPTER THIRTY-THREE

It was late, so we didn't stay long. Nancy escorted Pops, Duke, Koshka, and me to the street, where Duke had hung my umbrella on the tree branch.

"I'll take this gentleman home where he belongs," Pops said, elbowing Duke.

"And this one too," Duke said. He picked up Koshka and kissed me chastely on the cheek. Pops was watching us after all. "See you soon, darling?"

"Wait," I said. I wanted to tell him that he couldn't run from his mother and family obligations forever. He needed to go back to England and face the past he'd left behind. But when I tried to get the words out, nothing. Silence.

I looked at Nancy. "You're right. You can't tell a fictional character how to change."

She shrugged. "Told you so."

"What was that all about?" Duke demanded.

"Nothing," I said, then grabbed his face and kissed him hard (but not too hard, because this was still a Nancy Drew novel, after all).

"What was that for?" he asked. "Not that I'm complaining."

"Congratulations," I said. "You have now solved every mystery you've ever attempted to solve, including the mystery of us."

"Well done me," he said, beaming.

"Now go on. Get back in your books. I'll be there soon."

"Promise?"

"Promise."

Then he and Pops and Koshka disappeared before our eyes.

And there I was, all alone with Nancy Drew by the picket fence in front of her picturesque River Heights home lit by a single ancient streetlamp.

"As much as I hate to admit it," I said, "it's probably for the best I didn't learn all this about my mother and father and you until now. If I'd learned at age fifteen? I would have disappeared into this book and never looked back."

And since I was fictional . . . no one could've stopped me.

"Your grandparents would've been devastated to lose you," Nancy said. "And all those books you restored, all those Burners you defeated . . ."

"And I never would've met Duke either. But I'm glad to know my mother was so happy here."

"Very happy," Nancy said. "When she left to go visit her parents, she promised to come back. She would've come back if she hadn't gotten sick."

"But if you had a mother or a stepmother keeping an eye on you," I told her, "you never would've gotten away with all the wild shenanigans you got up to. Your father gave you a lot of leeway."

"I know why my writers didn't want me to have a mother. I needed my freedom to get into trouble and, well, this was a hundred years ago. Losing a parent was much more common then. But losing your Mums in any era . . . it's terribly unfair."

"Peripartum cardiomyopathy," I said, because you never forget the name of the monster that killed your mother. "Pops said she was home just two days before she started struggling to breathe. They delivered me immediately, but the damage to her heart was already done. She was in and out of the hospital, but only got sicker and weaker. Five months later, she was gone. No reason or rhyme. That's what I hate about the real world. Death is so meaningless."

I thought of my mother, young and in love, newly married, desperate to get back to her husband and stepdaughter. But I was premature and she was dying. We were both too weak to leave the house, much less the real world. Every waking moment, my mother must've ached for the family she'd found in the pages of *The Secret of the Old Clock*, the book in the photograph of us on the mantel. That was my mother—even sick, even dying, even lonely and trapped in a world that was not her own anymore . . . she still read to me.

The story of my life was a story.

"I don't think it's meaningless," Nancy said. "But it is a mystery, one we're all trying to solve. How do you turn something terrible into something meaningful? I dare say it's the greatest mystery of them all."

I nodded but said nothing.

"Rainy?" she asked. "Are you all right?"

"Can I tell you something? Without you hating me for it?"

"I could never hate you," Nancy said. "Remember, if you were a worm, I'd rescue you off the sidewalk—"

"—and give me a leaf for an umbrella."

She nodded. "What is it, Rainy?"

I sighed. "I have a father now and a sister. I have answers to questions I've been asking my whole life. I even know how Duke and I can be together."

"All good things, I hope."

"All good," I said. "So why isn't it enough? I should be thrilled. I should be dancing in the streets. But I'm . . . I don't know. I'm sorry. I'm being greedy."

Nancy moved to stand in front of me. She searched my face. "Rainy, what are you saying?"

"I guess I'm saying . . . I want my mom."

"Oh, Rainy." Nancy put her arms around me. It felt like something broke in me, a dam of words. Like a child having a tantrum, hammering fists and feet on the ground, I said it again and again.

I want my mom. I want my mom. I want my mom. I want my mom.

I said it for every birthday party she missed, for every Christmas and Halloween and Easter. I said it for every boo-boo she never kissed, for every fever I ran that she never soothed with the back of her hand and a Popsicle in bed.

I want my mom. I want my mom. I want my mom.

I said it for every fight we never had over something stupid we laughed about later. I said it for the homework she never reminded me to do and the tests she never helped me study for and for every assembly where I'd won a dumb child's prize or attendance certificate without her in the audience to cheer for me.

I want my mom.

I want my mom.

I want my mom.

I said it for Duke, who would never meet her.

I said it for the grandchildren she would never hold.

I said it for Pops and Grandma, who'd had to pick out their daughter's gravestone the same week they took their granddaughter to her six-month checkup.

I said it until I couldn't say it anymore, until I could only feel it, like a child's deepest, most primal need—not food or shelter but to reach out her hands and have her mother take them in hers.

"I want my mom, too," Nancy said. "My writers never even let me mourn her. I had to do all my grieving between the lines."

We looked at each other.

"I'm sorry," I said. "Today should be the happiest day of my life."

"The best days are the worst days," she said. "Because she's not here."

"I thought my mother left me your book to tell me to be strong and not be sad, to carry on and get to work."

"No, no," Nancy said. "I know there's not a story in the world that can take away the pain. But there is one thing books can do."

She reached up and pulled a maple leaf off the tree, then held it over my head like an umbrella.

"Right," I said. "They can remind you you're not alone."

"YOU AREN'T ALONE."

Nancy and I turned to see X standing under the streetlamp.

He clapped his hands. "It all makes perfect sense. You're a fictional character, March. No wonder I despise you so much. You're one of *them.*"

"What are you doing here?" I asked. "More advice? Revenge because I didn't take the bait last time? I know everything about my mother now and it makes me admire her more."

"No more advice," he said. "I'm here to end you. Since you're fictional, I can take the kid gloves off." He pulled out his gun.

"You wouldn't dare!" Nancy shouted, stepping between us. "I'll get my father and the town marshal!"

"I've got this," I said, placing a hand on her shoulder and moving her to the side. I stared X down. "I'm a self-aware fictional character. I can take over this story if I want. You forgot that part, didn't you?" I asked as his big scary stupid ugly gun suddenly turned into a . . .

Banana.

"What?" he looked at the banana in his hand, then threw it on the ground. Not only was he planning to murder me, but he wasted perfectly good fresh produce. Fiend!

I walked slowly, menacingly toward him. It's hard to be menacing in leggings, but I promise, I pulled it off. It helped that I also summoned a bolt of lightning, which hit the ground next to X, leaving a puff of smoke in the street.

He squealed and jerked away.

"Did you like that?" I asked. "How about this?"

A small but lethal meteor crashed into the concrete behind him, spraying him with glowing green shards.

I summoned fog. Invisible wolves growled from behind trees. X turned a circle in his panic, then faced me, terror writ in bold letters across his face. He pulled his silver lighter out of his pocket, but I wasn't about to give him a chance to escape. A giant bald eagle with the First Amendment written on his wings swooped in from the sky, snatching the lighter from his hand.

"No!" he cried out, leaping for it.

"Or how about this?" I asked, reaching behind my back. He held up his hands in terror. He knew I could pull anything out from behind my back—a knife, a ray gun, a venomous snake in a very bad mood.

"You're a Book Witch! You're not supposed to use violence."

"I'm also a fictional character. And in a story, a fictional character can do anything she wants! Like . . . this!"

I pulled out a book from behind my back and brandished it in his face.

"Dante's *Inferno*?" he asked, then laughed. "Finally, real literature. Your taste is improving, March."

"I'm not going to read it," I said. "I've already read it."

I tossed the book toward him, and it landed behind him on the ground, open.

With the tip of my umbrella, I shoved him backward into the book. A whirlwind of words captured him, dragging him down into the Seventh Circle of Hell, where those who do violence against art are punished for eternity. And as I did it, I said the three words every Book Witch in the world has wanted to say to every Burner since Savonarola's Bonfire of the Vanities.

"Go to Hell!"

Then with a sucking sound like the flushing of an industrial-strength toilet, he was gone.

I picked up the book, closed it, and locked X inside nice and tight with a spell.

Nancy stared at me, wide-eyed.

"I think you just turned my young adult series into horror," she said.

"Oops. Sorry! I can fix it."

"Don't apologize," she said. "I liked it!"

CHAPTER THIRTY-FOUR

Well, I suppose we can't end a Nancy Drew book without a Nancy Drew ending, can we? Time to skip ahead and tie everything up with a neat little bow.

Six months have now passed and everything is back to normal.

That was a lie. Everything is still very weird. But I am writing this case file in April, six months after the end of my adventure, so I do have a little perspective now.

To begin with, I still haven't told Carson Drew that he's my father. The spell Dr. Fanshawe put on him remains intact. But I visit often. He treats me like a daughter and doesn't mind at all that I call him Dad. In fact, I can tell he likes it.

Nancy visits me in the real world under the guise of Penny Nichols, apprentice Book Witch. With the umbrella my mother gave her, she can slip easily and safely between her books and our world for day trips. Although I'd love to live with her and our father in River Heights, we have to keep our visits short enough that we don't inadvertently rewrite over six hundred Nancy Drew books. But whenever we're together, she tells me stories about my mother, which I think Mom would've liked. Mom was a Book Witch, after all. She would've been honored to be a story.

As for Dr. Fanshawe . . . a day after the end of this adventure, the Ink and Paper Coven met in the Words, Words, Words stockroom.

Dr. Fanshawe was stripped of her leadership position and sentenced to ten years of the very worst sort of grunt work—removing price stickers from used books.

I don't feel sorry for her. Yes, she was just doing her job, and yes she did have to clean up the mess my mother had made of the Nancy Drew series. But she knew the whole time that I was half-fictional and kept it a secret from me. It's only fair she smell like Goo Gone for the rest of her natural life.

Professor Dodsworth threw his umbrella into the running for her position but came up one vote short. With the tiebreaker vote cast by "Penny," Pops became the new Coven leader. To Penny's surprise and delight, his first act was to instate Penny as a full-fledged Book Witch. His second act was to allow a little wiggle room into the Black and Whites. I'm happy to report that Pen and Ink Book Witches are now allowed to befriend—and fall in love with—fictional characters as long as it doesn't affect any existing books, which left open a very useful loophole. A loophole I took advantage of the very next day . . .

I KNOCKED ON MEDDA BAKER'S DOOR, AND WHEN SHE OPENED IT, she gasped with delight.

"Rainy! Who is that?"

I held a small black cat out to her.

"I don't know," I said as she took the cat into her arms. "I haven't named her. That's your job."

Medda cradled the cat to her shoulder. "Rainy, you're so sweet, but I can't take in another cat. I . . . I might not be here next year. I . . . I've been having some health scares."

"I know," I said. "But Pops and I promise we'll help out. And if, for any reason, something happens to you, I'll take her back. Koshka wouldn't mind a friend."

Medda kissed the flat spot between the cat's ears, the landing pad for kisses. "Thank you, Rainy. I'll name her Agatha."

"Don't thank me yet. That cat isn't a gift. She's a bribe."

Medda's eyes narrowed with suspicion.

"You said you were retired from writing," I said. "Would you mind *un*-retiring?"

She pursed her lips and glared at me. "You want me to finish that Duke of Chicago book Tom Hightower left behind."

"If you don't mind," I said with a painful grin.

"If I say no?"

"I'm taking Agatha back."

Her mouth fell open."You wouldn't!"

"All's fair in love, war, and fiction," I said. "Come on. It can be a novella. I don't care. All you have to do is write me in as a character in a new story."

"You want me to write Rainy March into a Duke of Chicago book? That's it?"

"Yes, that's it. Oh, and can you write in Mrs. Turner? I think she really misses being the housekeeper to a fictional detective."

"Anything else?" she asked. "And do I need my notebook for this?"

"Now that you mention it, I was thinking I could secretly be a rich, powerful socialite who's going undercover as Duke's secretary. And then we fall in love. And maybe on the last page, there's an epilogue where we get married or at least engaged? Oh, and Duke said he wants to finally take down Al Capone."

"That's more of a thriller plot than a mystery."

"That's fine. Duke looks very sexy when he's running for his life. You know, like Cary Grant in *North by Northwest*?"

She laughed. "Very well. Least I could do for a fellow Ducky. And for Agatha." She scratched her new cat under the chin.

"Thank you, Medda. You're saving my love life."

"I was getting bored being retired. And I love anything that keeps me from having to clean. Come on, Agatha. You can help me. Time for one last hurrah." She paused, tilted her head. "One last hurrah . . . I like the sound of that."

Without even saying goodbye, she turned and walked back into her house.

And before I knew it . . .

Book Six

THRILLER

CHAPTER THIRTY-FIVE

Ten girls had come and gone. Smart girls. Clever girls. Sweet girls. Bold and brassy and beautiful girls who fell in love with him before he'd even offered to take their coats. Girls that knew shorthand better than they knew longhand and could type a hundred words a minute with one hand while they answered the phone with the other.

But the minute the Duke told them what the job was all about, all ten of them headed for the hills like they'd heard there was real gold on the Gold Coast.

What a waste of a two-dollar advertisement in the paper.

The Duke sat at his desk and opened a drawer, pulled out a bottle of whiskey and a single shot glass. Awful stuff. More punishment than pleasure. He unscrewed the cap and lifted the bottle, but between the pour and the swallow, someone knocked on the door.

"This is why I need a secretary!" the Duke called out to God, the universe, and whoever had knocked. "So I don't have to answer my own bloody door!"

"Hire me then, and you won't have to."

A woman's voice. Calm, steady, sure of herself.

"You don't want the job," he called back. "Trust me. No one does."

"Why not?" the mystery woman replied.

"Two words," the Duke shot back. "Al Capone."

"Two words . . . Rainy March."

The Duke got out of his chair—reluctantly—walked to the door—hesitantly—and turned the knob—wearily.

"That the weather report or your name?" he asked, his voice trailing off at the sight of her. She had the sort of face that made a man straighten his tie, balance his checkbook, and see that his affairs were in order, because he'd either marry her or die trying.

"Both," the woman said with moxie by the acre. She had dark hair and storm-cloud eyes. Her skirt was tight as a miser's fist and she was showing just enough skin to make him want to see more before lunch.

"You're here for the secretary position?"

"I'm certainly not here for my health." She pushed past him, and he caught a glimpse of two trim ankles that made him want to write her mother a thank-you note.

He hurried to his desk and held out the chair for her. Then he sat down opposite her, behind the desk. "To be perfectly clear, you are here to be my secretary, Miss March?"

"I am," she said.

"Only my secretary?"

She gave a shrug. "I'm open to the possibilities."

"I only ask because I'm afraid I'm ten seconds away from falling in love with you. Then, of course, I'll ask you to marry me at some point."

She didn't answer, only lifted her wrist to stare at her wristwatch.

"Miss March?"

"I'm counting ten seconds," she said. "Time's up. Do you love me yet?"

"Madly."

"So I have the job?"

He smiled at her, and across the world, the toes of every woman curled even though they didn't quite know why.

"You're hired."

Book Seven

SCIENCE FICTION

CHAPTER THIRTY-SIX

The book was easy enough to find, displayed prominently in the window of A Long Story, the only bookstore within twenty miles of Frankie's hometown of Aurora, Nevada. On the colorful book cover, a man and a woman in vintage party clothes followed the shadow of a hare over a hill. The title was *The March Hare Mystery* and the author—no, *authors*—were Maxine Blake . . . and Jessa Charming.

Frankie had stopped there on her day off, relieved there were copies left. She snatched one off the New Release table and took it straight to the register.

"I finished this one last night," the woman behind the counter said, scanning the barcode.

"I don't need a bag," Frankie said. "I'll start it on the bus home."

She wanted to ask but didn't want to ask but finally she asked it.

"So . . . how is it?" Frankie said, nervously. "Does it read like a Book Witch book, or can you tell there's a new writer?"

"I couldn't tell," the bookseller said. "Jessa Charming was a good choice. Better than the alternative, right? No one wanted to see the series end."

"Definitely," Frankie said as she took the book, the receipt tucked inside alongside a free bookmark. "I need my Duke and Rainy fix."

She held out her arm, displaying her black umbrella tattoo to the bookseller.

"Nice," the bookseller said.

Frankie gave a polite wave as she left the store. While she waited for the bus to arrive, she opened the book to the first page and began reading . . .

All stories are love stories if you love stories.

She froze. A strange tingling sensation crept up the back of her neck. Where had she heard that before?

The girl . . . the girl at Maxine Blake's funeral had said that, right? Rachel, the girl who looked like Rainy March—not the one on the book covers, but like she'd always imagined Rainy March looked in her head.

For a split second, Frankie wondered if that had been the real Rainy March who'd crossed over into the real world to attend Maxine Blake's funeral. Of course not. That would never happen. Fictional characters coming to life? That was the stuff of science fiction.

Her bus arrived and Frankie got on, found her seat, and returned to the book. As she read, she time-traveled to the past and became sixteen again. She read a little further and the world around her disappeared, teleporting her onto the silver sidewalks of Fort Meriwether.

When she finally finished the book later that night in her own apartment, she looked up to find herself still in the life she'd always known. Too bad. For a few hours there, she'd been with Rainy March. She'd been young again, full of promise and possibility. Light-years ago, it felt like. A different time and place, before her father had died and she'd had to drop out of college and work at the coffee shop she still worked at to pay the bills. She'd wanted to be a librarian back then, but grad school was out of the question. Now . . . now she'd be happy with a little bookstore all her own, one closer than two towns away.

But she couldn't do that, could she? Open a bookstore? Start her own business? It would wipe out all of her savings. Then again, her town needed a bookstore, desperately. Bookstores were Frankie's sanctuary, her happy place. And every time she stepped into one, she dreamed of owning one of her own. Maybe she could rent a little storefront? The sort of place with an apartment on the second floor? She'd have the best selection of science fiction and fantasy novels in the entire Southwest. What would she call it? Otherworld Books? The Black Hole Bookstore? The Bookstore at the End of the World??

She smiled at the thought of it. But it would crazy, right? She was almost forty. Wasn't it too late to change her life like that? Take a risk like that? Go after a dream like that?

Frankie knew Rainy March would tell her to go for it. But Rainy March wasn't real. If only . . .

What wouldn't she give to slip through a crack in this universe to some other, friendlier universe where stories became real and the real world faded like a dream forgotten by breakfast?

There was a knock at her front door.

Frankie checked her watch.

Nearly three in the morning? The witching hour. Who would be knocking on her door this time of night?

From her front window, she could see a woman out front holding a black umbrella open even though it wasn't raining.

Frankie undid the dead bolt and opened the door enough to peer out at the mysterious figure. It was the woman from the funeral, the woman who looked exactly like the Rainy March in her head.

"Um . . . hi?" Frankie said. "You were at Maxine Blake's funeral, right? The Rainy March look-alike. What are you doing here?"

"I'm not a Rainy March look-alike. I am Rainy March. And I'm here to tell you—open the bookstore."

Frankie didn't know if she was awake or dreaming, but something told her to take this moment very seriously. "Um . . . okay?" Frankie said.

"You'll do it?"

"Yes. If you say so."

"I do say so," Rainy said. "Well, that was easy enough. Thanks again for fixing my umbrella for me. Bye now."

"Wait!" Frankie said. "What's happening? How can you be here? This is the real world, not a story."

"You sure about that?" she asked, but before Frankie could answer, Rainy March closed her umbrella with a flick of her finger and vanished.

Our revels now are ended.

ACKNOWLEDGMENTS

Mel Blanc, the legendary "man of a thousand voices," died in 1989. Shortly thereafter, Warner Brothers, the studio behind Looney Toons, released a tribute illustration by Darrell Van Citters. A microphone stands in a spotlight on a stage. Off to the left, Bugs Bunny, Daffy Duck, and other characters voiced by Blanc bow their heads in a moment of silent mourning. You can probably trace a direct line from this piece—entitled *Speechless*—to *The Book Witch*. It was certainly on my mind when I created Hugo Rees's tribute cartoon to Maxine Blake and Rainy March. I saw it printed in a magazine decades ago and the idea of characters mourning the creator who gave them voice has stayed with me ever since.

It's been a tough few years for books. Book challenges. Libraries being stripped bare of books. AI stealing and devaluing the human effort that goes into every work of art. Where is Rainy March when we need her? But books are resilient. Stories outlive their creators. Shakespeare created so much of our modern English language, we quote him constantly whether we realize it or not. And the pen will always be mightier than the sword, for a sword only destroys and a pen creates.

Of course, I must acknowledge my wonderful—and wonderfully patient—editor Shauna Summers at Ballantine Books, and the remarkable team there—Mae Martinez, Megan Whalen, and Emily Isayeff, plus Holly Overden, my incredible cover artist. And so much gratitude to Amy Tannenbaum and the whole team at the Jane Rotrosen Agency. Many thanks to beta readers Jenn LeBlanc and Bethany Hensel. And many hugs and kisses to my husband and obnoxiously talented illustrator Andrew Shaffer.

I'd be remiss if I didn't thank those people, real and imaginary, I never got to thank in person—Alexander Dumas and Edmond Dantès; Jane Austen and Lizzy Bennet; Toni Morrison and Sethe; Ray Bradbury and Douglas; Madeleine L'Engle and angry little Meg Murry; John Williams and Professor Stoner; Roald Dahl and Matilda; Agatha Christie and Poirot and Miss Marple; and, of course, Carolyn Keene and Nancy Drew.

I wish I could have met you all, shaken your hands, and said, "Thank you for the stories."

The real woman behind *The Secret of the Old Clock* was named Mildred "Millie" Wirt Benson. She wrote many of the earliest Nancy Drew novels under the pen name Carolyn Keene. She gave Nancy her spunk, her rebelliousness, and her little blue roadster. Millie was a character in her own right and deserves more recognition. In addition to reading lots of Nancy Drew novels—the originals and reboots—I read several excellent nonfiction works while researching this book:

Girl Sleuth: Nancy Drew and the Women Who Created Her by Melanie Rehak
Missing Millie Benson by Julie K. Rubini
The Girl Sleuth: On the Trail of Nancy Drew, Judy Bolton, and Cherry Ames by Bobbie Ann Mason

I must, obviously, thank my own feline familiars—MoonPie and Gizmo.

And, because I firmly believe in citing my sources, I must thank my favorite comedian, the legendary James Acaster, who said, "All triangles are love triangles if you love triangles." Truer words, James . . .

Finally, thank you to both my parents for working so hard so we could always afford books, and to my mom for reading to me and my sister every night before bed when we were kids.

Thanks, Mom. I love you.

ABOUT THE AUTHOR

MEG SHAFFER is a part-time creative writing instructor and the author of *The Wishing Game* and *The Lost Story.* She lives in Louisville, Kentucky, with her husband, author-illustrator Andrew Shaffer, and their two feline familiars, MoonPie and Gizmo.

Instagram: @meg_shaffer

ABOUT THE TYPE

This book was set in Berkeley, a typeface designed by Tony Stan (1917–88) in the early 1980s. It was inspired by, and is a variation on, University of California Old Style, created in the late 1930s by Frederic William Goudy (1865–1947) for the exclusive use of the University of California at Berkeley. The present face, in fact, bears influences of a number of Goudy's fonts, including Kennerley, Goudy Old Style, and Deepdene. Berkeley is notable for both its legibility and its lightness.

THE SECRET OF
THE OLD CLOCK
By
CAROLYN